ITALO SVEVO

Zeno's Conscience

Translated with an introduction by William Weaver

PENGUIN BOOKS

PENGUIN BOOKS

Published by the Penguin Group
Penguin Books Ltd, 80 Strand, London WC2R ORL, England
Penguin Putnam Inc., 375 Hudson Street, New York, New York 10014, USA
Penguin Books Australia Ltd, 250 Camberwell Road, Camberwell, Victoria 3124, Australia
Penguin Books Canada Ltd, 10 Alcorn Avenue, Toronto, Ontario, Canada M4V 3B2
Penguin Books India (P) Ltd, 11 Community Centre, Panchsheel Park, New Delhi – 110 017, India
Penguin Books (NZ) Ltd, Cnr Rosedale and Airborne Roads, Albany, Auckland, New Zealand
Penguin Books (South Africa) (Pty) Ltd, 24 Sturdee Avenue, Rosebank 2196, South Africa

Penguin Books Ltd, Registered Offices: 80 Strand, London WC2R ORL, England

www.penguin.com

La coscienza di Zeno published by L. Cappelli, Bologna 1923
This translation first published in the USA by Alfred A. Knopf, a division of Random House, Inc., 2001
First published in Great Britain in Everyman's Library 2001
Published in Penguin Classics 2002
8

This translation copyright © Alfred A. Knopf, a division of Random House Inc., 2001
Map on p. xxiii by Peter McClure

The moral right of the translator has been asserted

Printed in England by Clays Ltd, St Ives plc
ISBN-13: 978-0-140-18774-8

www.greenpenguin.co.uk

Penguin Books is committed to a sustainable future
for our business, our readers and our planet.
The book in your hands is made from paper
certified by the Forest Stewardship Council.

CONTENTS

TRANSLATOR'S INTRODUCTION

TAKE A LOOK at the author's name (his real name): Ettore Schmitz. The first half is Italian and, significantly, it is the name of a Greek hero, not of a Catholic saint. The surname is German. Then consider the birthplace: Trieste, a city that has had many masters, from ancient Romans to Austrians to Italians. In 1861, when Ettore Schmitz was born there, Trieste was an Austrian city, a vital one, the great empire's only seaport and a focus of trade between central Europe and the rest of the world. In this place of encounters and frontiers, young Ettore grew up to appreciate ambiguity, even contradiction; and, when he seriously began his career as a writer, he chose a pen name that reflected his complex background: Italo Svevo: Italus, the Italian; and Svevus, the Swabian (a duchy in medieval Germany, Swabia was also known as Alamannia).

His father Francesco Schmitz, was a German Jew, born in Trieste but closely linked to the German-speaking world. Ettore's mother was also Jewish and also from Trieste, but from an Italian family: her name was Allegra Moravia. Since the late eighteenth century Trieste had been a relatively serene place for its Jewish citizens, who were allowed to conduct business, accumulate wealth, occupy public office: some were even ennobled.

Francesco Schmitz was in the glassware business, and for much of Ettore's childhood that business went well. The boy, like his seven brothers and sisters, lived in comfort, if not affluence. Their father was something of an autocrat, and – like most other fathers in Trieste – he assumed his sons would follow him into the world of commerce. Francesco was a man of firm convictions, and one of these was the belief that success in affairs was dependent on a total mastery of the German language. So when Ettore was eleven he was sent with his adoring younger brother Elio to board at the Brusse'sche Handels und Erziehungsinstitut, a trade and education academy at Segnitz-am-Main, near Würzburg. Ettore did well there, but his real interest was reading, not commerce: he devoured Goethe, Schiller, Heine, Schopenhauer, and other classics, including Shakespeare in German translation.

In 1878 Schmitz returned to Trieste for two years and studied, in a somewhat random fashion, at the Istituto Revoltella, the closest thing Trieste then had to a university. At this time he also began writing, chiefly plays, evidence of an enduring passion for the theater that he was able to feed by attendance at the Teatro Communale. After some performances at Shakespeare there in 1880, he published a first article, "Shylock," in an Italian-language paper, *L'Indipendente*, an irredentist organ with which he was to be associated for several decades.

In that same year, after the failure of his father's business, Schmitz abandoned formal study and found a position in the Trieste branch of the Unionbank of Vienna, assigned to deal with its French and German correspondence. He remained, unhappily, at the bank for almost twenty years.

He continued to write (but rarely complete) plays, as his contributions to *L'Indipendente* became more frequent. Finally, in December of 1887, he began a novel. Its working title was characteristic: *Un inetto*. This could be translated literally as "an inept man," but perhaps Svevo meant something more like our modern term "a loser." The story is set in a bank; Svevo later admitted the work was largely autobiographical.

After an unhappy love affair a decade earlier, Schmitz's life seemed dully divided between home and office, but then he began meeting other young artists – notably the painter Umberto Veruda, who introduced him to Trieste's bohemian circles. In the winter of 1891 he had a serious affair with a

working-class woman, whom he later portrayed in his second
novel.

He completed the first novel, now retitled *Una vita* (*A Life*;
Svevo was unaware of the Maupassant novel of the same title).
In December of 1892 (after the manuscript had been rejected
by the prestigious Milanese firm of Treves), *Una vita* was published – at the author's expense – by the firm of Vram in
Trieste. The Trieste papers reviewed it benevolently; the critic
of Milan's *Corriere della sera*, Domenico Oliva, a sustaining
pillar of the Italian literary establishment, offered it mild praise.
But the book made no real impression.

Svevo's father had died in 1892, a few months before the
publication of *Una vita*. In October of 1895 Svevo's mother
died. At thirty-four he felt adrift. His brother Ottavio suggested that the two of them move to Vienna and go into business, but there were economic obstacles, and Schmitz was
reluctant to leave his part-time job with *Il Piccolo*, a leading
Italian daily paper, where he was responsible for scanning the
foreign press.

And there was another reason to stay in Trieste. During his
mother's last illness, he had come to admire his young cousin,
Livia Veneziani, who had impressed him with her gentle
manner and her thoughtfulness. He began giving her books; at
her insistence, he even promised to conquer his entrenched
habit of smoking (a promise often repeated, but never kept).
On 20 December 1895, despite strong objections from Livia's
parents, who considered the much older Schmitz a poor
prospect, Livia and Ettore became officially engaged. As a
festive gift, Livia presented him with a diary, a "keepsake"
album entitled *Blüthen und Ranken edler Dichtung* (*Blossoms and
Tendrils of Noble Poetry*), handsomely bound and illustrated
with watercolor reproductions of flowers, each day's page
headed by a sentimental poem. The pages for January and
February are dutifully filled in; a few March entries are written
up, then the writing peters out. Published posthumously under

the title *Diario per la fidanzata*, the diary offers many engaging insights into the character not only of Svevo but also of his fictional alter ego, Zeno Cosini. For instead of recording his day-to-day events, the diarist examines his conscience, analyzes his love of his fiancée, and describes his often wild fancies.

On the page for 3 January, under a soppy little poem by Georg Ebers, he wrote:

A man can have only two strokes of good luck in this world. That of loving greatly or that of combating victoriously in the battle for life. He is happy either way, but it is not often that fate grants both these happinesses. It seems to me therefore that ... the happy are those who either renounce love or withdraw from the battle. Most unhappy are those who divide themselves according to desire or activity between these two fields, so opposed. Strange: thinking of my Livia I see both love and victory.

A few days later, on 7 January, he wrote:

At the moment of waking I surely do not remember either the face or the love of Livia. Sometimes to recall one and the other in their entirety I need to see the photograph that has remained calmly watching me sleep. And then the serenity of waking is broken all at once by the recollection of life, of all life, and I am assailed simultaneously by all the joy of possession and the uneasiness that has always accompanied and will always accompany my love. Then I recall all the discussions of the day before in your company or else my just being silent, beside you. I am then calmed, and when I get up, I am whistling Wagner, the musician of love and of pain but I feel only the former, I leave the house with my hat a jaunty angle and ... a cigarette in my mouth. Poor Livia! Every pleasure and every displeasure that you give me increase my pharyngitis.

The frankness of the diary – which was submitted to Livia as he was writing it – did not diminish her love for her quirky future husband. She had developed a maternal fondness for his weaknesses, and she could smile at his many jokes and fancies.

Though she was one-quarter Jewish by birth, Livia had been brought up a Catholic and regularly attended Mass. So the prospective marriage involved a central conflict. Livia, after much debate, unhappily agreed to a civil ceremony. It took place on 30 July 1896. After a honeymoon – a month spent partly along the Adriatic coast and partly in Vienna – they moved into the large, somewhat pretentious villa of Livia's parents, in the outlying industrial town of Servola, where the Veneziani paint factory was also located. At first, Ettore and Livia occupied an independent apartment on the third floor of the villa. Later they moved downstairs and formed a single household with Olga and Gioachino, the senior Venezianis.

Svevo's in-laws played important roles in his life (and, to some extent, in his fiction). Gioachino is clearly the model for the ebullient, great-hearted Giovanni in *La coscienza di Zeno*. Olga – to whom Svevo sometimes referred, behind her back, as "the dragon" – was the moving force in the family and in the business (which, though founded by Gioachino, was to some extent descended from the chemicals firm of her father). It was Olga who ordered the workmen about, and it was she who – alone – mixed the secret ingredients of the formula for the underwater paint, used to protect the hulls of ships (including many naval vessels), that the Veneziani company produced and successfully marketed throughout Europe.

Despite Svevo's occasional ridiculous jealousy, the marriage was profoundly happy, and in 1897 Livia became pregnant; in that same year Svevo began a second novel, which he called *Il carnevale di Emilio* (*Emilio's Carnival*, later retitled *Senilità*). After the birth of their daughter, Letizia, Livia fell seriously ill, and Svevo decided to be baptized. On Livia's recovery they went through a marriage ceremony in church, though there is no evidence that Svevo took his new religion seriously.

Amid repeated vows to give up smoking, Svevo developed briefly another vice: gambling on the Exchange. In the spring of 1898, when he had lost 1,000 florins, he wrote out a solemn oath to give up trading and added that, to recoup the loss, he would "do without tobacco, coffee, and wine for the next ten years!" As he meticulously dated his frequent written resolutions to give up smoking, so he solemnly dated this sheet of paper: "7 March 1898."

Three months later, *L'Indipendente* began publishing *Senilità* in installments, and in the autumn of 1898, again at the author's expense, Vram brought out the volume. Again it caused no stir. Not for the first time, Svevo thought of giving up writing. But for him, writing was a vice as deeply rooted as smoking, and though he later claimed he had stopped writing for a long period, he was not telling the whole truth. While it was many years before he essayed another novel, he constantly wrote little stories, fables, observations.

His life at the bank continued to be unhappy, and, at just about this time, his supplementary teaching position at the Revoltella fell through. Unexpectedly, Olga invited – or commanded – him to work for the family firm. He was initiated into the secret of the paint formula. Veneziani submarine paint was in demand far beyond Trieste, and the family set up branches, first in Italy (at nearby Murano), then in England. Svevo was often deputed to organize and control these outposts of Olga's empire. To Olga's satisfaction (and his own), he proved good at his job; and in the course of time, he achieved financial ease. He and Livia and their daughter could live in near-luxury. In his leisure moments – partly as a substitute for writing – he devoted himself to the violin. His success as a musician was less than brilliant, but he was able to put together an amateur quartet, which performed at social gatherings at their hospitable Veneziani villa.

His foreign travels were putting his command of languages to the test, and he felt that his English, in particular, needed improvement. Toward the end of 1906, Svevo was told of a young tutor, James Joyce, an Irishman who had been in

Trieste since the previous March and had achieved a certain popularity, especially among the Jewish haute bourgeoisie. Since the penniless Joyce and his wife, Nora, often had to change dwellings, Joyce taught his pupils at their homes. Sometime in the autumn of 1906 he and Svevo began meeting, with reciprocal pleasure.

Joyce had recently managed (like Svevo, at his own expense) to publish a collection of his poems, *Chamber Music*, and had completed the stories of *Dubliners*, for which he was having trouble finding a publisher. He was also trying to get on with his more ambitious work, the novel then thought of as *Stephen Hero*. He showed his work to Svevo, and at one of their meetings actually read aloud his great story "The Dead" to Livia and Ettore, who immediately felt its power. After the reading, Livia went into the garden, picked some flowers, and handed the bouquet to Joyce as a sign of her admiration.

Eventually Svevo confessed to his young teacher that he also had – or had once had – literary ambitions. Joyce asked to read *Una vita* and *Senilità* and was profoundly impressed. He even quoted some passages of the latter work from memory to the thrilled author. (Svevo, it must be added, became one of several sources of "loans" to the young Irishman.)

Joyce discussed his own work more and more freely with Svevo. As he began planning *Ulysses*, he frequently consulted his pupil about Jewish beliefs and practices; and thus Svevo contributed to the characterization of Leopold Bloom. Livia – or, at least, her much-admired long blond tresses – was later a model for the personification of Dublin's river Liffey, as Anna Livia Plurabelle.

As the First World War began, Joyce had to leave Trieste, but from his exiles – first in Switzerland and later in Paris – he kept in touch with his friend. Joyce's continued moral support may have contributed to Svevo's first great postwar undertaking, *La coscienza di Zeno*, which was begun in March of 1919, more than twenty years after the completion of *Senilità*.

The years of the war were profoundly disruptive for Svevo, for Trieste, and for the underwater paint business. Even before hostilities began, many Italians fled the city, where the Austrian authorities had imposed a number of restrictions, including a severe censorship of the press. Gioachino and Olga, both Italian citizens, left for England, so Ettore remained in charge at the factory. Wanting to be near her Italian fiancé, Letizia – now in her teens – joined some family members in Florence.

The Austrians tried to confiscate the factory and wanted to know the secret formula; Ettore thwarted these efforts, first by concealing the ingredients and then by supplying a false formula. Finally he had to travel to Vienna to protest the confiscation of the factory. He was successful, but there was little business to be done in the beleaguered city.

Finally, well after the war's end and Trieste's annexation to Italy, the Schmitzes – including Letizia, now married and with a growing family – were able to take a vacation together. In the summer of 1922 they rented a villa in the hills north of Trieste. Here, in an access of fervid inspiration, Svevo went seriously to work on *La coscienza di Zeno*. Smoking furiously, he finished the book in a matter of months, and in May of 1923 the novel was published – again at the author's expense – by the firm Cappelli in Bologna. Once more Svevo's book aroused scant interest: a few local reviews, a brief and lukewarm notice in the *Corriere della sera*.

But the tide was soon to turn, dramatically. The last few years of Svevo's life would be radically different; he would come close to achieving victory in the battle of life. Though he had seen little of Joyce after his departure from Trieste and their correspondence had been desultory, Svevo had sent a copy of *La coscienza di Zeno* to his former English teacher. The response from Paris was immediate. Joyce's letter is dated 30 January 1924, and it reads, in part:

Thank you for the novel with the inscription. I am reading it with great pleasure. Why be discouraged? You must know it is by far your best work. As to Italian critics I can't speak. But send copies to Valéry Larbaud, Benjamin Crémieux, T. S. Eliot (Editor Criterion), F. M. Ford. I will speak or write to them about it also. I shall be able to write more when I've finished the book. So far two things interest me. The theme: I should never have thought that smoking could dominate a man like that. Secondly, the treatment of time in the book. You certainly don't lack penetration, and I see that the last paragraph of *Senilità* . . . has been growing and blossoming in secret.

Joyce, who knew something about promoting literary work, especially his own, was as good as his word. He did speak with Larbaud and Crémieux, prodding them to read and publicize the book. An important new Parisian review, *Le Navire d'Argent*, was soon planning a "Svevo number" with an essay by Larbaud and a translation of excerpts from *Senilità* and *La coscienza*. Svevo was the talk of literary Paris, and a young Italian poet, Eugenio Montale, visiting the city, heard of him there for the first time. On his return to Italy, Montale procured copies of the three novels and took up the cause, writing articles on Svevo for Italian reviews and enthusiastically spreading the word. Soon Svevo was a prominent literary figure, or rather a "case", debated at length in papers and in literary cafés. On one occasion, when Svevo was to pass through Milan en route to Trieste during a return trip from abroad, Montale arranged for a group of young writers to gather at the Milan train station and pay him homage. Svevo was also fêted by Florentine literary circles, and in Trieste he was now a respected member of the Caffè Garibaldi intellectual group.

The official literary establishment still regarded him with some suspicion and belittled his foreign fame, but that fame was undeniable. Translations of his works were already in progress. After his death an acquaintance, A. R. Ferrarin, recalled and quoted some remarks of his at this time:

"Until last year I was the ... least ambitious old man in the world," Svevo said. "Now I am overcome by ambition. I have become eager for praise. I now live only to manage my own glory. I went to Paris ... and all I could see was Italo Svevo: Italo Svevo among the treasures of the Louvre; Italo Svevo on the stage of the fifty-some Parisian theaters. Italo Svevo on the Elysées, and Italo Svevo at Versailles ... The ville lumière ... seemed to exist only as a function of my glory."

Svevo, in the last, satisfying years of his life, often visited Milan and frequented the literary salons there. In 1926 he gave a lecture on Joyce at the offices of *Il convegno*, an important review that also sponsored a club and a theater. Though Svevo, who had never spoken in public before, had grave misgivings, the occasion went well and reinforced his relationship with the review, which published some of his stories.

In the flush of excitement at his fame, he was not only writing stories but contemplating a sequel to *La coscienza di Zeno*. In the winter of 1927 a social event crowned this happy phase: Crémieux organized a dinner in Paris to honor Svevo, its guests including Isaak Babel, Ilya Ehrenburg, and other illustrious Paris residents, with Jules Romains presiding. Ehrenburg's account of the dinner emphasized the bad food and marveled at Svevo's incessant smoking.

His fame could not dispel an increasing pessimism. His conversation and his writing now contained frequent premonitions of death; his concern with old age – his "*senilità*," which had been a spiritual more than a physical state – was now real. He had to cut down on his eating, for he had developed a heart condition. Nevertheless he continued to go to the office and, in good moments, to write. He did not give up smoking.

In late August of 1928, Ettore and Livia decided to spend some time at the Alpine spa Bormio, where he had previously taken a cure. They traveled by motorcar, their chauffeur at the wheel, and took with them their six-year-old grandson, Paolo.

Having set out on 11 September, they broke the trip overnight and on the twelfth resumed the journey despite pouring rain. As the car was crossing a bridge not far from Motta di Livenza, it skidded and crashed into a tree. Only Svevo seemed badly hurt, though Livia and Paolo were also bleeding.

Svevo had a broken leg, some cuts and bruises, but he was also suffering from severe shock; the doctor quickly realized that the injured man was dying. Letizia and her husband arrived the next morning. At a certain point one of his visitors was smoking, and Svevo asked him for a cigarette. It was refused. Svevo replied: "That really would have been the last cigarette." He died that afternoon at half past two.

Livia survived him for almost thirty years and became the alert custodian of his fame. His death was the first of many family tragedies. In March of 1943 Letizia's two eldest sons died as prisoners of war in Russia. Another son, Sergio, was killed in partisan street fighting in Trieste in 1945. Earlier that year the Villa Veneziani and the factory had been destroyed in an Allied bombing.

Livia herself spent much of the war hiding from the Nazis. During that time she began writing a biography of Svevo. Later, a friend, Lina Galli, helped her complete it. But she had as much trouble finding a publisher as Ettore had had. At last it appeared, as *Vita di mio marito* (*Life of My Husband*) in Trieste in 1950. A charming, affecting, usefully informative work, it has subsequently been reissued and translated.

Svevo's widow lived to see her husband established as a modern Italian classic, but the "Svevo case" continued to provoke discussion. One of the thorniest questions surrounding Svevo was, quite simply, his Italian. In *La coscienza di Zeno*, the narrator complains about his own Italian. Like all his fellow Triestines, Zeno's first language is the local dialect. For Ettore Schmitz, his first language was also Triestino; his second, German. Italian was an acquired tongue, and from the beginning of his career critics have insisted that his Italian is clumsy.

"The Italian of a bookkeeper" is a recurrent jibe. In his preface to a reissue of Livia's *Vita di mio marito*, Montale tackles the question:

But the smell of warehouse and cellar, the almost Goldonian chatter of the Tergesteo, the unmistakable "late Ottocento" painting in some of his rare expanses of landscape and his numerous "interiors" – are they not the sure presence of a style? A commercial style, true, but also the only one natural to his characters.

If Svevo – or rather, Zeno Cosini – writes like a book-keeper, that may be because he *is* a bookkeeper. At the suggestion of the Bolognese publisher Cappelli, Svevo actually took the step of having a professional, non-Triestine writer, Attilio Frescura, examine his manuscript. For some time Svevo's papers have not been accessible. They are in packing-cases stored in the Trieste library, which is being "renovated" (renovation, in institutional Italy, is likely to be an endless process). So we have no idea what Frescura's proposed revisions were, nor do we know to what extent Svevo accepted them.

In making this translation – and here I must adopt the first person singular – I have steadfastly resisted the temptation to "prettify" Svevo's prose. And as I progressed, the temptation became less frequent, as that prose worked its charm on me. What could sometimes at first seem flat, unaccented, even opaque was, I realized, an essential part of Zeno's character, like his subtle irony, his cockeyed ratiocination, his quiet humor. In his important study, *In Praise of Antiheroes*, Victor Brombert devotes an acute chapter to Zeno, an antihero in the great European tradition, where the bumbling importer Zeno Cosini ranks with that other great creation, the good soldier Schweik.

I first read Svevo's novel when I was a college senior, in the English translation by Beryl de Zoete, under the title *Confessions of Zeno*. I fell in love with the book, and a few years later, when my Italian was more fluent, I read it again in the original and loved it even more. Beryl de Zoete must have been a fascinating woman. Her published works include scholarly studies of Oriental dance; she was the companion of the great translator and scholar Arthur Waley, and thus lived in the magic circle of Bloomsbury. She also translated *Senilità* and, later, one of Alberto Moravia's early novellas, the splendid *Agostino*.

In the 1920s, when she worked on *La coscienza di Zeno*, she was translating the work of an eccentric, virtually unknown Italian writer. Seventy years later, when I began my translation, I was dealing with a text of world renown, universally loved. There are times when a translator must also be something of a salesperson, and I suspect that Beryl de Zoete, in her admiration for Svevo, was also eager to sell him to an uninstructed public. Her translation did just that, and she must have been pleased, rightfully, with her achievement.

But, more than novels, translations age. The translators whose work illuminated my youth – Constance Garnett, Helen Lowe-Porter, Dorothy Bussy, C. K. Scott Moncrieff – have all been challenged and, in some cases, replaced. And I expect – admittedly without enthusiasm – that a new generation will retranslate the works of Gadda, Calvino, Eco, whom I introduced to English readers.

While I was working on this translation, I left my old, college-days copy of *Confessions of Zeno* on the shelf. When I had finished, or almost finished the job, I took two or three peeks at de Zoete's work, to compare a few of her solutions to mine. It was clear to me that she had had similar trouble with passages that troubled me. I had been ready to use (and duly acknowledge) any felicitous solutions of hers, but as it turned out, her words regularly drove me to press on and find new solutions of my own.

The first and perhaps greatest problem is the very title of the book. In Italian, "*coscienza*" means both "conscience" and "consciousness," and the word recurs often in the body of the novel. De Zoete's choice of "confessions," skirting the original word deftly, was inspired but, I felt, finally misleading, placing Zeno Cosini in a line descended from Augustine and Rousseau. (To one of my Catholic background, the word also had a religious, sacramental connotation that I felt was unsuitable.) Then, one day, in an article in *The Times Literary Supplement*, I read that in the past, the English word "conscience" had also had the meaning of "consciousness." The article quoted Shakespeare ("conscience doth make cowards of us all"). And I decided that my title would be *Zeno's Conscience.*

Translation is often described as a lonely profession. I have never found it so. True, during most of the work, I am alone in my study, facing the blank screen and the printed page. But I also have the pleasure of discussing work and words with others, with colleagues and friends. I began this translation years ago in Italy and completed it at Bard College, where the campus teems with Svevians, always ready to talk about his great novel. At Bard, I must thank my valued colleagues James Chace, Frederick Hammond, Robert Kelly, William Mullen, Maria Assunta Nicoletti, and Carlo Zei. I am also grateful to my student Jorge Santana for his help, and to my former student Kristina Olson for collaborating on the bibliographical note. In New York, my old friend Riccardo Gori Montanelli (who helped me with some of my first translations, in Charlottesville, Virginia, fifty years ago) came to my assistance with some stock-market terminology, and my editor, LuAnn Walther, and her assistant, John Siciliano, helped with the final stages of the long process of seeing *Zeno's Conscience* into print.

William Weaver

BIBLIOGRAPHICAL NOTE

THERE ARE COUNTLESS editions of *La coscienza di Zeno* available in any Italian bookstore. Among these one of the best is a paperback issued by the firm of Einaudi, in Turin, with a stimulating preface by the Svevo scholar Mario Lavagetto. The volume also contains the "continuations" of *La coscienza* (five stories Svevo wrote at the end of his life). Another leading Svevo scholar, Bruno Maier, has supervised the essential and impressive opera omnia edition of Svevo's work (including many letters and his plays and scattered pages), brought out by the enterprising, devoted Milanese firm dall'Oglio. The prestigious Meridiani series, published by Mondadori in Milan, has brought out a volume containing the three Svevo novels, with an important introduction by Franco Gavazzeni, a good chronology, many notes, and a bibliography. In preparing my translation, I also consulted a scholarly edition of the novel published by Principato (Milan), with invaluable footnotes.

In English, P. N. Furbank's biography, *Italo Svevo: The Man and the Writer*, published in 1966 (University of California Press), remains indispensable: thoroughly researched, elegantly written, eminently readable. It has more recently been complemented by John Gatt-Rutter's *Italo Svevo: A Double Life* (Oxford, 1988).

For Svevo's relations with James Joyce, see Richard Ellmann's biography, *James Joyce* (Oxford, 1959), and, more specifically, the recent, excellent study, *The Years of Bloom: James Joyce in Trieste, 1904–1920* by John McCourt (University of Wisconsin Press, 2000). McCourt is also the author, with

Renzo Crivelli, of *Joyce: In Sveno's Garden* (International Scholars Publication, 1997).

Important essays on Svevo include Renato Poggioli's introduction to the New Directions edition of the de Zoete translation, *Confessions of Zeno* (1947), and the above-mentioned chapter on Zeno in Victor Brombert's *In Praise of Antiheroes* (University of Chicago Press, 1999).

ITALY

AUSTRIAN EMPIRE

Udine
Tucinico
Gorizia
Carso
Trieste
ISTRIA
Fiume
Verona
Venice
Mantua
R. Po
Pola
Modena
Adriatic
Sea
Bologna

English miles   80

Zeno's Trieste

VIA BELVEDERE

Opicina Cable Tramway

Central Railway Station
Dogana

Public Gardens

VIA FABIO SEVERO
VIA CORONEO
CORSO STADION
Synagogue
VIA DEL ACQUEDOTTO
VIA CHIOZZA
VIA FARNETO

Post Office

VIA CARDUCCI

Assicurazioni Generali

PORTO NUOVO

Canal Grande

S. Antonio

Hospital

Borsa
VIA DEL CORSO

PORTO VECCHIO

Tergesteo

VIA DEL BOSCO

Pal. di Lloyd Triestino

RIVA DEL MANDRACCHIO

Jewish Cemetery
Convent

S. Maria Maggiore

Castello

Sartorio Pier
Pescheria

Piazza Cavana
CITTA VECCHIA

S. Giusto

Beacon

Museo Revoltella, (Higher School of Commerce)

RIVA GRUMULA

Sacchetta

RIVA OSP MATTIA

S. Giacomo

500 metres

Military Baths

Arsenal d'Artiglieria

CHIARBOLA

To Klagenfurt

Gas Works

To Servola

PASSEGGIO DI S. ANDREA
PASS° DI S. ANDREA

Porto Nuovo di Franz Josef I

Arsenal del Lloyd

ZENO'S CONSCIENCE

PREFACE

I AM THE doctor occasionally mentioned in this story, in unflattering terms. Anyone familiar with psychoanalysis knows how to assess the patient's obvious hostility toward me.

I will not discuss psychoanalysis here, because in the following pages it is discussed more than enough. I must apologize for having suggested my patient write his autobiography; students of psychoanalysis will frown on this new departure. But he was an old man, and I hoped that recalling his past would rejuvenate him, and that the autobiography would serve as a useful prelude to his analysis. Even today my idea still seems a good one to me, for it achieved results far beyond my hopes. The results would have been even greater if the patient had not suspended treatment just when things were going well, denying me the fruit of my long and painstaking analysis of these memories.

I am publishing them in revenge, and I hope he is displeased. I want him to know, however, that I am prepared to share with him the lavish profits I expect to make from this publication, on condition that he resume his treatment. He seemed so curious about himself! If he only knew the countless surprises he might enjoy from discussing the many truths and the many lies he has assembled here!...

Doctor S.

PREAMBLE

REVIEW MY CHILDHOOD? More than a half-century stretches between that time and me, but my farsighted eyes could perhaps perceive it if the light still glowing there were not blocked by obstacles of every sort, outright mountain peaks: all my years and some of my hours.

The doctor has urged me not to insist stubbornly on trying to see all that far back. Recent things can also be valuable, and especially fantasies and last night's dreams. But there should be at least some kind of order, and to help me begin *ab ovo*, the moment I left the doctor, who is going out of town shortly and will be absent from Trieste for some time, I bought and read a treatise on psychoanalysis, just to make his task easier. It's not hard to understand, but it's very boring.

Now, having dined, comfortably lying in my overstuffed lounge chair, I am holding a pencil and a piece of paper. My brow is unfurrowed because I have dismissed all concern from my mind. My thinking seems something separate from me. I can see it. It rises and falls . . . but that is its only activity. To remind it that it is my thinking and that its duty is to make itself evident, I grasp the pencil. Now my brow does wrinkle, because each word is made up of so many letters and the imperious present looms up and blots out the past.

Yesterday I tried to achieve maximum relaxation. The experiment ended in deepest sleep, and its only effect on me was a great repose and the curious sensation of having seen, during that sleep, something important. But it was forgotten by then, lost forever.

Today, thanks to the pencil I'm holding in my hand, I remain awake. I can see, or glimpse, some odd images that surely have nothing to do with my past: a puffing locomotive dragging countless coaches up a steep grade. Who knows where it's coming from or where it's going or why it has now turned up here?

As I doze, I remember how my textbook claims that this method will allow you to recall your earliest infancy, your cradle days. I see immediately a baby in a cradle, but why should that baby be me? He doesn't look anything like me; on the contrary, I believe he was born a few weeks ago to my sister-in-law, who displayed him as a miracle because he has such tiny hands and such big eyes. Recall my infancy? Hardly. Poor baby! I can't even find a way to warn you, now living in your own infancy, how important it is to remember it, for the benefit of your intelligence and your health. When will you discover that it would be a good idea to memorize your life, even the large part of it that will revolt you? Meanwhile, unconscious, you are investigating your tiny organism in search of pleasure, and your delightful discoveries will pave the way toward the grief and sickness to which you will be driven even by those who would not wish them on you. What is to be done? It is impossible to keep constant watch over your crib. In your breast – you poor little thing! – a mysterious combination is forming. Every passing minute provides a reagent. Too many probabilities of illness surround you, for not all your minutes can be pure. And besides – poor baby! – you are the blood relation of people I know. The minutes now passing may actually be pure, but all the centuries that prepared for your coming were certainly not.

Here I am, quite far from the images that precede sleep. I will make another attempt tomorrow.

SMOKE

THE DOCTOR WITH whom I discussed the question told me to begin my work with a historical analysis of my smoking habit.

"Write it down! And you'll see yourself whole! Try it!"

I believe I can write about smoking here at my desk, without having to sit and dream in that chair. I can't seem to begin, so I must seek help from my cigarettes, all very like the one I am now holding.

Today I discover immediately something I had forgotten. The cigarettes I first smoked are no longer on the market. Around 1870 in Austria there was a brand that came in cardboard boxes stamped with the two-headed eagle. Now, around one of those boxes I see a few people gathering, each with some characteristic, so distinct that I can recall their names, but not distinct enough to prompt any emotion at this unforeseen encounter. I want to delve deeper, so I go to the armchair: the people fade and are replaced by some clowns, who mock me. Dejected, I return to the desk.

One of those figures, with a somewhat hoarse voice, was Giuseppe, a youth my own age, and with him was my brother, a year younger than I, who died many years ago. It seems Giuseppe received a generous allowance from his father, and used to give us some of those cigarettes. But I am certain he offered more of them to my brother than to me. Hence I was faced with the necessity of procuring some for myself. So I stole. In summer my father hung his waistcoat over a chair in the breakfast room, and in its pocket there was always change. I procured the ten pennies necessary to purchase the precious

7

little packet, and I smoked its ten cigarettes one after the other, rather than hold on to the compromising fruit of my theft.

All this lay in my consciousness, within reach. It resurfaces only now because previously I didn't know that it could be of any importance. So I have recorded the origin of the filthy habit and (who knows?) I may already be cured of it. Therefore, I light a last cigarette, as a test; perhaps I will throw it away at once, revolted.

Then, I remember, one day my father caught me with his waistcoat in my hands. With a shamelessness I could not muster today, which still disgusts me (perhaps – who knows? – that disgust is highly significant in my life), I told him I had felt a sudden impulse to count the buttons. My father laughed at my mathematical or sartorial leanings, failing to notice that I had my fingers in the watch pocket. It should be said, to my credit, that this laughter, inspired by my innocence when it no longer existed, sufficed to keep me from ever stealing again. Or rather ... I stole again, but unawares. My father left some half-smoked Virginia cigars around the house, perched on table edges and armoires. I believed this was how he threw them away, and I believe our old maidservant, Catina, did then fling them out. I carried them off and smoked them in secret. At the very moment I grabbed them I was overcome by a shudder of revulsion, knowing how sick they would make me. Then I smoked them until my brow was drenched in cold sweat and my stomach was in knots. It cannot be said that in my childhood I lacked energy.

I know perfectly well also how my father cured me of this habit. One summer day I returned home from a school outing, tired and soaked in sweat. My mother helped me undress, and wrapping me in a big towel, she made me lie down to sleep on a sofa where she was also seated, busy with some sewing. I was almost asleep, but the sun was still in my eyes, and it was taking me a while to lose consciousness. The sweetness that, in those tender years, accompanied repose after great weariness is clear to me, like an image on its own, as clear as if I were there now, beside that beloved body that no longer exists.

I remember the big, cool room where we children used to play; now, in these times when space has become so precious, it is subdivided into two parts. In this scene my brother doesn't appear, and I am surprised because I think he must also have participated in that excursion, and should have shared in the rest afterwards. Was he also sleeping, at the other end of the sofa? I look at that place, but it seems empty to me. I see only myself, in the sweetness of that repose, my mother, then my father, whose words I hear re-echoing. He had come in and hadn't immediately seen me, because he called aloud: "Maria!"

Mamma, with a gesture accompanied by a faint sound of the lips, nodded toward me, whom she believed immersed in sleep, though I was only afloat on the surface, fully conscious. I was so pleased that, for my sake, Papà had to control himself that I kept absolutely still.

In a low voice my father complained, "I think I'm going mad. I could swear that, not thirty minutes ago, I left half a cigar on that cupboard, and now I can't find it. I'm getting worse. I'm losing track of things."

Also in a low voice, yet betraying an amusement restrained only by her fear of waking me, my mother replied, "But no one's been in that room since dinner."

My father murmured, "I know that, too, and that's why I feel I'm going mad!"

He turned and went out.

I half opened my eyes and looked at my mother. She had resumed her work, but was still smiling. Surely she didn't think my father was about to go mad, if she could smile at his fears like that. Her smile was so imprinted on my mind that I recalled it immediately one day when I saw it on the lips of my wife.

Later, it wasn't lack of money that made it difficult for me to satisfy my craving, but prohibitions that helped stimulate it.

I remember I smoked a great deal, hiding in every possible corner. Because of the strong physical disgust that ensued, I recall once staying a full half hour in a dark cellar, together with two other boys of whom I remember nothing but their childish clothing. Two pairs of short socks that stand erect because there were then bodies inside them, which time has erased. They had many cigarettes, and we wanted to see who could consume the most in the shortest time. I won, and heroically I concealed the sickness produced by this strange exploit. Then we came out into the sun and air. Dazed, I had to close my eyes to keep from falling. I recovered, and boasted of my victory. One of the two little men said to me: "I don't care about losing: I smoke only when I need to."

I remember the healthy words but not the little face, also surely healthy, which he must have turned toward me at that moment.

At that time I didn't know whether I loved or hated cigarettes, their taste, the condition nicotine created in me. But when I came to realize that I hated all of those, it was worse. And I had this realization at the age of about twenty. Then for some weeks I suffered from a violent sore throat accompanied by fever. The doctor prescribed bed rest and absolute abstention from smoking. I remember that word, *absolute*! It wounded me, and my fever colored it. A great void, and nothing to help me resist the enormous pressure immediately produced around a void.

When the doctor left me, my father (my mother had been dead for many years), his cigar clenched firmly between his teeth, remained a little longer to keep me company. As he went out, after gently running his hand over my blazing brow, he said: "No smoking, eh!"

A huge uneasiness came over me. I thought: "It's bad for me, so I will never smoke again. But first I want to have one last smoke." I lit a cigarette and felt immediately released from the uneasiness, though my fever was perhaps increasing, and at every puff I felt my tonsils burning as if they had been touched by a red-hot coal. I finished the whole cigarette dutifully, as if fulfilling a vow. And, still suffering horribly, I smoked many others during my illness. My father came and went with his cigar in his mouth, saying: "Bravo! A few more days without smoking and you'll be cured!"

These words alone made me yearn for him to leave, to go out at once, allowing me to rush to my cigarettes. I even pretended to fall asleep, to induce him to leave more quickly.

That illness provoked the second of my troubles: the effort to rid myself of the first. In the end, my days were full of cigarettes and of resolutions to smoke no more; and to make a long story short, from time to time my days are the same now. The whirl of last cigarettes, begun at twenty, continues still. My resolutions are less extreme, and my weakness finds greater indulgence in my elderly soul. When we are old, we smile at life and at everything it contains. I can say also that for some time I have been smoking many cigarettes . . . and they are not the last.

On the flyleaf of a dictionary I find this note of mine, recorded in an elegant, even ornate, hand:

"Today, 2 February 1886, I am transferring from the school of law to the faculty of chemistry. Last cigarette!!"

That was a very important last cigarette. I remember all the hopes that accompanied it. I had become infuriated with canon law, which seemed to me so remote from life, and I was rushing to science, which is life itself, perhaps condensed in a beaker. That last cigarette actually signified my desire for activity (even manual) and for serene thought, sober and solid.

To escape the chain of carbon compounds in which I had no faith, I returned to the law. An error – alas! – also marked by a last cigarette, which I find recorded in a book. This one was also important, and I became resigned yet again to those complications of the mine, the thine, and the theirs, always with the best intentions, finally throwing off the carbon chains. I had demonstrated scant inclination for chemistry, thanks in part to my lack of manual dexterity. How could I possibly have been dextrous, when I continued smoking like a Turk?

Now that I am here, analyzing myself, I am seized by a suspicion: Did I perhaps love cigarettes so much because they enabled me to blame them for my clumsiness? Who knows? If I had stopped smoking, would I have become the strong, ideal man I expected to be? Perhaps it was this suspicion that bound me to my habit, for it is comfortable to live in the belief that you are great, though your greatness is latent. I venture this hypothesis to explain my youthful weakness, but without any firm conviction. Now that I am old and no one demands anything of me, I still pass from cigarette to resolve, and from resolve to cigarette. What do those resolutions mean today? Like that old doctor described by Goldoni,* can I expect to die healthy, having lived with illness all my life?

Once, as a student, when I changed lodgings, I had to have my old room repapered at my own expense, because I had covered the walls with dates. Probably I left that room precisely because it had become the graveyard of my good intentions and I believed it no longer possible to conceive any further such intentions in that tomb of so many old ones.

I believe the taste of a cigarette is more intense when it's your last. The others, too, have a special taste of their own, but less intense. The last one gains flavor from the feeling of victory over oneself and the hope of an imminent future of strength and health. The others have their importance because, in lighting them, you are proclaiming your freedom, while the future of strength and health remains, only moving off a bit.

---

*Carlo Goldoni (1707–93), Venetian playwright. This prolific writer of comedies of Venetian life (as well as libretti, memoirs, and other works) has remained in the repertoire, not only in Italy.

The dates on the walls of my room were written in the most varied colors, even painted in oil. The resolution, reaffirmed with the most ingenuous good faith, found suitable expression in the strength of the color, which was to make the previous vow look pale. Certain dates were favorites of mine because of the harmony of the numbers. From the last century I remember one date that I felt should seal forever the coffin in which I wanted to bury my habit: "Ninth day of the ninth month of 1899." Significant, isn't it? The new century brought me dates of quite a different musicality: "First day of the first month of 1901." Today I still believe that if that date could be repeated, I would be able to begin a new life.

But the calendar is never lacking for dates, and with a little imagination any one of them can be found suitable for a good resolution. I remember the following, because it seemed to contain a supreme categorical imperative for me: "Third day of the sixth month of 1912, 2400 hours." It sounds as if each number were doubling the stakes.

The year 1913 gave me a moment's pause. There was no thirteenth month, to harmonize with the year. But you must not think so many harmonies are required for a date to lend significance to a last cigarette. Many dates that I find written down in volumes or in favorite notebooks stand out became of their dissonance. For example, the third day of the second month of 1905, at six o'clock! It has a rhythm of its own, when you think about it, because each number contradicts its predecessor. Many events, indeed all, from the death of Pius IX to the birth of my son, seemed to me worthy of being celebrated by the usual ironclad vow. All of my family are amazed at my memory for our anniversaries, sad and happy, and they believe me so considerate!

To reduce its outlandish appearance, I even tried to give a philosophical content to the last-cigarette disease. Striking a beautiful attitude, one says: "Never again." But what becomes of that attitude if the promise is then kept? It's possible to strike

13

the attitude only when you are obliged to renew the vow. And besides, for me, time is not that inconceivable thing that never stops. For me, and only for me, it retraces its steps.

*

Disease is a conviction, and I was born with that conviction. Of the disease I had at twenty, I would remember very little if I hadn't had it described for me at that time by the doctor. It's odd how you remember spoken words better than emotions, which cannot stir the air.

I went to that doctor because I had been told he cured nervous disorders with electricity. I thought that electricity could endow me with the strength necessary to give up smoking.

The doctor had a big belly, and his asthmatic breathing accompanied the clicking of the electric mechanism he employed immediately, at the first session: a disappointment, because I had expected that the doctor would study me and discover the poison polluting my blood. On the contrary, he pronounced my constitution healthy, and when I complained of difficulty in digesting and sleeping, he opined that my stomach lacked acids and that my peristaltic action (he used that adjective so many times that I have never forgotten it) was rather sluggish. He administered also a certain acid that ruined me; ever since then, I have suffered from excess acidity.

When I realized that on his own he would never arrive at discovering the nicotine in my blood, I decided to help him, expressing the suspicion that my illness could be attributed to this cause. With some effort he shrugged his heavy shoulders: "Peristaltic action . . . acid. Nicotine has nothing to do with it!"

Seventy applications of electricity followed, and they would continue to this day if I hadn't decided seventy were enough. Expecting no miracles, I still hurried to those sessions in the hope of persuading the doctor to forbid me to smoke.

I wonder how things would have turned out if my resolve had been strengthened then by such a prohibition.

And here is the description of my illness that I gave the doctor: "I'm unable to study, and even on the rare occasions when I go to bed early, I remain awake until the small hours strike. So I vacillate between law and chemistry because both these disciplines involve work that begins at a set time, whereas I never know at what hour I may get up."

"Electricity cures any form of insomnia," my Aesculapius averred, his eyes always on the dial rather than on the patient.

I went so far as to talk with him as if he were equipped to understand psychoanalysis, into which, timidly and precociously, I had ventured. I told him of my unhappiness with women. One wasn't enough for me, nor were many. I desired them all! In the street my agitation was immense; as women went by, they were all mine. I looked them up and down, insolently, out of a need to feel myself brutal. In my mind I undressed them, leaving only their boots on, I took them into my arms, and I let them go only when I was quite certain that I had known every part of them.

Sincerity and breath wasted! The doctor was gasping: "I certainly hope the electrical treatments will not cure you of that illness. The very idea! I would never touch a Ruhmkorff* again if I had reason to fear such an effect."

He told me an anecdote that he considered delightful. A man suffering from my same illness went to a famous doctor, begging to be cured, and the doctor, after succeeding perfectly, had to leave the country because otherwise his former patient would have had his scalp.

"My agitation isn't the good kind!" I cried. "It comes from the poison that surges through my veins."

---

* Heinrich Daniel Ruhmkorff (1803–77), inventor of an electrical device, a "coil," popular around the end of the nineteenth century.

With a heartbroken expresson, the doctor murmured: "Nobody is ever content with his lot."

And to convince him, I did what he was unwilling to do, and I examined my disease, reviewing all its symptoms. "My distraction! It also prevents my studying. I was in Graz preparing for the first state examinations, and I made a careful list of all the texts I would require until the last examination was over. Then, as it turned out, a few days before the examination I realized I had studied subjects I would need only several years later. So I had to postpone the exam. True, I had studied even those other things only scantily, thanks to a young woman in the neighborhood who, for that matter, conceded me little beyond some brazen flirtation. When she was at her window, I could no longer keep my eyes on the textbook. Isn't a man who behaves like that an imbecile? I remember the little, white face of the girl at the window: oval, framed by fluffy, tawny curls. I looked at her and dreamed of pressing that whiteness and that russet gold against my pillow."

Aesculapius murmured, "Flirtation always has something good about it. When you're my age, you won't flirt anymore."

Today I am certain that he knew absolutely nothing about flirtation. I am fifty-seven, and I'm sure that if I don't stop smoking or if psychoanalysis doesn't cure me, my last glance from my deathbed will express my desire for my nurse, provided she is not my wife and provided my wife has allowed the nurse to be beautiful!

I spoke sincerely, as in Confession: a woman never appeals to me as a whole, but rather . . . in pieces! In all women I loved feet, if well shod: in many others, a slender neck but also a thick one, and the bosom, if not too heavy. I went on listing female anatomical parts, but the doctor interrupted me.

"These parts add up to a whole woman."

I then uttered an important statement: "Healthy love is the love that embraces a single, whole woman, including her character and her intelligence."

At that time I surely hadn't yet known such a love; and when I did encounter it, it was unable to give me health; but it's important for me to remember that I identified disease where a man of science found health, and that later my diagnosis proved true.

In a friend who was not a physician I then found the person who best understood me and my disease. I derived no great advantage from this association, but in my life it struck a new note that still echoes.

This friend was a gentleman of means who enriched his leisure with study and literary projects. He talked much better than he wrote, and therefore the world was never to know what a fine man of letters he was. He was big and heavyset, and when I met him he was undergoing a strenuous cure to lose weight. In a few days he had achieved a considerable result, so that in the street everyone came up to him, hoping to enhance their own feeling of health, in contrast to his obvious illness. I envied him because he was capable of doing what he wanted, and I remained close to him for the duration of his cure. He allowed me to touch his belly, which shrank every day, and, in my malevolent envy, wanting to sap his determination, I would say to him: "When your cure's over, what's going to happen to all this skin?"

With great calm, which made his emaciated face comical, he replied: "In two days' time, massage therapy begins."

His cure had been planned in every detail, and he would certainly respect every date.

I developed a great faith in his wisdom, and I described my disease to him. I remember this description, too. I explained to him that I thought it would be easier to renounce eating three times a day than to give up smoking my countless cigarettes, which would require repeating the same wearisome decision every moment. Having such a decision on your mind leaves no time for anything else; only Julius Caesar was able to do several things at the same moment. True, I am not asked to

17

work, not while my accountant Olivi is alive, but why is a person like me unable to do anything in this world except dream or scratch at the violin, for which he possesses no talent?

The thinned fat man did not reply at once. He was methodical, and he first pondered for a long time. Then, with a learned mien that was rightfully his, given his great superiority in the field, he explained to me that my real disease lay not in the cigarette but in the decision-making. I should try giving up the habit without any resolutions or decisions. In me – he felt – over the course of the years two persons had come into being, one of whom commanded, while the other was merely a slave who, the moment surveillance weakened, flouted his master's will out of a love of freedom. This slave was therefore to be granted absolute freedom, and at the same time I should look my habit squarely in the face, as if it were new and I had never seen it before. It should not be fought, but neglected and forgotten in a certain way; abandoning it, I should turn my back on it nonchalantly, as on a companion now recognized as unworthy of me. Quite simple, really.

In fact, it did seem simple to me. It's true, moreover, that having then succeeded with great effort in dispelling all decisiveness from my spirit, I succeeded in not smoking for several hours, but when my mouth was cleansed and I felt an innocent taste such as a newborn infant must know, and a desire for a cigarette came over me, and when I smoked it I felt a remorse for which I renewed the decision I had tried to abolish. It was a longer way round, but it arrived at the same place.

One day that scoundrel Olivi gave me an idea: I would strengthen my resolve by making a bet.

I believe Olivi has always looked the way I see him today. I have always seen him a bit stooped but solid, and to me he has always appeared old, as I see him now, at eighty. He has worked for me and still works for me, but I don't love him, because in my view he has prevented me from doing the work that he does.

We made a bet! The first one of us who smoked would pay, and then each would regain his own freedom. So the accountant, who had been imposed on me to keep me from squandering my father's legacy, tried to diminish my mother's, which I controlled freely on my own!

The bet proved extremely pernicious. I was no longer occasionally the master, but only a slave, the slave of that Olivi, whom I didn't love! I smoked immediately. Then I thought to defraud him by continuing to smoke in secret. But, in that case, why should I have made the bet? To smoke a last cigarette, I hastily sought a date that might have some attractive tie with the date of the bet, which I could somehow imagine had also been recorded by Olivi himself. But the rebellion continued and I smoked so much I became short of breath. To free myself of this burden, I went to Olivi and confessed.

The old man, smiling, collected the money and immediately took from his pocket a thick cigar, which he lighted and smoked with great gusto. I had no doubt that he had observed the conditions of the bet. Obviously, other men are made differently from me.

Just after my son's third birthday, my wife had a fine idea. She suggested I have myself confined for a while in a clinic, to rid myself of the habit. I agreed at once, first of all because when my son reached an age at which he would be able to judge me, I wanted him to find me stable and tranquil, and also for the more urgent reason that Olivi was ill and threatening to abandon me, hence I might be forced to take his place at any moment, and I considered myself ill-suited for such great activity with all that nicotine inside me.

At first we thought of going to Switzerland, the traditional land of clinics, but then we learned that in Trieste a certain Dr. Muli had opened an establishment. I sent my wife to see him, and he offered to reserve for me a locked apartment where I would be guarded by a nurse, assisted also by other staff. As my wife told me about it, she smiled and even laughed out loud, amused at the idea of having me locked up, and I laughed heartily along with her. This was the first time she had participated in my attempts at treatment. Until now she had never taken my disease seriously, and she used to say that smoking was only a somewhat odd and not entirely boring way of life. I believe that after marrying me, she had been pleasantly surprised at never hearing me express any nostalgia for my freedom; I was too busy missing other things.

We went to the clinic on the same day Olivi told me that nothing could persuade him to stay on with me beyond the following month. At home, we prepared some fresh linen in a trunk, and that same evening we went to Dr. Muli's.

He welcomed us at the door, in person. At that time Dr. Muli was a handsome young man. It was midsummer; small, nervy, his lively, shining black eyes even more prominent in his sun-burnished face, he was the picture of elegance in his white suit, trim from his collar to his shoes. He roused my wonder, but obviously I was also the object of his.

A bit embarrassed, understanding the reason for his wonder, I said: "Of course. You don't believe in the necessity of the treatment, or in my seriousness in undertaking it."

With a slight smile, which somehow hurt me, the doctor replied: "Why not? It may be true that cigarettes are more harmful to you than we doctors admit. Only I don't understand why, instead of giving up smoking *ex abrupto*, you haven't decided simply to reduce the number of cigarettes you smoke. Smoking is all right, provided you don't overdo it."

To tell the truth, in my desire to stop smoking altogether, I had never even considered the possibility of smoking less. But this advice, arriving now, could only weaken my resolve. I spoke firmly: "Since it's been decided, let me give this cure a try."

"Try?" The doctor laughed with a superior manner. "Once you undertake it, the cure must succeed. Unless you employ brute force to overpower poor Giovanna, you will be unable to leave here. The formalities to release you would take so long that in the meantime you would forget your addiction."

We were in the apartment reserved for me, which we had reached by returning to the ground floor, after having climbed up to the third.

"You see? That barred door prevents any communication with the other part of the ground floor, where the exit is located. Not even Giovanna has the keys. To go outside, she also has to climb to the third floor, and only she has the keys to the door that was opened for us on that landing. In any case, there are always guards on the third floor. Not bad, eh? In a clinic originally designed for babies and expectant mothers?"

And he started laughing, perhaps at the thought of having shut me up among the babies.

He called Giovanna and introduced me. She was a tiny little woman of indeterminate age: anywhere between forty and sixty. She had small eyes, intensely aglow, and a cap of very gray hair.

The doctor said to her: "With this gentleman you must be ready to use your fists."

She looked at me, studying me, turned bright red, and shouted in a shrill voice, "I will do my duty, but I certainly can't fight with you. If you threaten me, I'll call the orderly, a strong man, and if he doesn't come at once, I'll let you go where you like, because I certainly don't want to risk my neck."

I learned later that the doctor had given her this assignment with the promise of a fairly generous bonus, which had only increased her fright. At that moment her words irked me – fine position I had put myself in, and of my own free will!

"Neck, indeed!" I cried. "Who's going to touch your neck?"

I turned to the doctor: "I would like you to instruct this woman not to disturb me. I have brought some books along, and I want to be left in peace."

The doctor uttered a few words of warning to Giovanna. Her only apology was to continue her attack: "I have children, two little daughters, and I have to live."

"I wouldn't condescend to murder you," I replied in a tone surely not calculated to reassure the poor creature.

The doctor got rid of her, sending her to fetch something or other from the floor above, and to soothe me, he offered to replace her with someone else, adding: "She's not a bad sort, and when I've instructed her to be a little more tactful, she will give you no cause for complaint."

Wishing to show what scant importance I attached to the person charged with watching over me, I declared my willingness to put up with her. I felt the need to calm down, I took from my pocket my next-to-last cigarette and smoked it greedily; I explained to the doctor that I had brought with me only two, and that I wanted to stop smoking at midnight on the dot.

My wife took her leave of me along with the doctor. Smiling, she said: "This is your decision, so be strong."

Her smile, which I so loved, seemed a mockery; and at that very moment a new feeling germinated in my spirit, with the result that an enterprise undertaken with such seriousness was doomed perforce to fail at once. I felt ill immediately, but I did not realize what was making me suffer until I was left alone. A mad, bitter jealousy of the young doctor. Handsome he was, and free! He was called the Venus of doctors. Why wouldn't my wife love him? Following her, as they left, he had looked at her elegantly shod feet! This was the first time since my marriage that I had felt jealous. What misery! It was no doubt a part of my condition as a wretched prisoner. I fought back! My wife's smile was her usual smile, not mockery after having eliminated me from the house. It was she, indeed, who had caused me to be locked up, though she attached no importance to my habit; but she had surely arranged this to please me. And, furthermore, I should recall that it wasn't so easy to fall in love with my wife. The doctor may have looked at her feet, but certainly he had done so to see what sort of boots to buy for his mistress. Still, I promptly smoked the last cigarette; and it wasn't yet midnight, only eleven o'clock, an impossible hour for a last cigarette.

I opened a book. I read without comprehending, and I actually had visions. The page on which I had fixed my gaze was occupied by a photograph of Dr. Muli in all his glory, beauty, elegance. I couldn't bear it! I summoned Giovanna. Perhaps if I could converse, I would calm down.

She came, and at once gave me a suspicious look. She cried with her shrill voice: "You needn't think you can persuade me to neglect my duty."

Meanwhile, to soothe her, I lied, assuring her I wasn't thinking any such thing, but I no longer felt like reading and would rather have a little chat with her. I made her sit down opposite me. Actually, she repelled me, with her old crone demeanor and her youthful eyes, shifty like the eyes of all weak animals. I felt sorry for myself, having to put up with such company! It's true that even when I'm free, I can never choose the company most suitable for me; as a rule it's the others who choose me, as my wife did.

I begged Giovanna to entertain me, and when she insisted she could say nothing worthy of my attention, I asked her to tell me about her family, adding that nearly everybody in this world has at least one.

She then obeyed, and started telling me that she had had to put her two little girls in the Institute for the Poor.

I was beginning to enjoy her story because her brisk way of dealing with those eighteen months of pregnancy made me laugh. But her temperament was too argumentative and I simply couldn't go on listening to her when, first, she tried

ZENO'S CONSCIENCE

to convince me that she had no other course, what with her scant wages, and then that the doctor had been wrong, a few days before, to assert that two crowns daily were enough for her, since the Institute supported her entire family.

She was shouting. "And what about the rest? Even after they've been fed and clothed, they still don't have all they need!" And out she came with a whole stream of things she had to provide for her daughters, all of which I have now forgotten, since to protect my hearing from her shrill voice, I deliberately directed my thoughts elsewhere. But I was distressed all the same, and I felt entitled to a reward: "Wouldn't it be possible to have a cigarette? Just one? I'd pay you ten crowns. Tomorrow, that is. Because I don't have a penny with me."

Giovanna was hugely frightened by my proposal. Then, speaking purely at random, just to be talking and to maintain my composure, I asked: "In this prison there must at least be something to drink, isn't there?"

Giovanna responded promptly and, to my astonishment, in a genuinely conversational tone, without yelling. "Yes, indeed! Before leaving, the doctor gave me this bottle of cognac. Here it is, still unopened. You see? The seal hasn't been broken."

In my present position, the only avenue of escape I could then envision was drunkenness. To such straits had my confidence in my wife reduced me!

At that moment my smoking habit didn't seem worth all the effort to which I had subjected myself. Already I hadn't smoked for half an hour and I wasn't even thinking about it, concerned as I was with the idea of my wife with Doctor Muli. So I was entirely cured, but irreparably ridiculous!

I opened the bottle and poured myself a little glass of the yellow liquid. Giovanna watched me, her mouth agape, but I hesitated before offering her any.

"When I've finished this bottle, will I be able to have another?"

Still in her pleasant conversational tone, Giovanna reassured me, "As much as you want! To comply with your slightest wish, the housekeeper must get up, even at midnight!"

I have never suffered from miserliness, and Giovanna immediately had her glass filled, to the brim. Before she could finish saying thanks, she had drained it, and she immediately cast her bright eyes on the bottle. So it was she herself who gave me the idea of getting her drunk. But that was no easy undertaking!

I couldn't repeat exactly everything she said to me, in her pure Triestine dialect, after she had drained all those glasses, but I had the profound impression of being with a person to whom, if I hadn't been distracted by my own concerns, I could have listened with pleasure.

First of all, she confided to me that this was precisely the way she liked to work. Everybody in this world should be entitled to spend a couple of hours every day in just such a comfortable chair, facing a bottle of good brandy, the kind that doesn't cause any ill effects.

I also tried to converse. I asked her if, when her husband was alive, her work had been organized in this same way.

She burst out laughing. When her husband was alive he had given her more beatings than kisses and, compared with the way she had had to work for him, any job had seemed a rest, long before I arrived at this place for my cure.

Then Giovanna became pensive and asked me if I believed that the dead could see what the living are up to. I nodded briefly. But she wanted to know if the dead, when they reach the other side, learned of everything that had happened back here during their lifetime.

For a moment the question actually did distract me. It had been asked, moreover, in a much softer tone because, to avoid being overheard, Giovanna had lowered her voice.

"So," I said, "you were unfaithful to your husband."

She begged me not to shout, then confessed that she had been unfaithful to him, but only during the first months of their marriage. Then she had grown accustomed to his blows and had loved her man.

To keep up the conversation, I asked: "So your older daughter owes her life to this other man?"

Again in a low voice, she admitted to believing as much, also because of a certain resemblance. She was very sorry she had betrayed her husband. She said this, but was still laughing because these are things you laugh about even when they hurt. But that was only after his death, because, before, since he didn't know about it, the matter couldn't have any importance.

Impelled by a certain fraternal friendliness, I tried to allay her sorrow; I told her I believed the dead do know everything, but certain things they don't give a damn about.

"Only the living suffer over them!" I cried, banging my fist on the table.

I bruised my hand, and there is nothing better than physical pain to provoke new ideas. It occurred to me that while I was here tormenting myself with the thought of my wife's taking advantage of my confinement in order to betray me, perhaps the doctor was still in the clinic, in which case I could recover my peace of mind. I asked Giovanna to go and see, saying that I felt a need to tell the doctor something, and promising her the whole bottle as a reward. Protesting that she wasn't all that fond of drinking, she still complied at once and I heard her climb unsteadily up the wooden steps to the upper floor, to emerge from our cloister. Then she came down again, but she slipped, making a great racket and screaming.

"The devil take you," I murmured fervently. Had she broken her neck, my position would have been greatly simplified.

Instead, she joined me, smiling, because she was in that state where pains aren't so painful. She told me she had spoken with the attendant, who was just going to bed; though, even there, he remained at her disposal, in the event that I turned nasty. She raised her hand, index finger pointed, but she tempered those words and that threatening gesture with a smile. Then, more sharply, she added that the doctor had not returned after seeing my wife out. Nct a sign! Indeed, for some hours, the attendant had hoped the doctor would return, because a patient needed to be looked at. Now the attendant had given up hope.

I looked at her, studying the smile that contorted her face, to see if it was habitual or if it was totally new, inspired by the fact that the doctor was with my wife rather than with me, his patient. I was seized by a fury that made my head spin. I must confess that, as always, in my spirit two persons were combating, one of whom, the more reasonable, was saying to me: "Idiot! What makes you think your wife is unfaithful? She wouldn't have to get you locked up to create the opportunity." The other, and this was surely the one who wanted to smoke, also called me an idiot, but shouted: "Don't you recall how easy things are when the husband is away? And with the doctor you are paying money to!"

Giovanna, taking another drink, said: "I forgot to lock the door upstairs. But I don't want to climb those steps again. Anyway, there are always people up there, and you'd look really foolish if you tried to run away."

"Yes," I said, with that modicum of hypocrisy now necessary to deceive the poor creature. Then I, too, gulped down some cognac, and declared that with all this liquor now at my disposal, I didn't give a damn about cigarettes. She believed me at once, and then I told her I actually wasn't the one who wanted me to break the smoking habit. It was my wife. Because when I smoked as many as ten cigarettes a day, I became something terrible. Any woman who came within reach of me then was in danger.

Giovanna began to laugh loudly, sinking back in the chair: "So it's your wife who prevents you from smoking the ten cigarettes you need?"

"That's exactly how it was! At least she used to keep me from smoking."

Giovanna was no fool once she had all that cognac inside her. She was seized by a fit of laughter that almost made her fall out of the chair, but when she had recovered enough breath to gasp out a few words, she painted a magnificent scene suggested to her by my illness. "Ten cigarettes . . . half an hour . . . you set the alarm . . . then . . . "

I corrected her. "For ten cigarettes I'd need an hour, more or less. Then, for the full effect, about another hour, give or take ten minutes . . . "

Suddenly Giovanna became serious and rose almost effortlessly from her chair. She said she would go and lie down because she was feeling a slight headache. I invited her to take the bottle with her, because I had had enough of that strong liquor. Hypocritically, I said that the next day I wanted to be provided with some good wine.

But she wasn't thinking about wine. Before leaving, as she held the bottle under her arm, she looked me up and down, with a leer that frightened me.

She left the door open, and a moment or two later a package landed in the center of the room. I picked it up immediately: it contained exactly eleven cigarettes. To make sure, poor Giovanna had chosen to be generous. Ordinary cigarettes, Hungarian. But the first one I lighted was very good. I felt enormously relieved. At once I thought, with smug pleasure, how I had outsmarted this place, fine for shutting up children, but not me. Then I realized I had outsmarted my wife too, and it seemed to me I had repaid her in her own coin. Why, otherwise, would my jealousy have been transformed into such acceptable curiosity? I remained in that room, calmly smoking those nauseating cigarettes.

After about half an hour, I remembered I had to escape from that clinic, where Giovanna was awaiting her reward. I took off my shoes and went out into the corridor. The door of Giovanna's room was ajar and, judging by her regular, noisy breathing, I imagined she was asleep. Cautiously I climbed up to the third story where, behind that door – Doctor Muli's pride – I slipped on my shoes. I stepped out onto a landing and started down the other stairs, descending slowly so as not to arouse suspicion.

I had reached the landing of the second floor when a young lady in a rather elegant nurse's uniform came after me, to ask politely: "Are you looking for someone?"

She was pretty, and I wouldn't have minded smoking the ten cigarettes in her company. A bit aggressively, I smiled at her: "Dr. Muli isn't in?"

She opened her eyes wide. "He's never here at this hour."

"Could you tell me where I might find him now? At my house there's someone ill who needs him."

Kindly, she told me the doctor's address, and I repeated it several times, to make her believe I wanted to memorize it. I wouldn't have been in any hurry to leave, but, irritated, she turned her back on me. I was actually being thrown out of my prison.

Downstairs, a woman was quick to open the door for me. I hadn't a penny on me, and I murmured: "I'll have to tip you some other time."

There's no knowing the future. With me, things are often repeated: it was conceivable that I might turn up there again.

The night was clear and warm. I took off my hat, the better to feel the breeze of freedom. I looked at the stars with wonder, as if I had only just conquered them. The next day, far from the clinic, I would give up smoking. Meanwhile, passing a café that was still open, I bought some good cigarettes, because it wouldn't be possible to conclude my smoker's career with one of poor Giovanna's cigarettes. The man who waited on me knew who I was and gave me the pack on credit.

Reaching my villa, I rang the bell furiously. First the maid came to the window, and then, after not such a short time, my wife. I waited for her, thinking, perfectly cool: Apparently Dr. Muli is here. But, recognizing me, my wife laughed, and her laughter, echoing in the deserted street, was so sincere that it would have sufficed to dispel all suspicion.

Once inside, I postponed any inquisitorial action. When I had promised my wife to tell my adventures, which she thought she knew already, the next day, she asked me: "Why don't you go to bed?"

As an excuse, I said: "I believe you've taken advantage of my absence to move that armoire."

It's true that, at home, I always believe things have been moved, and it's also true that my wife very often does move them; but at that moment I was peering into every corner to see if the small, trim body of Dr. Muli was concealed somewhere.

My wife gave me some good news. Returning from the clinic, she had run into Olivi's son, who had told her the old man was much better, having taken a medicine prescribed by a new doctor.

Falling asleep, I thought I had done the right thing in leaving the clinic, because I had plenty of time to cure myself slowly. And my son, sleeping in the next room, also was surely not preparing to judge me yet, or to imitate me. There was absolutely no hurry.

MY FATHER'S DEATH

THE DOCTOR HAS left town, and I really don't know if a biography of my father is necessary. If I describe my father in over-scrupulous detail, it might turn out that, to achieve my own cure, it would have been necessary to analyze him first. I am going bravely ahead, because I know that if my father had needed such treatment it would have been for an illness quite different from mine. In any case, to waste no time, I will tell only as much about him as is necessary to stimulate my memory of myself.

"15.4.1890. My father dies. L.C." For those who do not know, those last two letters do not stand for Lower Case, but for Last Cigarette. This is an annotation I find in a volume by Ostwald on positivistic philosophy, with which, full of hope, I have spent many hours and never understood. No one would believe this, but, despite its brevity, that annotation records the most important event of my life.

My mother died before I was fifteen. I wrote some poems dedicated to her – hardly the same as weeping – and, in my sorrow, I was accompanied always by the feeling that at this moment a serious, industrious life was to begin for me. My grief itself hinted at a more intense life. At that time a still-active religious feeling attenuated and softened the terrible misfortune. My mother continued to live, though far from me, and she would derive satisfaction from the successes for which I was preparing myself. Very convenient! I remember precisely my condition at that time. Thanks to my mother's death and the salutary emotion it inspired, everything was going to improve for me.

31

My father's death, on the contrary, was a great, genuine catastrophe. Heaven no longer existed, and furthermore, at thirty, I was finished. This was the end for me, too! I realized for the first time that the most important, the decisive part of my life lay behind me, irretrievably. My grief was not merely egoistic, as these words might suggest. Not at all! I wept for him and myself together, and also for myself alone, because he was dead. Until then I had gone from one cigarette to another and from one university department to another, with an indestructible faith in my ability. And I believe that faith, which made my life so sweet, would have endured perhaps even till today, if my father had not died. With him dead, there was no longer a tomorrow to which I could address my determination.

Time and again, when I think about it, I am amazed by the strange way this despair of myself and my future came into existence at my father's death and not before. Generally speaking, these are recent events, and to recall my great sorrow and every detail of that catastrophe, I certainly have no need to dream, as the analysis gentlemen would like. Until his death, I did not live for my father. I made no effort to be close to him and, when it was possible to do so without hurting him, I kept out of his way. At the university, everyone knew him by the nickname I had given him: "Old Silva Moneybags." It took his sickness to make me attached to him; the sickness that quickly became death, for it was very brief and the doctor gave him up for dead at once. When I was in Trieste, we saw each other perhaps an hour a day at most. We were never so close or so long together as in my time of mourning. If only I had taken more care of him and wept less! I would have been less sick myself. It was hard for us to be together, not least because intellectually we had nothing in common. Looking at each other, we both had the same pitying smile, his made more bitter by his keen paternal anxiety about my future, mine, on the contrary, all indulgence, convinced as I was that his weaknesses by now were inconsequential, as I attributed them in part to his age. He was the first to distrust my energy and – it seems to me – too soon. All the same, I suspect that even without the support of any scientific conviction, he distrusted me because he was self-made, and that was all I needed – now with confident scientific conviction – to increase my distrust of him.

He enjoyed, true, the reputation of being a clever business-man, but I knew that for many years his affairs had been handled by Olivi. Lack of talent for business was a point of resemblance between him and me, but there were no others; I can say that, of the two of us, I represented strength, and he weakness. What I have already recorded in these notebooks proves that I possess and always have possessed – perhaps my supreme misfortune – an impetuous drive toward the future. All my dreams of stability and strength can be defined only in those terms. My father knew nothing of all this. He lived in perfect harmony with the way he was made, and I must believe that he never exerted any effort to improve. He would smoke all day and, after Mamma's death, when he could not sleep, also at night. He drank a fair amount, too, like a *gentleman*, in the evening, at supper, so that he could be sure of finding sleep readily the moment he laid his head on the pillow. But, to hear him, smoking and alcohol were good medicines.

As for women, I learned from some relatives that my mother had had some cause for jealousy. Indeed, that mild woman apparently had sometimes to resort to violent measures to keep her husband in line. He allowed himself to be guided by her, whom he loved and respected, but apparently she never managed to wring any confession of infidelity from him, and thus she died in the conviction that she had been mistaken. Still, my good kinfolk tell how she caught her husband virtually *in flagrante* at her dressmaker's. He excused himself on the pretext of absentmindedness and so firmly that he was believed. The only consequence was that my mother never returned to that dressmaker, nor did my father. I believe that in his shoes I would have ended up confessing, but I would not have been able to abandon the dressmaker afterwards, for where I stand, I put down roots.

As a true *paterfamilias*, my father knew how to defend his peace and quiet. He possessed this peace and quiet both in his house and in his soul. The only books he read were bland and moral, not out of hypocrisy on his part, but from the most genuine conviction: I think he felt deeply the truth of those moralizing sermons, and his conscience was appeased by his sincere support of virtue. Now that I am growing old and turning into a kind of patriarch, I also feel that a preached immorality is more to be punished that an immoral action. You arrive at murder through love or through hate; you propagandize murder only through wickedness.

We had so little in common, the two of us, that he confessed to me how, among the people in the world who made him uneasy, I was number one. My yearning for health had driven me to study the human body. He, on the contrary, had been able to dispel from his memory any thought of that frightful machine. For him the heart did not beat and there was no need to recall valves and veins and metabolism, to explain how his organism lived. Exercise? No, because experience told him that whatever moved eventually stopped. The earth itself was, for him, unmoving and firmly attached to its hinges. Naturally he never said this, but he suffered if anything was said to him that did not conform to this view. He interrupted me, revolted, one day when I mentioned the antipodes to him. The thought of those people with their heads upside down made him queasy.

He reproached me for two other things: my absentmindedness and my tendency to laugh at the most serious matters. When it came to absentmindedness, he differed from me because he kept a little notebook in which he jotted down

34

everything he wanted to remember, reviewing its pages several times daily. In this way he thought he had overcome his ailment and didn't suffer from it anymore. He imposed that notebook method also on me, but in mine I jotted down nothing except a few last cigarettes.

As for my contempt for serious matters, I believe his great defect was to consider serious too many things in this world. Here is an example: When, after having transferred from the study of law to that of chemistry, I sought his permission to return to the former, he said to me amiably: "The fact remains that you are certifiably crazy."

I wasn't in the least offended, and I was so grateful to him for his acquiescence that I thought to reward him by making him laugh. I went to Dr. Canestrini for an examination and a certificate. It wasn't an easy matter because I had to submit to long and thorough tests. When I was given a clean bill of mental health, I triumphantly carried the document to my father, but he couldn't laugh at it. In a heartbroken voice, tears in his eyes, he cried: "Ah, you really are crazy."

And that was my reward for the laborious and innocuous little farce. He never forgave me and so never laughed at it. To persuade a doctor to examine you as a joke? To have a certificate drawn up, as a joke, complete with tax stamps? Madness!

In short, compared with him I represented strength, and at times I think that the disappearance of his weakness, which had strengthened me, was something I felt as a reduction.

I remember how he demonstrated his weakness when that rascal Olivi persuaded him to make a will. The will was important for Olivi, who wanted to have my affairs placed under his guardianship; and apparently he worked for a long time on the old man to induce him to perform that painful task. Finally my father made up his mind, but his broad, peaceful face turned grim. He thought constantly of death, as if that document had brought him into contact with it.

One evening he asked me: "Do you think everything stops when we're dead?"

The mystery of death is something I think about every day, but I was not yet in a position to give him the information he was asking of me. To please him, I invented the happiest faith in our future.

"I believe pleasure survives, because sorrow is no longer necessary. Decomposition could recall sexual pleasure. Certainly it will be accompanied by happiness and repose, since recomposition would be so toilsome. Decomposition should be the reward of life!"

I was a total failure. We were at table after supper. Without answering, he rose from his chair, drained another glass, and said, "This is no moment for philosophizing – least of all, with you!"

And he went out. Distressed, I followed him, thinking to stay with him and distract him from his sad thoughts. He sent me away, saying I reminded him of death and its pleasures.

He could dismiss the thought of his will until he was able to announce it to me as a fact. He remembered it every time he saw me. One evening he blurted: "I have to tell you something: I've made my will."

To relieve his nightmare, I immediately mastered my surprise at his communication and said to him: "I'll never have to undergo that nuisance, because I hope all my heirs will die before me!"

He was promptly disturbed by my laughing at such a grave matter, and he rediscovered all his desire to punish me. So it was easy for him to inform me of the fine trick he had played on me, making me Olivi's ward.

I must say I behaved like a good boy. I gave up any idea of objection, and to tear him from the thought that was making him suffer, I declared that I would comply with his last wishes, whatever they might be.

"Perhaps," I added, "my future behavior will lead you to alter your last wishes."

He liked that, also because he saw that I was attributing a very, very long life to him. Still, he actually wanted me to swear that, unless he decreed otherwise, I would never try to reduce Olivi's authority. I swore a formal oath, since my simple promise wasn't enough for him. I was then so meek that now, when I'm tortured by remorse for not having loved him enough before he died, I always summon up that scene. To be sincere, I have to add that it was easy for me to submit to his arrangements because at that time I found the idea of being forced not to work rather attractive.

About a year before his death, I once took rather vigorous action for the sake of his health. He confided to me that he felt unwell, and I forced him to go to a doctor, accompanying him there myself. The doctor prescribed some medicine and told us to come back the following week. But then my father refused, insisting that he hated doctors as much as undertakers, and he didn't even take the prescribed medicine because that also reminded him of doctors and undertakers. For a couple of hours he didn't smoke, and for a single meal, he gave up wine. He felt very well when he could say good-bye to the treatment, and I, seeing him happier, thought no more about it.

There were also times when I saw him sad. But I would have been amazed to see him really happy, alone and old as he was.

*

One evening toward the end of March, I was a bit late coming home. Nothing unusual: I had fallen into the hands of a learned friend, who wanted to expound to me some of his ideas about the origins of Christianity. For the first time I was obliged to think about those origins, yet I endured the long lesson to please my friend. It was cold and drizzling. Everything was unpleasant and gloomy, including the Greeks and the Jews of whom my friend spoke; still, I submitted to that suffering for a good two hours. My usual weakness! I could bet that even today I'd be equally incapable of resisting, if someone made a serious attempt to persuade me to study astronomy for a while.

I entered the garden surrounding our villa, which was reached by a short driveway. Maria, our maid, was waiting for me at the window and, hearing me approach, she cried into the darkness: "Is that you, Signor Zeno?"

Maria was one of those maidservants who are no longer to be found. She had been with us for about fifteen years. Every month she deposited a part of her wages in the savings bank against her old age: savings that proved of no use to her, however, for she died in our house, still on the job, shortly after my marriage.

She told me that my father had come home a few hours before, but had insisted on holding supper for me. When she protested that meanwhile he should begin eating, she was dismissed rather rudely. Afterwards he asked for me several times, anxious and uneasy. Maria hinted that she thought my father wasn't feeling well. He seemed to be having difficulty speaking and was short of breath. I must say that, being alone with him so much, she often got it into her head that he was ill. There were few things for the poor woman to observe in that lonely house, and − after the experience with my mother − she expected everyone to die before her.

I rushed to the dining room, somewhat curious, not yet concerned. My father rose immediately from the sofa where he was lying, and welcomed me with a great joy that did not move me because I first caught his expression of reproach. But at the same time his joy reassured me, as it seemed a sign of health. I didn't notice the stammering and shortness of breath Maria had mentioned. Then, instead of scolding me, he apologized for having been obstinate.

"I can't help it," he said, in a good-natured tone. "The two of us are alone in the world, and I wanted to see you before going to bed."

If only I had behaved with simplicity, putting my arms around my dear father, whom illness had made so meek and affectionate! Instead, I began coldly to make a diagnosis: Had the old Silva become so meek? Was he ill? I looked at him suspiciously and could find nothing better to do than scold him myself: "Why did you wait this long to eat your supper? You could have eaten, and then waited for me."

He laughed, very youthfully: "I eat better in company."

This jollity could also indicate a good appetite: I was reassured, and I started eating. In his house slippers, his legs unsteady, he came to the table and occupied his usual place. Then he sat and watched me as I ate, while he, after a few scant spoonfuls, took no more food and even pushed away the plate, which revolted him. But the smile persisted on his aged face. I remember only, as if it were something that had happened yesterday, how a couple of times, when I looked into his eyes, he avoided meeting my gaze. They say this is a sign of insincerity, but now I know it's a sign of illness. The sick animal will not allow himself to be observed at any orifice through which disease or weakness can be perceived.

He was still expecting to hear how I had spent all those hours during which he had waited for me. And seeing that it meant so much to him, I stopped eating for a moment and said curtly that until now I had been discussing the origins of Christianity.

He looked at me, dubious and perplexed: "So you, too, are thinking about religion these days?"

It was obvious that if I had agreed to think about it with him, I would have given him consolation. But, on the contrary, as long as my father was alive, I felt combative (afterwards no longer); and I replied with one of those trite remarks heard every day in the cafés around the University: "For me

39

religion is merely an ordinary phenomenon, something to be studied."

"Phenomenon?" he said, disoriented. He groped for a ready retort and opened his mouth to utter it. Then he hesitated and looked at the second dish, which at that moment Maria was offering him. He didn't touch it. Then, to gag himself, he stuck into his mouth a cigar stub and lighted it, allowing it to go out at once. He had granted himself a kind of interval, to reflect calmly. For an instant he looked at me resolutely: "Surely you don't mean to laugh at religion?"

Like the perfect idle student I had always been, I replied, with my mouth full: "Laugh? No, I study it!"

He was silent, and looked for a long time at the cigar stub he had laid on a plate. I understand now why he said that to me. Now I understand everything that passed through that already clouded mind, and I am surprised how I then understood nothing. I believe my spirit then lacked the affection that renders so many things comprehensible. Afterwards it was so easy for me! He avoided engaging my skepticism: a challenge too difficult for him at that moment, but he thought he could attack it on the flank, gently, as befitted a sick man. I remember that when he spoke, his breath came in gasps and impeded his speech. It's a great effort, to prepare yourself for combat. But I thought he would not resign himself to going to bed without pitching into me, and I prepared myself for discussions that then didn't take place.

"I . . . " he said, still looking at his now-spent cigar stub, "I feel how great my experience is, and my knowledge of life. A man doesn't live all these years for nothing. I know many things, and unfortunately I'm unable to teach them all to you as I would like. Oh, how I would like that! I see into things; and I see what is right and true and also what isn't."

I could raise no objection here. I mumbled, unconvinced, as I went on eating: "Yes, Papà."

I didn't want to hurt his feelings.

"Too bad you came home so late. I wasn't so tired before, and I could have said many things to you."

I thought he wanted to annoy me once again because I had been late, and I suggested saving that argument for the next day.

"It's not an argument," he replied, with a faraway look in his eyes. "It's something entirely different. Something that can't be discussed and that you'll know, too, as soon as I've told it to you. But it's hard to say!"

At this point I felt a suspicion: "You don't feel well?"

"I can't say I feel bad, but I'm very tired and I'm going off to bed at once."

He rang the bell and at the same time called out for Maria. When she came, he asked if everything was ready in his room. He then started off immediately, his slippers shuffling over the floor. When he was at my side, he bent his head to offer his cheek for my nightly kiss.

Seeing him move so unsteadily, I again suspected that he was ill and I asked him. We both repeated the same words several times, and he confirmed that he was tired but not ill. Then he added, "Now I'll think of the right words I'll say to you tomorrow. They'll convince you, you'll see."

"Papà," I declared with emotion, "I'll be happy to listen to you."

Seeing me so willing to bow to his experience, he hesitated to leave me: a favorable moment like this should be exploited! He ran his hand over his forehead and sat down in the chair he had been leaning on when he extended his cheek for the kiss. He was breathing with a little difficulty.

"Strange!" he said. "I can't say anything to you. Nothing at all."

He looked around as if he sought outside himself whatever he was unable to grasp within.

"And yet I know so many things. Indeed, I know everything. It must be the result of my great experience."

He wasn't suffering all that much at his inability to express himself because he smiled at his own strength, at his own greatness.

I don't know why I didn't call the doctor immediately. Instead, with sorrow and remorse, I must confess that I considered my father's words dictated by presumption, something I thought I'd observed in him several times. But I couldn't fail to notice his evident weakness, and only for that reason I didn't argue. I liked seeing him happy in his illusion of being so strong when, on the contrary, he was very weak. I was, besides, flattered by the affection he was displaying, showing his desire to pass on to me the knowledge he thought he possessed, though I was convinced I could learn nothing from him. And to encourage him and calm him, I said he shouldn't strive to find immediately the words he lacked, because in similar predicaments even the greatest scientists stored overcomplicated questions in some cranny of the brain until they simplified themselves.

He answered: "What I'm looking for isn't complicated. No, it's a matter of finding a word, just one, and I'll find it! But not tonight because I'm going to sleep straight through till morning, without the slightest concern."

Still he didn't rise from the chair. Hesitantly, after studying my face for a moment, he said: "I'm afraid I won't be able to tell you what I mean, thanks to your habit of laughing at everything."

He smiled as if to beg me not to take offense at his words, and got up from the chair and proffered his cheek for the second time. I abandoned any idea of arguing, of convincing him that in this world there are many things that could and should be laughed at, and I tried to reassure him with a strong embrace. Perhaps my action was too strong, because as he freed himself from my hug, he was even shorter of breath, but he surely understood my affection, because he said good night with a friendly wave of his hand.

"Off to bed!" he cried joyfully, and went out, followed by Maria.

And left alone (this, too, was strange) I didn't think about my father's health, but instead, moved and – I may say – filled with proper filial respect, I regretted that for such a mind, aspiring to lofty goals, a finer education had not been possible. Today, as I write, approaching the age reached by my father, I know for certain that a man can feel the existence of his own lofty intelligence, which gives no other sign of itself beyond that strong feeling. Thus, you take a deep breath, you accept yourself and you admire all nature as it is and as, unchanging, it is offered to us. This is a manifestation of the same intelligence that decreed all Creation. Certainly, in the last lucid moment of his life, my father's feeling of intelligence originated in his sudden religious inspiration, and in fact he was led to speak to me about it because I had told him of my discussion of the origins of Christianity. Now, however, I know also that this feeling of his was the first symptom of a cerebral hemorrhage.

Maria came back to clear the table and to tell me that my father had apparently fallen asleep immediately. So I also went off to bed, completely reassured. Outside, the wind was blowing and howling. I could hear it from my warm bed, like a lullaby gradually moving away from me, as I sank into sleep.

I don't know how long I slept. I was wakened by Maria. Apparently she had come into my room several times to call me and had then run out again. In my deep sleep I felt at first a certain agitation, then I glimpsed the old woman hopping about the room, and finally I understood. She had wanted to wake me, but by the time she succeeded, she was no longer in my room. The wind continued singing to me of sleep, and to tell the truth, I must confess that I went to my father's room with pain at having been wrenched from my sleep. God help her if he wasn't ill this time!

My father's room, not large, was somewhat overfurnished. After my mother's death, to lessen memories, he had changed rooms, taking all his furniture with him into the new, smaller room. Faintly illuminated by a little gas flame on the very low night table, the room was now immersed in darkness. Maria was supporting my father, who lay supine, but with a part of his torso extending from the bed. My father's face, covered with sweat, was ruddy in the light nearby. His head was resting on Maria's faithful bosom. He was growling with pain, and his mouth was so slack that saliva was trickling down his chin. Motionless, he stared at the wall opposite and didn't look around when I entered.

Maria told me she had heard his groans and had arrived in time to prevent his falling out of bed. At first — she assured me — he had been more distressed, but now he seemed relatively calm. Still she would not risk leaving him alone. Perhaps she meant to apologize for having called me, though I had already realized she had been right to wake me up. She wept as she spoke to me, but as yet I didn't weep with her; indeed, I admonished her to keep quiet and not to make the fright of this moment worse with her lamentations. I hadn't grasped the full situation. The poor woman made every effort to quell her sobs.

I put my lips to my father's ear and shouted: "Why are you groaning, Papà? Are you in pain?"

I believe he heard, because his moaning grew fainter and he looked away from the wall opposite as if he were trying to see me, though he couldn't manage to direct his gaze at me. Several times I shouted the same question into his ear, and always with the same result. My manly demeanor at once disappeared. My father, by that time, was closer to death than to me, so my shouting no longer reached him. A great fear overcame me, and I remembered first of all the words we had exchanged earlier in the evening. After just a few hours he had taken a step to see which of the two of us was right. Strange! My grief was accompanied by remorse. I hid my face in my father's pillow and wept desperately, the same sobbing for which I had reproached Maria a little earlier.

Now it was her turn to calm me, but she did this in a curious way. She begged me to be calm, but she spoke of my father, still moaning, his eyes all too open, as she might speak of a dead man.

"Poor thing!" she said, "to die like that! With that beautiful, full head of hair." She stroked him. It was true. My father's head was crowned by thick, white curls, whereas I, at thirty, was already balding.

I didn't remember that there were doctors in this world and that it was commonly supposed that they were sometimes agents of recovery. I had already seen death in that face distraught with pain, and I no longer had any hope. Maria was the first to mention the doctor, then she went out to wake our gardener and send him into the city.

I remained alone, supporting my father, for about ten minutes, which to me seemed an eternity. I remember how, as my hands touched that tormented body, I tried to impart to them all the tenderness that filled my heart. He couldn't hear words. What could I do to make him know how much I loved him?

When the gardener came, I went to my room to write a note; it was hard for me to put together those few words meant to give the doctor an idea of the situation so that he could bring some medicines with him at once. I saw constantly before me the certain, imminent death of my father and I asked myself: "What will I do now in this world?"

The long hours of waiting followed. I have a fairly precise recollection of those hours. After the first it was no longer necessary for me to support my father, who lay on his bed unconscious, unmoving. His groaning had stopped, but his insensibility was total. His respiration was hurried, and, almost unconsciously, I imitated it. I couldn't breathe for long at that pace, and I granted myself occasional pauses, hoping to induce the sick man also to repose. But he rushed ahead tirelessly. We tried in vain to give him a spoonful of tea. His unconsciousness lessened when he was obliged to defend himself against any intervention from us. Determined, he would clench his teeth. Even in his unconscious state, he was accompanied by that indomitable stubbornness of his. Long before dawn his breathing changed rhythm. It came in phases that began with slow respiration that could have seemed that of a healthy man, but this was followed by other, more rapid breaths ending in a long, frightening pause, which seemed to Maria and to me the announcement of death. But the first phase would resume, almost always the same, a musical line of infinite sadness, lacking any color. That respiration wasn't always the same, but it was always noisy and became virtually a part of that room. After that hour it remained always there, for a long, long time!

I spent a few hours sprawled on a sofa, while Maria was still seated by the bed. On that sofa I wept my most searing tears. Weeping obscures our guilt and allows us to accuse fate, without contradiction. I wept because I was losing the father for whom I had always lived. No matter that I had given him scant company. Hadn't my efforts to become a better man been aimed at affording him some satisfaction? The success I yearned for was to be my boast to him, who had always doubted me, but primarily it would be his consolation. And now, on the contrary, he could no longer wait for me and was going off, convinced of my incurable weakness. My tears were very bitter.

In writing, or rather, in setting down on paper these painful memories, I discover that the image that obsessed me at my first attempt to see into my past, that locomotive dragging a series of cars up a slope, had come to me initially on that sofa, as I listened to my father's breathing. That is how locomotives sound, as they pull enormous loads: they emit regular puffs that then accelerate, ending in a menacing pause as the listener fears he will see engine and train go hurtling downhill. Seriously! My first effort to remember had carried me back to that night, to the most important hours of my life.

Dr. Coprosich arrived at the villa some time before dawn, accompanied by an orderly carrying a medicine case. He had been obliged to come on foot because, in the violent hurricane, he hadn't found a cab.

I received him weeping, and he treated me with great kindness, also encouraging me to hope. Still, I should say at once: after that meeting, there are few men in this world who can arouse in me the keen dislike Dr. Coprosich inspires. He is still alive today, decrepit and surrounded by the respect of the entire city. When I glimpse him, so frail and hesitant, walking through the streets seeking a bit of exercise and air, even now my aversion is renewed.

At that time the doctor can't have been much over forty. He had devoted considerable study to forensic medicine, and though he was well known to be a good Italian, the Royal and Imperial authorities assigned the most important investigations to him. He was a thin, nervous man, his insignificant face crowned by a baldness that simulated a very high forehead. Another weakness of his gave him importance: as he raised his eyeglasses (and he always did this when he wanted to ponder something), his blinded eyes stared beyond or above his interlocutor, and they had the curious look of the colorless eyes of a statue, menacing or perhaps ironic. The eyes were then unpleasant. If he had something to say, even a single word, he would replace the glasses on his nose, and then his eyes would become once more those of a commonplace solid citizen, who carefully ponders the things of which he speaks.

He sat in the vestibule to rest for a few moments. He asked me to tell him exactly what had happened from the first alarm until his arrival. He removed his glasses, and his strange eyes gazed at the wall behind me.

I tried to be precise, and this was not easy, considering the state I was in. I remembered also that Dr. Coprosich could not tolerate people ignorant of medicine who used medical terminology, as if they knew something about the subject. And when I came to talk about what had seemed to me "cerebral respiration," he put on his glasses before saying to me: "Go slow with the definitions. We'll see later what it is." I had spoken also of my father's odd behavior, his anxiety to see me, then his haste to go to bed. I didn't report my father's strange talk: perhaps I was afraid of being forced to repeat some of the replies I had made to my father. But I did say that Papà had not managed to express himself with precision, and that he seemed to be thinking intensely about something going on in his head that he couldn't put into words. The doctor, his glasses squarely on his nose, exclaimed triumphantly: "I know what was going on in his head!"

So did I, but I didn't say so for fear of angering Dr. Coprosich: it was the hemorrhage.

We went to the sick man's bed. With the orderly's help, the doctor turned the poor inert body this way and that for a time that seemed to me interminable. He listened and examined. He tried to elicit the patient's help, but in vain.

"That's enough!" the doctor said at a certain point. He came over to me, his eyeglasses in his hand, as he looked at the floor and, with a sigh, said to me: "You must be brave. The situation is very serious."

We went to my room, where he washed his face.

He was thus without eyeglasses, and when he raised his face to dry it, his damp head seemed the curious head of an amulet made by unskilled hands. He remembered having seen us some months previously, and he expressed his surprise that we hadn't come back to him. Indeed, he thought then that we had left him for another doctor; on that occasion he had stated quite clearly that my father needed treatment. As he uttered these reproaches, without his glasses, he was impressive. He raised his voice and demanded explanations. His eyes sought them everywhere.

Of course he was right, and I had earned the reproach. I must say here that I am sure these words are not the reason why I hate Dr. Coprosich. I apologized, telling him of my father's aversion to doctors and medicines; I wept as I spoke, and the doctor, with generous kindliness, tried to calm me, saying that even if we had consulted him earlier, his skill might, at most, have been able to delay the catastrophe we were now witnessing, but not to prevent it.

However, as he went on inquiring about the first signs of the illness, he found new cause to reproach me. He asked if my father had complained in recent months about the state of his health, his appetite, his sleeping habits. I could give him no precise answers, and could not even tell him if my father had eaten much or little at that table where we sat down together daily. The obviousness of my guilt crushed me, but the doctor didn't insist with his questions. He learned from me that Maria had always thought the old man was at death's door, and that I had made fun of her for this.

He was cleaning his ears, looking upward. "In a couple of hours he will probably regain consciousness, at least partially," he said.

"So there's some hope?" I cried.

"None whatsoever!" he replied curtly. "The leeches are never wrong in these cases. He will surely regain a bit of consciousness, and perhaps then lose his mind."

He shrugged and replaced the towel. That shrug indicated a real dismissal of his own work, and encouraged me to speak. I was filled with terror at the idea that my father might come out of his daze in order to witness his death, but if it hadn't been for that shrug, I would never have had the courage to say as much.

"Doctor!" I implored. "Doesn't it seem a heartless thing, to make him regain consciousness?"

I burst out crying. The desire to cry lurked always in my shaken nerves, but I succumbed to it helplessly, to display my tears and to make the doctor forgive the criticism I had dared express of his treatment.

With great humanity he said to me, "Come now, calm yourself. The patient's awareness will never be sufficiently acute to allow him to recognize his condition. He's not a doctor. If we don't tell him he's dying, he won't know. On the other hand, we may run into something worse. I mean, he could lose his mind. I've brought a straitjacket with me, however, and the orderly will remain here."

More frightened than ever, I begged him not to apply the leeches. Then, quite calmly, he told me that the orderly had surely already applied them, because he had given the man instructions before leaving my father's room. I became angry. Could anything be more wicked than recalling a sick man to consciousness, without the least hope of saving him, only to plunge him into despair, or expose him to the risk of having to undergo – amid what suffering! – the straitjacket? With great violence, though still accompanying my words with those tears that craved compassion, I declared that it seemed to me an inconceivable cruelty not to allow a man to die in peace when he was definitively doomed.

I hate that man because he then became angry with me. This is what I was never able to forgive him. He became so agitated that he forgot to put on his glasses, and yet he discovered the exact spot where my head was, to fix it with his baleful eyes. He said that it seemed to him that I wanted to sever even the thin thread of hope that still existed. This is exactly how he said it, harshly.

We were on the verge of a fight. Weeping and shouting, I retorted that a few instants earlier he himself had rejected any hope of the sick man's being saved. My house and those living in it were not to be used in experiments; there were other places in this world for that sort of thing!

With great, ominously calm severity, he replied: "I explained to you the state of our knowledge at that instant. But who can say what may happen by tomorrow, or in half an hour's time? By keeping your father alive, I have left the door open to all possibilities."

Then he put on his glasses, and with his fussy clerk's mien, he added further, endless explanations about the importance that a doctor's intervention could have in the economic destiny of a family. An extra half hour of respiration could decide the fate of an inheritance.

I was weeping now also because I pitied myself for having to stand and listen to such things at such a moment. Exhausted, I stopped arguing. Anyway, the leeches had already been applied!

The doctor is a power when he is at a sick man's bedside, and toward Dr. Coprosich I exhibited all due respect. It must have been this respect that kept me from proposing that we seek a second opinion, a deference for which I reproached myself over many years. Now all remorse is dead, along with my other feelings of which I speak here as coldly as I would recount events that had befallen a stranger. In my heart, nothing of those days remains except my dislike for that doctor, who nevertheless stubbornly goes on living.

Later we went once again to my father's bed. We found him asleep, resting on his right side. They had placed a washcloth on his temple to cover the wounds made by the leeches. The doctor, eager to find out at once if the patient's consciousness had increased, shouted into his ears. The patient didn't react in any way.

"So much the better!" I said with great courage, though still weeping.

"The anticipated effect cannot fail!" the doctor replied. "Can't you see that his respiration has already changed?"

In fact, while gasping and labored, the respiration no longer followed those phases that had frightened me.

The orderly said something to the doctor, who nodded. It involved trying the straitjacket on the patient. They extracted the device from the case and pulled my father up, forcing him to remain seated in the bed. Then he opened his eyes: they were dull, not yet adjusted to the light. I sobbed again, fearing they would immediately look around and see everything. On the contrary, when the sick man's head was back on the pillow, those eyes closed, like the eyes of certain dolls.

The doctor exulted.

"It's an entirely different thing!" he murmured.

Yes: it was a different thing! For me, simply a serious threat. Fervently I kissed my father's brow, and in my mind I made a wish: "Now sleep. Sleep until the eternal sleep arrives!"

And this is how I wished for my father's death, but the doctor didn't divine it because he said to me, with good humor: "You, too, are pleased now, to see he has become himself again!"

By the time the doctor left, dawn had broken. A grim dawn, tentative. The wind, still blowing in gusts, seemed to me less violent, although it continued to raise the frozen snow.

I accompanied the doctor into the garden. I exaggerated these acts of politeness so that he wouldn't perceive my rancor. My face conveyed only consideration and respect. I allowed myself a grimace of disgust, relieving my strain, only when I saw him go off along the path leading to the gate of the house. Small and black in the midst of the snow, he staggered and stopped at every gust, to resist it better. My grimace wasn't enough for me, and I felt a need for other violent acts, after making that effort. For a few minutes I walked along the drive in the cold, bareheaded, angrily stamping my feet in the deep snow. I couldn't say, however, if this puerile wrath was directed at the doctor or at myself. First of all at myself, at me, who had wanted my father dead and hadn't dared say so. My silence converted that desire, inspired by the purest filial devotion, into a genuine crime that weighed on me horribly.

The patient went on sleeping. He uttered only a few words, which I didn't grasp, but in the calmest conversational tone, odd because he interrupted his breathing, still very fast, anything but calm. Was he approaching consciousness and desperation?

Maria had now sat down at the bed beside the orderly. He inspired my confidence, and displeased me only through a certain exaggerated conscientiousness. He rejected Maria's proposal to give the sick man a spoonful of broth, which she considered a good medicine. But the doctor had said nothing about broth, and the orderly wanted to wait for the doctor's return before taking such an important step. He spoke more imperiously than the matter warranted. Poor Maria didn't insist, nor did I. I made another grimace of disgust, however.

They persuaded me to lie down. Since I would have to spend the night with the orderly, tending the patient, who would need me and Maria both, one of us could now rest on the sofa. I lay down and fell asleep at once, with complete, pleasant loss of consciousness and − I'm sure of this − not interrupted by the slightest glimmer of a dream.

Last night, on the contrary, after spending part of yesterday collecting these memories, I had an extremely vivid dream that, with an enormous backward leap in time, carried me to those days. I saw myself again with the doctor in the same room where we had argued about leeches and straitjackets, a room that now looks completely different because it is the bedroom I share with my wife. I was telling Coprosich how to care for and cure my father, while the doctor (not old and decrepit as he is now, but vigorous and keen as he was then) wrathfully, spectacles in hand, his eyes unfocused, was shouting that it wasn't worth the trouble to do so many things. What he said exactly was this: "The leeches would recall him to life and to pain, and they mustn't be applied!" I, on the contrary, was banging my fist on a medical volume and yelling: "Leeches! I want leeches! And the straitjacket, too!"

Apparently my dream turned noisy, because my wife interrupted it, waking me. Distant shadows! I believe that to peer into them requires some optical aid, and this is what disorients you.

My calm sleep is the last memory of that day. Then other long days followed in which one hour resembled the next. The weather had improved; they were saying that my father's condition had also improved. He could move freely about the room and had begun his pursuit of air, from the bed to his easy chair. Through the closed windows, for some instants, he would look also at the snow-covered garden, dazzling in the sun. Every now and then, when I entered that room, I was ready to argue, to becloud that consciousness Coprosich was waiting for. But though my father showed signs of hearing and understanding better every day, that consciousness was still remote.

Unfortunately I must confess that at my father's deathbed I harbored in my soul a great resentment that strangely clung to my sorrow and distorted it. That resentment was addressed first of all toward Coprosich, and it was increased by my effort to conceal it from him. I felt some also toward myself, because I was unable to continue my argument with the doctor and tell him clearly that I didn't give a damn for his learning and that I was wishing for my father's death in order to spare him pain.

Finally I felt resentful also toward the sick man. Anyone who has had the experience of spending days and weeks with a restless patient, and who is untrained to act as nurse and therefore remains a passive spectator of the treatment given by others, will understand me. Further, while I should have had a long rest to clarify my feelings, to control and perhaps appreciate my suffering for my father and for myself, instead I now had to struggle to make him swallow his medicine and to prevent him from leaving the room. Struggle always produces resentment.

One evening Carlo, the orderly, summoned me to observe some new progress in my father. I rushed after him, my heart pounding at the idea that the old man might become conscious of his illness and reproach me for it.

My father was on his feet, in the middle of the room, dressed only in his underwear, his red silk nightcap on his head. Though his gasping was still very loud, he uttered from time to time some brief, intelligible words. When I came in, he said to Carlo: "Open!"

He wanted the window opened. Carlo replied that he couldn't do it because of the great cold. And for a while my father forgot his own demand. He went and sat down in an armchair by the window and stretched out, seeking relief. When he saw me he smiled and asked: "Did you sleep?"

I don't believe my reply reached him. This wasn't the consciousness I had feared so long. When a man dies, he has too many other worries to allow any thinking about death. My father's whole organism was concentrated on respiration. And instead of listening to me, he shouted again at Carlo: "Open!"

He could find no rest. He left the chair in order to stand up. Then, with great effort and with the attendant's help, he stretched out on the bed, settling first on his left side for a moment and then immediately on his right, but he could tolerate this position only for a few minutes. Once more he called for Carlo's help to stand on his feet again, and finally he went back to the chair, in which he occasionally stayed a bit longer.

That day, moving from bed to chair, he stopped at the mirror and, gazing at himself in it, murmured: "I look like a Mexican!"

I think it was to escape the ghastly monotony of the race from bed to chair that, on this day, he attempted to smoke. He managed to fill his mouth with a single puff, which he immediately expelled, breathless.

Carlo had called me to observe a moment of clear consciousness in the patient.

"Am I seriously ill, then?" he asked, with anguish. This clarity did not return. On the contrary, a little later he had a moment of delirium. He rose from the bed and thought he had wakened after a night's sleep in a Vienna hotel. His parched mouth and his desire for something cool must have led him to dream of Vienna, as he remembered the cold, icy water of that city. He immediately spoke of the good water awaiting him at the next drinking font.

In general, he was a restless patient, but docile. I was afraid of him because I always feared I might see him turn harsh if he came to understand his situation; so his docility did not ease my great strain. But he obediently accepted any suggestion given him, because he expected one of them might save him from his breathlessness. The attendant offered to fetch him a glass of milk, and he agreed with genuine joy. After waiting with great eagerness to receive that milk, he was equally eager to be rid of it, having taken barely a sip, and when he wasn't promptly obeyed, he dropped the glass on the floor.

During the night that followed, I felt for the last time my terror of witnessing that consciousness I so feared. He had sat down in the armchair by the window and was gazing through the panes into the bright night, the sky filled with stars. His breathing was still shallow, but he didn't seem to be suffering, absorbed as he was in looking up. Perhaps because of his respiration, his head seemed to be nodding repeated assent.

I thought fearfully: Now he is pondering the problems he always avoided. I tried to identify the exact point of the sky at which he was staring. He looked up, his trunk erect, with the effort of someone peering through an aperture too high for him. It seemed to me he was looking at the Pleiades. Perhaps in his whole life he had never looked so long at something so far off. Suddenly he turned to me and, still erect, he said: "Look! Look!" with an air of severe admonition. He went back immediately to staring at the sky, then he faced me once more: "You see? You see?"

He tried to return to the stars, but he couldn't: he sank back exhausted in the chair, and when I asked him what he had wanted to show me, he didn't understand, nor did he recall having seen anything or having wanted me to see it. The word he had sought so hard in order to pass it on to me had eluded him forever.

The night was long but, I must confess, not particularly tiring for me and the orderly. We let the patient do as he pleased, and he walked about the room in his strange garb, completely unaware that he was awaiting death. Once he tried to go out into the corridor, where it was very cold. I stopped him, and he obeyed me at once. Another time, on the contrary, he sat up, weeping and cursing, and I insisted he be allowed to move as he chose. He became calm at once, and resumed his silence and his vain pursuit of relief.

When the doctor returned, the patient let himself be examined, and even tried to take a deep breath as he was asked to do. Then he spoke to me: "What is he saying?"

He ignored me for a moment, but quickly turned to me again: "When will I be able to go out?"

Encouraged by such docility, the doctor urged me to tell him to make an effort and stay in bed as long as possible. My father heard only the voices to which he was accustomed: mine, Maria's, Carlo's. I didn't believe in the effectiveness of those orders, but still I repeated them, putting a threatening tone in my voice.

"Yes, yes," my father promised, and at that same moment he got out of bed and went to the chair.

The doctor looked at him and, with resignation, murmured: "Obviously changing his position gives him some relief."

A little later I was in bed, but I couldn't close my eyes. I looked into the future, seeking to discover why and for whom

57

I could continue my efforts at self-improvement. I wept a great deal, but rather for myself than for the hapless man who was rushing around his bedroom without peace.

When I got up, Maria went to bed and I stayed at my father's side with Carlo. I was dejected and tired; my father was more restless than ever.

It was then that the terrible scene occurred which I shall never forget and which was to cast a long, long shadow, vitiating all my courage, all my joy. Before I could forget that sorrow, my every feeling was to be undermined for years.

The orderly said to me: "It would be such a good thing if we could manage to keep him in bed. The doctor considers that very important!"

Until then I had remained lying on the sofa. I got up and went to the bed, where, at that moment, the patient had lain down. I was determined: I would force my father to stay at least half an hour in the repose the doctor wanted. Wasn't this my duty?

Immediately my father tried to roll over toward the edge of the bed, to escape my pressure and get up. With a hand pressed firmly against his shoulder, I blocked him, while in a loud, imperious voice I ordered him not to move. For a brief moment, terrified, he obeyed. Then he cried out: "I'm dying!"

And he pulled himself erect. For my part, frightened by his cry, I had relaxed the pressure of my hand, so he could sit on the edge of the bed, directly facing me. I believe his wrath increased when he found himself − if only for one moment − prevented from moving, and he was sure I was also depriving him of the air he so needed, just as I was taking away the light by standing over him, while he remained sitting. With a supreme effort he managed to stand on his feet. He raised his hand high, as if he had learned he could endow it with no other strength beyond its mere weight, and let it fall against my cheek. Then he slipped to the bed and, from there, to the floor. Dead!

I didn't know he was dead, but my heart contracted with grief at the chastisement that, dying, he had meant to give me. With Carlo's help I lifted him and laid him on the bed again. Weeping exactly like a punished child, I shouted into his ear: "It's not my fault! It was that damned doctor who wanted to force you to stay on your back!"

It was a lie. Then, still childlike, I also promised never to do it again: "I'll let you move any way you please."

The orderly spoke: "He's dead."

They had to pull me out of the room by main force. He was dead, and I could no longer prove my innocence to him!

Alone, I tried to pull myself together. I reasoned: it was inconceivable that my father, still out of his mind, could decide to punish me and could direct his hand precisely enough to strike my cheek.

How could I be certain that my reasoning was correct? I actually thought of going to Coprosich. As a doctor, he could tell me something about a dying man's capacity for decision and action. I might even have been the victim of an act inspired by an attempt to ameliorate his respiration! But I didn't speak with Dr. Coprosich. It was impossible to go and reveal to him how my father had bidden me farewell. To that man! He who had already accused me of lack of affection for my father!

I received another serious blow when I heard Carlo in the kitchen that evening, telling Maria: "The father raised his hand high and, with all his remaining strength, he slapped his son." Carlo knew it, and therefore Coprosich would know it as well.

When I went into the mortuary chamber, I found that they had dressed the corpse. Carlo must also have combed the beautiful white hair. Death had stiffened that body, which lay there proud and menacing. The great, powerful, well-shaped hands were livid, but they lay so naturally that they seemed ready to seize and punish. I was unwilling, unable, to see him again.

Afterwards, at the funeral, I managed to remember my father weak and good as I had always known him from my infancy, and I convinced myself that the slap given me by a dying man hadn't been intentional. I became good as gold, and my father's memory accompanied me, growing sweeter all the time. It was like a delightful dream: now we were in perfect harmony, I had become the weaker and he the stronger.

I returned to the religion of my childhood and remained there for a long time. I imagined that my father heard me and I could tell him that the fault had been not mine but the doctor's. The lie was of no importance because now he understood everything, and so did I. And for quite some time the conversations with my father went on, tender and secret like an illicit love, because with everyone I continued to laugh at all religious practices, while it is true – and I wish to confess it here – that into someone's hands I daily and fervently commended my father's spirit. True religion, indeed, is that which does not have to be avowed in order to provide the solace that at times – if only rarely – you cannot do without.

THE STORY OF MY MARRIAGE

IN THE MIND of a young man from a middle-class family, the concept of human life is associated with that of a career, and in early youth the career is that of Napoleon I. This is not to say that the young man dreams of becoming emperor, for you can remain at a much lower level and still resemble Napoleon. The most intense life is narrated, in synthesis, by the most rudimentary sound, that of the sea-wave, which, once formed, changes at every instant until it dies! I expected therefore also to assume form and to dissolve, like Napoleon and like a wave.

My life could provide only a single note with no variation, fairly high and envied by some, but horribly tedious. Throughout my life my friends maintained the same opinion of me, and I believe that I, too, since arriving at the age of reason, have not much changed the notion I formed of myself.

The idea of marrying may therefore have come to me from the weariness of emitting and hearing always that one note. Those who have not yet experienced marriage believe it is more important than it is. The chosen companion will renew, improving or worsening, our breed by bearing children: Mother Nature wants this but cannot direct us openly, because at that time of life we haven't the slightest thought of children, so she induces us to believe that our wife will also bring about a renewal of ourselves: a curious illusion not confirmed by any text. In fact, we live then, one beside the other, unchanged, except for an acquired dislike of one so dissimilar to oneself or an envy of one who is our superior.

The strange thing is that my matrimonial adventure began with my meeting my future father-in-law and with the friendship and admiration I felt for him, before I learned he was the father of some nubile girls. Obviously, therefore, it was not a resolution on my part that caused me to advance toward the goal of which I was ignorant. I neglected one young girl who for a moment I might have thought suited for me, and I remained attached to my future father-in-law. It's almost enough to make you believe in destiny.

My deeply felt desire for novelty was satisfied by Giovanni Malfenti, so different from me and from all the people whose company and friendship I had sought in the past. Having gone though two university departments, I was fairly cultivated, thanks also to my long inertia, which I consider highly educational. He, on the contrary, was a great businessman, ignorant and active. But from his ignorance he drew strength and peace of mind, and I, spellbound, would observe him and envy him.

Malfenti at that time was about fifty, a man of iron constitution, huge body, tall and heavy, weighing perhaps two hundred pounds or more. The few ideas that stirred in his immense head would then be expounded with such clarity, examined so thoroughly, and applied to so many new situations every day, that they became part of him, of his limbs, his character. I was quite lacking in such ideas, and I hung on to him, to enrich myself.

I had come to the Tergesteo building on the advice of Olivi, who told me that I would get my commercial activity off to a good start by spending some time at the Bourse, and that I might also garner there some useful information for him. I sat down at that table where my future father-in-law reigned, and I never left it afterwards, since it seemed to me I had really come upon a classroom of commerce, such as I had long been seeking.

He soon became aware of my admiration and repaid it with a friendship that immediately struck me as paternal. Can he have known at once how things were to end? One evening when, thrilled by the example of his great activity, I declared that I wanted to rid myself of Olivi and manage my own affairs, he advised against it and even seemed alarmed by my intention. I could devote myself to business, but I should always maintain my firm tie with Olivi, whom he knew.

He was more than willing to instruct me, and in my note-book he actually wrote in his own hand the three command-ments he considered sufficient to make any firm prosper: 1. There's no need for a man to know how to work, but if he doesn't know how to make others work, he is doomed. 2. There is only one great regret: not having acted in one's own best interest. 3. In business, theory is useful, but it can be utilized only after the deal has been made.

I know these and many other axioms by heart, but they were of no help to me.

When I admire someone, I try at once to resemble him. So I also imitated Malfenti. I wanted to be very clever, and I felt that I was. Indeed, I once dreamed I was smarter than he. I thought I had discovered a flaw in his business organization: I decided to tell him immediately in order to win his esteem. One day at the Tergesteo table I stopped him when, in a business argument, he was calling his interlocutor a jackass. I told him I thought it a mistake for him to proclaim his cleverness far and wide. In my view the truly clever man in business matters should take care to appear foolish.

Giovanni made fun of me. A reputation for cleverness was very useful. For one thing, many came to seek his counsel, bringing him the latest news, while he gave them the most helpful advice, confirmed by experience accumulated ever since the Middle Ages. At times he happened to gain, along with the news, the possibility of selling some merchandise. Finally – and here he started shouting because he felt he had at last hit upon the argument that should convince me – to sell or to buy profitably, everyone seeks out the most clever man. From the fool they could hope for nothing, except perhaps to persuade him to sacrifice his own interest, but his goods always cost more than the clever man's, because he has already been swindled at the moment of purchase.

For Giovanni, I was the most important person at that table. He confided in me his business secrets, which I never betrayed. His trust was well bestowed, and in fact he was able to deceive me twice, even after I had become his son-in-law. The first time his shrewdness cost me money, though, as it was Olivi who was deceived, I didn't complain much. Olivi had sent me to him to collect some information shrewdly, which I relayed to him. The information was such that Olivi never afterwards forgave me, and whenever I opened my mouth to tell him something, he would ask: "Who told you that? Your father-in-law?" To defend myself, I had to defend Giovanni, and in the end I felt more swindler than swindled. Quite a pleasant feeling.

But on the other occasion I myself was the imbecile, yet even then I couldn't bear my father-in-law any grudge. He provoked my envy one moment and my hilarity the next. In my misfortune I saw the precise application of his principles, which he had never illustrated to me more clearly. He also found the way to laugh with me, never confessing that he had deceived me and declaring that he had to laugh at the comic aspect of my ill luck. Only once did he admit he had played that trick on me. It was at the wedding of his daughter Ada (not to me), after he had drunk some champagne, which affected that great body whose usual beverage was pure water.

Then he told me the story, shouting to overcome the hilarity that almost robbed him of speech: "So then this decree comes along! Very depressed, I'm figuring out how much it's going to cost me. At that moment, in comes my son-in-law. He declares that he wants to go into business. 'Here's a fine opportunity,' I say to him. He falls on the document and signs it, afraid Olivi might arrive in time to stop him, and so the deal is done." Then he showered praise on me: "He knows the classics by heart. He knows who said this and who said that. But he doesn't know how to read the daily paper!"

It was true! If I had seen that decree, printed inconspicuously in the five newspapers I read every day, I wouldn't have fallen into the trap. I should have understood that decree immediately, and seen its consequences. This was no easy matter, because the decree reduced a certain tariff and thus reduced the cost of the merchandise involved.

The following day my father-in-law retracted his confession. On his lips the deal regained the character it had had before that supper. "Wine's a liar," he said seraphically, and it was tacitly understood that the decree in question had been published two days after the conclusion of our affair. He never again uttered the suggestion that, seeing that decree, I could have misunderstood it. I was flattered, but he didn't spare me out of kindness, but rather because he believed that everyone, reading the newspapers, has his own business interests in mind. I, on the contrary, when I read a paper, feel transformed into public opinion, and seeing the reduction of a tariff, I think of Cobden* and free trade. The thought is so important that it leaves no room for me to recall my wares.

Once, however, I happened to win his admiration for myself, for me as I truly am, and, indeed, precisely for my worst qualities. For some time he and I had held some shares in a sugar refinery, which we were expecting to produce miracles. Instead, the stock went down, slightly but steadily, and Giovanni, who was not a man to swim against the stream, sold off his shares and persuaded me I should unload mine. In perfect agreement, I meant to instruct my broker to sell, and meanwhile I jotted a reminder in a notebook that, in those days, I had resumed keeping. But, as everyone knows, during the day you never look into your pocket, and so, for several

*Richard Cobden (1804–65), English manufacturer and politician, firm believer in free trade.

65

evenings, on going to bed, I was surprised to find that memorandum, too late for me to act on it. Once I cried out in dismay, and to avoid giving my wife too many explanations, I told her I had bitten my tongue. Another time, amazed at my own negligence, I really bit my hands. "Watch out for your feet now!" my wife said, laughing. Then there were no further wounds because I became hardened. I looked, dazed, at that notebook, too slim to make its pressure felt during the day, and so I gave it no further thought until the next evening.

One day a sudden downpour forced me to seek shelter in the Tergesteo. There, by chance, I found my broker, who told me that in the past week the value of those shares had almost doubled.

"And now I'll sell!" I exclaimed in triumph.

I rushed to my father-in-law, who already knew about the increased value of that stock. He regretted having sold his shares and, if a bit less so, also regretted persuading me to sell mine.

"Don't take it too hard!" he said, laughing. "This is the first time you've lost anything by taking my advice."

The other matter had been the result not of his advice but of a mere suggestion from him, and in his opinion this was quite different.

I began laughing heartily.

"But I didn't act on that advice!" My luck wasn't enough for me, however: I tried to make it look like merit on my part. I told him the stock would not be sold until the next day, and, assuming a self-important manner, I tried to make him believe I had received some news I had forgotten to pass on to him, and it had led me to ignore his words.

Grim and offended, he spoke without looking me in the face. "A man with a mind like yours shouldn't go into business. And when he behaves so wickedly, he doesn't confess it. You still have a lot to learn, young fellow."

I disliked irritating him. It was much more amusing when he was doing me harm. I told him sincerely how matters had gone.

"As you see, a man with a mind like mine should absolutely go into business."

Mollified at once, he laughed with me. "What you earn from such a deal isn't a profit: it's a reward. That mind of yours has already cost you so much that it's only fair for it to reimburse you for a part of your losses!"

I don't know why I dwell here on our quarrels, which were so few. I was truly fond of him, and indeed I sought out his company despite his habit of yelling in order to think more clearly. My eardrums were able to bear his shouts. If he had shouted less loudly, those immoral theories of his would have been more offensive and, if he had been more gently brought up, his strength would have been less significant. And despite the fact that I was so different from him, I believe he reciprocated my affection with equal fondness. I would be more certain of this if he hadn't died so soon. He continued assiduously giving me lessons after my marriage and he often seasoned them with shouts and insults, which I accepted, convinced that I deserved them.

I married his daughter. Mysterious Mother Nature led me and it will be seen with what imperative violence. Now I sometimes study the faces of my children to see if, along with my narrow chin, which I have passed on to them, they possess at least some feature of the brute strength of the grandfather I chose for them.

I stood also at my father-in-law's grave, even though his last farewell to me hadn't been too affectionate. On his deathbed he told me he admired my shameless luck, which allowed me to move freely while he was crucified on that bed. Amazed, I asked him what I had done to him to make him wish me ill. And he answered me with these very words: "If I could pass my illness on to you and thus rid myself of it, I would give it to you immediately, even doubled! I have none of those humanitarian fancies of yours!"

There was nothing offensive in this: he would have liked to repeat that other transaction in which he had succeeded in loading off on me some worthless goods. But here, too, there was an affectionate pat on the head, because I wasn't sorry to hear my weakness described as the humanitarian fancies he attributed to me.

At his grave, as at all the others where I have wept, I grieved also for the part of myself that was buried there. What a loss it was for me, to be robbed of that second father, that common, ignorant, fierce fighter who underlined my weakness, my culture, my timidity. It's the truth: I'm timid! I would never have found this out if I hadn't studied Giovanni. God only knows how much better I would have come to know myself if he had continued living at my side!

Soon I realized that at the Tergesteo table, where he liked to reveal himself as he was and even a bit worse, Giovanni respected a self-imposed reservation: he never spoke of his home, or else he did so only when forced to, decorously and in a voice somewhat softer than usual. He nurtured a great respect for his family, and perhaps not everyone among those seated at that table seemed to him worthy of knowing anything about it. There I learned only that all four of his daughters had names beginning with A, a highly practical course, in his view, because in this way all the things on which that initial was embroidered could pass from one to the other without having to undergo any alteration. They were called (and I immediately learned those names by heart): Ada, Augusta, Alberta, and Anna. At that table, too, it was said that all four were beautiful. That initial made a much deeper impression on me than it should have. I dreamed of those four girls linked so firmly by their names. It was as if they were a bundle, to be delivered all together. The initial also said something else: my name is Zeno and I therefore had the sensation I was about to take a wife very far from my own country.

It was perhaps accidental that before presenting myself at the Malfentis', I had severed a fairly long-standing tie with a woman who might perhaps have deserved better treatment. But this accident provokes some thought. My decision to make this break was inspired by quite a frivolous motive. The poor girl had thought that a good way to bind me more tightly to herself was to make me jealous. On the contrary, the mere suspicion was enough to make me abandon her definitively. She couldn't have known at the time how possessed I was by the idea of marriage, and that I believed it impossible to enter that state with her simply because then the novelty would not have seemed great enough to me. The suspicion she deliberately inspired in me demonstrated the superiority of marriage, in which state such suspicions must not arise. When that suspicion, whose lack of substance I soon perceived, then vanished, I recalled that she spent money too freely. Today, after twenty-four years of honest matrimony, I am no longer of that opinion.

For her it proved a genuine stroke of luck because a few months later she married a very well-off man and achieved the desired change before I did. As soon as I was married, I met her in my home because her husband was a friend of my father-in-law. We ran into each other often, but for many years, all the time we were young, the greatest reserve reigned between us, and there was never any allusion to the past. The other day she asked me point-blank, her face crowned with gray hair youthfully hennaed: "Why did you drop me?"

I was sincere because I didn't have time to invent a lie: "I don't know anymore, but there are many, many other things in my life that I also don't know."

"I'm sorry," she said, and I was already bowing in response to the implied compliment. "In your old age you seem to me a very amusing man." I straightened up, with some effort. There was no need to thank her.

One day I learned that the Malfenti family had returned to the city after a fairly extended pleasure trip followed by their summer stay in the country. Before I could take steps toward being introduced into that household, Giovanni was ahead of me.

He showed me a letter from an intimate friend of his, asking for news of me. This man had been a classmate of mine and I had been very fond of him as long as I believed him destined to become a great chemist. Now, on the contrary, he mattered absolutely nothing to me because he had become a dealer in fertilizers, and now I hardly knew him. Giovanni invited me to the Malfenti house because I was a friend of that friend of his, and – obviously – I made no objection.

I remember that first visit as if it had taken place yesterday. It was a gloomy, cold autumn afternoon, and I even remember the relief I felt in ridding myself of my overcoat in the warmth of that house. I was actually about to reach my goal. Even now I remain bewildered by such blindness, which at the time seemed to me clairvoyance. I was pursuing health, legitimacy. True, that initial A embraced four girls, but three of them were to be eliminated at once, and as for the fourth, she, too, would be subjected to stern examination. Yes, I would be the sternest of judges. But meanwhile I would have been at a loss to name the qualities I would require of her and the characteristics I would loathe.

The vast and elegant drawing room was furnished in two different styles, some pieces were Louis XIV and others Venetian rich in gold-leaf impressed even on the leather. The furniture divided the room into two areas, as was then the fashion. There I found only Augusta, reading at a window. She gave me her hand, she knew my name, and even informed me that I was expected, as her Papà had announced my visit. Then she ran off to call her mother.

Of the four girls with the same initial, one was eliminated then and there as far as I was concerned. How could anyone have called her beautiful? The first thing you noticed about her was a squint so pronounced that if someone tried to recall her after not having seen her for a while, that defect would personify her totally. Her hair, moreover, was not abundant or blond, but a dull color, without luster; and her figure, while not graceless, was still a bit heavy for her age. During the few moments I remained alone I thought: "What if the other three look like this one! . . ."

A little later, the group of eligible girls was reduced to two. For another of them, entering with her mother, was only eight years old. She was a cute child with long, shining ringlets falling over her shoulders! Her plump, sweet face made her seem a little angel (as long as she kept silent), pensive in the way that Raphael's angels are pensive.

My mother-in-law . . . Ah! I feel a certain reluctance in speaking of her too freely. For many years I have been fond of her because she is my mother, but here I am telling an old story in which she does not appear as my friend, and even in this notebook, which she will never see, I have no intention of referring to her in terms less than respectful. For that matter, her intervention was so brief that I could even have forgotten it: a little push just at the right moment, no harder than necessary to make me lose my fragile balance. Perhaps I would have lost it even without her action, and anyway, who knows if she actually desired what then happened? She is so perfectly behaved that, unlike her husband, she will never, ever drink too much and consequently reveal things concerning me. And as nothing of the sort will ever happen to her, I am thus telling a story I don't know properly; that is, I don't know if it was because of her shrewdness or my own stupidity that of her four daughters, I married the one I didn't want.

What I can say is that at the time of my first visit my future mother-in-law was still a beautiful woman. She was also elegant in her way of dressing, with subtle luxury. Everything about her was understated and harmonious.

Thus my in-laws afforded an example of harmony between husband and wife such as I dreamed of. They had been very happy together: he always bellowing and she smiling a smile that signified agreement and sympathy at the same time. She loved her big, heavy man, and he must have won and retained her devotion with his successful transactions. Not self-interest but genuine admiration bound her to him, an admiration I shared and hence could easily understand. All that vivacity, which he infused into such confined space, a cage that held nothing but a single product and two enemies (the two contracting parties), where new combinations, new relations were constantly being discovered, wondrously animated their life. He told her about all his deals, and she was so well brought up that she never gave him advice because she would have feared misleading him. He felt a need for this mute support, and at times he rushed home to deliver a monologue, convinced he was going there to seek his wife's advice.

It came as no surprise when I learned he was unfaithful to her, and that she knew it and bore him no grudge. I had been married a year when one day Giovanni, very upset, told me he had misplaced a very important letter and he wanted to take another look at some papers he had given me, in the hope of finding it among them. Then, a few days later, in high spirits, he told me he had found it in his wallet. "Was it from a woman?" I asked him, and he nodded affirmatively, boasting of his good luck. Then, to defend myself, one day when he was accusing me of having lost some papers, I said to my wife and my mother-in-law that I didn't have Papà's luck, whose papers always found their way back into his wallet. My mother-in-law fell to laughing so heartily that I hadn't the slightest doubt it had been she who replaced that letter. We all love in our own way, and in my opinion, theirs was by no means the most stupid.

Signora Malfenti received me with great kindness. She apologized for having to keep little Anna with her, but there was always that quarter-hour when the child couldn't be left with others. *The little girl looked at me, studying me with grave eyes.* When Augusta came back and sat on a little sofa opposite the one where the Signora and I were seated, the child went and lay in her sister's lap, whence she observed me the whole time with a fixed gaze that amused me until I learned what thoughts were circulating in that little head.

The conversation was not immediately entertaining. The Signora, like all well-bred people, was fairly boring on first acquaintance. She asked me too many questions about the friend who we pretended had introduced me into that house and whose first name I couldn't even remember.

Finally Ada and Alberta came in. I breathed again: they were both beautiful, and brought into that drawing room the light that had been wanting till then. Both were dark and tall and slender, but they were quite different from each other. The choice I had to make was not difficult. Alberta was then no more than seventeen. Though dark, she had her mother's rosy, transparent skin, which enhanced the childishness of her appearance. Ada, on the contrary, was already a woman, with serious eyes, a face whose whiteness seemed all the more snowy, thanks to a faint blue cast, and a head of rich, curly hair, gracefully yet severely coiffed.

It is hard to retrace the tender origins of a feeling that was later to become so violent, but I am sure I did not feel the so-called *coup de foudre* for Ada. Instead of that lightning bolt, I felt a prompt conviction that this woman was the one I needed, the one who would lead me actually to moral and physical health through holy monogamy. When I think back, I am surprised that the lightning bolt was lacking and there was this conviction in its place. It is a known fact that we men do not seek in a wife the characteristics we adore and despise in a mistress. So apparently I didn't see at once all the grace and all the beauty of Ada; instead I stood there, admiring other qualities I attributed to her, seriousness and also energy, the same qualities, somewhat tempered, that I loved in her father. Since I later believed (as I believe still) that I wasn't mistaken and that Ada did possess those qualities as a girl, I can consider myself a good observer but also a blind observer. That first time, I looked at Ada with only one desire: to fall in love with her, for that was necessary if I was to marry her. I prepared to do this with the same energy I always devote to my hygienic practices. I cannot say when I succeeded, perhaps within the relatively brief time of that first visit.

Giovanni must have spoken to his daughters a great deal about me. They knew, among other things, that in the course of my studies I had transferred from law to chemistry, only to return – unfortunately! – to the former. I tried to explain: it was certain that when you confine yourself to one department, the greater area of knowledge remains blanketed by ignorance.

And I said: "If the seriousness of life were not now confronting me" – and I didn't add that I had been feeling this seriousness only a short time, since my resolution to marry – "I would have kept on transferring from one department to another."

Then, to make them laugh, I remarked on a curious thing: I always dropped a subject just at the moment when I had to face examinations.

"A coincidence," I said, with the smile of one who wants to hint he is telling a lie. And, indeed, the truth was that I had changed my courses in all seasons.

So I set out to win Ada and I continued my efforts to make her laugh at me, at my expense, forgetting that I had chosen her because of her seriousness. I am a bit eccentric, but to her I must have seemed downright unbalanced. The fault is not wholly mine, and this is clear from the fact that Augusta and Alberta, whom I had not chosen, judged me differently. But Ada, who at that very time was so serious that she was casting her beautiful eyes around in search of the man she would admit to her nest, was incapable of loving a person who made her laugh. She laughed, and she laughed for a long time, too long, and her laughter clothed in ridiculous garb the man who had provoked it. Hers was a genuine inferiority and in the end it was to harm her, but first it harmed me. If I had been able to keep silent at the right moment, perhaps things would have turned out differently. As least I would have given her time to speak and to reveal herself, and I could have steered clear of her.

The four girls were seated on the little sofa that could barely hold them, even though Anna was sitting on Augusta's lap. They were beautiful, all together like that. I observed this with inner satisfaction, considering that I was magnificently headed toward admiration and love. Really beautiful! Augusta's wan complexion served to heighten the dark color of the other girls' hair.

I had mentioned the University, and Alberta, who was in her last year of upper school, talked about her studies. She complained of finding Latin very difficult. I said I wasn't surprised, as it was not a language suited to women, and I actually thought that even in ancient Roman times the women spoke Italian. Whereas for me – I declared – Latin had been my favorite subject. A little later, however, I was foolish enough to quote a Latin saying, which Alberta had to correct. A real stroke of bad luck! I attached no importance to it, and informed Alberta that when she had perhaps a dozen semesters of university behind her, she would also have to be on her guard against quoting Latin tags.

Ada, who had recently spent some months in England with her father, observed that many girls there know Latin. Then, in the same serious voice, lacking any musicality, a bit deeper than one would have expected from her delicate figure, she said that English women were quite different from ours. They formed charitable organizations, and religious, even economic groups. Ada was urged to speak by her sisters, eager to hear again those things that seemed wondrous to young ladies of our city at that time. And to satisfy them, Ada told about those women who were club presidents or journalists, secretaries or political speakers, who mounted platforms to address hundreds of people without blushes or confusion when they were interrupted or when their arguments were contested. She spoke simply, with little color, with no intention of arousing wonder or laughter.

I loved her simple speech – I, who, when I opened my mouth, got things wrong or misled people because otherwise speaking would have seemed to me pointless. Without being an orator, I suffered from the disease of words. Words for me had to be an event in themselves and therefore could not be imprisoned in any other event.

But I harbored a special hatred for perfidious Albion, and I displayed it without fear of offending Ada, who, for that matter, had indicated neither hate nor love of England. I had spent some months there, but I hadn't met any English person of good society, since, in traveling, I had misplaced some letters of introduction obtained from business acquaintances of my father's. In London, therefore, I had frequented only a few French and Italian families, and in the end I decided that all the respectable people in that city came from the Continent. My knowledge of English was very limited. Still, with the help of my friends I could understand something of the life of those islanders and, especially, I learned of their dislike of all who are not English.

I described to the girls the fairly unpleasant impression I had derived from my stay amid enemies. I would, however, have stuck it out and put up with England for the six months my father and Olivi wanted to inflict on me so I could study English trade (which I never encountered because it is apparently conducted in recondite places), but then a disagreeable adventure had befallen me. I had gone into a bookseller's to look for a dictionary. In that shop, on the counter, a big, magnificent Angora cat was lying, whose soft fur simply begged to be stroked. Well! Simply because I gently stroked him, he treacherously attacked me and badly scratched my hands. From that moment on, England was intolerable and the following day I was in Paris.

Augusta, Alberta, and also Signora Malfenti laughed heartily. Ada, on the contrary, was dumbfounded and thought she had misunderstood. Hadn't it been the bookseller himself who had offended and scratched me? I had to repeat myself, which is always boring because repetitions never come off.

Alberta, the studious one, chose to come to my assistance. The ancients had also allowed their decisions to be guided by the movements of animals.

I rejected her help. The English cat had not been acting as an oracle: it acted as destiny!

Ada, her great eyes wide, wanted further explanations: "And you felt the cat represented the entire English nation?"

I was really unlucky! While it was true, that story seemed to me as instructive and interesting as if it had been invented for some specific purpose. To understand it, wasn't it enough to point out that in Italy, where I know and love so many people, the action of that cat would never have assumed such importance? But I didn't say this, and I said, on the contrary: "Certainly no Italian cat would be capable of such a thing."

Ada laughed for a long time, very long. My success seemed to me even too great because it diminished me, and I diminished my adventure with further explanations:

"The bookseller himself was amazed by the cat's reaction: it behaved well with everyone else. The misadventure fell to my lot because I was who I was, or perhaps because I was Italian. *It was really disgusting*, as I said in English, and I had to escape."

Here something happened that ought to have warned me and saved me. Little Anna, who till then had remained motionless, observing me, decided to express in a loud voice what Ada felt. She cried: "Is it true you're crazy? Completely crazy?"

Signora Malfenti threatened her: "Will you be quiet? Aren't you ashamed, interrupting the grownups' talk?"

The threat only worsened things. Anna shouted, "He's crazy! He talks with cats! We should get some ropes, quickly, and tie him up!"

Augusta, flushed with dismay, stood up and carried her out, scolding her and at the same time apologizing to me. But again at the door the little viper was able to stare into my eyes, make a face, and shout: "They'll tie you up! Wait and see!"

I had been assailed so unexpectedly that, for the moment, I could find no way of defending myself. I felt relieved, however, realizing that Ada was also sorry to hear her private feelings expressed in that way. The little girl's impudence brought us closer.

Laughing heartily, I said that I possessed a certificate, with an official seal, that attested to my complete sanity. Thus they learned of the trick my old father had played on me. I suggested bringing that certificate and showing it to little Annuccia.

When I made a move to leave, they wouldn't permit it. First they wanted me to forget the scratches inflicted on me by that other cat. They kept me there with them, offering me a cup of tea.

No doubt I felt immediately, in some obscure way, that if I wanted to appeal to Ada I would have to be a bit different from what I was; I thought it would be easy for me to become what she wanted. We went on talking about the death of my father, and it seemed to me that if I revealed the great sorrow that still oppressed me, the serious Ada might feel it with me. But at once, in my effort to resemble her, I lost my naturalness and therefore – as was quickly evident – I distanced myself from her. I said that the grief for such a loss was so great that if I were to have children I would try to make them love me less, so as to spare them great suffering later, at my passing. I was a bit embarrassed when the women asked me how I would act to achieve that aim. Maltreat them? Strike them?

Laughing, Alberta said, "The surest method would be to kill them."

I saw that Ada was animated by a desire not to displease me. So she hesitated: but all her best efforts could not lead her beyond hesitation. At last she conceded that it was clearly my goodness that led me to think of organizing my children's life in that way, but to her it seemed wrong to live only in preparation for death. I held my ground and asserted that death was the true organizer of life. I thought always of death, and therefore I had only one sorrow: the certainty of having to die. Everything else became of such scant importance that I accepted it all simply with a happy smile or with equally happy laughter. I let myself be carried away, saying things that were now less true, particularly because I was with her, already such an important part of my life. To tell the truth, I believe I said those things to her, meaning to let her know what a happy man I was. Often happiness had lent me a hand with women.

Thoughtful and hesitant, she confessed that she was not fond of such a state of mind. Diminishing the value of life, we also jeopardized life more than Mother Nature intended. What Ada had really told me was that I was not the man for her, but I had managed, all the same, to make her thoughtful and hesitant, and that seemed to me a success.

Alberta quoted an ancient philosopher who supposedly resembled me in his interpretation of life, and Augusta said that laughter was a wonderful thing. Her father, too, had a great store of laughter.

"Because he likes good business," Signora Malfenti said, laughing.

I finally broke off that unforgettable visit.

There is nothing more difficult in this world than to achieve a marriage exactly the way you want it. So much is clear from my case, where the decision to marry long ante-dated the choice of a betrothed. Why didn't I go out and see

countless girls before settling on one? No! It actually seemed
I would dislike seeing too many women, and I was reluctant to
tire myself. But even after choosing the girl, I might have
examined her a bit more closely and made sure at least that
she would be willing to meet me halfway, as they never fail to
do in romantic novels with happy endings. On the contrary,
I selected the girl with the deep voice and the slightly unruly
but severely coiffed hair, and I thought, serious as she was, she
wouldn't refuse an intelligent man like me, well-to-do, not
ugly, and of good family. From the very first words we
exchanged, I sensed something discordant, but discord is the
road to unison. I should confess what I thought: She must
remain as she is, because I like her this way and I will be the
one who changes, if she wishes. All things considered, I was
quite unenterprising because it's surely easier to change oneself
than to reshape others.

In a very short time the Malfenti family became the center
of my life. I spent every evening with Giovanni, who, after
introducing me into his home, had become also more cordial
and intimate with me. It was this cordiality that made me
aggressive. At first I visited his ladies once a week, then more
than once, until finally I was going to his house every day,
spending several afternoon hours there. I had numerous
excuses to become a fixture in that household, and I believe
I am right in declaring that they were also offered to me.
Sometimes I took my violin with me and spent a few hours
making music with Augusta, the only one in the house who
played the piano. It was a pity Ada didn't play, and it was a pity
I played the violin so badly, and to make matters still worse,
Augusta wasn't much of a musician, either. I had to eliminate
some bars of every piece because they were too difficult, on
the false pretext that I hadn't touched the violin for a long
time. The pianist is almost always superior to the amateur
violinist, and Augusta had a fair technique, but I, who played
so much worse than she, couldn't say I was pleased with her

and I thought: If I could play as well as Augusta, how much better I would play! While I was judging her, the others were judging me and, as I learned later, not favorably. Then Augusta would gladly have repeated our performance, but I realized that Ada had been bored and so I pretended several times to have forgotten my violin at home. Afterwards Augusta never mentioned it again.

Unfortunately I didn't spend with Ada only the hours I passed in that house. She soon accompanied me throughout the day. She was the woman I had chosen, she was therefore already mine, and I adorned her with all my dreams, so that the prize of my life would appear more beautiful to me. I adorned her, I bestowed on her all the many qualities I lacked and whose need I felt, because she was to become not only my companion but also my second mother, who would adopt me for a whole lifetime of manly struggle and victory.

In my dreams I also beautified her physically before handing her over to others. In reality, I pursued many women in my life, and many of them also allowed themselves to be over-taken. In my dreams I captured them all. Naturally I don't beautify them by changing their features, but I act like a friend of mine, a very refined painter who, when he portrays beauti-ful women, thinks intensely also of some other beautiful thing, for example of a piece of lovely porcelain. A dangerous dream, because it can endow the dreamed-of women with new power and, when seen again in the light of reality, they retain something of the fruits and flowers and porcelain with which they were clad.

It is hard for me to tell about my courtship of Ada. There came a long period in my life when I made an effort to forget that stupid adventure, which actually shamed me, with the shame that makes you shout and protest: No! I wasn't such a jackass! Well, then, who was it? But protest also affords some relief, and I persisted. It wouldn't have been so bad if I had acted like that ten years earlier, when I was twenty! But to be punished for such asininity simply because I had decided to marry seems to me downright unjust. I, who had already undergone every kind of adventure, always conducted with an enterprising spirit bordering on insolence, now had become again the timid youth who strives to graze his beloved's hand, perhaps without her noticing, then adores the part of his own body honored by such contact. This adventure, which was the purest of my life, I remember even today, when I am an old man, as the most despicable. It was out of place, out of time, the whole business, as if a boy of ten were to grope the breast of his wet-nurse. Disgusting!

How to explain, then, my long hesitation in speaking clearly and saying to the girl: Make up your mind!? Do you want me or don't you? When I went to that house I was arriving there from my dreams; I counted the steps that led me to that upper floor, telling myself that if their number was odd it would prove she loved me, and it was always odd because there were forty-three of them. I arrived at her side buoyed by this confidence, but I ended up speaking of something quite different. Ada had not yet found the opportunity to convey her disdain to me, and I remained silent! I, too, in Ada's place, would have received that youth of thirty with a swift kick in the behind!

I must say that in some respects I didn't resemble exactly the lovesick twenty-year-old, waiting in silence for his beloved to throw her arms around his neck. I awaited nothing of the sort. I was going to speak, but not yet. If I didn't go ahead, it was because of some doubts about myself. I was waiting to become nobler, stronger, worthier of my divine maiden. That could happen any day. Why not wait?

I am ashamed also of not having realized in time that I was heading for such a disaster. I was dealing with the simplest of girls, but thanks to my dreams of her, she appeared to me as the most consummate flirt. My enormous bitterness was unjust, when she finally made me see that she wanted nothing to do with me. But I had intermingled dreams and reality so closely that I was unable to convince myself she had never kissed me.

Misunderstanding women is a clear sign of scant virility. Before, I had never been mistaken, and I have to think that I was wrong about Ada, because from the very beginning I had established a false rapport with her. I had set out not to win her but to marry her, an unusual path for love to take, a very broad path, a very comfortable path, but one that doesn't lead to the goal, close though it may be. Love achieved in this way lacks the principal ingredient: the subjugation of the female. Thus the male prepares for his role in a great inertia that can affect all his senses, including sight and hearing.

I took flowers daily to all three girls, and on all three I lavished my fatuities and, above all, with incredible thought-lessness, I daily regaled them with my autobiography.

Everyone tends to remember the past with greater fervor as the present gains greater importance. It is said, indeed, that the dying, in their final fever, review their whole lives. My past now gripped me with the violence of a last farewell because I had the feeling I was moving far away from it. And I talked always about this past to the three girls, encouraged by the close attention of Augusta and Alberta, an attention that per-haps disguised Ada's lack of interest, of which I am unsure. Augusta, with her sweet nature, was easily moved, and Alberta listened to my descriptions of student japes, her cheeks flushed with the desire to experience similar adventures in the future.

A long time afterwards I learned from Augusta that none of the three girls had believed my stories were true. To Augusta they seemed all the more precious because, as I had invented them, they were more mine than if fate had visited them upon me. To Alberta the part she didn't believe was still enjoyable because she received some excellent hints. The only one out-raged by my lies was the serious Ada. For all my efforts I achieved the result of that marksman who hit the bullseye, but of the target next to his.

And yet to a great extent those stories were true. I can't at this point say to what extent because, as I had told them to many other women before the Malfenti daughters, through no wish of mine, they had changed and become more expressive. They were true inasmuch as I could not have told them in any other version. Today it's of no importance to me to prove their veracity. I wouldn't want to undeceive Augusta, who loves to consider them my invention. As for Ada, I believe that by now she has changed her mind and considers them true.

My complete lack of success with Ada became evident at the very moment when I judged that I should finally speak out clearly. I received the evidence with surprise and, at first, with incredulity. She had not uttered one word indicating her aversion toward me, and I had meanwhile shut my eyes so as not to see those little acts that suggested no great liking for me. And yet I myself hadn't said the necessary word, and I could always imagine that Ada didn't know I was there ready to marry her and she might believe that I – the eccentric and not very virtuous student – was seeking something quite different.

The misunderstanding kept being prolonged because of my intentions, which were too decidedly matrimonial. It is true that now I wanted all of Ada, whose cheeks I had assiduously polished, whose hands and feet I had made smaller, whose figure I had thinned and refined. I desired her as wife and as lover. But the way a woman is approached the first time is decisive.

Now for three times consecutively it so happened that I was received at the house by the other two girls. Ada's absence was explained the first time with the excuse of a call that had to be paid, the second with an indisposition, and the third I was given no excuse at all until, alarmed, I inquired. Then Augusta, whom I had addressed, didn't answer. In her place Alberta, at whom she had glanced as if seeking help, replied: Ada had gone to their aunt's.

My breath failed me. Obviously Ada was avoiding me. Even the day before, I had still tolerated her absence and had indeed prolonged my visit, hoping that in the end she would appear. This day, on the contrary, I stayed barely another few moments, unable to open my mouth, and then, pleading a sudden headache, I rose to leave. Strange: as I encountered Ada's resistance that first time, my strongest feeling was fury, outrage! I even thought of appealing to Giovanni to call the girl to order. A man who wants to marry is capable of such actions, repetitions of those of his ancestors.

This third absence of Ada was to become even more significant. By sheer chance I discovered she was in the house, but shut up in her room.

First of all I must say that in the house there was another person I hadn't succeeded in winning: little Anna. She no longer attacked me in the presence of others, because they had scolded her sharply. Indeed, at times she actually joined her sisters and listened to my stories. But when I left, she would overtake me at the door, politely ask me to bend down to her, then stand on tiptoe, and when she was actually able to press her little mouth to my ear, lowering her voice so that only I could hear her, she would say, calling me *tu*: "You are crazy, really crazy!"

The funny thing is that when the others were there, the little minx addressed me formally. If Signora Malfenti was in the room, the child would promptly take refuge in her mother's arms, and the Signora would stroke her, saying: "How polite my little Anna's become! Hasn't she?"

I never protested, and the polite Anna often would call me crazy again in the same fashion. I received her assertion with a cowardly smile that could have looked like thanks. I hoped the child wouldn't have the nerve to tell the grownups of her aggressions, and I was unwilling to inform Ada of her little sister's opinion of me. In the end that child really embarrassed me. If, when I was speaking with the others, my eye met hers,

I immediately had to find an excuse to look elsewhere, and this was difficult to do with any naturalness. I blushed, certainly. It seemed to me that the innocent little creature, with her opinion, could do me harm. I brought her presents, but they didn't mollify her. She must have been aware of her power and of my weakness, and in front of the others she looked at me, studying me with insolence. I believe we all have, in our conscience as in our body, some tender, concealed spots that we do not like to be reminded of. We don't even know what they are, but we know they're there. I turned my eye away from that childish gaze that wanted to delve into me.

But on this day as, alone and dejected, I was leaving the house, she overtook me, to make me bend down and hear the usual compliment, I leaned over to her and held out toward her my hands contracted into talons, with a face so distraught, a real madman's, that she ran off weeping and screaming.

So I managed to see Ada also this day, because it was she who came running at those cries. The child, sobbing, told her I had threatened her terribly because she had called me crazy.

"Because he really is crazy and I want to tell him so. What's wrong with that?"

I didn't listen to the girl, amazed to see Ada was at home. So her sisters had lied, or rather only Alberta had, to whom Augusta had handed over the duty, exempting herself! For a moment I had justice on my side, I was totally aware, guessing the whole story.

I said to Ada: "I'm glad to see you. I thought you had been at your aunt's for three days."

She didn't answer me at first because she bent over the weeping child. That delay in obtaining the explanation to which I felt entitled made my blood rush violently to my head. I was speechless. I took another step in the direction of the front door, and if Ada hadn't spoken to me, I would have gone away and would never have come back. In my wrath, this seemed an easy step, this renunciation of a dream that by now had gone on too long.

But at this point she turned to me, her face flushed, and said she had come in just a few moments before, because she hadn't found her aunt at home.

That sufficed to calm me. How dear she was, how maternally attentive to the child, who went on screaming! Ada's body was so supple that it seemed to have become smaller the better to reach the child. I lingered, admiring her, considering her again mine.

I felt so reassured that I wanted to make them forget my previous vexation, and I was very polite with Ada and even with Anna.

Laughing heartily, I said: "She calls me crazy so often that I wanted to show her a lunatic's real face and attitude. Do forgive me! You too, poor little Anna, don't be afraid: I'm a nice madman."

Ada, too, was very, very polite. She scolded the still-sobbing child, and apologized to me for her. If I had really been in luck, and, if in her anger, Anna had run away, I would have spoken. I would have uttered the sentence that is perhaps found even in certain foreign-language phrase books, ready-made, to facilitate the life of those who don't know the language of the country where they are staying: May I ask your father for your hand? This was the first time I wanted to marry, and so I found myself in a totally foreign land. Until then I had dealt differently with any women I encountered. I assaulted them, laying my hands on them right at the start.

But I didn't manage to say even those few words. Even they required a certain length of time! They had to be accompanied by a pleading facial expression, difficult to assume immediately after my conflict with Anna and also with Ada, and from the end of the hall Signora Malfenti was already advancing, summoned by the child's howls.

I held out my hand to Ada, who cordially and promptly gave me hers, and I said to her: "I'll see you tomorrow. My excuses to your mother."

I hesitated, however, to release that hand, resting trustfully in mine. I could sense that, leaving now, I would be rejecting a unique opportunity with this girl so intent on showing me every courtesy, compensating for her sister's rudeness. I followed the inspiration of the moment, I bent over her hand and brushed it with my lips. Then I opened the door and went out very quickly, after having seen that Ada, who until then had given me her right hand while her left supported Anna, clinging to her skirt, now looked with amazement at the tiny hand that had been subjected to the contact of my lips, as if she wanted to see if something were written there. I don't believe Signora Malfenti had glimpsed my action.

I stopped for a moment on the steps, amazed at my own absolutely unpremeditated act. Was it still possible to go back to that door I had closed behind me, ring the bell, and ask to be allowed to say to Ada those words she had sought in vain on her hand? No, I thought. My dignity would have suffered if I showed too much impatience. Besides, having informed her that I would come back, I had heralded my explanations. Now it was simply up to her to receive them, creating the opportunity for me to express them to her. Finally I had stopped telling stories to three young ladies and, instead, had kissed the hand of only one of them.

But then the day became rather unpleasant. I was restless and uneasy. I kept telling myself that my restlessness derived only from my impatience to see this matter resolved. I imagined that if Ada were to refuse me, I could then quite calmly go off in pursuit of other women. My attachment to her was totally the result of my own free determination, which now could be annulled by another woman, who would erase it! I didn't then understand that for the moment there were no other women in this world for me, and that I needed Ada and only her.

The night that followed also seemed to me very long; I lay awake for almost all of it. Since my father's death I had abandoned my noctambulist habits and now, when I had determined to marry, it would have been odd to resume them. I had therefore gone to bed early, wishing for sleep, which makes time pass so quickly.

During the day I had accepted with absolute blind faith Ada's explanations of those three absences from her living room in the hours when I was there, a faith born of my firm conviction that the serious woman I had chosen was incapable of lying. But during the night that faith was weakened. I suspected it was I myself who informed her that Alberta – since Augusta refused to speak – had supplied the excuse of that visit to her aunt. I didn't recall exactly the words I had addressed to her, my head aflame, but I believed I could be certain of having repeated that excuse. Too bad! If I hadn't, perhaps she, to excuse herself, would have invented something different, and having caught her out in a falsehood, I would already have had the clarification I was yearning for.

Here, too, I might have realized the importance Ada had for me by now, because to recover some calm I kept repeating to myself that if she wouldn't have me, then I would renounce marriage forever. Her refusal would thus change my life. And I went on daydreaming, comforting myself with the thought that perhaps this rejection would be a stroke of luck for me. I recalled that Greek philosopher who predicted regret both for those who married and for those who remained single. In short, I hadn't lost the capacity to laugh at my adventure; the only capacity I lacked was for sleep.

I dozed off as dawn was already breaking. When I woke up it was so late that only a few hours separated me from the time when I was allowed to visit the Malfenti house. Thus there would be no further need to daydream and collect other clues that might clarify Ada's thoughts for me. But it is hard to restrain one's own mind from brooding on a subject that is too important. Man would be a happier animal if he could do that. In the midst of the attentions to my person, which on that day I exaggerated, I thought of nothing else: In kissing Ada's hand, had I done the right thing? Or had I been wrong in not kissing her also on the lips?

That same morning I had an idea that I believe caused me great harm, robbing me of what little manly initiative my curiously adolescent state would have granted me. A painful suspicion: What if Ada were to marry me only because her parents prompted her to, without loving me or, indeed, feeling an aversion to me? For surely all the family, that is to say Giovanni, Signora Malfenti, Augusta, and Alberta, were fond of me; I could entertain doubts only about Ada. On the horizon the usual cheap novel was looming up: the young girl forced by her family into a hateful marriage. But I would never have allowed that. Here was another reason why I had to speak with Ada, indeed with Ada alone. It wouldn't be enough to say to her the words I had rehearsed. Looking into her eyes, I would ask: "Do you love me?" And if she said yes, I would clasp her in my arms, to feel the vibration of her sincerity.

So I seemed to be prepared for everything. But, on the contrary, I was to realize that I was about to be given a sort of exam, but had forgotten to go over the very pages of text on which I would be interrogated.

I was received by Signora Malfenti alone, who asked me to sit down in one corner of the great drawing room, then immediately began chattering vivaciously, preventing me even from asking for any news of the girls. I was therefore quite bewildered, but I reviewed my assignment to make sure I wouldn't forget it when the right moment came. All of a sudden I was recalled to attention as if by a trumpet blast. The Signora was delivering a preamble. She assured me of her friendship and her husband's, and of the affection of their whole family, including little Anna. We had known one another for such a long time. We had been seeing one another daily for four months.

"Five!" I corrected her, having counted them during the night remembering that my first visit had taken place in autumn, and now it was full spring.

"Yes, five!" the Signora said, thinking it over, as if to check my calculation. Then, in a reproachful tone: "It seems to me that you are compromising Augusta."

"Augusta?" I asked, believing I hadn't heard her correctly.

"Yes," she confirmed. "You lead her on, and you are compromising her."

Ingenuously, I revealed my feelings: "But I never see Augusta."

She made a gesture of surprise and, indeed (or was it just my imagination?), of pained surprise.

I was trying, meanwhile, to concentrate my thoughts in order to arrive rapidly at an explanation of what seemed to me a misunderstanding, whose importance, however, I had immediately grasped. In my mind, I saw myself again, visit by visit, during those five months, intent on studying Ada. I had played music with Augusta, and indeed at times I had talked more with her, who listened to me, than with Ada, but only so that Augusta could then explain my stories, enhanced by her approval, to Ada. Should I speak openly to the Signora and tell her of my designs on Ada? But a little earlier I had resolved to speak with Ada alone and plumb her heart. Perhaps if I had spoken openly with Signora Malfenti, things would have taken a different turn and, unable to marry Ada, I wouldn't have married Augusta, either. But following the resolution I had made before seeing Signora Malfenti, and hearing the surprising things she said to me, I was silent.

I thought hard, and therefore with a bit of confusion. I wanted to understand, I wanted to divine, and quickly. You see things less clearly when you open your eyes too wide. I could glimpse the possibility of their wanting to throw me out of their house. But I thought I could dismiss that. I was innocent, since I wasn't paying court to Augusta, whom they meant to protect. But perhaps they ascribed to me intentions regarding Augusta to avoid compromising Ada. And why protect Ada in this way, when, after all, she was no longer a child? I was sure I had seized her by the hair only in my dream. In reality I had done nothing more than touch her hand with my lips. I didn't want them to forbid me access to that house because, before leaving it for good, I wanted to speak with Ada. And so, in a tremulous voice, I asked: "Tell me, Signora, what I must do in order to offend no one."

She hesitated. I would have preferred to deal with Giovanni, who thought at the top of his lungs. Then, firmly, but with an effort to seem polite that was obvious in her tone of voice, she said: "For a while you should visit us less frequently – not every day, but perhaps two or three times a week."

Certainly, if she had told me curtly to leave and never return, I would have clung to my resolution, begging them to tolerate me in that house at least for another day or two, until I could clarify my situation with Ada. But instead, her words gave me the courage to display my pique: "Well, if you wish, I'll never set foot in this house again!"

What I had hoped for then occurred. She protested, again declaring the respect they all felt for me, and begging me not to be angry with her. And I made a display of my magnanimity, promising everything she wished, namely to stay away from that house for four or five days, then to come back regularly two or three times every week and, above all, not to harbor any resentment.

Having made these promises, I decided to show I meant to keep them, and I stood up to leave.

Laughing, the Signora protested: "With me there can be no compromising of any kind, and you may remain."

I begged her to allow me to leave, pleading an engagement I had only just remembered, while the truth was that I couldn't wait to be alone in order to ponder more comfortably this extraordinary adventure that had befallen me. The Signora actually implored me to stay, saying that I would thus give her the proof that I wasn't angry with her. So I remained, subjected constantly to the torture of listening to the idle chatter the Signora now indulged in, all about female fashion, which she didn't want to follow, about the theater, and also about this dry weather that was ushering in spring.

A little later I was glad I had remained, because I realized I needed a further explanation. Without any ceremony I interrupted the Signora, whose words I no longer heard, to ask her: "Will the whole family know that you have asked me to stay away from this house?"

At first she seemed not even to remember our agreement. Then she protested, "Away from this house? But only for a few days, mind you. I won't mention it to anyone, not even to my husband; in fact, I'd be grateful if you would use the same discretion."

I promised this, too, and I further promised that if I were asked to explain why I wasn't seen there so often, I would invent various excuses. For the moment I believed the Signora's words, and I imagined Ada might be amazed and grieved by my sudden absence. An attractive picture!

Then I stayed on, still awaiting some further inspiration, while the Signora talked about food prices, which had lately risen sky-high.

Instead of further inspiration, Aunt Rosina appeared, Giovanni's sister, older than he, but much less intelligent. She did possess some aspects of his moral physiognomy, enough to identify her as his sister. First of all, she had the same awareness of her own rights and of the duties of others – a fairly comical attitude, since she lacked any weapon with which to enforce it – and she also had the bad habit of abruptly raising her voice. She thought that in her brother's house her rights were such that – as I learned later – she considered

93

Signora Malfenti an intruder. She was a spinster, and she lived with just one maidservant, of whom she spoke always as her greatest enemy. When Aunt Rosina was dying, she charged my wife to keep an eye on the house until the maid, who had nursed her, was gone. Everyone in Giovanni's household put up with Aunt Rosina, fearing her aggressiveness.

Still I didn't leave. Aunt Rosina's favorite among her nieces was Ada. I felt a desire to win the old woman's friendship, too, and I searched for some engaging remark to address to her. I remembered vaguely that on the last occasion when I had seen her (or, rather, glanced at her, because then I had felt no need to look at her), the nieces, as soon as she had left, had remarked that she wasn't looking well. Actually, one of them had said: "She must have poisoned her blood in some rage with her maid."

I had found what I had sought. Looking affectionately at the old lady's broad, wrinkled face, I said to her: "You look much better, Signora."

I should have kept my mouth shut. She stared at me, amazed, and protested: "I'm the same as always. Better than when, according to you?"

She wanted to know when I had last seen her. I didn't remember that date exactly, and I had to remind her that we had spent a whole afternoon together, seated in that same living room with the three young ladies, not where we were now but on the other side. I had intended to show her my interest, but the explanations she demanded made it all last too long. My falsity oppressed me, producing genuine pain.

Signora Malfenti spoke up, smiling: "Surely you didn't mean to say that Aunt Rosina has put on weight?"

Good Lord! So this was the reason for Aunt Rosina's annoyance. She was very heavy, like her brother, and she hoped to grow thinner.

"Put on weight? No, indeed! I just wanted to say that Signora Rosina's color is better."

94

I tried to maintain an affectionate tone, whereas I had really to make an effort not to utter some piece of insolence.

Still, Aunt Rosina didn't seem satisfied. She had not been ill lately, and she couldn't see why she should have appeared ill. And Signora Malfenti agreed with her.

"Indeed, her color never alters: it's part of her," she said, turning to me. "Don't you think so?"

I thought so. Indeed, it was obvious. I left immediately. With great cordiality I held out my hand to Aunt Rosina, hoping to smooth her ruffled feathers, but she looked away as she gave her hand to me.

As soon as I had crossed the threshold of that house, my mood changed. What a liberation! I no longer had to ponder the meanings of Signora Malfenti, or make an effort to please Aunt Rosina. I actually think that if Aunt Rosina hadn't spoken up so sharply, that strategist Signora Malfenti would have achieved her purpose fully and I would have left that house, quite pleased with her cordial treatment. I skipped down the steps. Aunt Rosina had been a kind of gloss on Signora Malfenti. Signora Malfenti had suggested I stay away from her house for a few days. Too kind, dear lady! I would content her beyond her expectations, and she would never see me again! They had tortured me: the Signora, the aunt, and even Ada! With what right? Because I had wanted to marry? But I no longer gave it a thought! How beautiful freedom was!

For a good quarter of an hour I strode through the streets, accompanied by these feelings. Then I felt the need for an even greater freedom. I had to find a way to mark definitively my determination never to set foot in that house again. I rejected the idea of writing a letter in which I would take my leave. My abandonment became even haughtier if I didn't communicate my intention. I would simply forget to see Giovanni and his whole family.

I found the gesture, discreet and mannerly and therefore a bit ironic, with which I would thus seal my determination.

I rushed to a florist and selected a magnificent bouquet, which I addressed to Signora Malfenti accompanied by my card, on which I wrote only the date. Nothing more was needed. It was a date I would never forget thereafter, and perhaps Ada and her mother wouldn't forget it either: May 5, the anniversary of the death of Napoleon.

I insisted on immediate delivery. It was important for the flowers to arrive that very day.

And then? Everything had been done, absolutely everything, because there was nothing left to do! Ada remained separated from me, with all her family, and I had to live, doing nothing more, waiting for one of them to come seeking me, giving me the opportunity to do or say something else.

I rushed to my study to reflect and to shut myself away. If I had succumbed to my painful impatience, I would have immediately hurried back to that house, with the risk of arriving there before my flowers. There could be no lack of pretexts. I might even have forgotten my umbrella!

I didn't want to do anything of the sort. In sending that bouquet, I had taken a splendid stand, and it had to be maintained. Now I had to keep still, for the next move was up to them.

The introspection I achieved in my study, from which I had anticipated solace, only made clearer the reasons for my despair, exacerbated to the point of tears. I loved Ada! I didn't yet know if that was the right verb, and I continued my analysis. I wanted her not only to be mine, but to be my wife: she, with that marmoreal face and that unripe body, but only she, with her gravity, that made her unable to understand my wit, which I would not impart to her, but would renounce forever while she would instruct me in a life of intelligence and work. I wanted all of her, and I wanted all from her. In the end I concluded the verb was correct: I loved Ada.

It seemed to me that I had thought of something very important, which could guide me. Away with all hesitation!

It was no longer important to know if she loved me. I had to try to win her, and it was no longer necessary to speak with her if she was Giovanni's to bestow. Everything had to be cleared up promptly, to arrive at happiness at once or else to forget everything and be healed. Why did I have to suffer so much in this waiting? When I had learned – and I could learn it only from Giovanni – that I had definitively lost Ada, at least I would no longer have to battle with time, which would continue passing slowly without my feeling any need to push it. What's definitive is always calm, because it is detached from time.

I rushed at once to look for Giovanni. I sped in two directions. First toward his office, located in that street we continue to call New Houses, because that's what our ancestors called it. Tall old houses darkened the street, so close to the seashore, almost deserted at the sunset hour, and there I could proceed rapidly. As I walked on, I thought only of preparing as briefly as possible the sentence I would address to him. I had only to inform him of my resolve to marry his daughter. I didn't have to win him or convince him. That businessman would know what answer to give me the moment he had heard my question. Yet I was troubled by the problem of whether, on such an occasion, I should speak to him in dialect or in standard Italian.

But Giovanni had already left his office and had gone to the Tergesteo. I headed in that direction. More slowly, because I knew that at the Bourse I would have to wait longer to be able to speak to him alone. Then, arriving at Via Cavana, I had to slow down because of the crowd blocking the narrow street. And it was precisely when I was fighting my way through that crowd that I was finally granted, as if in a vision, the clarity I had been seeking for so many hours. The Malfentis wanted me to marry Augusta and didn't want me to marry Ada, and this for the simple reason that Augusta was in love with me and Ada didn't love me at all. Not at all, because otherwise they

97

wouldn't have intervened to separate us. They had told me I was compromising Augusta, but on the contrary, it was she who had compromised herself, in loving me. I understood everything at that moment, with vivid clarity, as if some member of the family had told me. And I guessed also that Ada had concurred in my being sent away from that house. She didn't love me, and she would never love me as long as her sister loved me. On the crowded Via Cavana, therefore, I had thought more purposefully than in my solitary study.

Today, when I cast my mind back to those five memorable days that led me to marriage, I am dumbfounded by the fact that my spirit was not affected on learning that poor Augusta loved me. Now cast out of the Malfentis' house, I loved Ada wrathfully. Why did I derive no satisfaction from the clear perception that Signora Malfenti had driven me away in vain, since I continued to dwell in that house, and very close to Ada, namely in the heart of Augusta? I actually considered a further insult Signora Malfenti's appeal to me not to compromise Augusta and, instead, to marry her. Toward the ugly girl who loved me I felt the very disdain I could not believe was addressed to me by her beautiful sister, whom I loved.

I walked still faster, but I turned aside and headed for my house. I no longer had to speak with Giovanni, because I now knew exactly how to behave; I saw it with a clarity so disheartening that perhaps it would at last give me peace, detaching me from time, which moved too slowly. It was even dangerous to talk about it with that boorish Giovanni. Signora Malfenti had spoken in a way I would understand only there in Via Cavana. Her husband was capable of behaving differently. He might even have said to me: "Why do you want to marry Ada? Let's see! Wouldn't you be better off marrying Augusta?" Because he had an axiom I remembered, one that might guide him in this situation: "You must always explain clearly any business transaction to your opponent, that's the only way you can be sure of understanding it better than he does!" Well, now what?

An open break would follow. Not until then would time be able to proceed at its chosen pace, because then I would have no reason to meddle with it: I would have arrived at the still point!

I remembered, too, another axiom of Giovanni's, and I clung to it because it gave me great hope. I was able to hang on to it for five days, those five days that transformed my passion into illness. Giovanni used to say you must never be in a hurry to close a transaction when you can't expect any gain: every transaction sooner or later arrives at its conclusion on its own, as is proved by the fact that the history of the world is so long and that so few transactions remain unsettled. Until the moment it is settled, any transaction may prove profitable.

I didn't remember that Giovanni had other axioms affirming the opposite, and I clung to that one. I had to cling to something. I made an ironclad resolution not to move until I learned that some new development had redirected my transaction to my advantage. And I was thus done such harm that, perhaps for this reason, no subsequent resolution of mine ever remained with me for so long a time.

No sooner had I made this resolution than I received a note from Signora Malfenti. I recognized the handwriting on the envelope, and before opening it, I flattered myself that my ironclad decision alone had sufficed to make her regret her maltreatment of me, inspiring her now to seek me out. When I found that the note contained only the letters *p.r.*,* which meant thanks for the flowers I had sent her, I was in despair. I flung myself on my bed and sank my teeth into the pillow as if to nail myself there and prevent myself from running out and breaking my vow. What ironic serenity emanated from those two letters! Far greater than that expressed by the date I had written on my card, which meant first a resolution and perhaps

---

* *p.r.*, for *per ringaziamento*: written on a calling card, these letters represented a correct but formal and cold way of saying thank you.

also a reproach. *Remember*, said Charles I, before they decapitated him, and he must have been referring to that day's date! I, too, had urged my adversary to remember and to fear!

Five terrible days and five terrible nights followed, and I observed the dawns and the sunsets that meant end and beginning and brought closer the hour of my freedom, the freedom to fight again for my love.

I was preparing for that combat. By now I knew how my fair maiden wanted me to be. It is easy to remember some resolutions I made then, first of all because I made some identical ones more recently, and further because I made a note of them on a sheet of paper I have kept. I was determined to become more serious. That meant not telling those jokes that made others laugh but discredited me, while they made the ugly Augusta love me and moved my Ada to contempt. Then there was the determination to be every morning at eight o'clock sharp in my office, which I hadn't seen for such a long time, and not to argue with Olivi about my rights, but to work with him and become capable of assuming in due course the management of my affairs. This would be essayed in a period more serene than the present; similarly, I would also stop smoking later, namely when I had regained my freedom, because it wouldn't do to make this horrible interval even worse. Ada was entitled to a perfect husband. So there were various plans to devote myself to serious reading, and to spend a half hour every day in the *salle d'armes*, and to go riding a couple of times each week. The day's twenty-four hours were not too many.

During those days of isolation, the most bitter jealousy was my constant companion. I had made the heroic vow to correct my every fault in preparation for my conquest of Ada in a few weeks' time. But for the present? For the present, as I subjected myself to the sternest discipline, would the other males of the city remain inactive, or would they try instead to take my woman away from me? Among them there was surely one who didn't need all these exertions in order to make himself welcome. I knew – I thought I knew – that when Ada found the man suited to her, she would immediately consent, without waiting to fall in love. During those days, when I encountered a well-dressed male, healthy and carefree, I hated him because to me he seemed to fit the bill for Ada. The thing I remember best from those days is the jealousy that descended like a fog on my life.

The horrid suspicion that I would see Ada taken from me in those days is nothing to laugh at, now that we know how things turned out. When I think back to those days of passion, I feel a great awe of my prophetic spirit.

Various times, at night, I walked beneath the windows of that house. Upstairs, they apparently continued amusing themselves as they had when I, too, had been there. At midnight or shortly before, the lights would go out in the living room. I would run off, afraid of being glimpsed by some visitor who would then be leaving the house.

But every hour of those days was torture also because of my impatience. Why did no one inquire after me? Why didn't Giovanni do something? Shouldn't he have been amazed, seeing me neither at his house nor at the Tergesteo? Was he, then, also in agreement about my banishment? I often interrupted my walks, day and night, to rush home and make sure no one had come asking for me. I couldn't go to bed if there was any doubt in my mind, so I would wake poor Maria and question her. I would spend hours waiting at home, the place where I was most easily found. But no one asked for me, and surely if I hadn't made up my mind to stir myself, I would still be a bachelor.

One evening I went to gamble at the club. For many years I hadn't put in an appearance there, respecting a promise I had made my father. It seemed to me the promise no longer had any validity, since my father couldn't have foreseen my painful circumstances and my urgent need for distraction. At first

I won, but with a luck that grieved me because it seemed a compensation for my bad luck in love. Then I lost, and I grieved again because I seemed to succumb to gambling as I had succumbed to love. I soon became fed up with the play. It was unworthy of me, and also of Ada. That was how pure my love made me!

In those days I also realized how my dreams of love had been annihilated by that harsh reality. Now my dream was quite different. I dreamed of victory rather than of love. My sleep was once embellished by a visit from Ada. She was in bridal attire and was coming with me to the altar, but when we were left alone, we didn't make love, not even then. I was her husband and I had gained the right to ask her: "How could you have allowed me to be treated like that?" No other rights mattered to me.

In one of my drawers I find drafts of letters to Ada, to Giovanni, and to Signora Malfenti. They date from that time. To Signora Malfenti I wrote a simple note, taking my leave before setting off on a long journey. I don't recall having had any such thing in mind, however. I couldn't leave the city when I wasn't certain no one would come looking for me. What a misfortune if they were to come and then not find me! None of those letters was sent. I believe I wrote them only to record my thoughts on paper.

For many years I had considered myself ill, but the illness made others suffer more than it did me. Now I finally came to know "painful" illness, a host of unpleasant physical sensations that made me genuinely unhappy.

This is how they began. At about one in the morning, unable to fall asleep, I would get up and walk around in the mild night until I came upon an outlying café, where I had never been and where I would thus not encounter any acquaintance: a welcome situation because I wanted to continue an argument with Signora Malfenti I had begun in bed, and I didn't want anybody interfering. Signora Malfenti had addressed further reproaches to me. She said I had tried to "play footsies" with her daughters. Actually, if I had attempted such a thing, I had surely done so only with Ada. I broke into a cold sweat at the thought that the Malfenti family was now reproaching me in such a fashion. The absent man is always wrong, and they could have taken advantage of my absence to band together against me. In the bright light of the café, I defended myself better. To be sure, there had been times when I would have liked to touch Ada's foot with mine, and once, indeed, I thought I had done so, with her acquiescence. But then it turned out I had pressed the wooden foot of the table, and that foot surely couldn't have told on me.

I pretended to take an interest in the billiards game. One gentleman, leaning on a crutch, came over and sat down right beside me. He ordered a lemonade, and since the waiter expected an order also from me, absently I also asked for lemonade, though I can't bear the taste of lemon. Meanwhile, the crutch, first propped against the sofa where we were seated, now slid to the floor, and I bent to pick it up with an almost instinctive movement.

"Oh, Zeno!" the poor cripple said, recognizing me as he turned to thank me.

"Tullio!" I cried, surprised, holding out my hand. We had been schoolmates, but hadn't seen each other for many years. I knew that, after finishing high school, he had gone into a bank, where he now held a good position.

I was nevertheless so distracted that I curtly asked him what had happened to shorten his right leg, making the crutch necessary.

With great good humor he told me that six months previously he had begun suffering from rheumatism so severe that it had finally affected his leg.

I quickly suggested many treatments. This is the ideal, effortless way to feign lively concern. He had tried them all. Then I interfered further: "In that case, why aren't you in bed, at this hour? I don't believe exposure to the night air can be good for you."

He joked, still good-naturedly, replying that he didn't believe the night air was good for me, either, and he was sure that those who haven't suffered from rheumatism, as long as they remain alive, can still fall victim to it. The right not to go to bed until the small hours was granted even by the Austrian constitution. For that matter, contrary to general opinion, heat and cold had nothing to do with rheumatism. He had studied his illness, and indeed he did nothing else in this world but investigate its causes and its remedies. He had been given an extended leave from the bank, not so much for treatment as for more thorough study. Then he told me he was following a strange cure. Every day he ate an enormous quantity of lemons. That day he had consumed about thirty, but with practice he hoped to be able to tolerate even more. He confided to me that lemons, in his opinion, were good also for many other diseases. Since he had begun taking them, he felt less irritation from the excessive smoking of which he, too, was a victim.

I felt a shudder run through me at the vision of all that acid, but immediately afterwards I had a somewhat happier vision of life: I didn't like lemons, but if they were to give me the liberty to do what I should do or wanted to do without suffering harm, freeing me from every other restraint, I would consume those countless lemons myself. Complete freedom consists of being able to do what you like, provided you also do something you like less. True slavery is being condemned to abstinence: Tantalus, not Hercules.

Then Tullio pretended to be equally eager for my news. I was quite determined not to tell him about my unhappy love, still I needed to unburden myself. I spoke with such exaggeration of my ailments (in this way I made a list of them, and I am sure they were slight) that in the end I had tears in my eyes, while Tullio was feeling better all the time, believing me worse off than himself.

He asked me if I was working. Everyone in the city said I did nothing, and I was afraid he would envy me, whereas at this moment I was in absolute need of commiseration. I lied! I told him I worked in my office, not much, but at least six hours daily, and then the extremely muddled questions inherited from my father and my mother kept me busy for another six hours.

"Twelve hours!" Tullio remarked, and with a contented smile he granted me what I sought: his commiseration. "You certainly aren't to be envied!"

His conclusion was correct, and I was so moved by it that I had to fight to restrain the tears. I felt unhappier than ever, and in that morbid state of self-pity, obviously I was vulnerable to injury.

Tullio had resumed talking about his illness, which was also his chief hobby. He had studied the anatomy of the leg and the foot. Laughing, he told me that when one walks at a rapid pace, the time in which a step is taken does not exceed a half-second, and that in that half-second no fewer that fifty-four muscles are engaged. I reacted with a start, and my thoughts immediately rushed to my legs, to seek this monstrous machinery. I believe I found it. Naturally I didn't identify the fifty-four moving parts, but rather an enormous complication went to pieces the moment I intruded my attention upon it.

I limped, leaving that café, and I went on limping for several days. For me, walking had become hard labor, also slightly painful. That jungle of cogs now seemed to lack oil, and in moving, they damaged one another reciprocally. A few days afterwards, I was assailed by a more serious illness, of which I will speak, that diminished the first. But even today, as I write about it, if someone watches me when I move, the fifty-four muscles become self-conscious and I risk falling.

This injury, too, is something I owe to Ada. Many animals become prey to hunters or to other animals when they are in love. I was then prey to illness, and I am sure that if I had learned of the monstrous machine at some other time, I wouldn't have suffered the slightest harm from it.

A few scribbles on a slip of paper that I preserved remind me of another strange adventure in those days. Besides the annotation of a last cigarette, accompanied by my confidence that I could be cured of the fifty-four-muscle disease, there is an attempted poem . . . about a fly. If I didn't know otherwise, I would believe that those verses had come from a proper young lady who was addressing in the familiar form the insects she sings about, but since I was the one who wrote them, I must believe, since I once followed that path, that a person can veer off in any direction.

Here is how those verses were born. Late one night I had come home and, rather than go to bed, I had entered my little study and turned on the gas. In the light a fly began to torment me. I managed to give it a tap – a light one, however, to avoid soiling my hand. I forgot about it, but then I saw it in the center of the table as it was coming to. It was motionless, erect, and it seemed taller than before, because one of its little legs was paralyzed and couldn't bend. With its two hind legs it assiduously smoothed its wings. It tried to move, but turned over on its back. It righted itself and stubbornly resumed its assiduous task.

I then wrote those verses, amazed at having discovered that the little organism, filled with such pain, was inspired in its immense effort by two errors: first of all, by the stubborn smoothing of its wings, which were unharmed, the insect revealed that it didn't know which organ was the source of its pain, and in the determination of that effort it revealed that its minuscule mind contained a fundamental belief that good health is the birthright of all and must surely return when it abandons us. These were errors that can easily be excused in an insect, which lives only a single season and hasn't time to accumulate experience.

Now Sunday arrived. The fifth day since my last visit to the Malfenti household. I, who work so little, retained always a great respect for the holiday, which divides life into brief periods, making it more tolerable. That holiday concluded also a tiring week for me, and I was entitled to joy. I didn't change my plans in the least, but they did not apply to that day, when I would see Ada again. I wouldn't endanger those plans by uttering the slightest word, but I had to see her because there was also the possibility that the situation had already turned in my favor, and then it would be a great pity to go on suffering for no purpose.

Therefore, at midday, with such haste as my poor legs permitted, I rushed downtown and to the street I knew Signora Malfenti and her daughters would have to take on their way home from Mass. It was a day of festive sunshine and, walking along, I thought that perhaps in the city a new development awaited me: Ada's love!

It was not so, but for another moment I had that illusion. Luck favored me incredibly. I came upon Ada face-to-face, Ada alone. My legs failed me, and so did my breath. What to do? My resolution should have made me step aside and allow her to pass with a measured greeting. But in my mind there was a bit of confusion because previously there had been other resolutions, among which I recalled one that involved me speaking to her clearly and learning my fate from her lips. I didn't step aside, and when she greeted me as if we had parted only five minutes before, I walked along with her.

What she had said to me was: "Good morning, Signor Cosini! I'm in something of a hurry."

And my reply was: "May I walk part of the way with you?"

She agreed, smiling. Should I have spoken then? She added that she was going straight home, and thus I understood I had only five minutes at my disposal to speak, and I even wasted a bit of that time in calculating if it would suffice for the important things I had to say. But to leave them unsaid was better than not to say all. I was confused further by the fact that in our city, for a young lady, it was in itself fairly compromising to allow a young man to accompany her in the street. She had allowed me to do so. Could I be satisfied with that? Meanwhile I looked at her, trying to feel once again my intact love, recently clouded by anger and doubt. Would I regain my dreams, at least? She seemed to me at once little and big, in the harmony of her lines. The dreams returned, pell-mell, even as I was beside her, in all her reality. This was my way of desiring, and I returned to it with intense joy. All traces of anger or bitterness vanished from my spirit.

But behind us a hesitant call was heard: "Signorina! May I – ?"

I turned, outraged. Who dared interrupt the explanations that I hadn't yet begun? A beardless young gentleman, dark-haired, pale, was looking at her with anxious eyes. In my turn I also looked at Ada, in the mad hope that she would call on me for assistance. A sign from her would have been enough to make me fall upon this individual and demand an explanation of his audacity. And if only he were to persist! My ailments would have been cured at once had I been allowed to give free rein to a brutal act of force.

But Ada didn't make that sign. With a spontaneous smile that slightly altered the line of her cheeks and mouth and also the light in her eyes, she held out her hand. "Signor Guido!"

That given name hurt me. Only a short time before, she had addressed me by my surname.

I took a closer look at this Signor Guido. He was dressed with an affected elegance, and in his gloved right hand he held a walking stick with a very long ivory handle, which I would never have carried, not even if they were to pay me a sum for every kilometer. I didn't reproach myself for having actually considered such a person a threat to Ada. There are some shady characters who dress elegantly and carry similar canes.

Ada's smile plunged me again into the most ordinary social intercourse. Ada introduced us. And I smiled, too! Ada's smile somehow suggested the wrinkling of clear water ruffled by a slight breeze. Mine also recalled a similar movement, but produced by a stone flung into the water.

His name was Guido Speier. My smile became more spontaneous because I was immediately offered the opportunity of saying something disagreeable to him: "You are German?"

He replied politely, admitting that because of his name, one might believe he was. But family documents proved they had been Italian for several centuries. He spoke Tuscan fluently, while Ada and I were condemned to our horrid dialect.

I looked at him to hear better what he was saying. He was a very handsome young man: his naturally parted lips allowed a glimpse of white, perfect teeth. His eyes were lively and expressive, and when he had bared his head, I had glimpsed his dark, slightly waving hair, which covered all the space Mother Nature had destined it for, while a good deal of my head had been invaded by my brow.

I would have hated him even if Ada hadn't been present, but that hatred made me suffer, and I tried to attenuate it. I thought: He's too young for Ada. And I also thought that the intimacy and courtesy in her attitude toward him were due to orders from her father. Perhaps the youth was important to Malfenti's business, and I had observed that in such cases the whole family was obliged to collaborate.

I asked him: "You are settling in Trieste?"

He answered that he had been there for a month and he was establishing a commercial firm. I breathed easy again! Perhaps I had guessed right.

I limped, but my walk was fairly nonchalant, seeing that no one noticed. I looked at Ada and tried to forget all the rest, including the other man walking beside her. After all, I live in the present and I don't think of the future when it isn't darkening the present with obvious shadows. Ada walked between the two of us, and on her face she had a fixed expression of vague happiness that almost arrived at a smile. That happiness seemed new to me. For whom was that smile? Wasn't it for me, whom she hadn't seen in such a long time?

I listened carefully to what was being said. They were talking about spiritualism, and I promptly learned that Guido had introduced the Malfenti household to the Ouija board.

I was burning with the desire to make sure that the sweet smile playing over Ada's lips was mine, and I plunged into the subject of their talk, making up a story about spirits. No poet could have improvised to set rhymes better. Before I knew where I was heading, I started out by declaring that I now believed in spirits, too, thanks to something that had happened to me the day before on this very street...no!...on the street we could glimpse, parallel to the one along which we were walking. Then I added that Ada, too, had known Professor Bertini, who had died recently in Florence, where he had moved on retiring. We learned of his death through a brief news item in a local paper, which I had forgotten about, and indeed, when I thought of Professor Bertini, I pictured him strolling in the Cascine, enjoying his well-earned rest. Well, just the day before, at a point I indicated in the street parallel to ours, I was approached by a gentleman who knew me and whom I was sure I knew. He had a strange, wriggling walk, like a certain kind of woman trying to smooth her progress...

"Of course! That would be Bertini!" Ada said, laughing.

Her laughter was mine, and, heartened, I continued: "I was sure I knew him, but I couldn't recall who he was. We discussed politics. It was Bertini, because he talked so much nonsense, with that sheeplike voice of his..."

"His voice, too!" again Ada laughed, looking at me, eager, to hear the conclusion.

"Yes! It must have been Bertini," I said, feigning fear, like the great actor the world has lost in me. "He shook my hand, taking his leave, and went off jauntily. I followed him for a few steps, trying to collect myself. It was only when he was out of sight that I realized I had spoken with Bertini. With Bertini, who had been dead for a year!"

A little later she stopped at the front door of her house. Shaking his hand, she said to Guido that she was expecting him that evening. Then, saying good-bye also to me, she added that if I weren't afraid of being bored I should join them that evening and help make the table dance.

I neither answered nor thanked her. I had to analyze that invitation before accepting. To me it had seemed to have the sound of forced good manners. Yes, perhaps for me the holiday would conclude with this meeting. But I wanted to appear polite, to leave every avenue open, also that of accepting the invitation. I inquired after Giovanni, with whom I had to talk. She replied that I would find him in his office, where he had gone to deal with some urgent matter of business.

Guido and I lingered for a short time, watching the elegant little form vanish into the darkness of the vestibule of her house. I don't know what Guido thought at that moment. For my part, I felt very unhappy: Why hadn't she issued that invitation first to me and then to Guido?

Together we retraced our steps, almost to the spot where we had found Ada. Polite and nonchalant (it was that same nonchalance that I most envied in others), Guido spoke further about that story I had improvised, which he took seriously. Actually, the only truth in the story was that in Trieste, also after Bertini's death, there lived a person who talked nonsense, who walked as if he were on tiptoe, and had a strange voice. I had made his acquaintance around that time, and for a moment he had reminded me of Bertini. I wasn't sorry that Guido should give himself a headache pondering that invention of mine. It was settled that I wouldn't hate him, because, for the Malfentis, he was simply an important merchant; but I disliked him because of his affected elegance and his walking stick. I disliked him so much, in fact, that I couldn't wait to be rid of him.

I heard him concluding: "It's also possible that the person with whom you spoke was much younger than Bertini, strode like a guardsman, with a manly voice, and that the resemblance was limited to his talking nonsense. That would have been enough to focus your thoughts on Bertini. But to accept this, it would be necessary to believe also that you are a very absent-minded person."

"Absentminded? Me? What an idea! I'm a businessman. What would become of me if I were absentminded?"

Then I decided I was wasting my time. I wanted to see Giovanni. Since I had seen the daughter, I could also see the father, who was much less important. I had to hurry if I wanted to find him still in his office.

Guido went on pondering how much of a miracle could be attributed to the absentmindedness of the one who works it or witnesses it. I wanted to take my leave and appear at least as nonchalant as he. Hence I interrupted him, leaving him there, with a haste quite close to rudeness: "For me, miracles either exist or they don't. They mustn't be complicated with a lot of stories. You believe or disbelieve, and in either case it's all very simple."

I didn't want to demonstrate any dislike for him, and indeed I felt that my words were conceding something to him, as I am a convinced positivist and do not believe in miracles. But it was a concession made with great ill humor.

I went off, limping worse than ever, and I hoped Guido didn't feel impelled to turn and watch me go.

I really had to talk with Giovanni. First of all, he would instruct me how to behave that evening. I had been invited by Ada, and from Giovanni's behavior I could understand whether I should go along with that invitation or remember, instead, that it went counter to the expressed wishes of Signora Malfenti. Clarity was essential in my dealings with these people, and if this Sunday weren't enough to give it to me, I would devote Monday to the same purpose. I kept contradicting my own resolutions, unaware. Indeed, it seemed to me I was acting on a decision reached after five days of meditation. That is how I categorized my activity during those days.

Giovanni greeted me with a shout, which did me good, and urged me to take a seat in the easy chair placed against the wall opposite his desk.

"Just five minutes, and I'll be right with you!" And a moment later he added: "Why, you're limping!"

I flushed. But I was in an improvisational mood. I told him I had slipped as I was leaving the café, and I named the very café where the accident had befallen me. I was afraid he might attribute my spill to a mind clouded by alcohol, and, laughing, I added the detail that when I fell, I was in the company of a person suffering from rheumatism, who limped.

A clerk and two porters were standing at Giovanni's desk. Some irregularity in a consignment of goods had to be checked, and Giovanni was interfering ponderously in the operation of his warehouse, with which he rarely concerned himself, preferring to keep his mind free – as he said – to do only what no one else could do in his place. He shouted more than usual, as if he wanted to engrave his instructions in his employees' ears. I believe it was a question of establishing the procedure of operations between office and warehouse.

"This paper! . . . " Giovanni shouted, passing from his right hand to his left a paper he had torn out of a ledger, "will be signed by you, and the clerk who receives it from you will give you one just like it, signed by him."

He glared straight at his interlocutors, through his eyeglasses and then over them, concluding with another shout: "Understand?"

He decided to repeat his explanation from the beginning, but it seemed to me he was wasting time. I had the curious feeling that if I hurried, I would be able to fight better for Ada, but then I realized to my great surprise that no one was expecting me and I was expecting no one, and nothing could be done for me.

I went toward Giovanni, with outstretched hand. "I'm coming to your house this evening."

He turned to me at once, as the others moved aside. "Why haven't we seen you for such a long time?" he asked simply.

I was overcome by an amazement that left me bewildered. This was the very question Ada had failed to ask me, and to which I would be entitled. If those other men hadn't been present, I would have spoken sincerely to Giovanni, who had asked me that question and had proved his innocence in what I now felt was a conspiracy against me. He alone was innocent and deserved my trust.

Perhaps I did not then think at once with such clarity, and the proof is the fact that I didn't have the patience to wait till the clerk and the porters had left. Besides, I wanted to see if Ada had perhaps been prevented from asking that question by the untimely arrival of Guido.

But Giovanni also prevented me from speaking, with a great show of haste to return to his work.

"We'll see each other this evening, then. You'll hear a violinist whose like you've never heard before. He claims to be an amateur only because he has so much money that he wouldn't condescend to making the violin his profession. He plans to go into business." He shrugged, with a gesture of contempt. "Much as I love business, in his place I would peddle nothing but notes. I don't know if you've met him. Name of Guido Speier."

"Oh, really? Really?" I said, pretending to be pleased, shaking my head and opening my mouth, in other words moving everything I could command with my will. That handsome youth could also play the violin? "Really and truly? That good, is he?" I was hoping Giovanni had been joking and, with the exaggeration of his praises, had wanted to suggest that Guido was no more than a tormentor of the violin. But he kept shaking his head with great awe.

I shook his hand. "Until later."

Limping, I went off to the door. A suspicion stopped me. Perhaps I would have been better advised not to accept that invitation, in which case I should inform Giovanni. I turned to go back to him, but I saw that he was watching me with great attention, leaning forward to see me more closely. I couldn't bear this, and I left!

A violinist! If it was true that he played so well, I, quite simply, was a man destroyed. If only I didn't play that instrument or at least hadn't allowed myself to be induced to play it at the Malfentis'. I had taken the violin into that house not to win people's hearts with my tone, but as an excuse to prolong my visits. How idiotic of me! I could have invented so many other, less compromising pretexts!

No one can say I succumb to illusions about myself. I know I have a profound feeling for music, and it is not affectation that makes me select the most complex pieces; however, that same profound musical feeling warns me and has warned me for years that I will never succeed in playing well enough to afford listeners pleasure. If I still go on playing, it's for the same reason that I continue to take care of my health. I could play well if I weren't ill, and I am pursuing health even when I ponder the equilibrium of the four strings. There is a slight paralysis in my organism, and on the violin it reveals its entire self and therefore is more easily treated. Even the lowest creature, when he knows what thirds are, or sixths, knows how to move from one to the other with rhythmic precision, just as his eye knows how to move from one color to the other. With me, on the contrary, when I have played one of those phrases, it sticks to me and I can no longer rid myself of it, and so it intrudes into the next phrase and distorts it. To put the notes in the right place, I have to beat time with my feet and my head, so nonchalance flies out the window, along with serenity, and with the music. The music that comes from a balanced organism is one with the tempo it creates and follows. When I achieve that, I will be cured.

For the first time I thought of abandoning the field, leaving Trieste, to go elsewhere in search of distraction. There was nothing more to hope for. Ada was lost to me. I was sure of that! Didn't I know she would marry a man only after having tested and judged him as if it were a matter of awarding him an academic honor? It seemed ridiculous to me because, honestly, among human beings the violin should not count in the choice of a husband, but that thought didn't save me. I felt the importance of that sound. It was decisive, as it is among songbirds.

I shut myself up in my study, though, for others, the holiday was not yet over! I took the violin from its case, undecided whether to smash it to smithereens or to play it. Then I tried it as if I wanted to bid it a last farewell, and finally I started practicing the eternal Kreutzer. In that same room I had made my bow travel so many kilometers that, in my bewilderment, mechanically, I began traveling some more.

All who have dedicated themselves to those accursed four strings know that as long as you live in isolation, you believe that each tiny effort produces a corresponding progress. If this weren't so, who would voluntarily subject himself to that regime of endless hard labor, as if he had had the misfortune to murder someone? After a little while it seemed to me that my battle with Guido was not definitively lost. Who knows? Perhaps I would be allowed to come between Guido and Ada through a victorious violin?

This was not presumption, but my usual optimism, of which I was never able to rid myself. Every threat of disaster at first terrifies me, but then is immediately forgotten in the greater certitude of being able to elude it. Now I had only to adopt a more benevolent opinion of my own talents as a violinist. In the arts generally, as everyone knows, confident evaluation comes from confrontation, which here was lacking.

And yet one's own violin, resounding so close to the ear, finds the shortest path to the heart. When I grew tired and stopped playing, I said to myself: "Good for you, Zeno. You've earned your keep."

Without the slightest hesitation, I went to the Malfentis'. I had accepted the invitation and now I couldn't fail to appear. I thought it a good omen when the maid welcomed me with a cordial smile, asking me if I had been ill; as I hadn't been there for so long, I gave her a tip. Through her mouth the whole family, whose representative she was, was asking me that question.

She led me into the living room, which was plunged into the deepest darkness. Arriving there from the bright light of the vestibule, I saw nothing for a moment and didn't dare move. Then I could discern several figures seated around a little table at the end of the room, at some distance from me.

I was greeted by Ada's voice, which, in the darkness, seemed sensual to me. Smiling, caressing. "Have a seat over there and don't disturb the spirits!" At this rate, I would surely not disturb them.

From another point at the table's rim, another voice resounded, Alberta's or perhaps Augusta's: "If you want to take part in the summoning, there's still a free place."

I was firmly determined not to let myself be ostracized, and I strode resolutely toward the point from which Ada's greeting had come. I banged my knee against a corner of that little Venetian table, which was all corners. The pain was intense, but I didn't allow it to stop me, so I went and sank onto a chair offered me by someone or other, between two young ladies, of whom I thought one, the one on my right, was Ada, and the other Augusta. Immediately, to avoid any contact with the latter, I shifted toward the other. I suspected, however, that I might be mistaken and, to hear the voice of my neighbor to the right, I asked her: "Have you already received some communication from the spirits?"

Guido, who seemed to be sitting opposite, interrupted me, shouting imperiously: "Quiet!"

Then, more mildly: "Collect your thoughts and concentrate intensely on the dead person you wish to summon."

I have nothing against any sort of attempt to peer into the world beyond. Indeed, I was annoyed that I hadn't been the one to introduce the little table into Giovanni's house, since it was obviously enjoying such a success. But I didn't feel like obeying Guido's orders, and therefore I didn't concentrate at all. Besides, I had already reproached myself so much for having let things reach this pass without ever speaking clearly to Ada that, as I now had the young lady at my side, in this favoring darkness, I intended to clarify everything. I was curbed only by the sweetness of having her so close after fearing I had lost her forever. I sensed the softness of the warm fabrics that brushed against my clothes, and I thought, too, as we were pressed so close to each other, my foot was touching her little foot, which, as I knew, in the evening was shod in a tiny patent leather boot. It was even too much after such long torture.

Guido spoke again: "Please concentrate, everybody. Now beg the spirit you are summoning to make his presence known by moving the table."

I was glad that he would go on dealing with the table. By now it was obvious that Ada was resigned to bearing almost all my weight! If she hadn't loved me, she wouldn't have borne me. The moment of clarification had come. I took my right hand from the table and, very slowly, I put my arm around her waist: "I love you, Ada!" I said in a low voice, moving my face close to hers to make myself more audible.

The girl did not answer immediately. Then, a wisp of a voice – Augusta's voice, however – said: "Why did you stay away so long?"

My surprise and dismay almost made me fall off my seat. Immediately I felt that, while I had finally to eliminate that irritating young lady from my destiny, I was still obliged to show her the consideration that a proper gentleman like myself must show the woman who loves him even if she is the ugliest female ever created. How she loved me! In my sorrow I felt her love. It could be only love that had led her not to tell me she wasn't Ada, and to ask me the question I had awaited in vain from Ada, while her sister certainly had been ready to ask me it the moment she saw me again.

I followed my instinct and did not answer her question, but, after a brief hesitation, said to her: "Actually, I'm glad I've confided in you, Augusta, because I believe you are so good!"

I immediately regained my balance on my stool. I couldn't have the clarification with Ada, but meanwhile there was now total clarity between me and Augusta. Here there would be no further misunderstandings.

Guido repeated his warning: "If you're not willing to be quiet, there's no point in spending our time here in the dark!"

He didn't know it, but I still needed a bit of darkness to isolate myself and collect my wits. I had discovered my mistake, and the only balance I had recovered was that of my seat.

I would talk with Ada, but in the clear light. I suspected it was not she on my left, but Alberta. How to verify this? The doubt almost made me fall to the left, and to recover my balance, I leaned on the table. The others all started to shout: "It moved! It moved!" My involuntary action could lead me to clarity. Where did Ada's voice come from? But Guido's voice now covered all the others, as he imposed the silence that I, quite willingly, would have imposed on him. Then, in a changed voice, pleading (the fool!), he spoke to the spirit, whom he believed present.

"I beg you! Tell us your name, spell it out in our alphabet!"

He thought of everything: He was afraid the spirit would use the Greek alphabet.

I kept up the farce, still peering into the darkness in search of Ada. After a slight hesitation I made the table move seven times so that the letter G was reached. It seemed a good idea to me, and though the U that followed required endless movements, I dictated quite distinctly the name of Guido. I have no doubt that, in dictating his name, I was led by a desire to relegate him to the spirit world.

When the name of Guido was complete, Ada finally spoke. "Some ancestor of yours?" she suggested. She was seated just at his side. I would have liked to move the table and shove it between the two of them, separating them.

"It could be!" Guido said. He thought he had ancestors, but that didn't frighten me. His voice was affected by a genuine emotion that afforded me the joy a fencer feels when he realizes his adversary is less fearsome that he had believed. He wasn't making these experiments in cold blood. He was a genuine fool! All weaknesses, except his, easily arouse my sympathy.

Then he addressed the spirit: "If your name is Speier, make one movement. Otherwise move the table twice." Since he wanted to have ancestors, I satisfied him, rocking the table two times.

"My grandfather!" Guido murmured.

After this, the conversation with the spirit proceeded more quickly. The spirit was asked if he had some news to communicate. He answered yes. Business or otherwise? Business! This answer was preferable because answering it required only a single movement of the table. Guido then asked if it was good news or bad. Bad was to be indicated by two movements, and I – without the slightest hesitation this time – chose to move the table twice. But the second movement encountered opposition, so there must have been someone in the group who wanted the news to be good. Ada, perhaps? To produce the second movement, I actually flung myself on the table and easily had my way! Bad news!

Because of the struggle, the second movement proved excessive and actually jolted the entire company.

"That's odd!" Guido murmured. Then, firmly, he cried: "That's enough! Somebody here is making fun of us!"

It was a command, which many obeyed at the same time, and the living room was suddenly flooded with light, as lamps were turned on in several places. Guido seemed pale to me! Ada was mistaken about that individual, and I would open her eyes.

In the room, besides the three girls, were Signora Malfenti and another lady the sight of whom made me feel embarrassed and uneasy because I believed it was Aunt Rosina. For different reasons the two ladies received from me a cool greeting.

The best of it was that I had remained at the table, alone at Augusta's side. It was again compromising, but I couldn't resign myself to joining all the others, clustered around Guido, who, with some vehemence, was explaining how he had realized the table was being moved not by a spirit but by a flesh-and-blood devil. It was he himself, not Ada, who had tried to arrest the table, as it had become too garrulous.

"I was restraining the table with all my might," he said, "to prevent its moving a second time. Someone must actually have leaned hard on it, to overcome my resistance."

Fine spiritualist, he was! As if a powerful force couldn't come from a spirit!

I looked at poor Augusta to see her expression after she had heard my declaration of love for her sister. She was very flushed, but looked back at me with a kindly smile. It was only now that she brought herself to confirm having heard that declaration.

"I won't tell anyone," she said to me in a low voice.

I was very pleased.

"Thank you," I murmured, pressing her hand, not small but perfectly shaped. I was prepared to become Augusta's good friend, whereas previously it would have been impossible, because I'm unable to be friends with ugly people. But I felt a certain fondness for her waist, which I had clasped and found slimmer than I had believed. Her face, too, wasn't bad, and it seemed malformed only because of that eye that looked in an errant direction. I had surely exaggerated that malformation, believing it extended also to the thigh.

They had ordered lemonade for Guido. I approached the group still surrounding him, and encountered Signora Malfenti as she was moving away from it.

Laughing heartily, I asked her: "Does he need a tonic?"

Her lips curled in a faint movement of scorn. "He doesn't seem much of a man," she said sharply.

I flattered myself that my victory could be of decisive importance. Ada couldn't think differently from her mother. The victory immediately produced the effect inevitable in a man of my temper. All bitterness vanished, and I didn't want Guido to suffer further. Certainly the world would be a sweeter place if more people resembled me.

I sat beside him, and without looking at the others, I said: "You must forgive me, Signor Guido. I allowed myself a little joke in bad taste. I was the one who made the table declare it was moved by a spirit bearing your name. I wouldn't have done it had I known your grandfather actually had that name, too."

Guido's complexion, which went pale, betrayed the importance my confession had for him. But he was unwilling to admit it, and he said: "These ladies are too kind! I really don't need any consolation. The matter is of no significance. I appreciate your sincerity, but I had already guessed that someone had put on my grandfather's wig."

He laughed smugly, saying: "You are very strong! I should have guessed the table was being moved by the only other man in the party."

I had proved myself stronger than he, in fact, but soon I was made to feel weaker. Ada looked at me with an unfriendly eye and attacked me, her lovely cheeks inflamed: "I pity you. How could you permit yourself to play such a trick?"

My breath failed me and I stammered: "I . . . I wanted to have a laugh. I didn't believe any of us would take the table business seriously."

It was a bit late to turn on Guido, and indeed, if my ear had been sensitive, I would have heard that never again, in a battle with him, could victory be mine. The wrath Ada displayed toward me was truly decisive. How could I have failed to realize that she was already completely his? But I persisted in the thought that he didn't deserve her because he was not the man she was seeking with her serious gaze. Hadn't even Signora Malfenti sensed this?

All the others united to protect me and thus worsened my position. Laughing, Signora Malfenti said: "It was only a joke, and quite a successful one."

Aunt Rosina's heavy body was still shaking with laughter, and she said with admiration: "Magnificent!"

I was sorry Guido was being so friendly. Of course, the only thing that mattered to him was making sure the bad news given him by the table hadn't been delivered by a spirit. He said to me: "I bet that at first you didn't move the table on purpose. You rocked it accidentally, then you decided to rock it deliberately. So the thing would be somehow important – that is, until the moment when you decided to sabotage your own inspiration."

Ada turned and looked at me with curiosity. She was about to display an excessive devotion to Guido, forgiving me because he had granted me his forgiveness. I forestalled her.

"No, no!" I said firmly. "I was tired of waiting for those spirits, who refused to appear, and I put myself in their place to have some fun."

Ada turned her back on me, shrugging her shoulders in such a way that I had the sensation of having been slapped. Even the curls on her nape seemed to me to express contempt.

As always, instead of looking and listening, I was concerned entirely with my own thoughts. I was oppressed by the fact that Ada was compromising herself horribly. I suffered keenly, as if faced by the revelation that my beloved was betraying me. Despite those demonstrations of affection for Guido, she could still be mine, but I felt that I would never be able to forgive her behavior. Is my mind too slow to be able to follow events that unfold without waiting until the impressions left in my brain by previous events have been erased? I had to proceed, nevertheless, along the path marked out by my decision. Downright blind stubbornness. Indeed, I wanted to make my resolution all the stronger, by recording it once again. I went to Augusta, who was looking at me anxiously with a sincere, encouraging smile on her face, and I said, serious and heartfelt: "This is perhaps the last time I will come to your house because, this very evening, I will declare my love to Ada."

"You mustn't do that," she said to me, pleading. "Don't you realize what's happening here? I would be sorry if it were to make you suffer."

She continued to place herself between me and Ada. Meaning to irk her, I said: "I will speak with Ada because I must. What she answers then is a matter of complete indifference to me."

I limped again toward Guido. When I was at his side, looking at myself in a mirror, I lit a cigarette. In the mirror I saw I was very pale, and for me this is a reason to turn even paler. I struggled to feel better and to appear nonchalant. In this double effort, my thoughtless hand grasped Guido's glass. Once I was holding it, I could think of nothing better to do than to drain it.

Guido burst out laughing. "Now you'll know all my thoughts, because I've just drunk from that glass myself."

I have never liked the taste of lemon. This time it must have seemed truly poisonous to me because, first of all, having drunk from his glass, I felt I had suffered an odious contact with Guido, and further, I was struck by the expression of wrathful impatience printed on Ada's face. She immediately called the maid and ordered another glass of lemonade, and repeated this order even though Guido declared he was no longer thirsty.

Then I was genuinely compassionate. She was compromising herself more and more. "Excuse me, Ada," I said to her in a low voice, looking at her as if expecting some explanation. "I didn't want to displease you."

Then I was filled with the fear that my eyes would become moist with tears. I wanted to spare myself ridicule. I shouted: "I got some lemon juice in my eye."

I covered my eyes with my handkerchief, thus I no longer needed to guard against my tears, and I had to be careful only not to sob.

I will never forget the darkness behind that handkerchief. I concealed my tears there, but also a moment of madness. I thought I would tell her everything, she would understand me and love me, and I would never, never forgive her.

I raised the handkerchief from my face, I let everyone see my teary eyes, and I made an effort to laugh and to provoke laughter: "I bet Signor Giovanni ships citric acid to the house for making lemonade."

At that moment Giovanni arrived, greeting me with his usual great cordiality. It afforded me some solace, which was short-lived, because he declared he had come home earlier than usual in his desire to hear Guido play. He broke off, asking me the reason for the tears that moistened my eyes. They told him my doubts about the quality of his lemonade, and he laughed.

Hypocrite that I was, I joined Giovanni in begging Guido to play. I reminded myself: Hadn't I come there that evening to hear Guido's violin? And the strange thing is that I know I meant to conciliate Ada through my pleas to Guido. I looked at her, hoping to be finally linked with her for the first time that evening. How odd! Wasn't I supposed to speak with her and not forgive her? Instead, I saw only her back and the scornful curls on her nape. She had rushed to remove the violin from its case.

Guido asked to be left alone for another quarter of an hour. He seemed hesitant. Later in the long years of our acquaintance I learned that he always hesitated before doing even the simplest things he was urged to do. He did only what he enjoyed, and before granting a request, he proceeded to search the depths of his soul, to discover there what he really desired.

Then, in that evening memorable for me, came the happiest quarter-hour. My whimsical chatter amused everyone, Ada included. It was certainly prompted by my excitation, but also by my supreme effort to defeat that menacing violin coming closer and closer...And that brief period of time that others, thanks to me, found so amusing, I recall as being devoted to a desperate struggle.

Giovanni told us that in the tram bringing him home, he had witnessed a pathetic scene. A woman had jumped off before the car had come to a stop, and thus had fallen clumsily and been injured. With some exaggeration, Giovanni described his anxiety on seeing the woman preparing to make that leap, and in such a way that she was obviously going to fall and perhaps be crushed. It was quite sad to foresee it all and to have no time to rescue her.

An idea came to me. I told how, for those dizzy spells that had caused me such suffering in the past, I had discovered a remedy. When I saw a gymnast performing his feats at too great a height, or when I witnessed the descent from a tram of a person too elderly or too awkward, I freed myself from all anxiety by wishing them harm. I actually came out and said in so many words that I wished they would fall and be shattered. This had an enormously calming effect on me and enabled me to observe the threat of an accident with total detachment. If my wish then didn't come true, I could consider myself even more satisfied.

Guido was enchanted by my idea, which seemed to him a psychological discovery. He analyzed it, as he did all trifles, and couldn't wait to put the cure to the test. But he expressed a reservation: the ill-wishes should not increase the number of accidents. Ada joined in his laughter and even gave me a glance of admiration. Like a fool, I was hugely pleased. But I discovered it was not true that I would never be able to forgive her: another great step forward.

We laughed a lot together, like nice young people all fond of one another. At a certain moment I remained at one side of the living room, alone with Aunt Rosina. She was still talking about the little table. Fairly stout, she sat motionless on her chair and spoke to me without looking at me. I managed to let the others know I was bored, and they all watched me, laughing discreetly, beyond the aunt's view.

To increase their amusement, it occurred to me to say to her, without any preamble: "You know, Signora, I find you much better? You're rejuvenated."

It would have been laughable if she had become angry. But, instead of feeling any anger, the Signora indicated her profound gratitude and told me that, indeed, she was much better now after a recent illness. I was so amazed by her reply that my face must have assumed a highly comical expression, so the hilarity I had hoped for was not wanting. A little later the puzzle was explained to me. I learned, in short, that this was not Aunt Rosina but Aunt Maria, a sister of Signora Malfenti's. I had thus eliminated from that living room one source of uneasiness for me, but not the greatest.

At a certain moment Guido asked for his violin. For that evening he would do without any piano accompaniment, and play the Chaconne. Ada handed him the violin with a grateful smile. He didn't look at her, but looked at the violin, as if he wanted to be alone with it and with his inspiration. Then he stood in the center of the room, turning his back to a good part of the company, lightly tapped the strings with his bow, tuning them, and played a few arpeggios. He stopped abruptly, to say with a smile: "I have a nerve! Imagine: I haven't touched the violin since the last time I played here!"

What a charlatan! He turned his back also to Ada. I glanced at her anxiously to see if she was suffering. Apparently not! She had put her elbow on the little table, her chin in her hand, intent on listening.

Then, siding against me, the great Bach himself intervened. Never again, neither before nor after, was I able to feel in that way the beauty of that music born from those four strings like a Michelangelo angel from a block of marble. Only my state of mind was new to me, and it led me to look up, ecstatic, as if at something totally new. Yet I struggled to keep that music distant from me. I never ceased thinking: "Careful! The violin is a siren and its player can produce tears even without possessing a hero's heart!" I was assailed by that music, which gripped me. It seemed to speak of my illness and my sufferings with indulgence, alleviating them with smiles and caresses. But it was Guido who spoke! And I sought to elude the music, saying to myself: "To be able to do that, you need only possess a rhythmic organism, a steady hand and a gift for imitation: things that I don't have. This is not inferiority: it is misfortune."

I was protesting, but Bach continued, as confident as fate. He sang on high, with passion, and descended to seek the basso ostinato that was surprising, though ear and heart had anticipated it: precisely in the right place! A moment later and the song would have faded, beyond the reach of resonance; a moment earlier, and it would have been superimposed on the song, stifling it. With Guido this didn't happen: his arm never wavered, not even in taking on Bach. This was true inferiority.

As I write today, I have all the evidence of that. I feel no joy for having seen things so clearly at that time. Then I was full of hatred, and that music, which I accepted as my own soul, could not allay it. Then the vulgar life of every day came and canceled it, without any resistance on my part. Of course! Vulgar life is capable of many such things. Thank God, geniuses are not aware of this!

Guido wisely stopped playing. No one applauded except Giovanni, and for a few moments no one spoke. Then, unfortunately, I myself felt the need to speak. How did I dare, before people who knew my own violin? It seemed my violin was speaking, yearning for music and scorning the other instrument on which – undeniably – music had become life, light, and air.

"Excellent!" I said, and it had all the tone of a grudging concession rather than applause. "But I don't understand why, toward the end, you played those notes staccato when Bach marked them legato."

I knew the Chaconne note by note. There had been a time when I believed that if I wanted to make progress, I would have to face similar challenges, and for long months I spent my time practicing some compositions of Bach measure by measure.

I felt that in the whole room there was nothing for me but contempt and derision. And yet I continued speaking, combating that hostility. "Bach," I added, "is so unassuming in his means that he doesn't contemplate a bow handled like that."

I was probably right, but it was also sure that I could never have handled a bow that way myself.

Guido, immediately, was as wide of the mark as I had been. He asserted: "Perhaps Bach didn't know that expressive possibility! It's my gift to him!"

He was climbing on the shoulders of Bach, but in that atmosphere no one protested, whereas I had been mocked because I had tried to climb only on Guido's.

Then something occurred, of slight importance, though for me it was decisive. From a distant room came little Anna's repeated cries. As we subsequently learned, she had fallen and cut her lip. So it happened that for a few minutes I found myself alone with Ada, as all the others ran out. Before leaving the room, Guido placed his precious violin in Ada's hands.

"Would you like me to hold that violin?" I asked Ada, seeing her hesitate before following the others. Truly I hadn't yet realized that the long-yearned-for opportunity had finally presented itself.

She hesitated, but then a strange mistrust prevailed in her. She clasped the violin still tighter to herself.

"No," she answered, "I don't have to go with them. I don't believe Anna has hurt herself very badly. She screams at any trifle."

She sat down with the violin, and it seemed to me that this gesture invited me to speak. In any case, how could I return home without having spoken? What would I have done afterwards, during that long night? I saw myself turning this way and that in my bed, or combing the streets or the taverns in search of distraction. No! I would not leave that house without having arrived at clarification and serenity.

I tried to be simple and brief. I had to be, anyway, as I was out of breath. I said to her: "I love you, Ada. Why don't you let me speak to your father?"

She looked at me, amazed and frightened. I feared she would start screaming like her baby sister in that other room. I knew that her tranquil gaze and her face, with its clean-cut lines, did not know love, but, so remote from love as she was now, I had never seen her. She began speaking, and she said something that must have been meant as a preface. But I wanted clarity: a yes or a no! Perhaps I was already offended by what could seem hesitation. To accelerate things and induce her to make up her mind, I opposed her right to gain time.

"You must have realized. You couldn't possibly have believed I was courting Augusta!"

I wanted to emphasize my words, but, in my haste, I emphasized the wrong ones and, as it turned out, poor Augusta's name was accompanied by a tone and a gesture of scorn.

Thus I rescued Ada from her embarrassment. She noticed nothing but the insult to Augusta. "What makes you think you're superior to Augusta? I don't think for a moment Augusta would agree to become your wife!"

Only then did she remember that she owed me an answer: "As for me . . . I'm amazed that you got such an idea into your head."

The harsh response was meant to avenge Augusta. In my great confusion I thought that the meaning of the sentence had only that purpose; if she had slapped me, I believe I would have paused to ponder the reason. Therefore I insisted once more: "Think about it, Ada. I'm not a bad man. I'm rich . . . I'm a bit odd, but it will be easy for me to improve."

"Think about it yourself, Zeno: Augusta is a fine girl and would really suit you. I can't speak for her, but I believe . . . "

It was very sweet to hear Ada call me by my given name for the first time. Wasn't this an invitation to speak even more clearly? Perhaps she was lost to me, or in any event she would not agree to marry me, but in the meantime she had to be saved from compromising herself further with Guido, about whom I should open her eyes. I was cautious and began by telling her that while I admired and respected Augusta, I absolutely did not want to marry her. I said this twice, to make myself clear: "I don't want to marry her." Thus I could hope to soothe Ada, who a moment before had believed I wanted to insult Augusta.

"A good, dear, lovable girl . . . Augusta. But she's not for me."

Then as I was about to rush matters, there was some noise in the hall; I could lose the floor at any moment.

"Ada! That man isn't right for you. He's a fool! Didn't you see how he suffered because of the table's answers? Did you see his cane? He plays the violin well, but there are even monkeys who can do that. Every word he says shows what a jackass he is . . . "

After listening to me with the expression of someone unable to grasp the sense of the words being spoken, she interrupted me. She sprang to her feet, still holding the bow and the violin, and hissed some offensive words in my face. I did my best to forget them, and I succeeded. I recall only that she began by asking me in a loud voice how I could speak in such a way of him and of her! My eyes were wide with surprise, because it seemed to me I had spoken only of him. I have forgotten the many scornful words she addressed to me, but not her beautiful, noble, and healthy face flushed with outrage, its lines made sharper as if chiseled by her indignation. This I never afterwards forgot, and when I think of my love and my youth, I see again the beautiful and noble and healthy face of Ada at the moment when she dismissed me definitively from her destiny.

All of them returned together, surrounding Signora Malfenti, who was carrying Anna in her arms, still crying. Nobody paid any attention to me or to Ada, and, without saying goodbye to anyone, I left the living room; in the hall I collected my hat. Strange! Nobody came to detain me there. I detained myself, on my own, remembering that I should not fail to observe the rules of good manners; thus, before going away I had to take my leave politely of one and all. The truth, I have no doubt, is that I was prevented from quitting that house by my conviction that, all too soon, a night was falling, far worse for me than the five nights that had preceded it. I, who had finally gained clarity, now felt another need: for peace, peace with everyone. If I were able to eliminate all bitterness from my relations with Ada and with all the others, it would be easier for me to sleep. Why did such bitterness have to exist? I couldn't be angry even with Guido, who, though he had no merit, surely was in no way to blame for being preferred by Ada!

She was the only one who had noticed me walk into the hall; when she saw me come back, she gave me an apprehensive look. Was she afraid of a scene? I wanted to reassure her at once. I passed her and murmured: "Forgive me if I offended you!"

She took my hand and, relieved, pressed it. It was a great comfort. For a moment I closed my eyes, to be alone with my soul and to see how much peace it had now gained.

As my fate would have it, while all the others were still concerned with the child, I found myself seated next to Alberta. I hadn't seen her, and I became aware of her presence only when she spoke to me, saying: "She didn't hurt herself. The only misfortune is with Papà. Whenever he sees her crying, he gives her a grand present."

I stopped analyzing myself, because I could see myself whole! To gain peace, I would have to behave in such a way that this room would no longer be forbidden me. I looked at Alberta. She resembled Ada! A bit smaller, and her body still bore some traces of childhood, not yet outgrown. She was quick to raise her voice, and her often excessive laughter contracted her little face and made it turn red. Strange! At that moment I recalled some advice of my father's: "Pick a young woman and it'll be easier for you to mold her as you wish." This memory was decisive. I looked at Alberta again. My mind was busy undressing her, and she appealed to me, sweet and tender as I supposed she was.

I said to her: "Listen, Alberta! I have an idea: Have you ever thought that you're at an age to take a husband?"

"I have no thought of marrying!" she said, smiling and looking at me meekly, without embarrassment or blushes. "I'm thinking of going on with my education. That's what Mamma wants, too."

"You could continue your studies after you're married."

I had an idea that seemed witty to me, and I said it at once: "I'm thinking of resuming my studies, too, after I'm married."

She laughed heartily, but I realized I was wasting my time; such foolishness was no use in winning a wife and gaining peace. I had to be serious. This was now easier because I was being treated quite differently from the way Ada had treated me.

I was truly serious. My future wife, in fact, had to know everything. In a choked voice I said to her: "A short while ago I made Ada the same proposal I've made to you. She refused, with scorn. You can imagine the state I'm in."

These words, accompanied by a sad expression, were nothing less than my final declaration of love for Ada. I was growing too serious, and with a smile I added: "But I believe that if you would agree to marry me, I would be most happy, and with you I would forget everybody and everything else."

She became very serious as she said: "You mustn't take offense, Zeno, because that would grieve me. I know you're a good sort and you know many things, without knowing it, whereas my professors know exactly what they know. I don't want to marry. Maybe I'll change my mind, but for the moment I have only one ambition: I'd like to become a writer. You see how much I trust you. I've never told anyone this, and I hope you won't give me away. For my part, I promise you I won't mention your proposal to anyone."

"Oh, you can tell everyone!" I interrupted her crossly. I felt threatened again with expulsion from that living room, and I hastily sought a remedy. There was only one way to lessen Alberta's pride in having been able to reject me, and I adopted it the moment I discovered what it was. I said to her: "Now I'll make the same proposal to Augusta, and I'll tell everyone that I married her because her two sisters refused me!"

I laughed with an excessive good humor that had come over me after my strange behavior. It wasn't into words that I put the wit of which I was so proud, it was into actions.

I looked around for Augusta. She had gone out into the hall, carrying a tray on which there was only a half-empty glass

134

with a sedative for Anna. I ran after her, calling her name, and she leaned back against the wall, waiting for me. I stood facing her and said: "Listen, Augusta. Would you like for the two of us to get married?"

The proposal was truly crude. I was to marry her, and she me, and I didn't ask what she thought, nor did I think that it might be up to me to offer some explanations. I was doing only what everyone wanted of me!

She raised her eyes, widened in surprise, so the skewed one was even more distinct than usual from the other. Her velvety smooth white face first blanched, then was immediately flushed. With her right hand she grasped the glass that was rattling on the tray. In a tiny voice she said to me: "You're joking, and that's not right."

I was afraid she would start crying, and I had the curious idea of consoling her by telling her of my sadness.

"I'm not joking," I said, serious and sad. "First I asked for the hand of Ada, and she rejected me angrily, then I asked Alberta to marry me, and with some fine words she also refused me. I don't bear either one a grudge. But I feel unhappy, yes, very unhappy."

Confronted by my sorrow, she regained her composure and began to look at me, touched, reflecting intensely. Her gaze resembled a caress, which gave me no pleasure.

"So I must know and remember that you don't love me?" she asked me.

What did this sybilline sentence mean? Was it the prelude to an acceptance? She wanted to remember! To remember for her whole life, which would be spent with me! I had the sensation of a man who, to commit suicide, has placed himself in a dangerous position and now has to make an immense effort to save his life. Wouldn't it be better if Augusta also rejected me and I was forced to return, safe and sound, to my study, where I hadn't felt too bad even on that day?

I said to her: "Yes! I love only Ada, and now I would marry you . . ."

I was about to tell her I couldn't resign myself to becoming a stranger to Ada, and therefore I would be content to become a brother-in-law. That would have been going too far, and Augusta might again have believed I wanted to make fun of her. So I said only: "I can't resign myself to being left alone."

She remained leaning against the wall, whose support perhaps she felt she needed; but she appeared calmer, and the tray was now held by a single hand. Was I saved? Did I have to abandon that living room, or could I stay, and would I have to marry? I said a few more words, only because I was impatiently awaiting hers, which were reluctant to come: "I'm a good sort, and I believe a person could easily live with me, even without any great love."

This was a sentence that in the long preceding days I had prepared for Ada, to induce her to say yes, even without feeling great love for me.

Augusta was a little short of breath and still remained silent. That silence could also mean refusal, the most delicate refusal imaginable: I was almost ready to rush off for my hat, still in time to put it on a rescued head.

But Augusta, her mind made up, with a dignified gesture I will never forget, stiffened her back and abandoned the support of the wall. In the narrow passage she moved still closer to me, who stood facing her. She said: "You, Zeno, need a woman who wants to live for you and help you. I want to be that woman."

She held out her plump hand, which I kissed, as if by instinct. Obviously it was impossible to do anything else. I must then confess that at that moment I was filled with a contentment that made my breast swell. I no longer had to resolve anything, because everything had been resolved. This was true clarity.

Thus it was that I became engaged. We were immediately, immensely fêted. My success resembled somewhat the huge success of Guido's violin, so great was the general applause. Giovanni kissed me and promptly started calling me *tu*. With an excessive display of affection, he said to me: "For a long time I have felt like a father to you, ever since I began giving you advice about your business."

My future mother-in-law also turned her cheek, which I grazed with the kiss I couldn't have eluded even if I had married Ada.

"You see? I had guessed everything," she said to me with incredible nonchalance, which went unpunished because I was unable and unwilling to protest.

She then embraced Augusta, and her immense fondness was revealed in a sob that escaped her, interrupting her display of joy. I couldn't elude Signora Malfenti, but I must say that her sob, at least for the duration of that evening, cast a pleasant and important light on my engagement.

Alberta, radiant, pressed my hand. "I mean to be a good sister to you."

And Ada said: "Bravo, Zeno!" Then, in a whisper: "Believe me: never did a man who thought he was acting hastily behave more wisely than you."

Guido gave me a great surprise. "Already this morning I realized you wanted one or the other of the Malfenti young ladies, but I couldn't figure out which."

They can't have been very intimate if Ada hadn't told him about my courting! Had I really acted hastily?

But a little later Ada also said to me: "I want you to love me as a sister. The rest must be forgotten; I will never say anything to Guido."

For the rest, it was wonderful to have provoked so much joy in a family. I couldn't enjoy it much myself, but only because I was very tired. I was also sleepy. That proved I had acted with great wisdom. I would have a good night.

At supper, Augusta and I witnessed silently the festivities in our honor. She felt it necessary to apologize for being unable to take part in the general conversation: "I can't say a thing. You must all remember that, half an hour ago, I had no idea of what was about to happen to me."

She always spoke the exact truth. She was between tears and laughter and she looked at me. I, too, wanted to caress her with my eyes; I don't know if I succeeded.

That same evening at that table, I suffered another wound. It was inflicted by Guido himself.

It seems that shortly before I arrived to participate in the séance, Guido had told the others how, that morning, I had declared I wasn't absentminded. They immediately gave him so many proofs of my falsehood that, in revenge (or perhaps to show he knew how to draw), he made two caricatures of me. In the first I was portrayed with my nose in the air while I leaned on an umbrella stuck in the ground. In the second the umbrella had broken and the handle had stabbed me in the back. The two caricatures achieved their purpose and provoked laughter through the simple device of making the individual meant to represent me – actually he bore no resemblance, and was distinguished only by great baldness – identical in both the first and second sketch; thus he could be considered so absentminded that he didn't change his expression even when he had been skewered by an umbrella.

They all laughed very much, indeed too much. I was deeply grieved by the highly successful attempt to ridicule me. And it was then that, for the first time, I was seized by my sharp pain. That evening it was my right forearm and hip that hurt. An intense burning pain, a numbness of the nerves as if they were threatening to snap. Dumbfounded, I put my right hand to my hip and with my left hand I gripped the affected forearm.

"What's wrong?" Augusta asked.

I replied that I felt a pain in my wrist, bruised by that fall in the café, which had been discussed earlier that evening.

I promptly made an energetic attempt to rid myself of that pain. I thought I would be cured of it if I avenged the offense to which I had been subjected. I asked for a piece of paper and a pencil, and I tried to draw a character being crushed by an overturned little table. Beside him I put a walking stick that he had dropped as a result of the catastrophe. Nobody recognized the stick, and therefore the insult didn't succeed as I would have liked. In order to clarify that individual's identity and explain how he happened to be in that position, I wrote beneath it: "Guido Speier turning the table." For that matter, all that could be seen of the wretch under the table was his legs, which might have resembled Guido's if I hadn't deliberately distorted them and if the demon of vengeance hadn't intervened to worsen my already childish drawing.

The persistent pain forced me to work in great haste. Certainly my poor organism had never been so pervaded by the desire to inflict a wound, and if I had had a sabre in my hand instead of that pencil I had no gift for using, perhaps the cure would have succeeded.

Guido laughed sincerely at my drawing, but then he mildly remarked: "I don't think the table did me any harm."

In fact, it hadn't, and it was this injustice that so pained me.

Ada took Guido's two drawings and said she wanted to keep them. I looked at her to convey my reproach, and she had to turn her gaze away from mine. I was entitled to reproach her because she exacerbated my pain.

I found a defense in Augusta. She asked me to write the date of our engagement on my drawing, for she, too, wanted to keep that scrawl. A hot wave of blood flooded my veins at this sign of affection, whose importance for me I realized for the first time. The pain, however, did not stop and I was forced to think that if that gesture of affection had come fom Ada, it would have caused such a rush of blood in my veins that all the flotsam accumulated in my nerves would have been swept away by it.

That pain was never thereafter to leave me. Now, in old age, I suffer less from it because, when it seizes me, I bear it indulgently: "Ah, here you are again, clear proof that I'm still young?" But in my youth it was another matter. I won't say the pain was great, though it sometimes impeded my free movement or kept me awake for whole nights. But it occupied a good part of my life. I wanted to be healed! Why should I have to bear all my life on my very body the stigma of defeat? Become the living, walking monument to Guido's victory? That pain had to be expelled from my body.

And so the treatments began. But, immediately afterwards, the angry origin of the disease was forgotten and it was now hard for me to retrace it. It couldn't have been otherwise: I had great faith in the doctors who treated me, and I believed them sincerely when they attributed that pain first to my metabolism and then to a circulatory defect, then to tuberculosis or to various infections, some of them shameful. I must also confess that all the cures afforded me some temporary relief, and thus each time the plausible new diagnosis seemed confirmed. Sooner or later it proved to be less exact, but not entirely mistaken, because with me nothing functions perfectly.

Only once were they really wrong: a kind of veterinarian in whose hands I had placed myself insisted for a long time on applying his blister papers to my sciatic nerve, but in the end he was outsmarted by my pain, which suddenly, during an examination, leaped from hip to neck, in any case, far from the sciatic nerve. The sawbones became angry and showed me the door and I went off – as I well remember – not in the least offended, but rather amazed that in its new position the pain hadn't changed at all. It remained angry and beyond reach as when it had tormented my hip. It's strange that all the parts of our body are able to ache in the same way.

The other diagnoses, absolutely exact, all persist in my body and fight among themselves for supremacy. There are days when I suffer from uric diathesis, and others when the diathesis is defeated, or rather healed, by an inflammation of the veins. I have whole drawers full of medicines, and they are the only drawers that I keep tidy. I love my medicines, and I know that when I abandon one of them, sooner or later I will return to it. In any event I don't believe I've wasted my time. Who knows how long ago and of what disease I would already have died if my pain hadn't simulated all my ailments in advance, persuading me to treat them before they overcame me?

But even though I can't explain its profound nature, I know when my pain took shape for the first time. Precisely because of that drawing so superior to mine. A straw that broke the camel's back! I'm sure I had never felt that pain before. I tried to explain its origin to a doctor, but he didn't understand me. Who knows? Perhaps psychoanalysis will throw some light on all the upheaval my organism underwent during those days and especially in the few hours following my engagement.

They weren't really so few, those hours!

Later, when the company broke up, Augusta said to me gaily: "Till tomorrow!"

I liked the invitation because it proved I had achieved my purpose and that nothing was over and everything would continue the next day. She looked into my eyes and found them filled with lively assent, consoling her. I went down those steps, which I no longer counted, asking myself: "I wonder – do I love her?"

This is a doubt that has accompanied me all through my life, and today I can believe that when love is accompanied by such doubt, it is true love.

But even when I had left that house behind, I was not allowed to go home to bed, to collect the fruit of that evening's activity in a long and refreshing sleep. It was hot. Guido felt the need of an ice, and he invited me to come with him to a café. He took my arm in a friendly gesture, and I, with equal friendliness, supported his. He was a very important person for me, and I would have been unable to refuse him anything. The great weariness that should have driven me to bed made me more accommodating than usual.

We went into the very place where poor Tullio had transmitted his disease to me, and we sat down at a secluded table. As we had walked along the street, my pain, which I didn't yet know was going to be such a faithful companion, had caused me great suffering, but for a few moments, after I was able to sit down, it seemed to abate.

Guido's company was downright terrible. He inquired with great curiosity about the story of my love for Augusta. Did he suspect I was deceiving him? I declared shamelessly that I had fallen in love with Augusta at once, on my first visit to the Malfenti house. My pain made me talkative, as if I wanted to shout it down. But I talked too much, and if Guido had paid more attention he would have realized I wasn't all that much in love with Augusta. I spoke of the most interesting feature of Augusta's body, namely that skewed eye that made one believe, mistakenly, that all the rest was similarly out of place. Then I tried to explain why I hadn't declared myself earlier. Perhaps Guido was surprised, having seen me arrive at that house only at the last minute and then become engaged.

I shouted: "The Malfenti young ladies are accustomed to great luxury, and I couldn't know if I was in a position to take on such a responsibility."

I was sorry that I had thus also included Ada, but there was nothing to be done now: it was so difficult to separate Augusta from Ada! I went on, lowering my voice the better to control myself: "So I had to make some calculations. I found that my money wasn't enough. Then I tried to figure out if there wasn't some way of expanding my business . . ."

I added that to make those calculations I had required a great deal of time, and so I had refrained from visiting the Malfentis for five days. Finally my tongue, given free rein, had arrived at a bit of sincerity. I was on the brink of tears and, pressing my hip, I murmured: "Five days is a long time!"

Guido said he was glad to discover I was such a prudent person.

I remarked curtly: "A prudent person is no more likable than a scatterbrain!"

Guido laughed. "It's odd that a prudent man should feel called upon to defend scatterbrains!"

Then, without any transition, he informed me briefly that he was about to ask for Ada's hand. Had he dragged me to the café to make this confession or, annoyed at having had to sit and listen to me go on about myself for so long, was he getting his revenge?

I am almost sure I managed to display the greatest surprise and the greatest pleasure. But a moment later I found a way of stinging him severely: "Now I understand why Ada liked that Bach piece so much, with all its distortions! It was well played, but Higher Authorities forbid profaning certain works."

It was a nasty blow, and Guido flushed with pain. His answer was subdued because he was now without his enthusiastic little audience. "For heaven's sake!" he began, to gain time. "Every now and then, when you play, you succumb to a whim. In that room very few were familiar with Bach, and I introduced him in a somewhat modernized form."

He seemed satisfied with his invention, but I was equally satisfied because it seemed to me an apology and a capitulation. This was enough to appease me, and in any case, nothing on earth could have made me quarrel with Ada's future husband. I declared that I had rarely heard an amateur play so well.

This didn't content him: he remarked that he could be considered an amateur only because he hadn't decided to appear as a professional.

Was that all he wanted? I agreed with him. It was obvious he couldn't be considered an amateur.

So we were friends again.

Then, point-blank, he started speaking ill of women. I was speechless! Now that I am better acquainted with him, I know he bursts into abundant discourse on any subject if he thinks he can be sure of pleasing his interlocutor. A little earlier, I had mentioned the luxury of the Malfenti young ladies, and he began there, only to continue talking about all womankind's other bad qualities. My weariness prevented me from interrupting him, and I confined myself to repeated gestures of assent that were themselves all too tiring for me. Otherwise, to be sure, I would have protested. I knew that I had every right to speak ill of women, who for me were represented by Ada, Augusta, and my future mother-in-law; but he could have no cause to nourish any resentment of the sex represented for him only by Ada, who loved him.

He was quite learned, and despite my fatigue I sat and heard him out with admiration. Long afterwards I discovered that he had borrowed the brilliant theories of the young suicide Weininger.* At that moment I suffered the burden of the Bach all over again. I even suspected he had some therapeutic aim. If not, then why would he want to convince me that a woman cannot possess genius or goodness? It seemed to me this treatment failed because it was administered by Guido. But I retained those theories and I amplified them by reading Weininger. They never heal you, but they come in handy when you are chasing women.

Having finished his ice, Guido felt he needed a breath of fresh air and he persuaded me to take a stroll with him towards the outskirts of the city.

I remember that for some days in the city we had been yearning for a bit of rain, hoping it would bring some relief from the premature heat. I hadn't even noticed the heat. That evening the sky had begun to be covered with fine, white clouds, the kind that lead simple people to hope for abundant rain, but a huge moon was advancing in the sky, intensely blue

* Otto Weininger (1880–1903), Austrian writer and philosopher, author of a book entitled *Sex and Character*.

where it was still clear, one of those moons with swollen cheeks that the same simple people also believe capable of devouring clouds. It was obvious, in fact, that where the moon passed, it dispelled and cleared.

I wanted to interrupt Guido's chatter, which kept me nodding constantly, a torture; and I described to him the moon's kiss, discovered by the poet Zamboni. How sweet that kiss was, in the heart of our nights, compared with the injustice that Guido was committing, at my side! As I spoke, stirring from the sluggishness I had fallen into with all this assenting, my pain seemed to diminish. It was the reward for my rebellion and I persisted in it.

Guido was obliged to leave women alone for a moment and look up. But not for long! Having discovered, thanks to my indications, the pale image of the woman in the moon, he returned to his subject with a joke, at which he – but only he – laughed loudly in the deserted street: "She sees plenty of things, that woman does! Too bad that, being a woman, she can't remember them."

It was part of his (or Weininger's) theory that no woman can be a genius because women are unable to remember.

We reached the foot of the Via Belvedere. Guido said a little climb would do us good. Once again I fell in with his wishes. Up there, in one of those acts best suited to very young boys, he stretched out on the low wall that separated the street from the one below. He thought he was being brave, risking a fall of about ten meters. At first I felt the usual horror, seeing him exposed to such danger, but then I recalled the method I had invented that evening, in a burst of improvisation, to free myself from such suffering, and I began to wish fervently that he would fall.

In that position he continued preaching against women. Now he said that, like children, they required toys, but costly ones. I remembered that Ada said she liked jewels very much. Was he actually talking about her? I had then a frightful idea!

Why didn't I cause Guido to fall those ten meters? Wouldn't it have been fair to exterminate the man who was robbing me of Ada without loving her? At that moment I felt that when I had killed him, I could rush to Ada and receive my recompense at once. In the strange, moon-filled night, it seemed to me she must have heard how Guido was defaming her.

I have to confess that, honestly, at that moment I was ready to kill Guido! I was standing beside him, as he lay full length on the low wall, and I coldly studied in what way I should grip him, to be sure I was doing the thing properly. Then I discovered that I didn't even have to grip him. He was lying with his arms folded beneath his head: a good shove would have sufficed to throw him irreparably off balance.

I had another idea, so important, I thought, that I could compare it to the huge moon that proceeded through the sky, clearing it: I had agreed to the betrothal with Augusta to make sure I could sleep soundly that night. How could I sleep if I were to kill Guido? This idea saved me and him. I chose to abandon at once my position standing over Guido, which was luring me toward that act. I bent my knees, sinking down until my head almost touched the ground.

"Oh, the pain! The pain!" I cried.

Frightened, Guido sprang to his feet, asking for an explanation. I went on groaning, more softly, without answering. I knew why I was groaning: because I had wanted to kill, and perhaps also because I had been incapable of doing so. The pain and the groan excused everything. It seemed to me I was shouting that I hadn't wanted to kill, and it also seemed I was shouting that it wasn't my fault if I hadn't been able to do it. It was all the fault of my illness and my pain. But I remember well how, at that very moment, my pain completely vanished and my groan remained nothing but histrionics, to which I tried in vain to give some content, recalling the pain and reconstructing it so as to feel it and suffer from it. But the effort was futile because it returned only when it chose.

As usual, Guido proceeded by hypothesis, and fondly he drew me to my feet. Then, with every consideration, still supporting me, he helped me down the little hill. When we reached the bottom, I declared I felt somewhat better and I believed that with his support I could move a bit faster. So it was possible to go to bed at last! Thus I was granted my first great satisfaction that day. Guido was working for me, almost carrying me. Finally it was I who imposed my will on him.

We found a pharmacy still open, and he thought to send me to bed accompanied by a sedative. He fabricated a whole theory about real pain and the exaggerated sense of it: a pain that multiplied through the exacerbation that it had itself produced. With that little bottle my collection of medicines began, and it was only right that Guido had been the one to choose it.

To provide a firmer basis for his theory, he postulated that I had suffered my pain for many days. I was sorry not to be able to content him. I declared that at the Malfentis', that evening, I had felt no pain. At the moment when I arrived at the fulfillment of my cherished dream, obviously I couldn't have been suffering.

And to be sincere I wanted actually to be what I claimed I was, and I said several times to myself: "I love Augusta, I do not love Ada. I love Augusta, and this evening I achieved the fulfillment of my cherished dream."

So we advanced in lunar night. I suppose that my weight tired Guido, because he finally fell silent. He offered, however, to see me all the way to my bed. I declined, and when I was allowed to close my door behind me, I heaved a sigh of relief. No doubt Guido heaved the same sigh.

I took the steps of my house four at a time, and ten minutes later I was in bed. I fell asleep quickly, and in the brief period preceding sleep, I remembered neither Ada nor Augusta, but only Guido, so sweet and good and patient. True, I had not forgotten that a little earlier I had wanted to kill him, but that had no importance because things that no one knows, things that leave no trace, do not exist.

The following day I went, a little hesitant, to my bride's house. I was not sure that the commitments made the night before had the value I thought I must attribute to them. I discovered that they did, in everyone's mind. Augusta also considered herself engaged, even more confidently than I.

It was a toilsome betrothal. I have the feeling of having broken it off several times and then reconstructed it with great effort, and I am surprised that nobody else was aware of this. Never did I have the certitude that I was actually heading for marriage, but nevertheless I apparently behaved like a sufficiently loving fiancé. In fact, I kissed and clasped to my bosom the sister of Ada whenever I had the opportunity. Augusta submitted to my aggressions as she believed a bride should, and I acted relatively well, simply because Signora Malfenti never left us alone for more than a few brief moments. My bride was much less ugly than I had thought, and I discovered her most beautiful feature only when I began kissing her: it was her blush! Where I kissed her a flame appeared in my honor, and I kissed more with the curiosity of the experimental scientist than with the fervor of the lover.

But desire was not wanting, and it made that burdensome time a bit easier. Thank God, Augusta and her mother prevented me from burning that flame in one single blaze as I often would have wished. How would we have continued to live afterwards? This way at least my desire continued to give me, on the front steps of that house, the same eagerness I had felt when I used to climb them to win Ada. The odd steps promised me that on this day I would be able to display to Augusta the nature of the betrothal she had wanted. I dreamed of a violent action that would give me back all the feeling of my freedom. I wanted nothing else, and it is quite strange that when Augusta learned what I wanted, she interpreted it as a sign of love-fever.

In my memory that period divides into two phases. In the first, Signora Malfenti often had Alberta keep an eye on us, or else she sent little Anna, with a schoolmistress, into the living room where we sat. Ada was never then associated with us in any way, and I told myself I should be pleased at this – whereas, on the contrary, I remember vaguely having once thought it would be a great source of satisfaction for me if I could kiss Augusta in the presence of Ada. Heaven knows what violence I would have subjected my fiancée to.

The second phase began when Guido became officially engaged to Ada, and Signora Malfenti, practical woman that she was, united the two couples in the same living room so that they could keep a reciprocal eye on each other.

In the first phase, I know Augusta declared herself perfectly satisfied with me. When I didn't assail her, I became extra-ordinarily loquacious. Loquacity was a necessity of mine. I created the occasion for it by persisting in the thought that since I was to marry Augusta, I should also take her education in hand. I lectured her about being sweet, affectionate, and above all faithful. I don't precisely recall the form I gave these sermons of mine, some of which she has repeated to me, as she has never forgotten them. She would listen to me, intent and docile. Once, in the enthusiasm of my teaching, I declared that if she were to discover an infidelity on my part, she would then be entitled to repay me in the same coin. Outraged, she protested that not even with my permission would she ever be capable of betraying me, and that after any infidelity of mine, she would have only the freedom to weep.

I believe that these sermons, which I preached for no purpose except to be saying something, had a beneficent influence on my marriage. The sincere thing about them was their effect on Augusta's spirit. Her fidelity was never put to the test because she never knew anything of my infidelities, but her affection and her sweetness remained unchanged over the long years we spent together, just as I had induced her to promise me.

When Guido made his proposal, the second phase of my betrothal began, with a resolution I could express in these terms: "Now! I am quite cured of my love for Ada!" Until then I had believed that Augusta's blushing had sufficed to heal me, but obviously no healing is complete! The recollection of those blushes led me to believe that they would now occur also between Guido and Ada. This, far more than any earlier blushing, would dispel any desire of mine.

The desire to violate Augusta belongs to the first phase. In the second I was much less aroused. Signora Malfenti had surely not been mistaken in organizing our surveillance at such slight cost to herself.

I remember that once, in jest, I started kissing Augusta. Instead of joking with me, Guido, in return, began kissing Ada. This seemed to me indelicate on his part, because he was not kissing chastely as I had done, out of respect for the other pair: he was kissing Ada on the mouth, actually sucking her lips. I am sure that, by then, I had already become fairly accustomed to regarding Ada as a sister, but I was not prepared to see her used so. I suspect a real brother would hardly like to see his sister manipulated like that.

Hence, in Guido's presence, I never kissed Augusta again. Guido, on the contrary, in my presence, tried once more to draw Ada to him, but it was she who defended herself, and he didn't repeat the attempt.

Very hazily I recall the many, many evenings we spent together. The scene was repeated to infinity, until it became imprinted on my mind: the four of us seated around the elegant little Venetian table, on which a large kerosene lamp was burning, covered by a green cloth shade that cast everything in shadow, except the embroidery work on which the two girls were engaged, Ada working on a silk handkerchief held loosely in her hand, Augusta at a little circular frame. I can see Guido perorating, and often I must have been the only one to encourage him. I remember also Ada's head, the gently curled black hair emphasized by the strange effect of the greenish yellow light.

We argued about that light, and about the true color of that hair. Guido, who could also paint, explained to us how a color should be analyzed. This lesson of his was something else I never afterwards forgot, and even today, when I want to understand the color of a landscape more clearly, I half-close my eyes until many lines disappear and only the lights can be seen, darkening also into the one true color. When I devote myself to such an analysis, however, on my retina, immediately after the real images, in a kind of personal physical reaction, the yellow-green glow reappears, and the dark hair on which for the first time I trained my eye.

I cannot forget one evening, distinguished from all the other evenings by an expression of jealousy from Augusta and immediately thereafter by a deplorable indiscretion on my part. Playing a joke on us, Guido and Ada had gone to sit far off, at the other end of the living room, by the Louis XIV table. So I quickly developed an ache in my neck, which I had to twist in order to talk with them. Augusta said to me: "Leave them alone! Over there they're really making love."

And I, with great sluggishness of mind, whispered to her that she shouldn't believe this, for Guido didn't like women. In this way, it seemed to me, I was apologizing for having interfered in the talk of the lovers. But, instead, it was a wicked indiscretion, reporting to Augusta the talk about women that Guido indulged in when he was with me, but never in the presence of any other member of our brides' family. The recollection of my words poisoned my mind for several days, while I may say that the recollection of having wanted to kill Guido hadn't troubled me for so much as an hour. But killing, even treacherously, is more virile than harming a friend by betraying a confidence.

By now Augusta was wrong to be jealous of Ada. It wasn't to see Ada that I twisted my neck in that fashion. Guido, with his chatter, helped me pass those long hours. I was already fond of him, and I spent a part of my days with him. I was bound to him also by the gratitude I felt for his high opinion of me, which he communicated to others. Even Ada listened to me with attention when I spoke.

Every evening, with some impatience, I awaited the sound of the gong that summoned us to supper, and what I remember chiefly of those suppers is my perennial indigestion. I overate in my necessity to keep active. At supper I lavished affectionate words on Augusta, insofar as my full mouth would allow, and her parents must have had the nasty impression that my great affection was diminished by my bestial voracity. They were surprised, on my return from our wedding journey, that I hadn't brought back the same appetite. It disappeared when I was no longer required to display a passion I didn't feel. The bride's parents must not find you cold at the moment when you are preparing to go to bed with the bride! Augusta particularly remembers the fond words I murmured to her at that table. Between mouthfuls I must have invented some magnificent ones, and I am amazed when I am reminded of them, because they do not seem mine.

Even my father-in-law, the sly Giovanni, let himself be deceived, and as long as he lived, whenever he wanted to furnish an example of great amorous passion, he would cite mine for his daughter. For Augusta, that is. He smiled blissfully at it, good father that he was, but it increased his contempt for me because, in his view, a man who places his entire destiny in a woman's hands is not a real man at all, especially if he remains unaware that, besides his own, there are also some other women in this world. This demonstrates how I was sometimes unfairly misjudged.

My mother-in-law, on the other hand, didn't believe in my love, not even when Augusta herself settled into it, with total trust.

For long years the Signora scrutinized me with a distrusting eye, dubious about the fate of her favorite daughter. Also for this reason, I am convinced she guided me in the days leading up to my betrothal. It was also impossible to deceive her, as she must have known my mind better than I did myself.

Finally came the day of my wedding, and on that very day I felt a last hesitation. I was to be at the bride's house at eight in the morning, but at seven-forty-five I was still in bed, smoking furiously and looking at my window, where, taunting me, the early morning sun shone brightly. I was pondering the idea of abandoning Augusta! The absurdity of my marriage was becoming obvious now that remaining close to Ada no longer mattered to me. Nothing of great moment would happen if I failed to turn up at the appointed hour! And besides: Augusta had been a lovable fiancée, but there was no way of knowing how she would behave after the wedding. What if she were immediately to call me a fool because I had let myself be snared like that?

Fortunately Guido came, and instead of resisting, I apologized for my delay, declaring that I thought a different hour had been set for the wedding. Rather than reproach me, Guido started telling me about himself and the many times that he had failed to keep engagements. Even when it came to absentmindedness he wanted to be superior to me, and I had to stop listening to him in order to get out of the house. So it was that I went to my wedding at a run.

I arrived very late, all the same. Nobody scolded me, and all except the bride were satisfied with some explanations that Guido offered in my place. Augusta was so pale that even her lips were livid. Though I couldn't say I loved her, certainly I would never want to cause her any pain. I tried to make up for my enormity and I was fool enough to blame my tardiness on three different causes. That was too many, and they revealed so clearly what I had been pondering in my bed while looking at the winter sun that we had to delay our leaving for the church to allow Augusta time to regain her composure.

At the altar I said yes absently, because in my real sympathy for Augusta, I was confecting a fourth explanation for my delay, and it seemed to me the best of all.

But then, as we came out of the church, I realized that Augusta had regained all her color. I was a bit irked, because that yes of mine certainly shouldn't have sufficed to reassure her of my love. And I was preparing to treat her very roughly if she were to recover enough to call me a fool because I had allowed myself to be ensnared like that. But, on the contrary, at her home, she took advantage of a moment when they had left us alone, to say to me, in tears: "I will never forget that, even without loving me, you married me."

I didn't protest because the matter was so obvious that protest was impossible. But, filled with compassion, I embraced her.

None of this was ever discussed again between Augusta and me because a marriage is far simpler than an engagement. Once married, you don't talk anymore about love, and when you feel the need to speak of it, animal instincts quickly intervene and restore silence. Now, these animal instincts may become so human that they also become complex and artificial, and it can happen that, bending over a woman's head of hair, you also make the effort to find in it a glow that is not present. You close your eyes and the woman becomes another, only to become herself again when you leave her. She is all gratitude, still greater if the effort has been successful. This is why, if I were to be born again (Mother Nature is capable of anything!), I would agree to marry Augusta; but never to be engaged to her.

At the station Ada held up her cheek for my fraternal kiss. I saw her only then, dazed as I was by all the people who had come to say good-bye, and I thought at once: You're the very one who got me into this! I held my lips to her velvety cheek, while taking care not even to graze it. This was my first satisfaction that day, because for an instant I felt the advantage I was deriving from my marriage: I had avenged myself, refusing to exploit the only opportunity offered me to kiss Ada! Then, as the train was speeding along, seated next to Augusta, I suspected I had done the wrong thing. I feared that my friendship with Guido had been jeopardized. But I suffered even more when I thought that Ada perhaps hadn't even noticed that I had not kissed the cheek she offered me.

She had noticed, but I learned this only when, in her turn, many months later, she set off with Guido from that same station. She kissed everyone. But to me she held out her hand, with great cordiality. I clasped it coldly. Her vengeance actually arrived late, because circumstances had completely changed. Since my return from my wedding journey, our relations had been those of brother and sister, and there could be no explanation for her having denied me the kiss.

IN MY LIFE I believed at various times that I was on the path to health and happiness. But never was this belief stronger than during the period of my wedding journey, and for a few weeks after our return home. It began with a discovery that stunned me: I loved Augusta and she loved me. At first, still dubious, I would enjoy one day and expect the next to be something quite different. But the next day followed and resembled the previous one, radiant, all filled with Augusta's tenderness and also — this was the surprise — my own. Every morning I rediscovered in her the same touching affection and in myself the same gratitude that, if it was not love, still bore a close resemblance to it. Who could have foreseen this, when I was limping from Ada to Alberta, to arrive at Augusta? I discovered I had not been a blind fool manipulated by others, but a very clever man. And, seeing my amazement, Augusta said to me: "Why are you so surprised? Didn't you know this is how marriage is? Even I knew it, and I'm so much more ignorant than you!"

I'm not sure whether it came before or after my affection, but in my spirit a hope was formed, the great hope finally to come to resemble Augusta, who was the personification of health. During our engagement I hadn't even glimpsed that health, because I was totally absorbed in studying myself first and, after myself, Ada and Guido. The glow of the oil lamp in that drawing room had never reached Augusta's thinnish hair.

Her blush was nothing! When it vanished as simply as the dawn colors vanish in the direct light of the sun, Augusta confidently followed the same path that all her sisters on this earth had followed, those sisters who can find everything in law and in order, or who otherwise renounce everything. Even though I knew her security was precarious, as it was based on me, I loved, I adored that security. Faced with it, I had to act at least with the modesty I assumed when faced with spiritualism. The latter could exist, and so faith in life could also exist.

Still it amazed me; her every word, her every action made it clear that, deep in her heart, she believed in eternal life. Not that she called it that: indeed, she was surprised when, on one occasion, I, who was repelled by errors until I began to love hers, felt obliged to remind her of life's brevity. What?! She knew everyone had to die, but all the same, now that we were married, we would remain together, together, together. She was thus unaware that when two are joined in this world, the union lasts for a period so very, very short that we cannot comprehend how we arrived at intimacy after an infinite time when we hadn't known each other, and we were now prepared never to see each other again for an equally infinite time. I understood finally what perfect human health was when I realized that for her the present was a tangible truth within which one could curl up and be warm. I sought admission and I tried to remain there, resolved not to make fun of myself and her, because this attack could only be my old sickness and I should at least take care not to infect anyone entrusted to my charge. Also for this reason, in my effort to protect her, for a while I was capable of acting like a healthy man.

She knew all the things that could drive me to despair, but in her hands these things changed their nature. Just because the earth rotates, you don't have to get seasick! Quite the contrary! The earth turned, but all other things stayed in their proper place. And these motionless things had enormous importance: the wedding ring, all the jewels and dresses, the green, the black, the dress for the afternoon stroll, which had to go straight into the closet on her return home, and the evening dress that was never under any circumstances to be worn during the day, or when I was unwilling to don my tailcoat. And the meal hours were strictly observed, as were the hours intended for sleeping. They existed, those hours, and were always in their place.

On Sunday she went to Mass, and sometimes I accompanied her to see how she could bear the representation of suffering and death. For her it wasn't there; and that visit filled her with peace for the entire week. She went there also on certain feast days, which she knew by heart. And that was all — whereas I, had I been religious, would have guaranteed my eternal bliss by spending the whole day in church.

There was a world of authorities also here below that reassured her. To begin with, the Austrian or Italian authority that guaranteed our safety in the streets and in our houses, and I always did my best to share that respect of hers. Then came doctors, those who had pursued their studies in order to save us when — God forbid — we came down with some illness. I employed that authority every day; she, on the contrary, never. But for this reason I knew what my ghastly fate would be when mortal illness struck me, whereas she believed that even then, firmly sustained up on high and here below, there would be salvation.

I am analyzing her health, but I fail, because I realize that in analyzing it I convert it into sickness. And in writing about that health, I begin to suspect it perhaps needed some treatment or instruction in order to heal. But when I was living at her side for so many years, I never harbored that suspicion for a moment.

Ah! the importance attributed to me in her little world! On every question I had to express my wishes, in the choice of food or dress, company or reading matter. I was forced into great activity, which didn't annoy me. I was collaborating in the construction of a patriarchal family, and I myself was becoming the patriarch I had once hated, but who now appeared to me as the emblem of health. It's one thing to be a patriarch and another to have to revere someone who claims that distinction. I wanted health for myself even at the price of sloughing off sickness onto the non-patriarchs, and especially during our journey, sometimes I gladly struck the pose of an equestrian statue.

But already during that journey it was not always easy for me to carry off the imitation I had prescribed for myself. Augusta wanted to see everything, as if this were an educational expedition. It was by no means enough just to go to the Pitti Palace: it was necessary to pass through all those numberless galleries, stopping at least for a moment or two at each work of art. I refused to leave the first room and I saw nothing further, assuming only the burden of finding excuses for my laziness. I spent half a day before the portraits of the founders of the house of Medici, and I discovered that they resembled Carnegie and Vanderbilt. Wonderful! So we belonged to the same race! Augusta didn't share my amazement. She knew that those two were Yankees, but she didn't yet know clearly who I was.

Here her health failed to triumph, and she had to renounce museums. I told her that once, at the Louvre, I became so confused in the midst of all those works of art that I was about to smash the Venus to bits.

With resignation, Augusta said: "Thank goodness museums are something you do on your honeymoon, then never again!"

In fact, in real life we lack the monotony of museums. Days go by, suitable for framing; they are rich in sounds that daze you, and besides their lines and colors, they are also filled with real light, the kind that burns and therefore isn't boring.

Health impels us to activity, to take on a world of nuisances. When the museums were closed, shopping began. She, who had never lived there, knew our villa better than I did, and she remembered that one room needed a mirror, another a rug, and in a third there was a place for a little statue. She bought furniture for a whole drawing room, and from every city we visited, at least one shipment was arranged. It seemed to me that it would have been more convenient and less annoying to make all those purchases in Trieste. Now we had to think of transport, insurance, customs clearance.

"But don't you know that all goods have to travel? Aren't you a merchant?" She laughed.

She was almost right, but I rebutted: "Goods are shipped in order to be sold, to make a profit. Otherwise they're left undisturbed, and they disturb nobody."

But her enterprise was one of the things I loved most about her. It was delightful, that enterprise, so naïve! Naïve because she had to be ignorant of the history of the world to be able to believe that she had made a clever transaction simply by buying an object: it's when you sell the object that you judge the wisdom of the purchase.

I thought I was well into my convalescence. My wounds had become less infected. Starting at that time, my unvaried attitude was one of happiness. It was as if, in those unforgettable days, I had made a vow to Augusta, and it was the only promise I never broke except for brief moments, times when life laughed louder than I. Our relationship was and remains a smiling one because I smiled always at her, believing her ignorant, and she at me, to whom she attributed much learning and many errors that she – so she flattered herself – would correct. I remained apparently happy even when my sickness overwhelmed me again. Happy as if my pain were no more than a kind of tickling.

In our long progress through Italy, despite my new-found health, I was not immune to many sufferings. We had set out with no letters of introduction, and very often it seemed to me that many of the strangers among whom we moved were my enemies. It was a ridiculous fear, but I was unable to master it. I could have been attacked, insulted, and, especially, slandered; and who would have protected me?

This fear reached a real crisis, which fortunately no one, not even Augusta, noticed. I was accustomed to buying almost all the newspapers that were offered to me along the street. One day, having stopped at a news vendor's kiosk, I felt the suspicion that he hated me and might easily have me arrested as a thief, for I had acquired only one paper from him, while under my arm I was holding many others, bought elsewhere and as yet unfolded. I fled, followed by Augusta, to whom I gave no reason for my running off.

I made friends with a coachman and with a guide; in their company at least I was assured of not being accused of absurd thefts.

Between me and the cabbie there were some obvious points of contact. He was very fond of the Roman Castelli wines, and he told me that from time to time his feet swelled up. He would go to the hospital, and then, cured, he would be discharged with many admonitions to give up wine. He would make an oath that he called ironclad because, along with it, he made a knot, which he tied to his metal watch chain. But when I knew him, the chain was hanging, without any knots, over his vest. I invited him to come and stay with me in Trieste. I described the taste of our wine, so different from his, to guarantee the success of this drastic cure. He wouldn't hear of it, and refused with an expression already filled with homesickness.

I became friends with the guide because he seemed superior to his fellows. It's easy enough to know more history than I do, but Augusta also, with her precision and her Baedeker, verified the accuracy of many of his observations. Besides, he was young and strode confidently along the allées sown with statues.

When I lost those two friends, I left Rome. The cabbie, having received a great deal of money from me, proved how wine sometimes also affected his brain, and he caused us to crash against a very solid ancient Roman construction. Later, the guide took it into his head one day to declare that the ancient Romans knew all about electricity and employed it extensively. He even recited some Latin verses to bear out what he said.

But then I was stricken by a minor ailment from which I was never to recover. A trifle, really: the fear of aging and, above all, the fear of dying. I believe it was generated by a special form of jealousy. Aging frightened me only because it brought me closer to death. As long as I was alive, Augusta would surely not be unfaithful to me; but I imagined that as soon as I was dead and buried, after making sure my grave would be properly tended and the necessary Masses said, she would promptly start looking for my successor, whom she would then surround with the same healthy and regulated world that now made me blissful. Her lovely health couldn't die just because I had died. My faith in that health was so great that I felt it could never perish, unless it was crushed beneath an entire speeding train.

I remember one evening in Venice as we were in a gondola moving along one of those canals whose profound silence is occasionally interrupted by the light and the noise of a street suddenly opening onto them. As always, Augusta was looking at things and objectively recording them: a cool, green garden rising from a filthy foundation revealed by the retreating water; the murky reflection of a spire; a long, dark alley ending at a stream of light and people. I, on the contrary, in the darkness, totally disheartened, was feeling an awareness of myself. I spoke to her of how time was passing and soon she would repeat that wedding journey with another man. I was so convinced of this that I seemed to be telling her a story that had already happened. And I felt it was unwarranted for her to start crying, to deny the truth of that story. Perhaps she had misunderstood me, and thought I was charging her with the intention of killing me. Quite the contrary! To make myself clearer, I described to her a possible manner of my dying: my legs, in which the circulation was surely already defective, would become gangrenous, and the gangrene, spreading rapidly, would arrive at some organ indispensable to my keeping my eyes open. Then I would close them, and it would be good-bye, Patriarch! A new one would have to be produced.

She went on sobbing, and to me those tears of hers, in the enormous sadness of that canal, seemed very important. Were they perhaps provoked by her despair at my precise view of that ghastly health of hers? Later I learned that, on the contrary, she hadn't the slightest idea of what health was. Health doesn't analyze itself, nor does it look at itself in the mirror. Only we sick people know something about ourselves.

It was then that she told me how she had loved me before she ever met me. She had loved me from the moment she heard my name, uttered by her father in this form: Zeno Cosini, an ingenuous fellow who widened his eyes when he heard any kind of commercial stratagem mentioned, and hastened to make a note of it in an order book, which he would then misplace. And if I hadn't noticed her confusion at our first meeting, then I must have been confused myself.

I remembered that on first seeing Augusta, I was distracted by her ugliness, since in that house with the four girls sharing the initial A, I had expected to find four great beauties. Now I learned she had loved me for a long time, but what did that prove? I didn't give her the satisfaction of changing my mind. When I was dead, she would find another.

When her tears abated, she leaned closer to me and, suddenly laughing, asked: "Where would I find your successor? Can't you see how ugly I am?"

In fact, in all likelihood I would be allowed some time to rot in peace.

But fear of aging never abandoned me thereafter, I lived always with the fear of passing my wife on to another man. The fear was not mitigated when I was unfaithful to her, nor was it increased by the thought of losing my mistress in the same way. That was an entirely different thing, and one had nothing to do with the other. When the fear of dying seized me, I would turn to Augusta for comfort, like children who hold out their little scratched hand for their mother to kiss. She found always new words to comfort me. On our honeymoon she gave me another thirty years of youth, and today she does the same. I, on the contrary, knew that the joyful weeks of our wedding trip had already brought me substantially closer to the horrible grimaces of the deathbed. Augusta could say whatever she liked, the calculation was still simple: every week I was one week nearer.

When I realized that I was afflicted too often by the same pain, I avoided tiring her by saying the same things over and over, and to inform her of my need for comfort, I had only to murmur: "Poor Cosini!" She knew then exactly what was upsetting me, and she hastened to envelop me in her great fondness. In this way I was able to receive her comfort also when I suffered quite different pain. One day, sick with the pain of having betrayed her, I murmured inadvertently: "Poor Cosini!" I derived great benefit from it because even then her comfort was precious to me.

On returning from the honeymoon, I was surprised because I had never lived in such a warm and comfortable home. Augusta brought into it all the conveniences she had had in her own home, but also many others she invented herself. The bathroom, which since time immemorial had always been at the end of a long corridor, half a kilometer from my bedroom, was now next to our room, and it was supplied with a greater number of faucets. Then a little area near the pantry was converted into a coffee room, furnished with padded carpets and great leather armchairs. We spent an hour or so there every day after lunch. Against my wish, it contained everything necessary for smoking. My little study, too, though I did everything to defend it, underwent alterations. I was afraid the changes would make it hateful to me, but, on the contrary,

I quickly realized that only now had it become possible to live in. She arranged its lighting so that I could read while seated at my desk or sprawled in a chair or stretched out on the sofa. She even provided a music stand for the violin, with its own little light that illuminated the music without hurting my eyes. There too, and also against my wishes, I was accompanied by all the equipment required for a peaceful smoke.

So there was much construction at home, and there was a certain amount of disorder that affected our tranquillity. To her, working toward eternity, this brief inconvenience couldn't matter, but for me it was quite different. I put up stiff opposition when she conceived the desire to create a little laundry in our garden, which would involve the actual building of a shed. Augusta insisted that having a laundry at home guaranteed the health of the *bébés*. But at present there were no *bébés* and I saw no need to be disturbed by them before their arrival. But she brought to my old house an instinct that came from the open air, and, in love, she resembled the swallow, who immediately thinks of the nest.

But I also made love, and brought flowers and jewels to the house. My life was entirely changed by my marriage. After a weak attempt at resistance, I gave up the idea of arranging my time as I pleased, and I adhered to the strictest schedule. In this respect my education brought excellent results. One day, shortly after our honeymoon, I innocently allowed myself to be detained from going home to lunch, and after eating something in a café, I remained out until evening. Coming home well after dark, I found that Augusta had had no lunch and was destroyed by hunger. She uttered no reproach, but she could not be convinced that she had done the wrong thing. Sweetly but firmly, she declared that unless she had advance notice, she would await me for lunch, even until dinnertime. This was no joking matter! On another occasion I let a friend persuade me to stay out until two in the morning. I found Augusta up, waiting for me, her teeth chattering from the cold, as she had neglected to tend the stove. She was slightly indisposed, afterwards making the lesson imparted to me unforgettable.

One day I decided to give her another great present: I would work! It was something she desired, and I myself thought that work would be beneficial to my health. Obviously those who have less time for sickness are less sick. I went to work, and if I didn't persist at it, that wasn't my fault. I went with the best intentions and with true humility. I didn't insist on sharing in the management of the business, asking instead just to keep the ledger. Facing the thick volume in which all the clerical work was laid out with the regularity of streets and houses, I was filled with respect, and I began to write, my hand trembling.

Olivi's son, an elegant, bespectacled young man, erudite in all the commercial sciences, took over my instruction, and I honestly can't complain about him. He annoyed me a little with his economic science and his law of supply and demand, which seemed to me more self-evident than he would admit. But he showed a certain respect for me as the owner, and I was all the more grateful because he couldn't possibly have learned that from his father. Respect for ownership must have been part of his economic science. He never scolded me for the mistakes I often made in posting entries; he simply ascribed them to ignorance and then gave me explanations that were really superfluous.

The trouble came when, what with looking at all those transactions, I began to feel like making some of my own. In the ledger, very clearly, I came to visualize my own pocket, and when I posted a sum under "debit" for our clients, instead of a pen, I seemed to hold in my hand a croupier's rake, ready to collect the money scattered over the gaming table.

Young Olivi also showed me the incoming mail; I read it with attention and – I must say – at first, in the hope of understanding it better than others. A perfectly commonplace offer one day commanded my impassioned attention. Even before reading it I felt something stir in my bosom, which I recognized immediately as that obscure presentiment that sometimes came to me at the gaming table. It is hard to describe this precognition. It consists of a certain expansion of the lungs whereby you breathe the air voluptuously, no matter how smoke-filled it may be. But there is more: You know at once that when you have doubled your stake you will feel even better. However, it takes some experience to grasp all this. You have to have abandoned the table with empty pockets and with regret at not having heeded it; then the table can no longer elude you. And if you have neglected it, that day is beyond salvation, because the cards take their revenge. However, it is much more pardonable not to heed the green table than to disregard the ledger before your eyes; and in fact I heard the call clearly, inside me, crying: "Buy that dried fruit at once!"

In all humility I spoke of it to Olivi, naturally without mentioning my inspiration. Olivi replied that he handled such transactions only for third parties, when he might make a small percentage. Thus he denied my dealings any possibility of inspiration, which was to be saved for third parties.

Night strengthened my conviction; the presentiment was then inside me. I breathed so well that I couldn't sleep. Augusta sensed my restlessness, and I had to tell her the reason. She immediately felt my inspiration, and in her sleep she even murmured, "Aren't you the master?"

True, in the morning, before I left, she said to me, concerned: "It wouldn't do for you to vex Olivi. Shall I speak with Papà?"

I wouldn't permit that, because I knew that Giovanni also attached very little significance to inspirations.

I reached the office fully determined to fight for my idea, not least to avenge the insomnia I had suffered. The battle raged until noon, when the deadline for accepting the offer expired. Olivi remained irremovable and dismissed me with the usual remark.

"Would you perhaps like to reduce the authority vested in me by your late father?"

Offended, I went back to my ledger for the moment, quite determined not to meddle in business anymore. But the taste of sultana raisins lingered on my palate, and every day at the Tergesteo I inquired about the price. Nothing else mattered to me. It rose slowly, very slowly, as if it needed to gather strength before breaking into a dash. Then in a single day it made a spectacular leap. The grape harvest had been wretched, and that fact became known only now. Funny thing, inspiration! It hadn't foreseen the poor harvest, but only the increase in price.

The cards took their revenge. In any event I couldn't stay put at my ledger, and I lost all respect for my instructors, especially now that Olivi no longer seemed so sure he had done the right thing. I laughed and jeered; it was my chief occupation.

A second offer came in, the price almost doubled. Olivi, to appease me, asked my opinion, and I said, triumphant, that I wouldn't eat raisins at that price.

Offended, Olivi murmured: "I stick to the system I've followed all my life."

And he went off to look for a buyer. He found one for a very small quantity, and again with the best of intentions, he came back to me and asked hesitantly: "Shall I cover this little purchase?"

Nasty as before, I answered: "I'd have covered it before making it."

In the end Olivi lost the strength of his own conviction and left the sale uncovered. The raisins continued to rise, and we lost everything we could lose on that small quantity.

But Olivi became angry with me and declared that he had gambled only to please me. The sly fox was forgetting that I had advised betting on the red and he, to outsmart me, had bet on the black. Our quarrel was beyond mending. Olivi appealed to my father-in-law, saying that between me and himself the firm would be harmed, and if my family so wished, he and his son would step down and leave me a free hand. My father-in-law immediately decided in Olivi's favor.

He said to me: "This dried-fruit deal is all too instructive. You two men will never be able to get along. Now who has to step down? The man who, without the other, would have concluded only one good transaction? Or the man who has been running the firm by himself for half a century?"

Augusta, too, was led by her father to persuade me not to meddle again in my own affairs. "Your goodness and your innocence," she said, "seem to make you unsuited to business. Stay home with me."

Enraged, I sulked in my tent – or, rather, my study. For a while I did some reading, I played music, then I felt a desire for more serious activity, and I nearly returned to chemistry, then to jurisprudence. Finally, and I don't know why, I devoted myself to the study of religion. I seemed to be resuming the studies I had already begun at the death of my father. Perhaps this time they were undertaken as a vigorous attempt to draw closer to Augusta and her health. Going to Mass with her was not enough; I had to proceed in a different way, namely by reading Renan and D. F. Strauss, the former with pleasure, the latter as punishment. I say this here to underline the immense desire that bound me to Augusta. And she never guessed this desire when she saw me with the critical edition of the Gospels in my hands. She preferred indifference to knowledge, and so she was unable to appreciate the greatest sign of affection I had given her. When she interrupted her toilette or her household occupations, as she regularly did, to peep in at the door of my room with a word of greeting, seeing me bent over those texts, she would make a grimace.

"Still bothering with that stuff?"

The religion that Augusta needed did not require any time to be learned or practiced. A quick bow of the head, then back to life at once! No more than that. For me, religion assumed quite a different aspect. If I had possessed true faith, I would have had only that and nothing else in this world.

Still, into my magnificently organized little room boredom sometimes entered. It was more like anxiety, because that was precisely when I seemed to feel the strength to work; but I was waiting for life to assign me some task. While I waited, I frequently went out and I spent many hours at the Tergesteo or in some café.

I was living in a simulation of activity. Very boring activity.

A university friend, who had been forced to come home in haste from a little town in Styria to be treated for a serious illness, became my nemesis, although he hardly looked the part. He came to see me after having spent a month in Trieste, in bed, which had sufficed to transform his disease from acute nephritis to chronic and probably incurable nephritis. But he believed he was better and was gaily preparing to move immediately, during that spring, to some place with a climate milder than ours, where he expected to be restored to complete health. It had probably been fatal for him to linger so long in our bleak native town.

The visit of that man, sick but happy and smiling, I consider a dire event for me; but perhaps I am wrong. It only marks a time in my life that I would have had to live through in any case.

My friend, Enrico Copler, was amazed that I had heard nothing about him or about his illness, of which Giovanni must have been informed. But Giovanni, since he was also sick, had no time for anyone and had said nothing to me, even though he came to my house every sunny day to nap for a few hours in the open air.

With the two sick men there, we all spent a very merry afternoon. They talked about their sicknesses, which provide the greatest diversion for the sick, while the subject is not too sad also for the healthy who are listening. There was only one disagreement, because Giovanni required fresh air, which was forbidden the other guest. The disagreement vanished when a slight wind rose, persuading Giovanni also to stay with us, in the warm little room.

Copler told us about his sickness, which caused no pain but sapped his strength. Only now that he was better did he realize how sick he had been. He talked about the medicines that had been administered to him, and then my interest grew keener. Among other things, his doctor had recommended an effective method to allow him long sleep, without having to poison himself with actual sleeping potions. But they were the very thing I needed most!

My poor friend, hearing that I needed medicines, flattered himself for a moment, thinking I might be suffering from his own disease, and he advised me to have myself looked at, listened to, and treated.

Augusta burst into hearty laughter and declared that I was nothing but an imaginary sick man. Then Copler's emaciated face betrayed something similar to resentment. Immediately, in a virile fashion, he freed himself from the condition of inferiority to which he was apparently condemned, attacking me with great energy.

"Imaginary sick man? Well, I prefer to be genuinely sick. In the first place, an imaginary sick man is a ridiculous monstrosity, and furthermore there are no medicines for him, whereas the pharmacy, as you can see in my case, always has something efficacious for those of us who are really ill."

His speech seemed that of a well man, and – here I must be honest – it made me suffer.

My father-in-law energetically agreed with Copler, but his words stopped short of heaping contempt on the imaginary sick man, because they betrayed all too clearly Giovanni's envy of the healthy man. He said that if he were healthy, as I was, instead of boring his fellow man with complaints, he would have rushed to his beloved, beneficent transactions, especially now that he had managed to reduce his girth. He was unaware that his loss of weight was not considered a favorable symptom.

Thanks to Copler's attack, I really did look like a sick man, and an ill-treated sick man at that. Augusta felt called upon to intervene on my behalf. Stroking my hand as it lay limp on the desk, she said my sickness didn't trouble anybody and she wasn't even convinced I did believe I was sick, because in that case I wouldn't be so filled with the joy of living. Thus Copler returned to the condition of inferiority to which he was doomed. He was quite alone in this world, and while he might be my rival in the matter of health, he possessed nothing similar to the devotion Augusta offered me. Feeling deeply the need for a nurse, he resigned himself to confessing to me later how much he had envied me for this reason.

The discussion continued over the next few days in a calmer key, while Giovanni slept in the garden. And Copler, having given the question some thought, now declared that an imaginary sick man was genuinely sick, but more intimately and even more radically than the genuinely sick. In fact, the former's nerves were reduced to such a state that he felt sickness when it wasn't there, while the normal function of the nerves would consist of giving the alarm through pain and leading the sufferer to seek aid.

"Yes," I said. "Like the teeth, where the pain is felt only when the nerve is exposed, and then it has to be destroyed to effect the cure."

In the end we agreed that a truly sick man and an imaginary sick man were equal. In his nephritis, in fact, a warning sign from the nerves had been absent, and still was; whereas my nerves, on the contrary, were perhaps so sensitive that they were alerting me to the sickness I would die of some decades later. So they were perfect nerves and had the sole disadvantage of not allowing me many happy days in this world. Now that he had managed to catalog me among the sick, Copler was quite content.

I don't know why the poor man had a mania for talking about women, but when my wife was not present, he talked of nothing else. He claimed that in the truly sick man, at least with the diseases we know of, there was a weakening of the sex drive, which was a good defense of the organism, whereas in the imaginary sick man, who suffered only a disorder of the overexerted nerves (this was our diagnosis), that same drive was pathologically strong. I corroborated his theory with my experience, and we commiserated with each other reciprocally. I don't know why I didn't feel like telling him I was far removed from any excess and had been for a long time. I could have at least confessed that I considered myself, if not healthy, then convalescent, without offending him too much, for to proclaim oneself healthy while one knows all the complications of our organism is a difficult thing to do.

"You desire all the beautiful women you see?" Copler questioned me further.

"Not all!" I murmured, to tell him I was not that sick. For a start I didn't desire Ada, whom I saw every evening. For me she was truly the forbidden woman. The rustle of her skirts said nothing to me, and if I had been allowed to move them with my own hands, it would have been the same. Luckily I hadn't married her. This indifference was, or so it seemed to me, a manifestation of genuine health. Perhaps my desire for her at one time had been so violent that it had burned itself out. However, my indifference extended also to Alberta, though she was very pretty in her tidy, sober little school-dress. Could the possession of Augusta have sufficed to still my desire for the entire Malfenti family? That would really have been very moral!

Perhaps I didn't mention my virtue because I was constantly being unfaithful to Augusta in my thoughts, and even now, speaking to Copler, with a shudder of desire I thought of all the women that I was neglecting on her account. I thought of the women hurrying along the streets, all bundled up, and whose secondary sexual organs for that reason became too important, whereas those of woman possessed then vanished as if possession had atrophied them. I still felt keenly the desire for adventure: that adventure that began with the admiration of a boot, a glove, a skirt, of all that covers and alters shape. But this desire was not in itself guilty. Copler, however, was wrong in analyzing me. To explain to someone the sort of man he is somehow authorizes that man to act as he pleases. Copler did even worse, but still, when he spoke or when he acted, he couldn't foresee where he would be leading me.

Copler's words remain so important in my memory that when I recall them, they summon up all the sensations associated with them, and all the things and the people. I stepped into the garden with my friend, who had to go home before sunset. From my villa, which stands on a hill, there was a view of the port and the sea, a view now blocked by recent construction. We paused to take a long look at the sea, ruffled by a slight breeze, reflecting in myriads of red light the calm glow of the sky. The Istrian peninsula afforded the eye repose, with its green tenderness that extended in an enormous arc on the sea like a solid penumbra. The docks and the breakwaters were small and insignificant in their strictly linear forms, and the water in the basins dark in its immobility, or was it perhaps murky? In the vast panorama, peace was small, compared to all that animated red on the water; and after a little while, dazzled, we turned our backs to the sea. On the little lawn before the house, in contrast, night was already descending.

In front of the porch, on a big chair, his head covered by a cap and protected also by the raised lapel of his fur coat, his legs wrapped in a blanket, my father-in-law was asleep. We stopped to look at him. His mouth was agape, the lower jaw slack like that of something dead, his respiration noisy and too rapid. Every so often his head fell on his chest, and without waking, he would raise it again. There was then a movement of his eyelids, as if he wanted to open his eyes, to find his balance more easily, and his breathing would change rhythm. A genuine interruption of his sleep.

It was the first time the gravity of my father-in-law's illness was revealed to me so clearly, and I was deeply distressed.

In a low voice Copler said to me: "He should be under treatment. Probably he also suffers from nephritis. He isn't actually sleeping: I know that condition. Poor devil!"

Concluding, he advised me to send for his doctor.

Giovanni heard us and opened his eyes. He immediately seemed less ill, and joked with Copler: "You're staying out here, defying the open air? Won't it be bad for you?"

He thought he had slept soundly, and he had no idea that he could lack for air here, facing the vast sea from which so much air was wafted to him! But his voice was faint and his words interrupted by gasps; his face was ashen and, rising from his chair, he felt frozen. He had to take refuge in the house. I can still see him, the blanket under his arm, as he crossed the lawn, short of breath but laughing, as he waved to us.

"You see what a genuinely sick man is like?" Copler said, unable to dispel his dominating thought. "He's dying, and he doesn't know he's sick."

It seemed to me, too, that the genuinely sick man was not suffering much. My father-in-law and also Copler have been at rest for many years in the Sant'Anna cemetery, but there was a day when I passed their graves and the fact of their having lain beneath their tombstones for so many years did not vitiate the thesis of one of them.

Before leaving his old house, Copler had liquidated his affairs, and so, like me, he had no business concerns. However, once out of bed, he was unable to remain still and, not having any business of his own, he began to busy himself with that of others, which seemed far more interesting to him. He devoted himself to charity, but because he had decided to live entirely off the interest of his capital, he couldn't permit himself the luxury of doing everything at his own expense.

So he organized collections and taxed his friends and acquaintances. He recorded everything, like the good businessman he was, and I thought that book was his viaticum and that, had I been in his situation, sentenced to a brief life and without family as he was, I would have enriched that life by delving into capital. But he was the imaginary healthy man and he touched only the interest due him, unable to concede that the future was brief.

One day he came at me with a request for a few hundred crowns, to purchase a little piano for a poor girl who had already been often subsidized by me and by others through him, providing her a small monthly allowance. We now had to act quickly, to take advantage of a bargain. I couldn't exempt myself but a bit sullenly I remarked that I would have made a profit if I had stayed home that day. From time to time I am subject to fits of stinginess.

Copler took the money and went off with a word of thanks, but the effect of my remark became evident a few days later and it was, unfortunately, significant. He came to tell me that the piano had been installed and that Signorina Carla Gerco and her mother begged me to call on them so they could thank me. Copler was afraid of losing his client and wanted to obligate me, allowing me to savor the gratitude of the two women I had benefited. At first I tried to escape this nuisance, assuring him that I was convinced he distributed his benefaction wisely; but he was so insistent that I finally had to agree.

"Is she beautiful?" I asked, laughing.

"Very beautiful," he replied, "but she's not your cup of tea."

Curious, his mentioning cups, as if we could have drunk from the same one and he might communicate his pyorrhea to me. He told me how honest this family was, and how unfortunate, having lost its mainstay a few years ago, and how they continued to live in the direst poverty, though always with the strictest propriety.

176

It was an unpleasant day. A damp wind was blowing, and I envied Copler, who was wearing his fur coat. I had to hold my hat on with my hand; otherwise it would have flown off. But I was in a good humor because I was going to collect the gratitude owed to my philanthropy. We went on foot along Corsia Stadion, we crossed the Public Garden. It was a part of the city I never saw. We entered one of those so-called developer's houses, which our forefathers had set about building some forty years ago, in places remote from the city, which promptly invaded them; its appearance was modest, but still more impressive than the houses built today with the same intentions. The stairs occupied a cramped space and were therefore very steep.

We stopped at the second floor, which I reached well before my companion. I was surprised that of the three doors that gave on that landing, two, one on either side, were marked by the visiting card of Carla Gerco, pinned there with tacks, while the third also had a card, but with another name. Copler explained to me that the Gerco ladies had their kitchen and bedroom to the right, while, to the left, there was only one room, Signorina Carla's studio. They had been able to rent out the central rooms of the apartment, and so their own rent was very low, but they suffered the inconvenience of having to cross the landing to go from one room to the other.

We knocked on the door at the left, the study, where mother and daughter, advised of our visit, were waiting for us. Copler made the introductions. The mother, a very shy person in a poor black dress, her head distinguished by her snowy white hair, made me a little speech that she must have prepared in advance: they were honored by my visit, and they thanked me for the considerable present I had given them. After that she didn't open her mouth again.

Copler observed everything like a professor at a state examination, hearing the repeated lesson that he had taught with great effort. He corrected the speaker, telling her that I had not only provided the money for the piano, but had also contributed to the assistance he had collected for them. Devoted to precision, Copler was.

Signorina Carla rose from the chair by the piano where she had been sitting, extended her hand to me, and said simply: "Thank you."

This, at least, was sufficiently brief. My philanthropic burden was beginning to weigh on me. I, too, concerned myself with other people's business, like any truly sick man! What would that pretty young woman see in me? A person eminently respectable, but not a man! And she was really pretty! I believe she wanted to seem younger than she was, wearing a skirt too short for the current fashion, unless around the house she wore a skirt dating from the time when she hadn't attained her full growth. But her head was a woman's, and displayed the somewhat elaborate coiffure of a woman who wishes to please. The rich brown braids were arranged to cover her ears and also, in part, her neck. I was so concerned with my dignity, and so afraid of Copler's inquisitorial eye, that at first I didn't even take a good look at the girl; but now I know her completely. There was a musical quality in her voice when she spoke, and with an affectation by now a part of her nature, she deliberately elongated her syllables as if she wanted to caress the sound she put into them. For this reason, and also because of certain vowels, excessively broad even for Trieste, her speech had something foreign about it. I learned later that certain coaches, to teach voice production, alter the value of vowels. Her pronunciation was something quite different from Ada's. Her every sound seemed to be one of love.

During that visit, Signorina Carla smiled all the time, perhaps imagining that she had the expression of gratitude imprinted on her face. It was a slightly forced smile: the true look of gratitude. Then, a few hours later, when I began to dream of Carla, I imagined that in her face there had been a struggle between happiness and sorrow. Subsequently I found none of this in her, and once again I learned that female beauty simulates feelings that are totally unrelated to it, just as the canvas on which a battle is portrayed has no heroic feeling.

Copler seemed pleased by the introduction, as if the two women had been his creation. He described them to me: they remained happy with their lot and they were working. He spoke some words that seemed quoted from a scholastic text and, nodding mechanically, I seemed bent on confirming that I had done my homework and therefore knew how poor, virtuous women without money ought to be.

Then he asked Carla to sing something for us. She was reluctant, insisting she had a cold. She suggested postponing it to another day. I felt, sympathetically, that she feared our judgment, but I wished to prolong the meeting, so I joined my pleas to Copler's. I added that I didn't know if she would ever see me again, as I was very busy. Copler, though he knew I had absolutely no obligations in the world, confirmed with great seriousness everything I said. It was then easy for me to deduce that he didn't want me to see Carla again.

Again she tried to beg off, but Copler insisted, with a word that sounded like a command, and she obeyed. How easy it was to force her!

She sang *La mia bandiera*. From my soft sofa I followed her singing. I desired ardently to be able to admire it. How beautiful it would have been to behold her clad in genius! But on the contrary I was surprised to hear that her voice, when she sang, lost all musicality. Effort distorted it. Nor was Carla able to play, and her inept accompaniment made that poor music even poorer. I reminded myself that I was hearing a student, and I analyzed the volume of the voice to see if it sufficed. I decided, in order to be able to continue encouraging her, that only her training had been bad.

When she stopped, I seconded Copler's abundant and talkative applause. He said, "Imagine the effect of this voice if it were accompanied by a good orchestra."

This was certainly true. An entire, powerful orchestra was needed over that voice. I said with great sincerity that I would wait to hear the young lady in a few months' time, when I could give my opinion about the value of her training. Less sincerely, I added that the voice surely deserved schooling of the first rank. Then, to attenuate anything disagreeable that there may have been in my first words, I philosophized about how it was necessary for a superb voice to find a superb school. This superlative covered everything. But later, when I remained alone, I was amazed at having felt the necessity to be sincere with Carla. Did I love her already? Why, I hadn't even taken a good look at her!

On the stairs, with their dubious odor, Copler spoke again: "Her voice is too strong. It's a voice for the theater."

He didn't know that by now I had learned something different: that voice belonged in a very small space, where the listener could enjoy the impression of naïveté in that singing and could dream of adding art to it, through life and suffering.

Leaving me, Copler said he would let me know when Carla's teacher organized a public concert. This maestro was not yet much known in the city, but he would surely become a great celebrity in the future. Copler was sure of it, even though the maestro was fairly old. It seemed that celebrity would be awarded him now, after Copler had come to know him. Two illusions characteristic of the moribund, the maestro's and Copler's.

The curious thing is that I felt it necessary to tell Augusta about this visit. One could think I did so out of prudence, since Copler knew about it and I didn't feel like asking him to keep it quiet. But actually I was only too eager to talk about it. It was a great relief. So far I had had nothing to reproach myself with except my having remained silent with Augusta. Now I was completely innocent.

She asked me a few questions about the girl, and whether she was beautiful. It was hard for me to answer: I said that the poor girl had seemed very anemic to me. Then I had a good idea: "What if you took her in hand a bit?"

Augusta had so much to do in her new house and in her old family, where they called on her to help out in the care of her sick father, that she thought no more about it. My idea had therefore been truly good.

Copler, however, learned from Augusta that I had told her about our visit, and he also therefore forgot the qualities he had attributed to the imaginary sick man. He said to me, in Augusta's presence, that in a short time we would pay another visit to Carla. He trusted me completely.

In my idleness I was promptly seized by a desire to see Carla again. I didn't dare rush to her, fearing Copler would find out. But I was never at a loss for pretexts. I could go to offer her further assistance, unknown to Copler, but I would first have to be sure that, in her own interest, she would agree to remain silent. And what if that genuine sick man were already the girl's lover? I knew absolutely nothing about the truly sick, and it could easily be their habit to have their mistresses paid for by others. If so, a single visit to Carla would be enough to compromise me. I wouldn't endanger the peace of my family; or, rather, it was in no danger unless my desire for Carla increased.

But it did increase, constantly. I already knew that girl much better than when I had shaken her hand to take my leave of her. I remembered especially that black braid that covered her snowy neck, and how it would have to be pushed aside with the nose if one wanted to succeed in kissing the skin it concealed. To stimulate my desire, I had only to remember that on a certain landing, in my own little city, a beautiful girl was available, and a short walk would be enough for me to go and take her! The battle with sin in some circumstances becomes very difficult because you have to renew it every day and every hour: as long as the girl remains on that landing, in other words. Carla's long vowels summoned me, and

ZENO'S CONSCIENCE

perhaps it was their very sound that had instilled the conviction in my soul that when my resistance had disappeared, there would be no other resistances. However, it was clear to me that I could deceive myself, and perhaps Copler saw things with greater precision. This suspicion also helped reduce my resistance, since poor Augusta could be saved from my possible betrayal by Carla herself, whose mission as a woman was to offer resistance.

Why should my desire have caused me any remorse, when it seemed actually to have arrived just in time to save me from the menacing tedium of those days? In no way did it harm my relations with Augusta: quite the contrary, in fact. I spoke to her now not only with the affectionate words I had always had for her, but also with those that, in my thoughts, were being formed for the other. There had never been such a wealth of tenderness in my house, and Augusta seemed enchanted by it. I was always strict regarding what I called the family schedule. My conscience is so delicate that, with my present behavior, I was already preparing to attenuate my future remorse.

That my resistance was not totally lacking is proved by the fact that I reached Carla not in one outburst, but by degrees. First, for several days I arrived only as far as the Public Garden, and with the sincere intention of delighting in that greenery that seems so pure in the midst of the grayness of the streets and houses that surround it. Then, not having had the good luck to run into her casually, as I had hoped, I left the Garden and walked until I was directly under her windows. I did this with great emotion, which recalled that delightful excitement of a youth approaching love for the first time. For a long while I had been deprived not of love, but of the thrill of rushing to it.

I had barely left the Public Garden when I came upon my mother-in-law, face to face. At first I had a curious suspicion: in the morning, so early, in this neighborhood, so far from ours? Perhaps she was also betraying her sick husband. I immediately learned that I was doing her an injustice, because

182

she had called on the doctor, for consolation after having spent a bad night with Giovanni. The doctor had had good words for her, but she was so distressed that she soon left me, forgetting even to be surprised at having come upon me in that place frequented only by old people, children, and nannies.

But just the sight of her was enough to make me feel the grip of my family again. I turned toward home with a firm step, to which I beat time, murmuring: "Never again! Never again!" At that moment Augusta's mother, with her grief, had given me the sense of all my duties. It was a good lesson, and it lasted the whole day.

Augusta wasn't at home because she had hurried to her father and had stayed with him all morning. At table she told me that they had discussed whether, given Giovanni's condition, they shouldn't postpone Ada's wedding, which had been set for the next week. Giovanni was already better. Apparently at supper he had let himself be induced to overeat, and indigestion had assumed the appearance of a worsening of his sickness.

I told her I had already had the news from her mother, whom I had encountered that morning in the Public Garden. Augusta, too, was not surprised by my walk, but I felt called upon to furnish an explanation. I told her that for a while now I preferred the Public Garden as the destination of my strolls. I could sit on a bench and read my paper.

Then I added: "That Olivi! He's really fixed me! Condemning me to such inactivity."

Augusta, who on this score felt a bit guilty, had an expression of sadness and regret. I then felt fine. But I was truly quite pure because I spent the whole afternoon in my study and could honestly believe I was definitively cured of any perverse desire. I was now reading the Apocalypse.

And despite the fact that I had thus established my right to go every morning to the Public Garden, my resistance to temptation had become so great that the next day, when I went out, I headed in exactly the opposite direction. I went to look for some music, wanting to try a new violin method that had been recommended to me. Before going out, I learned that my father-in-law had passed an excellent night and would come to us in a cab that afternoon. I was pleased both for my father-in-law and for Guido, who would finally be able to marry. All was going well: I was saved, and so was my father-in-law.

It was that very music that led me back to Carla! Among the methods the shopkeeper offered me was one written not for the violin but for the voice. I carefully read the title: *Complete Manual of the Art of Singing (school of Garcia) by M. Garcia (junior), comprising a paper on the Human Memory and Physiological Observations on the Human Voice, read at the Academy of Sciences in Paris*.

I allowed the clerk to serve other customers, and I began reading the little book. I must say that I read it with an agitation that at first resembled that of a depraved youth approaching pornography. Yes! This was the way to reach Carla; she needed that book, and it would be a crime on my part not to acquaint her with it. I bought it and returned home.

Garcia's opus consisted of two parts, one theoretical and the other practical. I continued reading it, determined to understand it well enough to be able to give my own advice to Carla when I eventually went to see her with Copler. Meanwhile I would gain some time and sleep in peace, while still diverting myself with the thought of the adventure in store for me.

But Augusta herself brought things to a head. Coming in to greet me, she interrupted my reading, bent down, and brushed my cheek with her lips. She asked me what I was doing, and, hearing something about a new manual, she thought it was for the violin and didn't trouble to take a second look. When she left me, I exaggerated the risk I had run, and I thought it would be best not to keep that book in my study. I should deliver it immediately to its destiny, and so I was forced to head straight for my adventure. I had found something more than a mere pretext for doing what it was my desire to do.

I no longer had the slightest hesitation. Having reached that landing, I turned at once to the door on my left. But I stopped for a moment at that door to listen to the sounds of the song *La mia bandiera*, that echoed gloriously in the stairwell. It was as if, for all this time, Carla had continued singing the same thing. I smiled, filled with affection and desire by such childishness. I then cautiously opened the door without knocking, and entered the room on tiptoe. I wanted to see her right away, then and there. In the confined space her voice was really unpleasant. She sang with great enthusiasm and with greater warmth than on the occasion of my first visit. She had actually flung herself against the back of the chair, to be able to expel all her breath from her lungs. I saw only the delicate head bound by the thick braids, and I retreated, overcome with deep emotion at my own daring. She meanwhile had reached the final note, which she was reluctant to cut off, and I was able to go out on the landing again and shut the door behind me without her noticing. That last note had wavered up and down, before being securely anchored. So Carla was able to hear the correct note, and it was now Garcia's job to take over and teach her how to find it more promptly.

I knocked when I felt calmer. She came immediately to open the door, and I will never forget her slender form, leaning against the jamb, as she fixed me with her great dark eyes until she could recognize me in the darkness.

But meanwhile I had grown calm and could thus be seized again by all my misgivings. I was on the way to betraying Augusta, but I was thinking that if, on the previous days, I had been content to go no farther than the Public Garden, now, all the more easily, I could stop at this door, deliver the compromising book, and leave, completely satisfied. It was a brief moment, full of the best intentions. I even remembered some strange advice once given me to rid myself of the habit of smoking, and it might work also on this occasion: some-times, to be satisfied, it was enough to light the match, then throw away both match and cigarette.

It would have been easy enough to do this, because Carla herself, when she recognized me, blushed and seemed about to flee, embarrassed — as I later learned — at being found wearing a cheap, threadbare house dress.

Once recognized, I felt called upon to apologize: "I've brought you this book, which I think will interest you. If you like, I can leave it with you and go away at once."

The tone of the words was — or so it seemed to me — rather curt, but not the sense, because all in all I left it up to her to decide whether I should leave, or remain and betray Augusta.

She decided at once, because she grasped my hand, the better to detain me, and she ushered me inside. Emotion clouded my vision, and I believe the cause was not so much the soft contact of that hand, but rather the familiarity that seemed to decide my fate and Augusta's. Therefore I believe I entered with some reluctance, and when I recall the story of my first infidelity, I have the feeling that I committed it because I was dragged into it.

Carla's face was truly beautiful, flushed as it was. I was delightfully surprised to realize that while she hadn't been expecting me, she had still been hoping for me to visit. She said, with great satisfaction: "So you felt the need to see me again? To see the poor little girl who owes you so much?"

Surely, had I wanted to, I could have taken her into my arms immediately, but the thought never crossed my mind. The thought was so far from me that I didn't even answer her words, which seemed compromising to me, and I began again to talk about Garcia and the necessity of that book for her. I spoke of it with a haste that led me to utter some ill-considered words. Garcia would teach her how to make the notes as firm as metal and as sweet as air. He would explain to her how a note can represent only a straight line – indeed, a plane, a truly polished plane.

My fervor vanished only when she interrupted me to express a painful suspicion: "Then you don't like the way I sing?"

I was dumbfounded by her question. I had uttered a harsh criticism, but I wasn't aware of it, and I protested in all sincerity. I protested so well that I seemed, while speaking only of singing, to return to the love that had so imperiously drawn me into that house.

And my words were so loving that they still allowed a measure of sincerity to shine through: "How can you believe such a thing? Would I be here if that were so? I stood on that landing for a long time, enjoying your singing, delicious and sublime in its innocence. Only I believe that, to reach perfection, something further is needed, and I have come to bring it to you."

Such was the power that the thought of Augusta had over my spirit that it made me go on protesting that I had not been swept here by my desire!

Carla listened to my flattering words, which she was quite incapable of analyzing. She was not very cultivated, but, to my great surprise, I realized she was not lacking in common sense. She told me that she herself had grave doubts about her talent and her voice: she felt she was not making any progress. Often, after a certain number of hours of study, she allowed herself the pleasure and the reward of singing *La mia bandiera*, hoping to discover some new quality in her voice. But it was always the same: no worse, and perhaps always fairly good, as those who heard her insisted, as I had, too (and here her lovely dark eyes addressed me a humble question, revealing how she needed to be reassured as to the meaning of my words, which still seemed ambiguous to her), but there was no real progress. The maestro said that in art progress was never slow, but rather came in great leaps that brought you to the goal, and thus one fine day she would wake up, a great artist.

"It's a long business, all the same," she added, looking into space and perhaps seeing again all her hours of boredom and pain.

Honesty is considered first of all that which is sincere, and it would have been very honest on my part to advise that poor girl to give up studying voice and become my mistress. But I had not yet ventured that far beyond the Public Garden, and moreover, all else aside, I was not very confident of my judgment in the realm of singing. For some moments now I had been worried about only one person, that tiresome Copler, who spent every Sunday at my villa with my wife and me. This would have been the moment to find some pretext for asking the girl not to tell Copler about my visit. But I refrained, not knowing how to disguise my request, and it was just as well, because a few days later my poor friend took a turn for the worse and died almost immediately.

Meanwhile, I told her that in Garcia she would find everything she was looking for, and for a single instant, and only for an instant, she eagerly expected miracles from that book. Soon, however, confronted by all those words, she doubted the effectiveness of its magic. I read the theories of Garcia in Italian, then in Italian I explained them to her, and when that wasn't enough, I translated them into Triestine, but she felt nothing happen in her throat, and she could have found that book's true efficacy only if it had then become manifest. The trouble is that I, too, soon became convinced that the book, in my hands, was of little value. Going over those sentences fully three times and not knowing what to make of them, I avenged my incapacity by criticizing them freely. Here was this Garcia, wasting his time and mine, to prove that inasmuch as the human voice could produce various sounds, it was wrong to consider it a single instrument. Then the violin, too, should be considered a conglomerate of instruments. I was perhaps mistaken to communicate this criticism of mine to Carla, but in the presence of a woman you want to win, it is hard not to exploit an opportunity, when you have one, to exhibit your own superiority. She, in fact, admired me; actually physically, she thrust away from herself the book that had been our Galeotto, though it did not lead us as far as sin. I still couldn't resign myself to renouncing that, so I postponed it until my next visit. When Copler died, there was no longer any need. Any link between that house and mine was broken, and so any further action would be restrained only by my conscience.

But meanwhile we had become rather intimate, in an intimacy greater than might have been expected in that half hour of conversation. I believe that agreement on a critical opinion forges an intimate bond. Poor Carla took advantage of this intimacy to confide her troubles to me. After Copler's intervention they had lived simply in that house, but without great privations. The heaviest burden for the two poor women was the thought of the future, for Copler brought them his assistance at very specific intervals, but he didn't allow them to rely on it with certainty; he didn't want worries, and he preferred the women to have them. And, further, he didn't give that money for nothing: he was the real master in that house, and he had to be informed of every slightest thing. Woe to them if they allowed themselves some expenditure without his approval in advance! Carla's mother, a short time before, had been indisposed, and Carla, the better to take care of the household tasks, had neglected her singing for a few days. Informed by the maestro, Copler made a scene and went off, declaring it was not worth their while importuning gentlemen to lend them assistance. For several days they lived in terror, afraid they had been abandoned to their fate. Then, when he returned, he renewed agreements and conditions and established exactly how many hours every day Carla was to sit at the piano and how many she could devote to the house. He also threatened to pay them a surprise visit at any hour of the day.

"To be sure," the girl concluded, "he only wants what is best for us, but he becomes so angry over trivial things that one of these times, in his fury, he'll finally turn us out on the street. But now that you have also taken an interest in us, this danger doesn't exist anymore, does it?"

And again she pressed my hand. As I didn't answer immediately, she was afraid I felt some solidarity with Copler, and she added: "Signor Copler says how good you are, too!"

These words were meant as a compliment to me, but also to Copler.

His personality, so disagreeable in Carla's portrayal, was new to me, and it prompted my appreciation. I would have liked to resemble him, whereas the desire that had drawn me into this house made me so unlike him! It was quite true that the money he brought the two women came from other people, but he contributed all his own efforts, a part of his own life. That anger, which he devoted to them, was truly paternal. But I had a suspicion: What if those efforts had been inspired by desire? Without hesitation, I asked Carla: "Has Copler ever asked you for a kiss?"

"Never!" Carla replied with spirit. "When he is satisfied with my behavior, he expresses his approval gruffly, presses my hand for an instant, then leaves. Other times, when he's angry, he refuses even to shake my hand and doesn't even notice how I'm crying, in my fear. A kiss, at such a moment, would be a liberation for me."

Seeing me laugh, Carla made herself clearer: "I would gladly accept a kiss from a man that old, to whom I owe so much!"

There's an advantage of the truly sick: they look older than they are.

I made a weak attempt to look like Copler. Smiling so as not to frighten the poor young woman too much, I told her that I, too, when I took an interest in someone, ended up by becoming very imperious. Generally speaking, I too believed that when you study an art you must study it seriously. Then I became so caught up in my role that I even stopped smiling.

Copler was right to be stern with a young person who couldn't understand the value of time: she should also remember how many people were making sacrifices to help her. I was truly serious and stern.

And so the time came for me to go to lunch and, especially on that day, I didn't want to keep Augusta waiting. I held out my hand to Carla and then I noticed how pale she was. I wanted to console her: "You can rest assured that I will always do my best to plead your cause with Copler and with everyone else."

She thanked me, but she still seemed downcast. Later I learned that, seeing me arrive, she had immediately guessed something close to the truth and had thought I was in love with her and she was therefore saved. But then – just as I was preparing to leave – she thought I was in love only with art and singing, and so, if she didn't sing well and didn't improve, I would abandon her.

She seemed very downcast indeed. I was overcome with compassion, and since there was no time to waste, I reassured her in the way she herself had described as the most effective. I was already at the door when I drew her to me, carefully shifted with my nose the thick braid from her neck, which I then reached with my lips and even grazed with my teeth. It looked like a joke, and in the end she laughed, too; but only when I left her. Until that moment she had remained inert and dazed in my arms.

She followed me onto the landing, and as I started down the stairs, she asked me, laughing: "When will you come back?"

"Tomorrow, or perhaps later!" I replied, already unsure. Then, with greater decision, I said: "Definitely, I'll come tomorrow." But, not desiring to compromise myself too far, I added: "We'll continue our reading of Garcia."

She didn't change expression in that brief moment: she nodded assent to the first, hesitant promise, assented gratefully to the second, and assented also to my third proposal, smiling the whole time. Women always know what they want. There was no hesitation on the part of Ada, who rejected me, or of Augusta, who accepted me, or of Carla, who let me have my way.

On the street, I found myself immediately closer to Augusta than to Carla. I breathed the fresh, open air and I was filled with the sensation of my freedom. I had done nothing that went beyond a joke, and so it would remain, because it had ended on that neck and beneath that braid. Finally Carla had accepted that kiss as a promise of affection and, especially, of assistance.

That day at table, however, I began really to suffer. Between me and Augusta lay my adventure, like a great, grim shadow, which to me seemed impossible for her not to see. I felt small, guilty, and sick, and I felt the pain in my side as a sympathetic pain reverberating from the great wound in my conscience. As I absently pretended to eat, I sought solace in an iron resolution: "I will never see her again," I thought, "and if, out of concern, I have to see her, it will be the last time." After all, not much was demanded of me: just one effort, not to see Carla ever again.

Augusta, laughing, asked me: "You look so worried. Have you been to see Olivi?"

I laughed, too. It was a great relief, being able to talk. The words were not such as to confer total peace, for to say such words I would have had to confess and then promise; but since I could not do that, it was a great relief even to say something else. I spoke copiously, full of goodness and cheer. Then I found something even better: I talked about the little laundry that she so desired and that I had refused her until then, and I promptly gave her permission to build it. She was so moved by my unsolicited permission that she got up and came to give me a kiss. It was a kiss that obviously erased that other one; and I promptly felt better.

So it was that we acquired the laundry, and even today, when I pass the little building, I remember how Augusta wanted it and Carla made it possible.

An enchanting afternoon ensued, filled with our affection. In solitude, my conscience was far more irritating. Augusta's words and affection came and soothed it. We went out together. Then I accompanied her to her mother's and I also spent the whole evening with her.

Before going to sleep, as often happened with me, I looked for a long while at my wife, already sleeping, concentrated in her light respiration. Even asleep, she was in perfect order, the covers drawn to her chin, and her less-than-abundant hair collected in a short braid knotted at her nape. I thought: I don't want to cause her pain. Never! I fell asleep serenely. The next day I would clarify my relations with Carla and I would find the way to reassure the poor girl about her future, without being obliged to give her kisses in consequence.

I had an eerie dream. Not only was I kissing Carla's neck: I was also eating it. But the neck was made in such a way that the wounds I inflicted on it with angry lust did not bleed, and with its slightly curved shape, the neck still remained covered by white, intact skin. Carla, sinking in my arms, seemed not to suffer from my bites. The one who suffered, on the contrary, was Augusta, who suddenly arrived running. To reassure her, I said: "I won't eat it all; I'll leave a piece for you, too."

The dream seemed a nightmare only later, when I woke up and my befuddled mind could remember it – but not before then, because while it lasted, not even Augusta's presence had taken away the sense of satisfaction it brought me.

Once awake, I was fully aware of the force of my desire and of the danger it represented for Augusta and also for me. Perhaps in the womb of the woman sleeping at my side, another life, for which I would be responsible, was beginning. Who knows what Carla would want if she were my mistress? To me she seemed desirous of that pleasure that so far had been denied her, and how would I be able to provide for two families? Augusta wanted the useful laundry, the other woman would want something different but no less costly. I saw Carla again as she waved to me from the landing, laughing, after having been kissed. She already knew I would be her prey. I was frightened and now, alone and in the darkness, I couldn't suppress a moan.

My wife, immediately awake, asked me what was wrong and I answered with brief words, saying the first thing that came into my mind when I could recover from my fright, finding myself questioned at a moment when I felt I had shouted a confession.

"I'm thinking of my approaching old age!"

She laughed and tried to console me without, at the same time, truncating the sleep to which she was clinging. She addressed me with the same words she always repeated when she saw me frightened by the passage of time: "Don't think about it, not now, while we are young . . . Sleep is so good!"

The exhortation helped: I gave it no more thought, and I fell asleep again. A word in the night is like a shaft of sunshine. It illuminates a stretch of reality and, confronted by it, the constructions of the imagination fade. Why did I have so much to fear from poor Carla, when I was not yet her lover? It was obvious I had done everything to frighten myself with my own situation. Finally, the bébé that I had evoked in Augusta's womb had so far given no sign of life beyond the construction of the laundry.

I got up, still accompanied by the best intentions. I rushed to my study and prepared an envelope containing a bit of money I wanted to give Carla at the very moment when I announced I was abandoning her. However, I would declare myself ready to send her more money by mail at any time she asked for it, writing to me at an address I would give her. Just as I was about to go out, Augusta, with a sweet smile, invited me to accompany her to her father's house. Guido's father had arrived from Buenos Aires to be present at the wedding, and we should go and make his acquaintance. She surely was less concerned about Guido's father than about me. She wanted to renew the sweetness of the previous day. But it was no longer the same thing: to me it seemed wrong to allow time to pass between my good resolve and its execution. Meanwhile, as we were walking along the street side by side and, to all appearances, secure in our affection, the other woman considered herself already the object of my love. That was wrong. I felt this walk as an actual constraint.

We found Giovanni really better. Only he couldn't put on his boots because of a certain swelling of the feet; he attached no importance to it, so neither did I. He was in the living room with Guido's father, to whom he introduced me. Augusta promptly left us to go to her mother and sister.

Signor Francesco Speier seemed to me a much less educated man than his son. He was small, crude, about sixty, with few ideas and little vitality, perhaps also because, as a consequence of an illness, his hearing was severely impaired. He dropped an occasional Spanish word into his speech.

"*Cada vez* I come to Trieste . . ."

The two old men were talking about business, and Giovanni listened carefully because this business was very important to Ada's future. I listened absently. I heard that old Speier had decided to wind up his business in Argentina and to give Guido all his *duros*, to use in setting up a firm in Trieste; then Francesco would return to Buenos Aires, to live with his wife and daughter on a little farm he had inherited. I didn't understand why, in my presence, he was telling Giovanni all this, and I don't know why even today.

At a certain point it seemed to me both men stopped talking, looking at me as if they expected some advice; and, to be polite, I remarked, "The farm can't be all that small, if it brings in a living."

Giovanni immediately shouted: "What are you talking about?"

The explosion of his voice recalled his better days, but surely if he hadn't shouted so, Signor Francesco wouldn't have noticed my remark. But instead he paled and said: "I hope Guido will not fail to pay me the interest on my capital."

Giovanni, shouting again, tried to ressure him: "I should say so! Double the interest if you need it. Isn't he your son?"

Signor Francesco still didn't seem quite reassured, and he was expecting from me some word of reassurance. I provided it at once, and more, because now the old man could hear less.

Then the discussion between the two businessmen continued, but I was careful to take no further part in it. Giovanni looked at me from time to time over his eyeglasses, to observe me, and his heavy respiration seemed a threat. He spoke at last, and asked me at a certain point: "Don't you agree?"

I nodded eagerly.

My agreement must have seemed all the more eager, for my every action was now made more expressive by the anger mounting within me. What was I doing in this place, allowing the passage of time that was needed for carrying out my good resolution? I was obliged to neglect a task so valuable for me and for Augusta! I was preparing an excuse to leave, but at that moment the living room was invaded by the women, and by Guido accompanying them. Shortly after his father's arrival, he had given his bride a magnificent ring. Nobody looked at me or greeted me, not even little Anna. Ada already wore the splendid jewel on her finger, and resting her arm on her fiancé's shoulder, she showed the ring to her father. The women also looked at it, ecstatic.

Rings also held no interest for me. Why, I didn't even wear my own wedding band, because it impeded the circulation of the blood! Without saying good-bye, I left the living room, went to the front door, and was about to go off. But Augusta noticed my flight and overtook me in time. I was amazed by her distraught look. Her lips were as pale as they had been on the day of our wedding, just before we entered the church.

I told her I had some pressing business. Then, recalling in time that a few days before, on a whim, I had bought some very weak glasses, for the nearsighted, and I had not yet tried them out, having slipped them into my vest pocket, where I could now feel them, I told her I had an appointment with an oculist to have my eyes examined, since for some while my sight had seemed weaker to me. She answered that I could go at once, but she begged me first to bid a proper good-bye to Guido's father. I shrugged with impatience, but still I did as she wished.

I went back into the living room and everyone politely said good-bye to me. As for myself, sure that now they would send me off, I even had a moment of good humor. Guido's father, somewhat bewildered by all this family, asked me: "Will we meet again before I leave for Buenos Aires?"

"Oh!" I said, "*cada vez* that you come to this house, you will probably find me here!"

They all laughed and I went off triumphantly, with a fairly happy good-bye also from Augusta. I left in such good order, after having performed all the required formalities, that I could proceed with confidence. But there was another reason why I was freed of the doubts that until then had held me back: I was running away from my father-in-law's house to be somewhere as far from it as possible, namely Carla's house. In the Malfenti household, and not for the first time, they suspected me of ignobly conspiring against Guido's interests. Innocently, quite absently, I had spoken of that farm in Argentina, and Giovanni had immediately interpreted my words as if they had been deliberately intended to cause Guido trouble with his father. It would have been easy for me to explain myself to Guido if necessary; for Giovanni and the others, who believed me capable of such machinations, vengeance was sufficient explanation. Not that I had decided to hurry to be unfaithful to Augusta. But, in full daylight, I was doing what I desired. A visit to Carla still implied nothing wrong. On the contrary. If I were once again to encounter my mother-in-law in that neighborhood, and if she were to ask me what I was doing there, I would immediately reply: "Why, naturally, I'm going to Carla's." So that was the only time I went to Carla without a thought of Augusta. My father-in-law's attitude had so offended me!

On the landing I didn't hear the sound of Carla's voice. I had a moment of terror: What if she had gone out? I knocked and entered immediately, before anyone had invited me. Carla was there, but so was her mother. They were sewing together, in a pairing that could have been habitual, though I had never seen it before. Each quite separate from the other, they were working on the same large sheet, hemming it. Thus I had rushed to find Carla, and had found her with her mother. That was quite a different thing. Neither good resolutions nor bad could be carried out. Everything remained suspended.

Flushing deeply, Carla stood up as the old woman slowly removed her eyeglasses and put them in a case. I then thought I was entitled to be indignant for a reason other than that of seeing myself prevented from clarifying my feelings promptly. Weren't these the hours that Copler had assigned to study? I greeted the old woman politely, but even this act of politeness was hard for me to bear. I greeted Carla, too, almost without looking at her.

I said to her: "I came to see if this book" – and I nodded to the Garcia, still lying on the table where we had left it – "could provide us with some other useful ideas."

I sat in the place I had occupied the day before, and I immediately opened the book. Carla tried at first to smile at me, but seeing that I didn't respond to her courtesy, she sat down beside me with a certain solicitous obedience, to read. She was hesitant; she didn't understand. I looked at her and saw on her face an expression spreading that could denote scorn and stubbornness. I imagined this was the way she usually received Copler's reproaches. Only she was not yet sure that my reproaches were exactly those Copler addressed to her because – as she told me later – she remembered that the previous day I had kissed her, and so she believed herself forever protected against my wrath. Therefore she was still ready to convert that scorn into a friendly smile. I must say here, because later I won't have the time, that her confidence, the notion that she had definitively tamed me with that one kiss she had granted me, displeased me enormously; a woman who thinks like that is very dangerous.

But at that moment my mood was exactly the same as Copler's, charged with reproof and ill-feeling. I began reading aloud the very part that we had already read the day before, which I myself had demolished, pedantically and without other comment, emphasizing some words that seemed the most significant.

With a slightly tremulous voice, Carla interrupted me: "I believe we've already read this!"

So I was finally obliged to say words of my own. One's own words can also provide a bit of health. Mine were not only milder than my thoughts and my behavior, but they actually restored me to the life of society.

"You see, Signorina," and I immediately accompanied the coy title with a smile that could also have been a lover's, "I would like to review this material before continuing. Perhaps yesterday we judged it a bit hastily, and a friend of mine just now warned me that to understand everything Garcia says, he must be studied thoroughly."

I felt finally also the need to show some consideration for the poor old lady, who certainly in the course of her life, however unfortunate she had been, had never found herself in a similar situation. I addressed to her a smile that cost me more than the one I had bestowed on Carla.

"It's not very amusing," I said to her, "but even someone not interested in singing can profit by listening to it."

I continued stubbornly reading. Carla surely felt better, and something that resembled a smile played on her fleshy lips.

The old woman, on the contrary, still seemed a poor captured animal, and she stayed in that room only because her shyness prevented her from finding an excuse to leave. And as for me, nothing in the world could have made me betray my desire to throw her out. It would have been a grave and compromising action.

Carla was more determined: with great respect she begged me to interrupt that reading for a moment and, turning to her mother, told her that she could go and that they would continue their work on that sheet in the afternoon.

The Signora came over to me, undecided whether or not to give me her hand. I clasped it with real fondness and said: "I realize this reading is not at all amusing."

It seemed as if I wanted to regret her leaving us. The Signora went out after placing on a chair the sheet that until then she had held on her lap. Then Carla followed her for a moment onto the landing to say something, while I yearned to have her beside me finally. She came back in, closed the door behind her, and returning to her chair, she again had a rigidity around the mouth that recalled the face of a stubborn child.

She said: "Every day at this hour I study. It would happen that today I had to work on that urgent task!"

"But can't you see that I don't care a thing about your singing?" I shouted, and I assailed her with a violent embrace that drove me to kiss her first on the mouth, then at once on the same spot where I had kissed her the day before.

Strange! She burst into floods of tears and pulled away from me. She said, sobbing, that she had suffered too much, seeing me come in like that. She wept with that self-compassion usual in those who see their suffering sympathized with. The tears are produced not by grief, but by their own story. One weeps when one protests against injustice. It was, in fact, unjust to impose studying on that beautiful girl who could be kissed.

All in all, things went worse than I had imagined. I had to explain myself, and to be brief, I didn't allow myself the time required for invention, and I told the exact truth. I told her of my impatience to see her and to kiss her. I had decided to come to her early; I had even passed the night with that determination. Naturally I was unable to say what I had imagined happening when I came to her, but that was of scant importance. It was true that when I was determined to come and tell her I meant to abandon her forever, I had felt the same painful impatience as when I was rushing to her to take her into my arms. Then I told her about the events of the morning, and how my wife had made me go out with her and had taken me to my father-in-law's, where I was forced to listen to their discussion of business matters that didn't affect me. Finally, with great effort, I manage to free myself and hurry all the long way here – and what do I find? . . . The room all cluttered with that sheet!

Carla burst out laughing because she realized that there was nothing of Copler in me. On her lovely face that laughter seemed a rainbow, and I kissed her again. She didn't respond to my caresses, but she accepted them meekly, an attitude I adore perhaps because I love the weaker sex in direct proportion to its weakness. For the first time she told me she had learned from Copler that I loved my wife very much.

"Therefore," she added, and I saw the shadow of a serious purpose pass over her face, "between the two of us there can be a sincere friendship and nothing more."

I had little faith in that very wise determination, because the same mouth that uttered it could not even then evade my kisses.

Carla spoke at length. Obviously she wanted to arouse my compassion. I remember everything she said to me, which I believed only when she vanished from my life. As long as I had her close, I constantly feared her as a woman who would sooner or later take advantage of her power over me to ruin me and my family. I didn't believe her when she assured me that she asked nothing beyond security for her own life and her mother's. Now I know for certain that she never intended to obtain from me more than she needed, and when I think of her I blush with shame at having understood and loved her so inadequately. She, poor child, had nothing from me. I would have given her everything, because I am one of those people who pay their debts. But I always waited for her to ask something of me.

She told me of the desperate condition in which she had found herself at her father's death. For months and months she and the old lady had been forced to work day and night on embroidery commissioned from them by a merchant. Ingenuously she believed that help had to come from divine providence, and in fact at times she would remain for hours at the window, looking down at the street, from whence that help should arrive. Instead, Copler came. Now she said she was content with her condition, but she and her mother spent uneasy nights because the help given them was quite precarious. What if, one day, it should turn out that she had neither the voice nor the talent to be a singer? Copler would abandon them. Further, he spoke of having her perform in a theater in a few months' time. And what if that proved a total fiasco?

Continuing this effort to stir my compassion, she told me that the financial misfortune of her family had also shattered her dream of love: her fiancé had abandoned her.

I was still a long way from compassion. I said to her: "I suppose that fiancé kissed you a lot? Like me?"

She laughed because I was preventing her from speaking. Thus I saw before me a man pointing out the way to me.

The hour at which I should have been home for lunch was long past. I would have liked to leave. Enough for that day. I was quite far from the remorse that had kept me awake during the night, and the uneasiness that had drawn me to Carla had totally disappeared. But I was not calm. It is, perhaps, my fate never to be. I felt no remorse because Carla had promised me all the kisses I wanted in the name of a friendship that couldn't offend Augusta. I thought I was discovering the cause of the discontent that as usual was sending vague pains through my organism. Carla saw me in a false light! Carla might despise me, seeing me so desirous of her kisses when I loved Augusta! That same Carla who made a show of respecting me so much because she had such need of me!

I decided to win her esteem, and I spoke words that should pain me like the memory of a cowardly crime, like a betrayal committed in complete freedom, without necessity and without benefit.

I was almost at the door, and with the look of someone who is serene and is reluctantly confessing, I said to Carla: "Copler has told you how fond I am of my wife. It's true, I have the greatest respect for my wife."

Then I told her, in complete detail, the story of my marriage, of how I had fallen in love with Augusta's older sister, who would have nothing to do with me because she was in love with someone else, and how I had then tried to marry another of her sisters, who also rejected me, and how finally I came to marry Augusta.

Carla immediately believed the accuracy of this story. Then I learned that Copler had heard some of it at my house and had repeated to her various details not entirely, but almost, true, which I had now rectified and confirmed.

"Is your wife beautiful?" she asked, pensive.

"It's a matter of taste," I said.

There was some prohibiting core still active inside me. I had said I respected my wife, but I hadn't yet said I didn't love her. I had said neither that she attracted me nor that she couldn't attract me. At that moment I felt I was being quite sincere; now I know that with those words I was betraying both women and all love, theirs and mine.

Frankly, I wasn't yet at ease; therefore something was still wanting. I remembered the envelope of my good resolution, and I handed it to Carla. She opened it and gave it back to me, saying that only a few days before, Copler had brought their monthly allowance and for the moment she had no need of money. My uneasiness increased thanks to an idea I had conceived long ago, that truly dangerous women never accept small sums. She became aware of my discomfort, and with delightful naïveté, which I appreciate only now as I write, she asked me for a few crowns with which she could buy some crockery that the two women had been deprived of after a disaster in the kitchen.

Then something happened that left an indelible mark in my memory. At the moment of leaving, I kissed her, but this time with complete intensity, she returned my kiss. My poison had worked. She said, in all innocence: "I'm fond of you because you are so good and not even wealth could spoil you."

Then she added, slyly: "Now I know I must never keep you waiting but, beyond that danger, there's nothing else to fear from you."

On the landing she asked again: "Can I send the singing teacher to the devil, along with Copler?"

Rapidly descending the stairs, I said to her: "We'll see!"

So something still remained unresolved in our relations; all the rest had been clearly defined.

It caused me such discomfort that when I came out into the open air, undecided, I turned in the direction opposite my home. I would almost have wanted to go back at once to Carla and explain something else to her: my love for Augusta. It could be done because I hadn't yet said to Carla that I loved her. Only, as conclusion to that true story I had told her, I had forgotten to say that now I truly loved Augusta. Carla, then, had deduced that I didn't love Augusta at all, and therefore she had returned my kiss so ardently, underlining it with her own declaration of love. It seemed to me that if this episode hadn't occurred, I could have borne more easily Augusta's trusting gaze. And to think that, a short time before, I had been happy to learn that Carla knew of my love for my wife and thus, through Carla's decision, the adventure I had sought was being offered me in the form of a friendship spiced with kisses.

At the Public Garden I sat on a bench, and with my cane I absently traced that day's date in the gravel. Then I laughed bitterly: I knew that date would not mark the end of my infidelities! On the contrary, they were just beginning on that day. Where was I to find the strength not to return to that desirable woman who was expecting me? Further, I had already assumed some obligations, obligations of honor. I had received kisses and I had not been allowed to return their value except in the form of a few dishes! It was an unpaid invoice that now bound me to Carla.

Lunch was sad. Augusta sought no explanation for my tardiness, and I offered her none. I was afraid of giving myself away, especially because, during the brief walk between the Public Garden and home, I had toyed with the idea of telling her everything, and the story of my infidelity might therefore be written on my honest face. That would have been the only way of saving myself. Telling her everything, I would have placed myself under her protection and under her surveillance. It would have been such a decisive act that then, in good faith, I could have marked that day's date as a start toward honesty and health.

We talked of many indifferent things. I tried to be light-hearted, but I couldn't even attempt to be affectionate. She was short of breath; surely she was waiting for an explanation that didn't come.

Then she left the room, to continue her great task of storing the winter clothing in special wardrobes. I glimpsed her often in the afternoon, intent on her work, there at the end of the long corridor, assisted by the maid. Her great suffering didn't interrupt her healthy activity.

Restless, I passed often from my bedroom to the bath. I would have liked to call Augusta and tell her at least that I loved her, because for her – poor simple thing! – this would have been enough. But instead I continued meditating and smoking.

I naturally went through various phases. There was even a moment when that access of virtue was curtailed by a lively impatience for the next day to come, so I could rush to Carla. It may be that this desire also was inspired by some good resolve. After all, the great difficulty was to be able to commit myself, alone as I was, to something and be bound by my duty. The confession that would have won me my wife's collaboration was unthinkable; so there remained Carla, on whose lips I could have sworn my vow, with a last kiss! Who was Carla? Not even blackmail was the greatest danger I risked with her! The next day she would be my mistress: Who could say what would then ensue? I knew her only through what that imbecile Copler had told me; and on the basis of such information, a more clever man than I, Olivi for example, wouldn't agree even to stipulate a contract.

All of Augusta's beautiful, healthy activity throughout my house was wasted. The drastic marriage cure I had undertaken in my desperate search for health had failed. I remained sicker than ever and married as well, harming myself and others.

Later, when I was in fact the lover of Carla, returning in my mind to that sad afternoon I was unable to understand why, before making any further commitment, I hadn't stopped myself with a manly decision. I had wept so over my infidelity before committing it, that it should conceivably have been easy to avoid it. But hindsight can always be ridiculed and so can foresight, because they are of no use. In those anguished hours, in big letters in my dictionary at the letter C (Carla) that day's date was written, with the words "last infidelity." But the first genuine infidelity, which committed me to subsequent infidelities, followed only the next day.

At a late hour, knowing nothing better to do, I took a bath. I felt my body was defiled and I wanted to wash it. But when I was in the water I thought: "To be clean, I would have to dissolve completely in this water." Then I dressed, so devoid of willpower that I didn't even dry myself properly. The day vanished, and I remained at the window looking at the new green leaves on the trees in my garden. I suddenly started shivering, and with a certain satisfaction I thought I had a fever. It was not death I desired, but sickness, a sickness that would serve me as a pretext to do what I wanted, or that would prevent me from doing it.

After having hesitated for such a long time; Augusta came looking for me. Seeing how sweet she was, without any bitterness, I felt my shivering increase until my teeth began to chatter. Frightened, she made me go to bed. My teeth were still chattering from the cold, but I already knew I didn't have a fever, and I prevented her from calling the doctor. I asked her to turn off the light, to sit beside me, and not to speak. I don't know how long we remained there: I regained the necessary warmth and also some confidence. My mind, however, was still so befuddled that when she again spoke of calling the doctor, I told her I knew the reason for my ill health, and I would tell her later what it was. I was returning to my resolution to confess. No other way remained open for me to rid myself of all this oppression.

So we stayed there somewhat longer, mute. Later I realized that Augusta had risen from her chair and was beside me. I was afraid that perhaps she had guessed everything. She took my hand, stroked it, then lightly placed her hand on my head, to see if it was feverish, and finally she said to me: "You should have expected it. Why this painful surprise?"

I was amazed at these strange words and, at the same time, at hearing them through a stifled sob. It was obvious she wasn't referring to my adventure. How could I have foreseen something like this? With a certain asperity I asked her: "What do you mean? What should I have foreseen?"

Confused, she murmured: "The arrival of Guido's father for Ada's wedding..."

Finally I understood: she believed I was suffering at the imminence of Ada's marriage. It seemed to me she was wronging me: I was not guilty of such a crime. I felt as pure and innocent as a newborn babe, and freed immediately from all oppression. I leaped out of bed.

"You think I'm suffering because of Ada's marriage? You're crazy! Ever since I've been married I haven't given her another thought. I didn't even remember that Señor Cada Vez had arrived here today!"

I kissed her and embraced her with total desire, and my tone was so obviously sincere that she was ashamed of her suspicion.

Her ingenuous face, too, was freed of every cloud and we quickly went to supper, both hungry. At that same table where we had suffered so much, we now sat like two good companions on a holiday.

She reminded me that I had promised to tell her the reason for my indisposition. I feigned sickness, that sickness that supposedly entitled me to do, blamelessly, anything I liked. I told her that, earlier, in the company of the two old gentlemen that morning, I had felt profoundly dejected. Then I had gone to collect the glasses that the oculist had prescribed for me. Perhaps that sign of age had depressed me still further. And I had walked through the streets of the city for hours and hours. I also told her something of the fantasies that had made me suffer so, and as I recall, they contained even a hint of confession. I don't know in what connection with the imaginary illness, I talked also about our blood, which flowed round and round, kept us erect, capable of thought and action and therefore of guilt and remorse. She didn't understand that this was all about Carla, but to me it seemed as if I had told her everything.

After supper I put on the eyeglasses and pretended for a long time to read my paper, but those glasses blurred my vision. I felt a surge of emotion, the happiness of an alcoholic.

I said I couldn't understand what I was reading. I continued acting the sick man.

I spent an almost sleepless night. I was awaiting Carla's embrace with complete, immense desire. I desired her specifically, the girl with the thick, crooked braids and the voice so musical when the note wasn't forced on her. She had been rendered desirable also by everything I had already suffered for her. I was accompanied all night by an ironclad resolution. I would be sincere with Carla before making her mine, and I would tell her the whole truth about my relations with Augusta. In my solitude I started laughing: it was very original to set out on the conquest of one woman with a declaration of love for another on your lips. Perhaps Carla would revert to her passivity! And then what? For the moment no action of hers could have lessened the value of her submission, which I felt I could count on.

The following morning, as I dressed, I murmured the words I would say to her. Before becoming mine, Carla had to know that Augusta, with her character and also with her health (I could have spent many words to explain what I meant by health, and they would have contributed to Carla's education), had been able to win my respect, and also my love.

Taking my coffee, I was so absorbed in preparing an elaborate speech that Augusta received no sign of affection from me beyond a light kiss before I left. But I was all hers! I was going to Carla in order to rekindle my passion for Augusta.

As soon as I entered the room serving as Carla's studio, I felt such relief at finding her alone and ready that I immediately drew her to me and passionately embraced her. I was frightened by the energy with which she repelled me. Downright violence! She would have none of this, and I remained agape in the middle of the room, painfully disappointed.

But Carla, promptly recovering, murmured: "Can't you see that the door's been left open and somebody's coming down the stairs?"

I assumed the mien of a formal visitor until the intruder had passed. Then we closed the door. She paled, seeing me also turn the key. Thus all was clear. A little later, in my arms, she murmured in a choked voice: "You want this? You really want it?"

She had called me *tu*, and this was decisive. I then answered promptly: "I want nothing else!"

I had forgotten that I would have liked to clarify something first.

Immediately afterwards I would have liked to begin talking about my relationship with Augusta, having neglected to do so before. But it was difficult just then. Talking with Carla about something else at that moment would have seemed like diminishing the importance of her devotion. Even the most deaf of men knows that such a thing cannot be done, though all men know there is no comparison between the importance of that devotion before it happens and immediately afterwards. It would have been a great insult for a woman, opening her arms to a man for the first time, to hear him say to her: "First of all I must clarify those words I said to you yesterday..." Yesterday?! Anything that happened the day before must seem unworthy of being mentioned, and if a gentleman happens not to sense this, then so much the worse for him, and he must behave in such a way that nobody realizes it.

Certainly I was the gentleman who didn't feel that, because in my pretense I erred as sincerity would not have been capable of erring. I asked her: "How did you come to give yourself to me? How did I merit such a thing?"

Did I want to show my gratitude, or to reproach her? Probably it was only an attempt to embark on the explanations.

A bit amazed, she looked up, to see my expression: "I had the impression that you took me," and she smiled affectionately, to prove that she was not reproaching me in any way.

I remembered how women insist on being told you have taken them. Then, she herself realized she had made a mistake

– things are taken, but people come to an agreement – and she murmured: "I was waiting for you! You were the knight who was to come and set me free. Of course it's a pity you're married, but since you don't love your wife, at least I know my happiness isn't destroying the happiness of anyone else."

I was seized by the pain in my side, so intense that I had to stop embracing her. Then I hadn't exaggerated the importance of my ill-considered words? Was it precisely my falsehood that had led Carla to become mine? So now, if I were to think of describing my love for Augusta, Carla would be entitled to reproach me actually for deceit! Rectifications and explanations were no longer possible. But later on there would be an opportunity for explanation and clarification. Waiting for it established a new bond between me and Carla.

There, at Carla's side, my passion for Augusta was reborn completely. Now I would have had only one desire: to rush to my true wife, only to see her intent on her task, like an industrious ant, storing away our things in an atmosphere of camphor and naphthalene.

But I remained with my duty, which was very grievous because of an episode that disturbed me greatly at first, for it seemed another threat from the sphinx with whom I was dealing. Carla told me that, immediately after I had left the previous day, the singing teacher had come and she had simply shown him the door.

I couldn't repress a gesture of vexation. It amounted to informing Copler of our liaison!

"What will Copler say to that?" I cried.

She began laughing and took refuge, on her own initiative this time, in my arms. "Didn't we decide to get rid of him, too?"

She was pretty, but she could no longer conquer me. I promptly found also a suitable attitude for myself, the pedagogue's, because it allowed me to release the bitterness I felt deep in my heart against the woman who prevented me from speaking of my wife as I would have liked. "We have to work in this world," I said to her, because, as she should already know, it is a wicked world, where only the fittest survive. And what if I were to die now? What would become of her? I had suggested the prospect of my abandonment in a way at which she absolutely could not take offense, and in fact she was moved. Then, with the obvious intention of demoralizing her, I told her that, with my wife, I had only to express a wish and I saw it fulfilled.

"Very well!" she said, resigned. "We'll send word to the maestro to come back!" Then she tried to communicate to me her dislike of that teacher. Every day she had to tolerate the presence of that disagreeable old man who made her repeat a thousand times the same exercises that were of no use at all, absolutely none. She didn't recall having had a pleasant day except during the times when the maestro fell ill. She had even hoped he would die, but she had been unlucky.

She became downright violent in her despair. She repeated, expanding it, her complaint of ill luck: she was a poor helpless creature, past hope. When she recalled that she had loved me immediately because it seemed to her that my actions, my words, my eyes offered the promise of a less harsh life, less rigorous, less boring, she wanted to cry.

Thus I became immediately acquainted with her sobs, and they annoyed me; they were so violent that they shook her weak organism, invading it. I felt I was undergoing at once an abrupt attack on my wallet and on my life. I asked her: "Do you think my wife does nothing in this world? Now, while the two of us are talking, her lungs are being polluted by camphor and naphthalene."

Carla sobbed. "Possessions, a household, clothes . . . lucky woman!"

Irritated, I thought she wanted me to rush out and buy her all those things, only to provide her with an occupation she preferred. I displayed no anger, thank God, and obeyed the voice of duty, which shouted: Caress the girl who has abandoned herself to you! I caressed her. I ran my hand lightly over her hair. As a result the sobs ceased, and her tears flowed copiously and freely, like rain after a thunderstorm.

"You are my first lover," she went on to say, "and I hope you will go on loving me."

That information, that I was her first lover, a designation implying a possible second one, did not move me greatly. It was a declaration that came late because for a good half hour that subject had been left behind. Still, it was a new threat. A woman believes herself entitled to everything with her first lover. Softly I murmured in her ear: "You're my first lover, too . . . since my marriage."

The sweetness in my voice disguised the attempt to make the two of us even.

A little later I left her, because under no circumstances did I want to arrive late for lunch. Before leaving, I again took out the envelope that I called "of good intentions" because an excellent intention had created it. I felt the need to pay, in order to feel freer. Carla again gently refused that money, and I then became very angry, but I was able to restrain myself from revealing that anger only by shouting very sweet words. I said that I had achieved the summit of my desires in possessing her, and that now I wanted to have the sense of possessing her even further by supporting her completely. Therefore she should take care not to make me angry because I then suffered too much. Wanting to rush off, I summarized in a few words my notion, which became – shouted like this – very curt.

"Are you my mistress? Then your maintenance is my duty."

Frightened, she stopped resisting and accepted the envelope, while she looked at me anxiously reckoning what might be the truth, my outcry of hate or the words of love with which she was granted everything she had desired. She was a bit reassured when, before leaving, I touched her brow with my lips. On the stairs I had the suspicion that now, with the money at her disposal, having heard me assume responsibility for her future, she would show Copler the door as well if he were to come to her that afternoon. I would have liked to climb back up those stars and exhort her not to compromise me by such an action. But there was no time and I had to run off.

I fear that the doctor, who will read this manuscript of mine, may think that Carla, too, would have been an interesting subject for psychoanalysis. It will seem to him that her submission, preceded by the dismissal of the voice teacher, was perhaps too quick. It seemed to me also that as a reward for her love she had expected too many concessions from me. It required many, many months for me to understand the poor girl better. Probably she had allowed herself to be possessed in order to be free of Copler's upsetting tutelage, and it must have been a very painful surprise for her to realize that she had given herself in vain because her heaviest burden, namely having to sing, would continue to oppress her. She was still in my arms when she learned that she would have to go on singing. Whence the rage and the grief that couldn't find the right words. For different reasons each of us thus uttered some very strange words. When she loved me, she regained all the naturalness that calculation had robbed her of. I was never natural with her.

Running away, I thought still: "If she knew how much I love my wife, she would behave differently." When she did come to know it, she behaved, in fact, differently.

In the open air I breathed freedom and didn't feel the sorrow of having compromised it. I had time until tomorrow, and I would perhaps find some refuge from the difficulties that were threatening me. Hurrying home, I even had the courage to blame it all on the social order, as if it had been responsible for my past behavior. It should have been capable, I felt, of allowing a man to make love now and then (not always), without his having to fear the consequences, even with women he doesn't love at all. There was no trace of remorse

in me. Therefore I believe remorse is generated not by regret
for a bad deed already committed, but by the recognition of
one's own guilty propensity. The upper part of the body bends
over to study and judge the other part and finds it deformed.
The repulsion then felt is called remorse. Even in ancient
tragedy the victim wasn't returned to life, and yet the remorse
passed. This meant that the deformity was cured, and that the
tears of others had no further importance. Where could there
be any room for remorse in me, when, with so much joy and
so much affection, I was speeding to my legitimate wife? For a
long time I had not felt so pure.

At lunch, making no effort at all, I was happy and affectionate with Augusta. That day there was not a false note
between us. Nothing excessive: I was as I should be with the
woman honestly and surely mine. At other times there
were excessive shows of affection on my part, but only when
there was a struggle going on in my spirit between the two
women. Then, through excessive displays of affection, it was
easier for me to keep Augusta from seeing that between the
two of us there lay the shadow, momentarily fairly powerful,
of another woman. I can also say that for this reason Augusta
preferred me when I was not entirely and most sincerely hers.

I myself was somewhat amazed by my calm, and I attributed
it to the fact that I had succeeded in making Carla accept that
envelope of good intentions. Of course, I didn't believe that,
with it, I had paid her off. But it seemed to me that I had begun
to buy an indulgence. Unfortunately, for the entire duration of
my affair with Carla, money remained my principal concern.
At every opportunity I laid some aside in a well-hidden place
in my library, to be ready to deal with any demands from the
mistress of whom I was so afraid. Thus, when Carla abandoned
me and left me holding that money, it served to pay for
something quite different.

We were to spend the evening at my father-in-law's house,
at a dinner to which only family members had been invited

and which was meant to replace the traditional banquet, prelude to the wedding being celebrated two days later. Guido
wanted to take advantage of Giovanni's improvement in order
to be married, for he was afraid the condition wouldn't last.

I went with Augusta to my father-in-law's early in the
afternoon. Along the way I reminded her that, the day before,
she had suspected I was unhappy because of that wedding. She
was ashamed of her suspicion and I went on at length about
that innocence of mine. Hadn't I come home, without even
remembering that the same evening there was the celebration
preparatory to the wedding?

Although there were no other guests except us family members, the older Malfentis wanted the banquet to unfold in all
solemnity. Augusta had been asked to come and supervise the
dining room and the table. Alberta would have nothing to do
with such matters. A short time before, she had been awarded a
prize for a one-act play, and now she was eagerly girding herself
to reform the nation's theater. So we bustled around that table,
I and Augusta, assisted by a maid and by Luciano, a boy from
Giovanni's office, who showed as much feeling for order in the
household as he did for order in the office.

I helped carry some flowers to the table and arranged them
neatly.

"You see?" I said, joking, to Augusta, "I even contribute to
their happiness. If they asked me also to make up the nuptial
bed, I would do it with the same untroubled brow!"

Later we went to see the bridal pair, who had just returned
from a formal visit. They had occupied the most secluded corner
of the living room, and I suppose that until we arrived they had
been cuddling. The bride hadn't even changed her afternoon
dress and was very pretty, flushed as she was by the heat.

I believe that the couple, to hide any sign of the kisses they
had exchanged, wanted to persuade us that they had been
discussing science. It was nonsense, perhaps even improper!
Did they want to exclude us from their intimacy, or did they

believe their kisses could cause someone pain? In any case, this didn't spoil my good humor. Guido told me Ada wouldn't believe him when he said that certain wasps could, with their sting, paralyze other insects even stronger than they, then preserve them, paralyzed, alive and fresh, as nourishment for their offspring. I thought I recalled that something so monstrous did exist in nature, but at this point I was unwilling to give Guido any satisfaction.

"You think I'm a wasp, so you're aiming at me?" I said to him, laughing.

We left the couple so they could devote themselves to happier things. I, however, was beginning to find the afternoon quite long, and I wanted to go home and await the dinner hour in my study.

In the vestibule we found Dr. Paoli, coming out of my father-in-law's bedroom. He was a young doctor who, nevertheless, had already been able to acquire a good clientele. He was very blond and ruddy and white, like an overgrown boy. His powerful physique, however, was so dominated by his eyes that his whole person seemed serious and imposing. His eyeglasses made him appear bigger, and his gaze clung to things like a caress. Now that I know very well both him and Dr. S. – the psychoanalysis man – it seems to me that the latter's eyes are more deliberately inquiring, whereas in Dr. Paoli they indicate his tireless curiosity. Paoli sees his patient precisely, but also the patient's wife and the chair on which he is sitting. God only knows which of the two men treats his patients better! During my father-in-law's sickness, I often went to Paoli to persuade him not to tell the family that the threatened catastrophe was imminent, and I remember one day, looking at me longer than I liked, he said to me, smiling: "Why, you adore your wife!"

He was a good observer, because I did indeed at that moment adore my wife, who was suffering so much because of her father's illness and whom I was betraying daily.

He told us Giovanni was even better than the day before. Now he had no other reservations because the season was very favorable, and he believed the bridal couple could set off on their journey without concern. "Naturally," he added cautiously, "there could be unpredictable complications." His prognosis came true, because unpredictable complications followed.

As he was taking his leave, he remembered that we knew a man named Copler, to whose bedside he had been called that very day for a consultation. He found that the man had been seized with a kidney paralysis. He told us the paralysis had been heralded by a horrible toothache. Here his prognosis was grave but, as usual, attenuated by a doubt.

"His life could even be prolonged, if he survives to see the sun tomorrow morning."

Augusta, in her compassion, had tears in her eyes and begged me to hurry at once to our poor friend. After some hesitation, I obeyed her wish, and gladly, because my spirit was suddenly filled with Carla. How hard he had been on our poor girl! And now, with Copler gone, she was left there, alone, on that landing, not compromising in the least, because cut off now from any communication with my world. I had to hasten to her and erase the impression my harsh attitude must have made that morning.

But, prudently, I went first to Copler. I had, after all, to be able to tell Augusta I had seen him.

I already knew the modest but comfortable and decent little apartment where Copler lived in Corsia Stadion. An old pensioner let him have three of the five rooms. I was received by this landlord, a heavy man, short of breath, with red eyes, who paced restlessly up and down a short, dark corridor. He told me the regular doctor had only just left, after having verified that Copler was in the throes of death. The old man spoke in a low voice, always gasping, as if he were afraid to disturb the peace of the dying man. I lowered my voice as well. It is a form of respect, this way we men feel, though it is not exactly certain whether the dying would not prefer to be accompanied along the last stretch of their path by bright, strong voices that would remind them of life.

The old man told me the patient was being tended by a nun. Filled with awe, I stopped for some while at the door of that room where poor Copler, with his death-rattle, its rhythm so precise, was measuring out his final hours. His noisy respiration was composed of two sounds: the one produced by the air he inhaled seemed hesitant; the other, born from the exhaled air, seemed precipitous. A haste to die? A pause followed the two sounds, and I thought that when the pause was lengthened, then the new life would begin.

The old man wanted me to go into the room, but I wouldn't. I had had my fill of dying men who glared at me with an expression of reproach.

I didn't wait for that pause to lengthen, and I hurried to Carla. I knocked at the door of her study, which was locked, but nobody answered. Losing patience, I started kicking the door, and then, behind me, the door of the living room opened. The voice of Carla's mother asked: "Who is it?"

Then the timorous old woman looked out, and when, in the yellow light that came from her kitchen, she recognized me, I realized that her face was covered by an intense flush heightened by the transparent whiteness of her hair. Carla wasn't in, and she offered to go fetch the key to the study to admit me to that room, which she considered the only one worthy of receiving me. But I told her not to take the trouble, I entered the kitchen and sat down unceremoniously on a wooden chair. Under a pot on the stove, a modest little mound of charcoal was glowing. I told her not to neglect supper on my account. She reassured me. She was preparing some beans, which can never be overdone. The humble food being cooked in the house, whose cost I would now have to sustain by myself, moved me and allayed the irritation I felt at not having found my mistress ready.

The Signora remained standing despite my repeated invitations to her to sit down. Brusquely I told her I had come bearing some very bad news for Signorina Carla: Copler was dying.

The old woman's arms dropped to her sides, and she immediately felt the need to sit.

"Oh, my goodness!" she murmured. "What will we do?"

Then she remembered that what lay ahead of Copler was worse than what was in store for her, and she added a lament: "Poor gentleman! Always so kind!"

Her face was already bathed in tears. Obviously she didn't know that if the poor man hadn't died at the right moment, she would have been thrown out of that house. This thought also reassured me. How surrounded I was by the utmost discretion!

I wanted to reassure her, and I told her that what Copler had done for them till now, I would continue doing. She protested that it wasn't for herself that she was crying, since she knew the two of them were surrounded by such good people, but for the fate of their great benefactor.

She wanted to know what illness he was dying of. Telling her how the catastrophe had been announced, I remembered that discussion I had had with Copler some time before on the utility of pain. So the nerves of his teeth had been agitated and had begun calling for help because, a meter away from them, his kidneys had ceased functioning. I was so indifferent to the fate of my friend, whose death-rattle I had heard only a short while before, that I was beginning to play with his ideas. If he had still been present to hear me, I would have told him that, after this, we could understand how, in the imaginary sick man, the nerves could legitimately ache for a sickness that had burst out at a distance of some kilometers.

Between the old woman and me there was very little left to talk about, and I agreed to go and wait for Carla in her study.

I picked up the Garcia and tried to read a few pages. But the art of singing had little effect on me.

The old woman joined me again. She was uneasy because she didn't see Carla arriving. She told me that the girl had gone to buy some dishes that they urgently needed.

My patience was just about exhausted. Angrily I asked her: "Did you break some dishes? Couldn't you be more careful?"

And so I rid myself of the old woman, who went off, muttering: "Only two . . . yes, I broke them . . ."

This procured me a moment of hilarity because I knew that all the crockery in the house had been destroyed, and not by the old woman, but by Carla herself. Later I learned that Carla was anything but gentle with her mother, who therefore was deathly afraid of talking too much about her daughter's business with her protectors. It seems that once, naïvely, she had told Copler how Carla was irritated by the voice lessons. Copler became enraged with Carla, who then took it out on her mother.

And so, when my delightful mistress finally came to me, I loved her violently and angrily. Enchanted, she stammered: "And I was doubting your love! The whole day I was tormented by a wish to kill myself for having succumbed to a man who immediately afterwards treated me so badly!"

I explained to her that I was often gripped by severe headaches. I found myself in a state that, if I hadn't bravely resisted, would have had me racing back to Augusta, so I spoke again of those pains, and thus I could control myself. I continued, constructing myself. Meanwhile, we mourned poor Copler together, really together!

For that matter, Carla wasn't indifferent to the horrible end of her benefactor. As she spoke, she went pale: "I know what I'm like," she said. "For a long time I'll be afraid to be alone. Even when he was alive, he frightened me so!"

And, for the first time, shyly, she suggested I spend the whole night with her. I wasn't even thinking about it, and

I couldn't have prolonged my stay in that room even for another half hour. But, always careful not to reveal to the poor girl my soul, of which I was the first to complain, I raised some objections, saying such a thing was impossible because in this house there was also her mother. With genuine disdain she pursed her lips. "We would bring the bed in here; Mamma wouldn't dare spy on me."

Then I told her about the wedding dinner awaiting me at home, but then I also felt obliged to tell her I would never be able to spend the night with her. Observing the vow to be kind that I had just made, I succeeded in controlling my every tone, so I sounded affectionate, but it seemed to me that any other concession I might grant her, or even lead her to hope for, would be the equivalent of a renewed betrayal of Augusta, which I didn't want to commit.

At that moment I sensed what my strongest bonds to Carla were: my affectionate intentions and then the lies I told about my relations with Augusta, which gradually, as time went on, would have to be revised or rather expunged. Therefore I began the process that very evening, naturally with all due prudence because it was still too easy to recall the fruit that my falsehood had borne. I told her that I strongly felt my obligations toward my wife, who was such an admirable woman that she surely deserved to be loved better, and I would never want her to learn how I betrayed her.

Carla embraced me.

"This is how I love you: kind and sweet, the way I imagined you the first time. I will never try to do any harm to that poor thing."

I didn't like to hear Augusta called a poor thing, but I was grateful to poor Carla for her meekness. It was good that she didn't hate my wife. I wanted to show her my gratitude, and I looked around for a sign of affection. In the end I found it. I gave her, too, a laundry: I permitted her not to recall the singing teacher.

Carla had a burst of affection, which rather annoyed me, but I bravely endured it. Then she told me that she would never give up singing. She sang all day long, but in her own way. In fact, she wanted me to hear a song of hers immediately. But I would have none of it and, like a coward, I ran off. So I think that she contemplated suicide also that night, but I didn't give her time to tell me.

I went back to Copler, because I had to take Augusta the latest news of the sick man, to make her believe I had spent all that time with him. Copler had died about two hours previously, almost immediately after I left him. Accompanied by the old pensioner, who had continued pacing up and down the little corridor, I entered the mortuary chamber. The corpse, already dressed, lay on the bed's bare mattress. He held a crucifix in his hands. In a low voice the pensioner told me that all the formalities had been taken care of, and that a niece of the departed would come and stay through the night by the corpse.

I could go away then, knowing my poor friend was being given those few attentions he might need, but I remained for a moment to look at him. I would have liked to feel a sincere tear spring from my eyes, in mourning for the poor man who had struggled hard against his disease until he tried to come to an agreement with it. "It's so sad!" I said. The disease for which so many medicines existed had brutally killed him. It seemed a mockery. But my tears were absent. Copler's emaciated face had never seemed to me so strong as it did in the rigidity of death. It seemed fashioned by a chisel in a colored marble, and no one could foresee the imminent putrefaction looming over it. It was still a real life that his face displayed: it disapproved of me haughtily perhaps, or perhaps also of Carla, who didn't want to sing. For a moment I started, when it seemed that the corpse's death-rattle was recommencing. I immediately regained my critical calm as I realized that what had seemed a rattle to me was only the pensioner's gasping, exacerbated by his emotion.

He then saw me to the door and begged me to recommend him if I found anyone who might need these lodgings: "As you have seen, even in a situation like this, I was able to do my duty, and even more, much more!"

For the first time he raised his voice in which there echoed a resentment, no doubt directed at poor Copler, who had left the rooms vacant without proper advance notice. I rushed off, promising everything he wanted.

At my father-in-law's, I found the party had gone to the table at that moment. They asked me for news, and, rather than mar the gaiety of that feast, I said Copler was still alive and so there was still some hope.

It seemed to me the gathering was quite sad. Perhaps I formed this impression when I saw my father-in-law condemned to clear broth and a glass of milk, while around him the others were heaping their plates with the choicest foods. He had nothing but free time, and he spent it watching the mouths of the others. Seeing how Signor Francesco devoted himself actively to the antipasto, he murmured: "And to think, he's two years older than me!"

Then, when Signor Francesco arrived at his third glass of white wine, Giovanni grumbled in a low voice: "That makes three! I hope it turns to gall!"

The augury wouldn't have bothered me if I, too, had not eaten and drunk at that table, and if I hadn't known that the same metamorphosis would be wished for the wine that passed my lips. Therefore I started eating and drinking covertly. I exploited every moment when my father-in-law stuck his big nose into the cup of milk, or replied to some remark addressed to him, to swallow some great morsels or to gulp down huge glasses of wine. Alberta, simply out of a desire to make people laugh, warned Augusta that I was drinking too much. My wife, jokingly, wagged a threatening forefinger at me. This in itself wasn't bad, but it was bad because now it was no longer worth the trouble to eat in secret. Giovanni, who until then had almost forgotten about me, peered over his eyeglasses at me with a look of genuine hatred.

He said: "I've never overindulged in drinking or eating. Anyone who does isn't a real man, he's a – " and he repeated several times the last word, which was by no means a compliment.

Thanks to the effect of the wine, that offensive word, hailed by general laughter, kindled in my soul a truly unreasonable desire for revenge. I attacked my father-in-law at his weakest point: his sickness. I shouted that it wasn't the drinker or eater who wasn't a real man, it was the man who feebly obeyed the doctor's orders. I, in his case, would have been independent, quite different. At my daughter's wedding – out of love, if for no other reason – I wouldn't have allowed anyone to prevent me from eating and drinking.

Enraged, Giovanni said: "I'd like to see you in my shoes!"

"Isn't it enough to see me in my own? Have I given up smoking, by any chance?"

It was the first time I managed to boast of my weakness, and I immediately lit a cigarette to illustrate my words. They all laughed and told Signor Francesco how my life was full of last cigarettes. But that one wasn't the last, and I felt strong and mettlesome. However, I immediately lost the others' support when I poured some wine for Giovanni, into his large water glass. They were afraid Giovanni would drink and shouted to stop him, until Signora Malfenti managed to seize that glass and move it out of the way.

"You really would like to kill me?" Giovanni asked mildly, looking at me with curiosity. "Wine turns you nasty!" He hadn't made the slightest move toward the wine I had offered him.

I felt really downcast and defeated. I would almost have flung myself at my father-in-law's feet to beg his forgiveness. But that, too, seemed a gesture prompted by the wine, and I rejected it. In begging his forgiveness, I would have confessed my guilt, whereas the banquet was continuing and would still last long enough to afford me the opportunity to make amends for this first joke, which had come off so badly. In this world there's time for everything. Not all drunks succumb immediately to wine's every prompting. When I have drunk too much, I analyze my retching as when I am sober and probably with the same result. I went on observing myself, to understand how I had conceived that evil idea of harming my father-in-law. And I realized I was tired, mortally tired. If they knew the sort of day I'd been through, they would forgive me. I had possessed and violently abandoned a woman two separate times, and I had twice returned to my wife, only to betray her twice. It was my luck that, at this point, into my memory there intruded that corpse over which I had tried in vain to weep, and the thought of the two women vanished; otherwise I would have ended up talking about Carla. Didn't I always have a yearning to confess, even when I hadn't been made more magnanimous by the effect of wine? In the end I spoke about Copler. I wanted them all to know that I had lost my great friend that day. They would forgive my behavior.

I cried out that Copler was dead, really dead, and that I had kept silent about it till then, rather than sadden them. And lo and behold! Finally I felt tears come to my eyes, and I had to look away to conceal them.

The others all laughed because they didn't believe me, so then I became stubborn, wine's most obvious effect. I described the dead man: "He looked as if he'd been sculpted by Michelangelo: so hard, in the most enduring marble."

There was a general silence, interrupted by Guido, who cried: "And now you no longer feel obliged not to sadden us?"

The observation was fair. I had failed to keep a vow that I remembered! Was there no way to make amends? I fell to laughing uproariously.

"Fooled you! He's alive and getting better."

They all looked at me, trying to get their bearings.

"He's better," I added seriously. "He recognized me and he even smiled at me."

They all believed me, but there was general indignation. Giovanni asserted that if he weren't afraid of hurting himself in making such an effort, he would have thrown a plate at my head. In fact, it was unforgivable of me to trouble the party with an invented piece of news like that. If it had been true, there would have been no blame. Wouldn't it then be better for me to tell them the truth again? Copler was dead, and as soon as I was alone, I would find my tears ready to mourn him, spontaneous and abundant. I sought the words, but Signora Malfenti, with her *grande dame* gravity, interrupted me: "Let's leave that poor sick man alone for the present. We'll think about him tomorrow!"

I obeyed at once, even with my thoughts, which broke away from the dead man definitively: Good-bye! Wait for me! I'll come back to you the moment this is over!

It was the time for toasts. Giovanni had obtained the doctor's permission to sip a glass of champagne at this moment. Gravely he superintended the pouring of his wine, and he refused to raise the glass to his lips until it was brimming. After having expressed serious, straightforward wishes for Ada and Guido, he drained it slowly to the last drop. Glowering at me, he said he had dedicated that final sip to my health. To ward off this augury, which I knew was not benevolent, under the table I crossed my fingers, on both hands.

My recollection of the rest of the evening is a bit muddled. I know that a little later, prompted by Augusta, everyone around that table said all sorts of good things about me, holding me up as a model husband. I was forgiven everything, and even my father-in-law grew more mellow. He added, however, that he hoped Ada's husband would prove good like me, but at the same time also a better businessman and, especially, one who . . . and he groped for the word. He couldn't find it, and no one among us tried to supply it, not even Signor

Francesco, who, having seen me for the first time that very morning, could know me only slightly. For my part I didn't take offense. How the spirit is soothed by the knowledge that one has done great wrongs and must make up for them! I accepted all the insolences in a grateful spirit, provided that they were accompanied by affection, which I didn't deserve. And in my mind, confused by weariness and wine, serene on every score, I cherished the picture of myself as the good husband, who never becomes less good for being adulterous. It was important to be good, very, very good, and nothing else mattered. With my hand I blew a kiss to Augusta, who received it with a grateful smile.

Then there were some at the table who wanted to take advantage of my drunkenness for a good laugh, and I was forced to propose a toast. I finally agreed because at that moment it seemed to me it would be a fine thing to be enabled to express thus in public my good intentions. Not that I had any self-doubt at that moment, because I felt myself to be exactly as described, but I would become even better were I to assert a resolution in front of so many people who, in a certain sense, would be underwriting it. And so it was that in the toast I spoke only of myself and of Augusta. For the second time in those days I related the story of my marriage. I had falsified it for Carla, keeping silent about my being in love with my wife; here I falsified it differently because I didn't mention the two people so important in the story of my marriage, namely Ada and Alberta. I told of my hesitation, for which I could never console myself, as it had robbed me of so much time for happiness. Then, out of gallantry, I attributed some hesitations also to Augusta. But she denied them, laughing merrily.

With some difficulty I recovered the thread of my speech. I narrated how at last we had gone on our honeymoon and how we had made love in all the museums of Italy. I was so totally immersed, up to my neck, in falsehood that I also added this lying detail that served no purpose. And yet they say that in wine there is truth.

Augusta interrupted me a second time to set things straight, and told how she had had to avoid museums because of the danger that the masterpieces were risking from me. She didn't realize that in this way she was revealing the falsity of more than just that detail! If there had been an observer at the table, he would quickly have discovered the nature of that love I was portraying in a setting where it could not have taken place.

I resumed the long, drab speech, telling of the arrival at our house and how both of us had begun perfecting it, adding this or that, even including a laundry.

Still laughing, Augusta interrupted me again: "This party isn't in our honor; it's in honor of Ada and Guido! Talk about them!"

All agreed noisily. I also laughed, realizing that thanks to me we had achieved a genuine, noisy jollity that is the norm on such occasions. But I could find nothing more to say. I felt as if I had talked for hours. I swallowed several more glasses of wine, one after the other.

"Here's to Ada!" I straightened up for a moment to see if she had crossed her fingers under the tablecloth.

"Here's to Guido!" And I added, after gulping down the wine: "With all my heart," forgetting that at the first glass I hadn't added a similar declaration.

"Here's to your firstborn!"

And I would have drunk a number of those glasses for all their children, if I had not finally been stopped. For those poor innocents I would have drunk all the wine remaining on that table.

Then everything turned even darker. I recall clearly only one thing: my chief concern was not to seem drunk. I held myself erect and spoke little. I distrusted myself, I felt the need to analyze every word before saying it. While the general talk continued, I had to renounce taking part in it because I wasn't given time to clarify my murky thinking. I wanted to broach a subject myself, and I said to my father-in-law: "Have you heard Extérieur has dropped two points?"

I had mentioned something that didn't trouble me in the least, something I had overheard at the Bourse; I wanted only to talk about business, serious matters that a drunk usually wouldn't recall. It seemed to me that for my father-in-law this was not a matter of such indifference, and he accused me of being a bird of ill omen. With him I could never get anything right.

Then I turned to my neighbor, Alberta. We talked about love. To her it was of interest in theory, and to me, for the moment, it was of no interest whatsoever in practice. Therefore it was the perfect subject to talk about. She asked me for some ideas, and I immediately discovered one that seemed to me obvious from my experience of that very day. A woman was an object whose value fluctuated far more than any stock on the market. Alberta misunderstood me and thought I meant to say something well-known to everyone: namely that a woman of a certain age had quite a different value from one of another age. I made myself clearer: a woman might have a high value at a certain hour of the morning, none at all at noon, and then in the afternoon be worth twice her morning value, only to end in the evening at an actually negative value. I explained the concept of negative value: a woman had that kind of value when a man was calculating how much he'd be willing to pay to send her very far away from himself.

Still the poor playwright didn't see the accuracy of my discovery, while I was sure of myself, recalling the shifts of value that, just today, Carla and Augusta had suffered. The wine then intervened when I chose to explain further, and I veered completely off course.

"You see," I said to her, "supposing that you now have the value of x and you allow me to press your little foot with mine, your value immediately increases by another x at least."

I accompanied immediately the words with the action.

Bright red, she withdrew her foot and, wishing to seem witty, she said: "But this is practice, not theory. I'll put it to Augusta."

I have to confess that I, too, felt that little foot as something quite apart from arid theory, but I protested, crying out with the most innocent manner in the world: "It's pure theory, the purest! And it is wrong on your part to take it as anything else."

The fancies of wine are authentic events.

For a long time Alberta and I didn't forget that I had touched a part of her body, informing her that I did so to feel pleasure. Word had underlined action; and action, word. Until she married, she always had for me a smile and a blush; afterwards, on the contrary, blush and wrath. That's how women are. Every day that dawns brings them a new interpretation of the past. Their life cannot be very monotonous. For my part, on the contrary, the interpretation of that action of mine remained always the same: the theft of a small object of intense flavor; and it was Alberta's fault if, at a certain time, I tried to make her recall that action whereas later I would have paid any sum for it to be forgotten completely.

I recall, too, that before I left that house, something else happened, far more serious. I remained, for a moment, alone with Ada. Giovanni had long since gone to bed and the others were saying good night to Signor Francesco, whom Guido was escorting back to the hotel. I looked for a long time at Ada, all dressed in white lace, her arms and shoulders bare. For a long time I was dumb, although I felt the need to say something to her; but, having studied it, I suppressed any phrase that came to my lips. I remember I pondered also if it were permissible for me to say to her: How happy I am that you are marrying at last and that you are marrying my great friend Guido. Now finally all will be over between us.

I wanted to utter a lie because everyone knew that between us all had been over for several months, but it seemed to me that the lie was a lovely compliment, and it is certain that a woman, dressed like that, requires compliments and basks in them. After long reflection, however, I did nothing. I suppressed those words because in the sea of wine in which I was swimming, I found a plank that saved me. I thought that I would be wrong to risk Augusta's affection in order to please Ada, who didn't love me. But, in the doubt that troubled my mind for a few instants, and even afterwards, when I wrenched myself free of those words, I gave Ada such a look that she rose and left, after turning to observe me with fear, ready perhaps to start running.

Actually a glance of one's own can be remembered as well as a word, perhaps even better. It is more important than a word because in all the dictionary there is no word that can undress a woman. I know now that my glance then falsified the words I had conceived, simplifying them. To Ada's eyes, it had tried to penetrate her clothing and also her epidermis. And it had certainly meant: Would you like to come to bed with me at once?

Wine is a great danger, especially because it doesn't bring truth to the surface. Anything but the truth, indeed: it reveals especially the past and forgotten history of the individual rather than his present wish; it capriciously flings into the light also all the half-baked ideas with which in a more or less recent period one has toyed and then forgotten; it ignores the erasures and reads everything still legible in our heart. And we know there is no way of canceling anything there radically, as you can cancel a mistaken endorsement on a promissory note. All our history is always readable there, and wine shouts it, overlooking whatever life has subsequently added.

To go home, Augusta and I took a cab. In the darkness it seemed to me that it was my duty to embrace and kiss my wife, because that was how I had behaved many times in similar circumstances, and I feared that if I were not to do it, she might think something had changed between us. Nothing had changed between us: the wine also shouted this! She had married Zeno Cosini, who, unchanged, was at her side. What did it matter if, that day, I had possessed other women, whose number the wine, to make me happy, was increasing, placing among them Ada or Alberta, I can't recall which?

I remember that, falling asleep, for a moment I saw again Copler's marmoreal face on his deathbed. He seemed to demand justice, namely the tears I had promised him. But he didn't receive them now, either, because sleep embraced me, annihilating me. First, however, I apologized to the ghost: Wait a little longer. I'll be with you at once!

I never was with him again, because I didn't even attend his funeral. We had so much to do in the house, and I also outside it, that there was no time for him. We talked about him on occasion, but only to laugh, recalling how my wine had killed him over and over, then resuscitated him. Indeed, he remained proverbial in the family, and when the newspapers, as often happens, announce, then retract someone's death, we say: "Like poor Copler."

The next morning I rose with a bit of a headache. I felt the pain in my side slightly, perhaps because, while the effect of the wine lasted, I hadn't felt it at all, and I had promptly lost the habit of it. But, basically, I wasn't sad. Augusta contributed to my serenity, saying that it would have been terrible if I hadn't come to that wedding supper, because, until I arrived, she had felt she was at a wake. So I had no remorse about my behavior. Then I sensed that one thing only had not been forgiven me: that look at Ada!

When we met in the afternoon, Ada gave me her hand with an anxiety that increased my own. Perhaps, however, on her conscience she had that escape of hers, which had been far from polite. But also my glance had been a nasty action. I remembered exactly the movement of my eye, and I understood how she couldn't forget that she had been pierced by it. I had to make amends, assuming a carefully fraternal demeanor.

They say that when you suffer the effects of drinking too much, the best remedy is to drink some more. That morning, to restore my spirits, I went to Carla's. I went to her with the specific desire of living more intensely, which is what leads you back to alcohol, but, walking toward her, I would have desired her to inspire in me an intensity quite different from that of the day before. I was accompanied by intentions that were not very precise, but all honest. I knew I couldn't give her up immediately, but I could head toward that highly moral action little by little. Meanwhile I would go on talking to her about my wife. With no surprise, one fine day she would learn that I loved my wife. I had in my pocket another envelope with some money, ready for any development.

I arrived at Carla's, and a quarter of an hour later she reproached me with a word that, in its justice, echoed for a long time in my ear: "How crude you are, in love!" I am not aware of having been crude just then. I had begun talking to her about my wife, and the praises attributed to Augusta had sounded to Carla's ears like so many reproaches addressed to her.

Then it was Carla who hurt me. To pass the time, I had told her how I had grown annoyed at the banquet, especially because of a toast I had proposed, which had been totally out of place.

Carla remarked: "If you loved your wife, you wouldn't make unsuitable toasts at her father's table."

And she gave me a kiss to reward me for the scant love I felt for my wife.

Meanwhile the same desire to intensify my life, which had brought me to Carla, would have led me at once back to Augusta, who was the only one with whom I could have talked about my love for her. The wine taken as antidote was already too much, or else more wine was needed. But that day my rapport with Carla was to become sweeter, finally to be crowned by that fondness which – as I learned later – the poor young girl deserved. She had volunteered several times to sing me a song, eager to have my opinion. But I wanted nothing to do with her singing, which no longer interested me, not even in its naïveté. I told her that since she refused to study, it wasn't worth her singing anymore.

My offense was serious, and it made her suffer. Seated beside me, to keep me from seeing her tears, she looked motionless at her hands, folded in her lap. She repeated her reproach.

"How rough you must be with someone you don't love, if you are like this with me!"

Good devil that I am, I let myself be touched by those tears, and I begged Carla to split my ears with her big voice in the little room. Now she turned reluctant, and I had to threaten to leave if she didn't oblige me. I have to admit that for an instant I thought I had found a pretext to regain my freedom, at least temporarily, but at that threat, my humble servant, her eyes lowered, went and sat at the piano. She then devoted a very brief moment to collecting her thoughts and ran her hand over her face as if to dispel every cloud. She succeeded with a promptitude that surprised me, and her face, when that hand revealed it, bore no sign of her earlier sorrow.

I immediately had a great surprise. Carla told her song, narrated it; she didn't shout it. The shouting — as she then told me — had been forced on her by her teacher; now she had dismissed it, along with him. The Triestine song she sang,

> *Fazzo l'amor xe vero*
> *Cossa ghe xe de mal*
> *Volè che a sedes'ani*
> *Stio là come un cocal ...*

is a kind of story or confession. Carla's eyes shone slyly and confessed even more than the words. There was no fear of shattered eardrums, and I went over to her, surprised and enchanted. I sat beside her and she then retold the song directly to me, half-closing her eyes to say, in the lightest and purest tone, that the sixteen-year-old wanted freedom and love.

For the first time I saw Carla's little face exactly: the purest oval marked by the deep, curved hollow of the eyes and the delicate cheekbones, made even purer by a snowy whiteness, now that she kept her face turned toward me and to the light, therefore not obscured by any shadow. And those soft lines in that flesh, which seemed transparent yet concealed the blood so well and the veins, perhaps too weak to appear, demanded devotion and protection.

Now I was ready to give her much devotion and protection, unconditionally, even at the moment when I would be so prepared to go back to Augusta, because Carla at that moment asked nothing but a paternal fondness that I could grant without betrayal. What satisfaction! I remained there with Carla, I gave her what her little oval face asked for, and yet I wasn't moving away from Augusta! My fondness for Carla became more delicate. After that, if I felt the need of honesty and purity, I no longer had to abandon her; I could stay with her and change the subject.

Was this new sweetness due to her little oval face, which I had then discovered, or to her musical talent? Undeniably, to the talent! The strange little Triestine song ends with a strophe in which the same young girl asserts that she is old and decrepit and that by now she needs no freedom except to die. Carla continued slyly to infuse gaiety into the poor verses. It was still youth feigning age, the better to proclaim its rights from that new point of view.

When she finished and found me filled with admiration, she, too, for the first time, while loving me, was also sincerely fond of me. She knew the little song would please me more than what her maestro taught her.

"Too bad," she added sadly, "that unless you want to sing in *cafés chantants*, there's no way you can earn a living from it."

I easily convinced her this wasn't how things stood. In this world there were many great artists who spoke their music and didn't sing.

She made me give her some names. She was overjoyed to learn how important her art might become.

"I know," she added naïvely, "that this kind of singing is much harder than the other kind, where you just have to yell at the top of your lungs."

I smiled and didn't argue. Her art was also difficult, surely, and she knew it because that was the only art she knew. That little song had cost her long hours of study. She had said it over and over, correcting the intonation of every word, every note. Now she was studying another, but she wouldn't have it mastered for a few more weeks. Until then she wouldn't let me hear it.

Delicious moments followed in that room where, previously, only scenes of brutality had taken place. Now a career was opening before Carla. The career that would free me from her. Very similar to the one Copler had dreamed of for her! I suggested I find her a maestro. At first the word frightened her, but then she let herself be convinced easily when I told her she could give it a try, remaining free to dismiss him when he seemed tiresome to her, or of little use.

With Augusta, too, I felt that day went very well. My spirit was calm, as if I had returned from a stroll and not from Carla's house, or as Copler's spirit must have been when he left that house on days when the women had given him no cause to become angry. I relished it as if I had come upon an oasis. For me and for my health, it would have been very grave if all my long affair with Carla had proceeded in eternal agitation. From that day on, as a result of this esthetic beauty, things progressed more calmly, with the slight interruptions necessary to rekindle my love for Carla and my love for Augusta. True, my every visit to Carla meant an infidelity to Augusta, but all was soon forgotten in a bath of health and of good intentions. And the good intention was not brutal and exciting as it had been when in my throat I had the desire to tell Carla I would never see her again. I was sweet and paternal: here, too, I was thinking of her career. Abandoning a woman every day only to come running after her the next day was an exertion that my poor heart would have been unable to withstand. So, on the contrary, Carla remained always in my power, and I turned her first in one direction, then in another.

For a long time the good intentions were not strong enough to make me rush around the city seeking the teacher who would be right for Carla. I toyed with the good intention, while remaining seated. Then one fine day Augusta confided in me that she felt she was to be a mother, and then my intention for a moment grew gigantic and Carla had her maestro.

I had hesitated so long because it was obvious that even without a teacher, Carla had been able to set to work seriously in her new art. Every week she learned a different song to sing for me, its words and its tone both carefully analyzed. Certain notes needed a bit more polish, but perhaps in the end they would be smoothed out. For me, a decisive proof that Carla was a true artist was the way she constantly perfected her songs, never renouncing the best features, which she had grasped at the very start. I often persuaded her to repeat her first song, and every time I found some new and effective accent had been added. Given her ignorance, it was marvelous that in her great effort to develop a strong expressiveness, she had never thought to cram false or exaggerated sounds into the song. Like a true artist, she added every day a pebble to her little edifice, and all the rest remained intact. The song was not stereotyped, but rather the sentiment that dictated it. Before singing, Carla always ran her hand over her face, and behind that hand there was a moment of thought, enough to immerse her in the little playlet she had to construct. A play that was not always puerile. The ironic mentor of

Rosina te xe nata in un casoto

threatened, but not too seriously. The singer seemed to suggest she knew this was an everyday story. Carla thought differently, but in the end she achieved the same result.

"I'm on Rosina's side, because otherwise the song wouldn't be worth singing," she said.

Sometimes Carla might unconsciously rekindle my love for Augusta, and my remorse. In fact, this occurred every time she ventured an offensive movement against the position so firmly occupied by my wife. Carla still harbored the desire to have me all to herself for a whole night; she confessed to me that since we had never slept side by side, it seemed to her we were not close. Wishing to acquire the habit of being sweeter to her, I didn't squarely refuse to content her, but almost always I thought it wouldn't be possible to do such a thing unless I was resigned to finding Augusta in the morning at a window, where she had waited for me the whole night. And anyway, wouldn't this be an added betrayal of my wife? At times, namely when I was rushing to Carla, filled with desire, I felt inclined to grant her wish, but immediately afterwards I saw how impossible and unsuitable it was. But in this way for a long time neither the prospect of the thing nor its achievement could be eliminated. Apparently we agreed: sooner or later we would spend a whole night together. Meanwhile it had become possible because I had induced the Gerco women to evict those tenants who separated their house into two parts, and Carla finally had her own bedroom.

Now it happened that shortly after Guido's wedding, my father-in-law was seized by the attack that was to kill him, and I unwisely told Carla that my wife had to spend a night at her father's bedside to allow my mother-in-law some rest. Carla insisted I spend with her that same night, so painful for my wife. I lacked the courage to rebel against this whim, and I resigned myself to it with a heavy heart.

I prepared for that sacrifice. I didn't go to Carla in the morning, and so I hurried to her in the evening with total desire, telling myself also that it was childish to believe I was betraying Augusta more gravely because I was doing it at a moment when she was suffering for other reasons. Therefore I managed even to become impatient when poor Augusta detained me, showing me how I should arrange the things I might need for supper, for the night, and also for my coffee the next morning.

Carla received me in the studio. A little later her mother, who was also her servant, served us a delicious little supper, to which I added the pastries I had brought with me. The old woman then returned to clear away and, to tell the truth, I would have liked to go to bed at once, but it was really still too early, and Carla persuaded me to wait and to hear her sing. She went through her entire repertoire, and that was surely the best part of those hours, because the eagerness with which I awaited my mistress served to increase the pleasure Carla's little songs had always given me.

"An audience would smother you with flowers and applause," I told her at a certain moment, forgetting that it would be impossible to put an entire audience in the state I was in.

Finally we lay down in the same bed in a little room, completely bare. It looked like a passage cut off by a partition. I still wasn't sleepy, and I was desperate at the thought that if I had been, I wouldn't have been able to sleep with so little air at my disposal.

Carla was called by her mother's shy voice. To answer, she went to the door and opened it a crack. I heard her angrily ask the old woman what she wanted. Shyly, the mother spoke some words whose meaning I couldn't grasp, and then Carla yelled before slamming the door in her mother's face: "Leave me alone! I told you before: tonight I'm sleeping in here!"

Thus I learned that Carla, tormented at night by fear, continued to sleep in her old bedroom with her mother, where she had a separate bed, while the one in which we were to sleep together remained empty. It was certainly out of fear that she had led me to behave so shamefully to Augusta. With a sly gaiety, which I didn't share, she confessed she felt safer with me than with her mother. I began to think a bit about this bed in such proximity to the solitary studio. I had never seen it before. I was jealous! A little later I was scornful also of the attitude Carla had assumed toward that poor mother of hers. She was made a bit differently from Augusta, who had renounced my company in order to help her parents. I am especially sensitive to lack of respect toward parents, I who bore my poor father's caprices with such resignation.

Carla couldn't be aware of my jealousy or of my scorn. I repressed the manifestations of jealousy, remembering how I had no right to be jealous, as I spent a good part of my days wishing that someone would relieve me of my mistress. Nor was there any purpose in displaying my scorn to the poor girl when I was already entertaining once more the wish to abandon her for good, though my scorn was now increased for the same reasons that a bit earlier would have provoked my jealousy. What I needed was to get away as soon as possible from that little room, containing no more than a cubic meter of air, which was also very hot.

I don't even remember clearly the excuse I invented to get away immediately. Breathless, I started getting dressed. I mentioned a key I had forgotten to give my wife, making it impossible for her to reenter our house, if she had to. I displayed the key, which was simply the one I always kept in my pocket, now offered as tangible evidence of the truth of my assertions. Carla didn't even try to stop me; she dressed and accompanied me downstairs, to light my way. In the darkness of the steps, she seemed to be studying me with an inquisitorial glance, which upset me. Was she beginning to understand me? It wasn't all that easy, seeing that I knew too well how to simulate. To thank her for allowing me to go, I continued applying my lips now and then to her cheeks, and I simulated being pervaded still by the same enthusiasm that had brought me to her. I then had no cause to doubt the success of my simulation. Shortly before, inspired by love, Carla had told me that the ugly name of Zeno, foisted on me by my parents, was certainly not what my appearance would lead anyone to imagine. She wanted me to be called Dario, and there, in the darkness, she said good-bye to me, calling me by that name. Then she noticed that the weather was threatening, and she offered to go and fetch me an umbrella. But I absolutely couldn't bear any more of her, and I ran off, still grasping that key, in whose authenticity I myself was beginning to believe.

The profound darkness of the night was broken every so often by dazzling flashes. The muttering thunder seemed very distant. The air was still calm and stifling as it had been in Carla's little room. Even the rare drops that fell were tepid. The sky, obviously, held a threat and I began running. In Corsia Stadion I was lucky to come upon a doorway still open and lighted, where I found refuge just in time! A moment later the cloudburst hit the street. The downpour was marked by a furious wind that seemed to bring with it also the thunder that, all of a sudden, was very very close. I started! It would have been truly compromising if I were killed by lightning, at this hour, in Corsia Stadion! Thank heaven my wife also knew that a man of eccentric tastes could run this far at night, and so there is always an excuse for everything.

I had to remain in that doorway for over an hour. It seemed constantly that the weather wanted to let up, but it would then promptly resume its fury in another form. Now it was hailing.

To keep me company, the building's concierge had come out, and I had to give him a few coins so he would postpone closing the great door. Then into the doorway came a gentleman dressed in white and dripping water. He was old, thin, bony. I never saw him again, but I cannot forget him thanks to the light in his black eyes and the energy that emanated from his whole person. He was cursing at having suffered such a soaking.

I have always enjoyed talking with people I don't know. With them I feel healthy and secure. It's actually restful. I have to be careful not to limp, and I'm safe.

When the weather finally let up, I went at once not to my house, but to my father-in-law's. At that moment I felt I had to report in at once and boast of being present.

My father-in-law had fallen asleep, and Augusta, assisted by a nun, could join me. She said I had done the right thing in coming, and she threw herself, weeping, into my arms. She had witnessed her father's horrible suffering.

She noticed how wet I was. She settled me in an easy chair and covered me with some blankets. Then she could stay with me for a while. I was very tired, and even in the short time she could spend at my side, I had to fight off sleep. I felt very innocent because, to begin with, I hadn't betrayed her by staying away from our conjugal domicile for a whole night. This innocence was so beautiful that I was tempted to enhance it. I began by uttering some words resembling a confession. I told her I felt weak and guilty, and, as she then looked at me, asking an explanation, I immediately drew my head back into my shell and, plunging into philosophy, I told her that I felt a sense of guilt at my every thought, my every breath.

"That's how monks and nuns think, too," Augusta said. "Who knows? Maybe we're punished like that for sins we're ignorant of!"

She spoke other words suited to accompany her tears, which continued to flow. It seemed to me she hadn't clearly understood the difference that lay between my thinking and that of those religious, but I didn't want to argue, and at the monotonous sound of the wind, which had risen again, and with the serenity given me also by my impulse toward confession, I sank into a long, restorative sleep.

*

When it came to the singing teacher, all was resolved in a few hours. I had long since chosen one, and to tell the truth, I had settled on his name first of all because he was the cheapest maestro in Trieste. In order not to compromise me, it was Carla herself who went to talk with him. I never saw him, but I must say that I now know a great deal about him and he is one of the people I most respect in this world. He must be a healthy simpleton, a rare thing for an artist who lived by his art, as did this Vittorio Lali. An enviable man, in other words, because he was talented and also healthy.

Meanwhile I sensed at once that Carla's voice had softened, becoming more flexible and secure. We had been afraid the maestro would impose some strain on her, as the man chosen by Copler had done. Perhaps this one adapted himself to Carla's wishes, but the fact is that he stuck to the genre she preferred. Only many months later did she realize that she had progressed from it slightly, becoming more refined. She no longer sang the little Triestine songs and then not even the Neapolitan one, but had moved on to old Italian songs and to Mozart and Schubert. I remember in particular a lullaby attributed to Mozart, and on days when I feel best the sadness of life and regret the unripe girl who was mine and whom I didn't love, the lullaby echoes in my ear like a reproach. Then I see Carla again, costumed as a mother who produces from her bosom the sweetest sounds to coax her baby to sleep. And yet she, who had been an unforgettable lover, couldn't be a good mother, any more than she had been a good daughter. But obviously the ability to sing like a mother is a talent that surpasses all others.

From Carla I learned her teacher's history. He had studied for a few years at the Conservatory in Vienna and had then come to Trieste, where he had the good fortune to work for our leading composer, who had gone blind. He wrote down the man's compositions at his dictation, but he also enjoyed the composer's trust, which the blind must grant totally. Thus he knew the man's intentions, his most mature convictions as well as his dreams, which remained always youthful. Soon the youth had absorbed into his spirit all music, including the music Carla needed. His appearance was also described to me: young, blond, fairly sturdy, carelessly dressed, a soft shirt not always freshly laundered, a cravat that must have been black, loose, and full, a slouch hat with exaggerated brim. A man of few words – according to what Carla told me, and I must believe her because a few months later he became talkative with her – as she informed me immediately – and completely intent on the task he had undertaken.

Soon my day suffered some complications. In the morning I brought to Carla's not only love but also a bitter jealousy, which became much less bitter in the course of the day. It seemed impossible to me that this youth did not take advantage of this fine, easy prey. Carla seemed amazed that I could think such a thing, but I was just as amazed to see her amazement. Had she forgotten how things had gone between me and her?

One day I came to her in a jealous rage and, frightened, she declared herself ready to discharge the maestro immediately. I don't believe her fright was produced only by the fear of seeing herself deprived of my support, because at that time I received from her demonstrations of affection beyond any possible doubt, which at times made me blissful, whereas, when I found myself in a different mood, they annoyed me, seeming acts hostile toward Augusta, in which, no matter how much it cost me, I was constrained to concur. Her offer embarrassed me. Whether I was in the moment of love or the moment of repentance, I was unwilling to accept a sacrifice from her. There had to be some communication between my two humors, and I didn't want to reduce my already scant freedom to pass from one to the other. Therefore I couldn't accept such a proposal, which instead made me all the more cautious, so that even when I was exasperated by jealousy, I could conceal it. My love became more wrathful, and in the end, when I desired her and even when I didn't desire her in the least, Carla seemed to me an inferior being. So she was unfaithful to me? I cared nothing about her. When I didn't hate her, I forgot her existence. I belonged to the atmosphere of health and honesty, the realm of Augusta, to whom I returned immediately in body and soul the moment Carla left me free.

Given Carla's absolute sincerity, I know exactly the extent of the long period in which she was completely mine, and my recurrent jealousy then cannot be considered anything but a manifestation of a recondite sense of justice. I should certainly be punished as I deserved. First the maestro fell in love. I believe the first symptom of his love consisted of certain words Carla repeated to me with a triumphant air, believing they marked her first great artistic success for which she merited a word of praise from me. He apparently told her that, if she was unable to pay him, he would continue her lessons for nothing. I would have given her a slap, but then the moment came when I could claim to be able to rejoice in that real triumph of hers. She forgot the cramp that at first had seized my whole face, like someone who sinks his teeth into a lemon, and she accepted serenely my belated praise. He had told her everything about himself, which didn't amount to much: music, poverty, and family. His sister had caused him many troubles, and he had managed to transmit to Carla a great dislike for that woman she didn't know. That dislike seemed very compromising to me. They now sang together some of his songs, which seemed poor stuff to me, both when I loved Carla and when I felt her like a chain. It is quite possible they were good, even though I never heard any mention of them afterwards. Later he conducted some orchestras in the United States, and perhaps over there those songs are sung, too.

But one fine day she told me he had asked her to become his wife and she had refused. Then I spent two really bad quarter-hours: the first when I felt so overwhelmed with wrath that I would have liked to wait for the maestro and throw him out with a sound kicking, and the second when I couldn't find the way of reconciling the possibility of continuing my liaison with that marriage, which was, after all, a good and moral thing and a much more reliable simplification of my position than the career Carla imagined launching under my patronage.

Why had this wretched maestro got so overheated, and in such a short time? Now, after a year's association, everything between me and Carla was smoother, even my frown when I left her. My remorse by now was quite bearable, and though Carla was still right to call me rough in love, it seemed she had become used to it. That must have been fairly easy for her, because I was never again as brutal as I had been in the first days of our affair, and, having tolerated that first excess, she must have found what followed quite mild in comparison.

Therefore, even when Carla no longer mattered so much to me, it was always easy for me to foresee that I would be displeased if I went to call on my mistress the next day and did not find her. Of course, it would then have been beautiful to be able to return to Augusta without the usual intermezzo at Carla's, and for the moment I felt entirely capable of that; but first I would have liked to try it out. My intention at that moment must have been more or less the following: "Tomorrow I will ask her to accept the maestro's proposal, but today I will prevent her." And with great effort I continued behaving like a lover. Now, as I speak of it, having recorded all the phases of my adventure, it might seem I was trying to make someone else marry my mistress and yet keep her on as mine, which would have been the policy of a man more shrewd than I and more balanced, though just as corrupt. But it's not true: she was to marry the maestro, but she was to reach that decision only the following day. And so it was not until then that this state of mine ended, which I stubbornly insist on calling innocence. It was no longer possible to adore Carla for a brief period of the day and then hate her for twenty-four consecutive hours, to rise every morning as ignorant as a newborn babe and to live through the day, so similar to the preceding ones, to be surprised by the adventures it brought, which I should have known by heart. This was no longer possible. Before me lay the prospect of losing my mistress forever if I weren't able to master my desire to rid myself of her. I mastered it at once!

And consequently, on that day, when she no longer mattered to me, I made Carla a jealous lover's scene that, in its falsity and its fury, resembled the one that, overwhelmed by wine, I had made to Augusta that night in the carriage. Only now the wine was lacking, and in the end I was truly moved by the sound of my own words. I declared to her that I loved her, that I couldn't go on without her, that I seemed to be demanding of her the sacrifice of her life, since I could offer her nothing that could equal what she was being offered by Lali.

This was actually a new note in our relationship, which had had nevertheless many hours of great love. She listened to my words, basking in them; much later she set about convincing me I shouldn't be so upset just because Lali was in love. She wasn't giving it a thought!

I thanked her, with the same fervor that now, however, no longer succeeded in moving me. I felt a certain heaviness in my stomach: obviously I was more compromised than ever. My show of fervor, instead of diminishing, increased, only to allow me to say a few words of admiration for poor Lali. I didn't want to lose him at all, I wanted to save him, but for the next day.

When it came to deciding whether to keep or dismiss the maestro, we were immediately in agreement. I wouldn't want to deprive her not only of a teacher but also of a career. She also confessed that the teacher was important for her, at every lesson she had the proof of the necessity of his help. She assured me I could go on living calmly and confidently: she loved me and no one else.

Obviously my betrayal had broadened and deepened. I had attached myself to my mistress by a new tenderness that bound with new bonds and invaded a territory until then reserved exclusively for my legitimate affection. But when I returned to my house, that tenderness no longer existed and, increased, was lavished on Augusta. Toward Carla I felt nothing but a deep distrust. Who knows how much truth there was in that marriage proposal? I wouldn't have been surprised if one fine day, without marrying that other man, Carla were to present me with a child endowed with great musical talent. And the ironclad resolutions began again, accompanying me on the way to Carla's, only to abandon me when I was with her, resuming then even before I had left her. All without consequences of any kind.

And there were no other consequences from these new developments. Summer went by and carried off my father-in-law. I then had a great deal to do in Guido's new firm, where I worked more than I had anywhere else, including the various university departments. I will tell more about this activity later. Winter also went by, and then in my little garden the first green leaves opened and they never saw me as dejected as those of the year before had. My daughter Antonia was born. Carla's teacher was always at our disposal, but Carla wouldn't give him any consideration and neither would I, yet.

Still there were serious consequences in my relations with Carla through events that really might not have been thought important. They occurred almost unnoticed, and were distinguished only by the consequences they left behind.

Specifically, at the beginning of that spring, I had to agree to go strolling with Carla in the Public Garden. It seemed to me gravely compromising, but Carla had such a desire to stroll in the sun on my arm that in the end I contented her. We were never to be allowed to live even for brief moments as husband and wife, and this attempt also came to a bad end.

The better to enjoy the new warmth that suddenly arrived from the heavens, where it seemed the sun had only recently regained its dominion, we sat down on a bench. The garden, on weekday mornings, was deserted, and I thought that by remaining in one place, the risk of being observed was further lessened. On the contrary, his armpit leaning heavily on a crutch, with slow but enormous steps, Tullio was approaching us, the man with the five hundred and four muscles; and without looking at us, he sat down right at our side. Then he raised his head, his gaze met mine, and he greeted me.

"After all this time! How are you? Are you less busy finally?"

He had sat just next to me, and in my first surprise I moved so as to block his view of Carla. But, after shaking my hand, he asked me: "And is this your lady wife?"

He was expecting to be introduced.

I submitted. "Signorina Carla Gerco, a friend of my wife's."

Then I continued lying, and I know, from Tullio himself, that the second lie was enough to reveal everything to him. With a forced smile, I said: "The Signorina also sat down beside me on this bench without seeing me."

The liar should always bear in mind that, if he would be believed, he must tell only essential lies. With his working-class common sense, the next time we met, Tullio said to me: "You explained too much, and I guessed you were lying and the beautiful young lady was your mistress."

By then I had already lost Carla, and with great pleasure I confirmed that he was right on the mark, but I told him sadly that by now she had abandoned me. He didn't believe me, and I was grateful to him for that. His incredulity seemed a good sign.

Carla was seized by an ill humor such as I had never remarked in her before. I know now that her rebellion began at this point. I wasn't aware of it immediately because, in order to hear Tullio, who had begun telling me about his sickness and the treatments he was trying, I turned my back on her. Later I learned that a woman, even one who allows herself to be treated with less courtesy, will never accept being denied in public, except at certain moments. She directed her outrage more toward the poor cripple than toward me, and wouldn't reply when he addressed her. Nor was I listening to Tullio; for the moment I couldn't take an interest in his cures. I was looking into his little eyes to divine what he was thinking of this encounter. I knew that by now he was pensioned off and, having the entire day free, he could easily spread his gossip through all the social world of our little Trieste of that time.

Then, after long meditation, Carla rose to leave us. "Good-bye," she murmured, and she went off.

I knew she was cross with me and, still taking Tullio's presence into account, I tried to gain the time necessary to pacify her. I asked permission to accompany her, since I had to go in her direction. Her sharp farewell implied definitive abandonment, and for the first time I seriously feared it. The stern threat robbed me of breath.

But Carla herself still didn't know where she was going with her firm steps. She was releasing the irritation of the moment, which in a little while would leave her.

She waited for me and then walked along beside me without a word. When we reached her home, she was overcome by a fit of weeping that didn't frighten me because it led her to take refuge in my arms. I explained to her who Tullio was and how much harm he could do me, thanks to his tongue. Seeing that she continued weeping, but remained in my arms,

I ventured a firmer tone: Did she really want to compromise me? Hadn't we always said we would do everything to avoid causing grief for that poor woman who was, after all, my wife and the mother of my daughter?

It seemed that Carla was coming round, but she wanted to be left alone, to regain her calm. I hurried away, overjoyed.

It must have been this adventure that gave her the constant wish to appear in public as my wife. It seemed that, not wanting to marry the maestro, she meant to force me to occupy a larger part of the role she denied him. She nagged me for a long time to take two seats at a theater, which we would occupy, arriving from separate directions, to find ourselves neighbors as if by chance. With her I went only – but often – to the Public Garden, that milestone of my misdeeds, where I now arrived from the opposite direction. Beyond that, never! Therefore my mistress ended up resembling me too much. For no other reason, at any moment she would become angry with me, in sudden outbursts of wrath. Soon she would recover, but they were enough to make me ever so good and meek. Often I found her dissolved in tears, and I could never succeed in extracting an explanation of her sadness from her. Perhaps the fault was mine because I didn't insist enough. When I knew her better, that is when she abandoned me, I needed no further explanations. Pressed by hardship, she had plunged into that affair with me, not really the right man for her. In my arms she had become a woman and – I like to suppose – an honest woman. Naturally this should not be attributed to any merit of mine, especially since the ensuing harm was all mine.

A new whim seized her, which surprised me at first, then, immediately afterwards, touched me: she wanted to see my wife. She swore not to approach her and to take care not to not be seen herself. I promised her that when I learned my wife was going out somewhere at a specific time, I would let her know. She was to see my wife not near my house, a deserted area where an individual is too readily noticed, but on some crowded city street.

At about that time my mother-in-law was afflicted with an eye ailment, which required her eyes to be bandaged for several days. She was bored to death, and to persuade her to observe the treatment strictly, her daughters took turns watching over her: my wife in the morning, and Ada until precisely four o'clock in the afternoon. With prompt decision, I told Carla that my wife left my mother-in-law's house precisely at four. Even now I don't know why I misrepresented Ada to Carla as my wife. What's certain is that after the marriage proposal made to her by the teacher, I felt a need to bind my mistress to me further, and I may have thought that the more beautiful she found my wife, the more she would appreciate the man who sacrificed (so to speak) such a woman to her. Augusta, at this time, was no more than a fine, healthy wet nurse. Caution may also have played a part in my decision. I certainly had reason to fear the moods of my mistress, and it would be of no importance if she were to let herself be swept into some rash act with Ada, who had indicated to me that she would never try to denigrate me to my wife.

If Carla were to compromise me with Ada, I would tell Ada the whole truth and, I must say, with a certain satisfaction.

But my tactic produced a truly unpredictable result. Impelled by some anxiety, the next morning I went to Carla earlier than usual. I found her completely changed from the day before. A great seriousness dominated the fine oval of her little face. I wanted to kiss her, but she repelled me, then let her cheeks be brushed by my lips, only to induce me to listen to her obediently. I sat facing her on the other side of the table. Without excessive haste, she picked up a piece of paper she had been writing on when I arrived, and placed it among some music lying on the table. I paid no attention to that paper and only later did I learn it was a letter she was writing to Lali.

And yet I know now that even at that moment Carla's spirit was torn by doubts. Her serious eyes rested on me, inquiring; then she turned to the light at the window, the better to isolate herself and study her own mind. Who knows? If I had immediately sensed more clearly the struggle within her, I might have been able to retain my delightful mistress.

She told me of her encounter with Ada. She had waited outside my mother-in-law's house and, when she saw the woman arrive, she recognized her at once.

"There could be no mistake. You had described her most important features to me. Oh! You know her well!"

She was silent for a moment to overcome the emotion that was choking her. Then she went on: "I don't know what there has been between the two of you, but I never want to betray that woman again, so beautiful and so sad! And I am writing to the maestro today to tell him I am ready to marry him!"

"Sad!" I cried, surprised. "You're mistaken, or else she was suffering just then because her shoe was too tight."

Ada, sad! Why, she was always laughing and smiling, even that very morning when I had seen her for an instant at my house.

But Carla was better informed than I: "Tight shoe! She walked like a goddess, stepping among the clouds!"

More and more moved, she told me that she had managed to receive a word – oh! how sweet – spoken to her by Ada, who dropped her handkerchief, which Carla picked up and handed to her. Her brief word of thanks moved Carla to tears. Then there was more between the two women. Carla insisted that Ada had also noticed she was crying and had moved off with a heartbroken glance of solidarity. For Carla, all was clear: my wife knew I was unfaithful to her and was suffering! Hence the resolve never to see me again and to marry Lali.

I didn't know how to defend myself! It was easy for me to speak with complete dislike of Ada but not of my wife, the healthy wet nurse who hadn't the slightest idea of what was going on in my spirit, completely intent as she was on her own ministry. I asked Carla if she hadn't noticed the hardness in Ada's eyes, and if she hadn't noticed the low, rough voice, lacking any sweetness. To regain Carla's love at once, I would gladly have attributed to my wife many other flaws, but I couldn't because, for about a year, with my mistress I had done nothing but praise my wife to the skies.

I saved myself in a different way. I, too, was overcome by a great emotion that brought tears to my eyes. It seemed to me I could legitimately pity myself. Involuntarily, I had enmeshed myself in a tangle where I felt terribly unhappy. That confusion between Ada and Augusta was unbearable. The truth was that my wife was not so beautiful and that Ada (for whom Carla was seized by such compassion) had done me a great wrong. Therefore Carla was really unfair in judging me.

My tears made Carla more tender: "Dario, dearest! Your tears make me feel so much better! There must have been some misunderstanding between you two, and the important thing now is to clear it up. I don't want to judge you too harshly, but I will never betray that woman again, nor do I want to be the cause of her tears. I've made a vow!"

Despite the vow, she ended up betraying Augusta for a last time. She wanted to part from me forever with a last kiss, but I would grant that kiss only in one form, otherwise I would have gone off filled with bitterness. So she resigned herself. We murmured both together: "For the last time!"

It was a delightful moment. The resolution made by both of us had an efficacy that canceled all guilt. We were innocent and blissful! My benevolent fate had reserved for me an instant of perfect happiness.

I felt so happy that I continued the playacting until the moment of our separation. We would never see each other again. She refused the envelope I always carried in my pocket and would have no memento of me. We had to dismiss from our new life every trace of our past misdeeds. Then I gladly kissed her on the forehead, paternally, as she had wanted me to do before.

Afterwards, on the stairs, I hesitated, because matters were becoming a bit too serious, whereas if I could know that the next morning she would still be at my disposal, thoughts of the future would not have come to me so quickly. From her landing, she watched me descend, and with a little laugh, I shouted up at her: "Till tomorrow, then!"

She drew back, surprised and almost frightened, and went off, saying: "Never again!"

I still felt relieved at having dared say the word that could lead me toward another last embrace whenever I wished. Without desires and without commitments, I spent a whole beautiful day with my wife, then in Guido's office. I must say that the lack of engagements brought me closer to my wife and my daughter. For them I was something more than the usual: not only sweet, but a true father who calmly arranges and commands, his mind entirely on his home. Going to bed, I said to myself, in the form of a proposal: All days should be like this one.

Before falling asleep, Augusta felt the need to confide a great secret to me: she had learned it from her mother that same day. Some days before, Ada had caught Guido embracing a maidservant of theirs. Ada had reacted haughtily, but then the maid turned impudent, and Ada discharged her. Yesterday they had been anxious to learn how Guido had taken the matter. If he had complained, Ada would have demanded a separation. But Guido had laughed and protested that Ada hadn't seen clearly; however, even though that woman was innocent, he honestly disliked her, and had nothing against her being dismissed from the house. Apparently things were now smooth again.

It was important for me to know whether Ada had been imagining things when she surprised her husband in that situation. Could there still be any possible doubt? Because the fact remains that when two people are hugging each other, they are in a position quite different from when one is cleaning the other's shoes. I was in excellent humor. I even felt required to seem impartial and calm in judging Guido. Ada was certainly jealous by nature, and it could be that she had seen distances diminished and people's positions altered.

In a heartbroken voice, Augusta told me she was sure Ada had seen clearly and that now, out of excessive devotion, she was using bad judgment. She added: "She would have done much better to marry you!"

Feeling more and more innocent, I remarked generously: "It remains to be seen if I would have done better to marry her instead of you!"

Then, before falling asleep, I murmured: "What a cad! Besmirching his own house like that!"

I was fairly sincere in reproaching him specifically for that aspect of his behavior for which I didn't have to reproach myself.

The next morning I got up with the strong desire that at least this first day should exactly resemble the preceding day. It was probable that the delightful resolutions of the day before wouldn't bind Carla any more than they did me, and I felt entirely free of them. Certainly the eagerness to know what Carla thought about it made me hurry. My desire would have been to find her ready for another resolution. Life would have sped away, rich indeed in pleasures, but even more in efforts for self-betterment, and my every day would have been devoted in a great degree to good and in the slightest degree to resolutions. Carla had had only one: to show that she loved me. She had kept it, and I had some difficulty making myself believe it would now be easy for her to maintain the new resolution while revoking the old one.

Carla wasn't at home. It was a great disappointment, and I gnawed my fingers in chagrin. The old woman showed me into the kitchen. She told me Carla would be back before evening. Carla had said she would eat out, and so on that stove there wasn't even the little fire that usually glowed there.

"You didn't know?" the old woman asked me, her eyes wide with surprise.

Pensive, distracted, I murmured: "I heard of it yesterday. I wasn't sure Carla actually meant today."

I left, after politely saying good-bye. I was gnashing my teeth, but in secret. It took some time to muster the courage to be angry publicly. I entered the Public Garden and strolled there for half an hour, to gain the time to understand things better. They were so clear that I couldn't make heads or tails of anything. All of a sudden, with no pity at all, I was forced to maintain such a resolution. I felt ill, really ill. I limped, and I struggled also with a kind of shortness of breath. I have those attacks: I can breathe perfectly, but I start counting the individual breaths, because I have to take them consciously, one after the other. I have the sensation that if I am not careful, I will die of suffocation.

At that hour I should have gone to my office, or rather to Guido's. But it was impossible for me to leave this place in my present state. What would I do now? This was very different from the day before! If I had only known the address of that wretched maestro who, while singing at my expense, had taken my mistress from me!

In the end I went back to the old woman. I would find a word to send to Carla, to persuade her to see me again. Now the main endeavor was to bring her within reach as quickly as possible. The rest wouldn't involve great difficulties.

I found the old woman seated at a window in the kitchen, intent on darning a stocking. She took off her eyeglasses and, almost timorously, cast an interrogative glance at me. I hesitated. Then I asked her: "Do you know if Carla has decided to marry that Lali?"

To me, it seemed I was breaking this news to myself. Carla had already told it to me twice, but the day before I had paid little attention. Those words of Carla's had struck my ear, and distinctly, because I had recalled them, but they had slipped away without penetrating more deeply. Now they barely reached my viscera, which were twisting in pain.

The old woman looked at me, also hesitant. Surely she was afraid of committing any indiscretions for which she could then be reproached. Finally she burst out, obviously and completely joyful: "Carla told you? Then it must be so! I believe she would be doing the right thing! What do you think?"

Now she was laughing happily, the cursed hag, who, I had always believed, was informed about my relations with Carla. I would gladly have struck her, but I confined myself to saying that first I would have waited until the maestro had made a position for himself. To me, in other words, it seemed they had rushed matters.

In her joy the Signora became talkative with me for the first time. She didn't share my opinion. When a couple marries young, the career has to be made afterwards. Why did it have to be made first? Carla had so few needs. Her voice, now, would cost less, since her husband would also be her teacher.

These words, which could have seemed a reproach to my niggardliness, gave me an idea that appeared magnificent and that for the moment raised my spirits. In the envelope I always carried in my breast pocket there should by now be a tidy sum. I took it from my pocket, sealed it, and handed it to the old woman to give to Carla. Perhaps I also had the desire to pay off my mistress finally in a seemly fashion, but the stronger desire was to see her again and possess her again. Carla would see me again whether she wanted to return the money to me or whether it suited her to keep it, because then she would feel the need to thank me. I could breathe: all was not over forever!

I told the old woman that the envelope contained a little money, what was left of the sum given to me for them by poor Copler's friends. Then, greatly reassured, I said to tell Carla that I would remain her good friend for the rest of my life, and that if she ever needed help, she could call on me freely. In this way I could send her my address, which was that of Guido's office.

I left with a far more buoyant step than the one that had brought me there.

But that day I had a violent quarrel with Augusta. It was over a trifle. I said the soup was too salty and she claimed it wasn't. I had a mad fit of rage because I had the impression she was making fun of me. I violently pulled the cloth toward me, making the dishes fly from the table to the floor. The baby, in her nurse's arms, began screaming, which mortified me greatly because the little mouth seemed to be reproaching me. Augusta blanched as only she could blanch, took the child in her arms, and went out. It seemed to me her reaction was also excessive: Would she now leave me to eat alone like a dog? But immediately, without the child, she came back, laid the table again, sat opposite me in her usual place, where she moved her spoon as if she wanted to resume eating.

Under my breath, I was cursing, but I already knew I was a plaything in the hands of the intemperate forces of nature. Nature, who found little difficulty in accumulating those forces, found even less in unleashing them. My curses now were directed against Carla, who pretended to act only in the interest of my wife. And this was what the girl had done to her!

Augusta, true to a system she has continued to follow, when she sees me in that state, didn't protest, didn't cry, didn't argue. When I meekly began to beg her pardon, she wanted to explain one thing: she hadn't laughed, she had only smiled in the very way that had so often pleased me and that I had so often praised.

I was profoundly ashamed. I begged for the child to be brought to us at once, and holding her in my arms, I played with her for a long time. Then I made her sit on my head, and under her little dress, which covered my face, I dried my eyes, wet with the tears that Augusta hadn't shed. I played with the baby, knowing that in this way, without humbling myself to apologize, I was drawing closer to Augusta, and in fact her cheeks had already regained their usual color.

So that day also ended very well, and the afternoon resembled the previous one. It was exactly the same as if that morning I had found Carla in the usual place. I hadn't lacked my relief. I had repeatedly begged forgiveness because I had to coax Augusta to resume her motherly smile when I said or did anything eccentric. It would have been dreadful if, in my presence, she had been forced to assume a fixed attitude or repress even one of those familiar, affectionate smiles that seemed to me the fullest and most benevolent judgment of me that could be expressed.

In the evening we talked again about Guido. Apparently his peace with Ada was complete. Augusta was amazed at her sister's goodness. This time, however, it was I who had to smile, because obviously she didn't realize her own goodness, which was immense.

I asked her: "And if I were to besmirch our home, wouldn't you forgive me?"

She hesitated. "We have our child," she cried, "whereas Ada has no children that bind her to that man."

She didn't love Guido; at times I think she bore him a grudge for having made me suffer.

A few months later, Ada presented Guido with twins, and Guido never understood why I congratulated him so warmly. Now that he had children, even in Augusta's opinion, the housemaids could be his without his risking any danger.

The following morning, however, at the office, when I found on my desk an envelope addressed to me in Carla's hand, I breathed again. Now nothing was finished and I could go on living supplied with all the necessary elements. In a few words Carla agreed to meet me at eleven that morning at the Public Garden, by the entrance just opposite her house. We would not be in her room, but still in a place very close to it.

I couldn't wait, and I arrived at the meeting place a quarter-hour early. If Carla was not there, I would go straight to her house, which would be far more comfortable.

This day, too, was steeped in the new spring, tender and radiant. When I turned off the noisy Corsia Stadion and entered the garden, I found myself in the silence of the countryside, which was not really broken by the light, constant rustle of the boughs stirred by the breeze.

With rapid steps I was nearing the gate of the garden when Carla came walking toward me. She had my envelope in her hand and she approached me without a smile of greeting, but rather with a stern determination on her pale face. She was wearing a simple cotton dress, coarsely woven, with pale blue stripes, which was very becoming. She, too, seemed a part of the garden. Later, in the moments when I hated her, I accused her of having dressed like that deliberately to make herself more desirable at the very moment when she was denying herself to me. It was, instead, the first day of spring that clothed her. It must also be remembered that in my long but brusque love, my woman's adornment played a very small part. I had always gone directly to that studio room of hers, and modest women are always very simple when they are staying home.

She held out her hand, which I pressed, saying to her: "I thank you for coming!"

How much more decorous it would have been for me if, during that conversation, I had remained so meek!

Carla seemed moved, and when she spoke, a kind of tremor affected her lips. At times, also when she sang, that movement of the lips impeded the note. She said to me: "I would like to oblige you and accept this money from you, but I can't, I absolutely can't. Please, take it back."

Seeing her close to tears, I immediately obeyed, accepting the envelope, which later I found still in my hand long after I had abandoned that place.

"You really want nothing more to do with me?"

I asked this question, not thinking that she had answered it the day before. But was it possible that, desirable as she appeared to me, she could refuse herself?

"Zeno!" the girl answered, with some sweetness. "Didn't we promise ourselves we would never see each other again? After that promise, I have made a commitment similar to the one you had before knowing me. It is as sacred as yours. I hope that by now your wife has realized you are entirely hers."

So in her thoughts Ada's beauty continued to be important. If I had been sure this abandonment was Ada's fault, I would have had a way of taking reparatory measures. I would have told Carla that Ada wasn't my wife and I would have let her see Augusta, with her asymmetrical eye and her healthy wet-nurse figure. But wasn't the commitment she had made now more important? That had to be discussed.

I tried to speak calmly while my lips were also trembling, though with desire. I told her she didn't yet realize how much she was mine and how she no longer had the right to dispose of herself. In my head was stirring the scientific proof of what I wanted to say, namely that famous experiment of Darwin's on an Arab mare, but, thank heaven, I am almost certain I didn't say anything about it. I must have talked about animals, however, and their physical fidelity, in a meaningless stammer. Then I gave up the more difficult arguments, inaccessible to her and also to me at that moment.

And I said: "What commitment can you have made? What importance can it have compared with an affection like the one that has united us for over a year?"

I grabbed her roughly by the hand, feeling the need of some energetic action, but finding no words to complement it.

She freed herself as vigorously from my grasp as if it were the first time I had taken such a liberty.

"Never!" she said, in the attitude of someone taking an oath. "I have made a holier pledge! With a man who also has made the same pledge to me."

There was no doubt! The blood that suddenly colored her cheeks had been driven there by rancor toward the man who had not made any commitment to her.

She made herself even clearer: "Yesterday we walked along the streets, arm in arm, in the company of his mother."

It was obvious that my woman was running away, farther and farther from me. I ran after her madly, leaping like a dog when he is denied a tasty morsel of meat. Again I seized her hand violently.

"Well," I suggested, "let's walk like this, hand in hand, through the whole city. In this unusual fashion, to make ourselves even more visible, we'll go along Corsia Stadion, then past the Chiozza arcades, and across the Corso as far as Sant'Andrea, then return to our room by another route, so the whole city can see us."

There, for the first time, I was renouncing Augusta! And it seemed a liberation to me because she was the one who wanted to take Carla from me.

Again she removed her hand from my grasp and said sharply: "That would more or less be the same walk he and I took yesterday!"

I started again: "And does he know? Everything? Does he know that you were mine yesterday, too?"

"Yes," she said proudly. "He knows everything, everything."

I felt lost, and in my anger, like the dog who, when he can't reach the desired morsel, bites the clothes of the one withholding it, I said: "This husband of yours has an excellent stomach. Today he digests me. Tomorrow he will be able to digest everything you like."

I didn't hear the exact sound of my words. I knew I was shouting in pain. She, on the contrary, had an expression of indignation of which I wouldn't have believed her dark, mild gazelle eyes capable.

"You say this to me? And why don't you have the courage to say it to him?"

She turned her back on me and rapidly walked toward the gate. I was already feeling remorse for the words I had said, bewildered, however, by my great surprise that I was forbidden to treat Carla less gently now. It kept me nailed to the spot. The little figure, blue and white, with quick, short steps, was already reaching the exit, when I made up my mind to run after her. I didn't know what I would say to her, but it was impossible for us to part like this.

I stopped her at the door of her building and spoke, sincerely, only of the great sorrow of that moment. "Are we going to part like this, after so much love?"

She went on without answering me, and I followed her up the steps. Then she looked at me with hostile eyes: "If you want to see my husband, come with me. Can't you hear? He's the one playing the piano."

I heard just then the syncopated notes of Schubert's *Abschied* in the Liszt transcription.

Though since my childhood I have never handled a sabre or a club, I am not a fearful man. The great desire that had impelled me thus far had suddenly vanished. Of the male character, all that remained in me was the combativeness. I had asked imperiously for something not rightfully mine. To lessen my error now I had to fight, because otherwise the memory of that woman threatening to have me punished by her husband would have been unbearable.

"Very well!" I said to her. "If you will allow me, I'll come with you."

My heart was pounding, with no fear — except the fear of not behaving properly.

I continued climbing the stairs with her. But suddenly she stopped, leaned against the wall, and started crying, wordlessly. Up above, the notes of the *Abschied* continued to resound on that piano which I had paid for. Carla's tears made that sound very moving.

"I'll do whatever you want. Do you want me to go?" I asked.

"Yes," she said, barely able to utter that brief word.

I slowly went down the stairs, also whistling Schubert's *Abschied*. I don't know if it was an illusion, but I seemed to hear her call me: "Zeno!"

At that moment she could even have called me by that strange name of Dario that she sometimes considered a pet name, and I wouldn't have stopped. I had a great desire to go away, and I was returning once again, pure, to Augusta – as the dog, when his approach to the female is fended off with kicks, runs away, totally pure for the moment.

When, the next day, I was again reduced to the state in which I had found myself at the moment I headed for the Public Garden, it seemed to me simply that I had been a coward: she had called me, though not by our pet name, and I hadn't answered! It was the first day of suffering, which was followed by many others of bitter desolation. No longer understanding why I had gone off like that, I blamed myself for having been afraid of that man or afraid of scandal. Now I was ready to accept any compromise, as I had been when I suggested to Carla that long walk through the city. I had lost an opportune moment, and I knew very well that, with certain women, such a moment occurs only once. For me that one time would have sufficed.

I decided promptly to write to Carla. It wasn't possible for me to allow even one more day to go by without making an attempt to return to her. I wrote and rewrote that letter, to condense into a few words all the intelligence of which I was capable. I rewrote it so many times also because writing it was a great comfort to me; it was the release I needed. I begged her forgiveness for my display of wrath, declaring that my great love needed some time to calm down. I added: "Every day that passes brings me another crumb of tranquillity," and I wrote this sentence many times, always clenching my teeth. Then I told her that I couldn't forgive myself for the words I had addressed to her and I felt the need to ask her pardon. I couldn't, unfortunately, offer her what Lali was offering her and of which she was so worthy.

I imagined that the letter would have a great effect. Since Lali knew everything, Carla would show it to him, and for Lali it could be advantageous to have a friend of my worth. I even dreamed we might begin a sweet three-sided life, because my love was such that for the moment I would have regarded my fate as mitigated if I were allowed simply to pay court to Carla.

The third day I received a brief note from her. It was not addressed at all, neither to Zeno nor to Dario. She said only: "Thank you! May you also be happy with your spouse, so worthy of all good things!" Naturally, she was speaking of Ada.

The opportune moment had not lasted, and with women it never lasts unless you grab it by the braids and hold it tight. My desire was distilled into a furious bitterness. Not toward Augusta! My spirit was so full of Carla that I felt remorse, and with Augusta I forced myself to maintain a foolish, stereo-typed smile, which to her seemed genuine.

But I had to do something. I surely couldn't wait and suffer like this every day! I didn't want to write her again. For women, written words have too little importance. I had to find something better.

With no specific intention, I hurried to the Public Garden. Then, much more slowly, to Carla's house and, arriving on that landing, I knocked at the kitchen door. If it were possible, I would have avoided seeing Lali, but I wouldn't have minded running into him. That would be the crisis I felt I needed.

The old woman, as usual, was at the stove, on which two great fires were burning. She was surprised to see me, but then she laughed like the good, innocent creature she was.

She said, "I'm glad to see you! You were so accustomed to see us every day, that obviously you can't bring yourself to give us up entirely."

It was easy for me to make her chatter on. She told me that Carla's love for Vittorio was immense. That day he and his mother were coming to have dinner with them. She added, laughing: "Soon he'll end by persuading her to come with him even to the many voice lessons he has to give every day. They can't bear to be apart, not even for a few moments."

She smiled at that happiness, maternally. She told me that in a few weeks' time they would be married.

I had a bad taste in my mouth, and I would almost have turned toward the door to leave. Then I lingered, hoping the old woman's nattering would inspire some good idea in me, or give me some hope. The last error I had committed with Carla had been to run away before I had studied all the possibilities that might have been available to me.

For an instant I believed I had my idea. I asked the old woman if she had actually decided to be her daughter's servant until she died. I told her I knew that Carla wasn't very gentle with her.

She went on working diligently at the fire, but she heard me out. She possessed an innocence I didn't deserve. She complained of Carla, who lost her temper over any trifle. She apologized: "Of course, I grow older every day and I forget everything. It's not my fault!"

But she hoped things would go better now. Carla's moods would be fewer, now that she was happy. And then Vittorio, right from the start, had shown her great respect. Finally, still intent on making some shapes with a mixture of flour and fruit, she added: "It's my duty to stay with my daughter. There's nothing else I can do."

With a certain anxiousness I tried to convince her. I told her that she could easily free herself from this bondage. Wasn't I here? I would continue to give her the monthly allowance that I had given Carla till now. I wanted to support somebody! I wanted to keep with me the old woman, who to me seemed part of the daughter.

The old woman showed me her gratitude. She admired my goodness, but she had to laugh at the idea that she could be advised to leave her daughter. It was something unthinkable.

The hard word struck my brow, forcing me to lower my head! I was returning to that great solitude where there was no Carla, nor was there any visible path that led to her. I remember making a final effort to delude myself that some sign of such a path might remain. I said to the old woman, before leaving, that after a while she might change her mind. I begged her to remember me then.

Leaving that house, I was filled with outrage and bitterness, as if I had been ill-treated when I was preparing to perform a good action. That old woman had actually offended me with that outburst of laughter. I could hear it still reechoing in my ears, and it signified more than mere mockery of my final proposal.

I didn't want to go to Augusta in this condition. I could foresee my fate. If I went to her, I would end up ill-treating her, and she would get her revenge with that great pallor that so hurt me. I preferred to walk the streets at a steady pace that might bring a little order to my spirit. And in fact that order came! I stopped complaining about my fate, and I saw myself as if a great light had projected me, full-figure, on the pavement I was looking at. I wasn't asking for Carla. I wanted her embrace, preferably her last embrace. How ridiculous! I dug my teeth into my lips to cast some sorrow, or rather a modicum of seriousness, on my ridiculous image. I knew everything of myself and it was unforgivable for me to suffer so much because I had been offered a unique opportunity to be weaned. Carla was gone, as I had so often wished.

With such clarity in my spirit, a little later in a remote street of the city, which I had reached without paying any attention, when a heavily painted woman made a sign, I rushed to her without hesitation.

I arrived quite late for lunch, but I was so sweet to Augusta that she was immediately happy. But I wasn't able to kiss my child, and for several hours I couldn't eat, either. I felt very soiled! I feigned no sickness as I had done other times to conceal and attenuate guilt and remorse. I couldn't seem to find solace in any resolve for the future, and for the first time I made none at all. It took many hours for me to return to the usual rhythm that drew me from the gloomy present to the luminous future.

Augusta realized there was something new in me. It made her laugh. "With you, there's never a chance of being bored. You're a different man every day."

Yes! That woman of the slums resembled no other, and I had her in me.

I spent the afternoon and also the evening with Augusta. She was very occupied, and I remained beside her, inert. I felt that, inert, I was being carried along by a current, a current of clear water: the honest life of my house.

I abandoned myself to that current that carried me but didn't cleanse me. Far from it! It emphasized my filth.

Naturally, in the long night that followed, I arrived at the resolution. The first was the most rigid. I would acquire a weapon to destroy myself at once if I caught myself heading for that part of the city. This resolution made me feel better and soothed me.

I didn't moan once in my bed, and on the contrary, I simulated the regular respiration of the sleeper. Thus I returned to the old idea of purifying myself through a confession to my wife, as I had thought to do when I had been on the verge of betraying her with Carla. But now the confession was very difficult, and not because of the gravity of the misdeed, but because of the complication in which it had resulted. Facing a judge like my wife, I would also have to adduce extenuating circumstances, and these would emerge only if I could tell of the unforeseen violence with which my relations with Carla had been ruptured. But then it would be necessary to confess also that now-ancient infidelity. It was purer than this latest one, but (who knows?), for a wife, more offensive.

Through studying myself, I arrived at more and more rational resolutions. I thought to avoid the repetition of a similar misdeed by hastening to organize another attachment like the one I had lost and of which I obviously had need. But the new woman also frightened me. A thousand dangers would have besieged me and my little family. In this world another Carla didn't exist, and with bitter tears I mourned her, Carla the sweet, the good, who had even tried to love the woman I loved and who had failed only because I had put before her another woman, precisely the one I didn't love at all!

THE STORY OF A BUSINESS PARTNERSHIP

IT WAS GUIDO who wanted me with him in his new business firm. I was dying to be a part of it, but I'm sure I never let him guess this desire of mine. Obviously, in my inertia, the proposal of this activity, in partnership with a friend, appealed to me. But there was more to it than that. I still hadn't abandoned the hope of becoming a good businessman, and it seemed to me easier to progress through teaching Guido than through being taught by Olivi. Many in this world learn only by listening to themselves; in any case, they are unable to learn by listening to anyone else.

There were also other reasons why I wished that association. I wanted to be useful to Guido! In the first place, I was fond of him, and although he wanted to appear strong and self-confident, he seemed to me helpless, in need of the protection I was glad to provide him. Further, to my own conscience and not only to Augusta's eyes, it seemed that the more attached I became to Guido, the more my absolute indifference to Ada was clear.

In short, I was awaiting only a word from Guido to place myself at his disposal, and this word would have come even earlier, but he didn't believe I was so inclined toward commerce, as I would have nothing to do with the business offered me at my own firm.

One day he said to me: "I've taken every course at the Higher School of Commerce, but still I'm a bit worried about having to handle competently all those details that ensure the smooth functioning of a firm. True, a businessman doesn't have to know anything, because if he needs books, he calls the bookkeeper and if he needs the law he calls a lawyer, and for his accounts he goes to an accountant. But it's hard to have to hand over my accounts to an outsider, right at the start!"

It was the first clear allusion to his intention of having me join him. To tell the truth, I had no experience of accounting beyond those few months when I kept the books for Olivi, but I was sure that, for Guido, I was the only accountant who wasn't an outsider.

The first time we openly discussed the eventuality of our partnership was when he went to pick out the furniture for his office. Without hesitation he ordered two desks for the director's office.

Blushing, I asked him: "Why two?

He replied: "The other one's yours."

I felt such gratitude that I could have hugged him.

When we had left the shop, Guido, a bit awkwardly, explained that he couldn't as yet offer me a position in his firm. He was leaving that space for me in his office, only to induce me to come and keep him company whenever I liked. He didn't want to commit me to anything and he too would remain free. If his business went well, he would give me a position in the management of the firm.

As Guido talked about his business, his dark, handsome face turned serious. It seemed he had already thought of all the procedures he wanted to adopt. He stared into the distance, above my head, and I had such faith in the seriousness of his meditations that I also turned to look at what he was seeing, namely those procedures that were to make his fortune. He didn't want to take the path our father-in-law had already followed so successfully, or the less adventurous and more secure route trod by Olivi. For him they were all old-fashioned merchants. He would strike out in a new direction and he was glad to have me with him because he considered me not yet ruined by the old men.

All this rang true to me. I was being offered my first commercial success, and I blushed with pleasure a second time. So it happened that, out of gratitude for the esteem he had shown me, I worked with him and for him, at times intensely, at other times less so, for a good two years, with no compensation beyond the glory of that position in the director's office. At that point it was surely the longest time I had ever devoted to one occupation. But I can't boast about it, because that work bore no fruit for me or for Guido, and in business – as everyone knows – you judge only by results.

I remained confident that I was on my way to a great business success for about three months, the time necessary to establish that firm. I knew it would be up to me not only to handle certain details such as correspondence and accounts, but also to keep an eye on our transactions. Guido still exerted such a great influence over me that he could also have ruined me, and only my good luck prevented him. At a sign from him I would come running. This provokes my amazement even now as I write, after I have had time to think about it for such a long part of my life.

And I write of those two years also because my attachment to him seems to me a clear manifestation of my sickness. Why should I attach myself to him to learn about big business, then immediately afterwards remain attached to him to teach him about small business? Why should I feel good in that position simply because I believed my great friendship for Guido signified a great indifference toward Ada? Who was demanding all this of me? Wasn't our reciprocal indifference sufficiently proved by all those tykes we kept bringing into the world? I had nothing against Guido, but he was surely not the friend I would have chosen freely. I saw his faults constantly and so clearly that his thinking often irked me, when some weakness of his didn't seem touching to me. For a long time I offered him the sacrifice of my freedom, and I allowed him to drag me into the most hateful situations only to assist him! A genuine,

outright evidence of sickness or of great goodness, two qualities that are very closely related.

This remains true even though in the course of time a great
affection grew up between us, as is always the case among
decent people who see each other every day. And my affection
was really great! After he left us, for a long time I felt how
much I missed him, and indeed my whole life seemed empty,
since such a large part of it had been taken over by him and
his business.

I have to laugh, recalling how, immediately, in our very first
venture, the purchase of the furniture, we mistook one of the
conditions in a certain way. We had acquired the furniture and
couldn't yet make up our minds to set up the office. On the
choice of office, between me and Guido there was a difference
of opinion which delayed us. From my father-in-law and from
Olivi I had always observed that in order to keep your eye on
the warehouse, your office should adjoin it.

Guido protested with a grimace of disgust: "Those Trieste
offices that stink of salt cod or tanned hides!" He guaranteed
that he could arrange surveillance also from a distance, but still
he hesitated. One fine day the furniture dealer ordered us to
collect our purchases, otherwise he would throw them into
the street, whereupon Guido rushed to decide on an office,
the last one offered us, without any storage space in the
vicinity, but right in the center of the city. And so we never
thereafter had a storeroom.

The office consisted of two vast rooms full of light, and one
little room without windows. To the door of this room was
fastened a board with the word ACCOUNTS in clear lettering.
One of the other two doors also had a sign: CASH, while
the third was adorned with the very English designation:
PRIVATE. Guido had also studied business in England, and
had come home with some useful ideas. The CASH room
was equipped, properly, with a magnificent iron safe and the
traditional cage. Our PRIVATE room became a luxurious

chamber, splendidly papered in a dark, velvety color and furnished with the two desks, a sofa, and several very comfortable easy chairs.

Then came the purchase of the books and the various utensils. Here my director's role was beyond debate. I ordered the things and they arrived. Actually I would have preferred not to be obeyed with such alacrity, but it was my responsibility to list all the things required in an office. Then I thought I had discovered the great difference between me and Guido. Whatever I knew enabled me to speak and him to act. When he came to know what I knew, and no more than that, he did the buying. It's true that in business sometimes he was quite determined to do nothing, neither buy nor sell, but this also seemed to me the resolve of a man who believes he knows a great deal. I would have been less decisive, even in my inertia.

In making these purchases I was very prudent. I rushed to Olivi to take the measurements of the correspondence register and the account books. Then young Olivi helped me set up the books and also once explained to me double-entry book-keeping, none of it difficult, but it was very easily forgotten. When it came time to balance the books, he would explain that to me as well.

We didn't yet know what we would do in that office (I know now that Guido, at that time, didn't know either), and we were debating every aspect of our organization. I remember that for days we discussed where we would put the other employees if we were to need them. Guido suggested fitting as many as possible into the CASH room. But young Luciano, our only employee for the time being, declared that if the cash box was kept in a room, nobody should be put there except those having actually to handle the cash. It was quite hard, having to accept lessons from our runner! I had a moment of inspiration: "I seem to recall that in England everyone is paid by check."

This was something I had been told in Trieste.

"Fine!" Guido said. "I remember that too, now. Strange, I had forgotten it!"

He started explaining to Luciano at great length how it was no longer the practice to handle so much cash. Checks passed from one to another in any amount you wanted. Ours was a splendid victory, and Luciano remained silent.

He benefited greatly from what he learned from Guido. Our runner is now a highly respected Trieste merchant. He greets me still with some humility, tempered by a smile. Guido always spent a part of the day teaching first Luciano, then me, and in due course the secretary. I remember that for a long time he had toyed with the idea of doing business on commission so as not to risk his own money. He explained the essence of this kind of business to me, and, seeing that I obviously understood it too quickly, he began explaining it to Luciano, who stood and listened to him at length with an expression of the liveliest interest, his big eyes shining in his still beardless face. It cannot be said that Guido wasted his time, because Luciano is the only one of us who has succeeded in that branch of commerce. And yet they say that knowledge is what wins!

Meanwhile from Buenos Aires came the *pesos*. This was serious! At first it seemed an easy matter to me, but on the contrary the Trieste market was not ready for that exotic valuta. Again we had to call on young Olivi, who taught us how to cash those checks. Then, at a certain point, when we seemed to be on our own, as Olivi had steered us safely into port, for several days Guido went around with his pockets stuffed with crowns, until we found our way to the bank, which relieved us of the uncomfortable burden, handing us a checkbook, which we quickly learned how to use.

Guido felt called upon to say to Olivi, who had helped him with what might be called the installation: "I assure you I will never compete with the firm of my friend!"

But the young man, who had a different concept of business, replied: "If only there were a larger number of contractors handling our articles! It would be better!"

Guido was agape, he had understood all too well, as he always tended to, and he clung to that theory, dishing it out to anyone who would have it.

For all his Higher School education, Guido had a rather hazy notion of credit and debit. He watched me with surprise as I set up the capital account, and also as I posted our expenditures. Then he was such an expert in bookkeeping that when a deal was offered him, he analyzed it first of all from the bookkeeping point of view. It actually seemed to him that a knowledge of accounting gave the world a new appearance. He saw debtors and creditors being born everywhere, even when two people were trading blows or when they kissed.

You could say that he went into business armed with the maximum prudence. He rejected a number of transactions, and indeed for six months he rejected them all, with the serene attitude of a man who knows more than he's letting on.

"No!" he would say, and the monosyllable seemed the result of precise calculation even when it concerned an article he had never seen. But all his reflection had been lavished on picturing how the deal and its eventual gain or loss would look in the accounts. Bookkeeping was the last thing he had learned, and it came to dominate all his ideas.

I am sorry to have to speak so ill of my lamented friend, but I must be truthful, also to understand myself better. I remember how much intelligence he employed to clutter our little office with daydreams that prevented us from pursuing any healthy activity. At a given point, to initiate the commission business, we sent out a thousand circulars in the mail. Guido expressed this thought: "Think of all the stamps we would save if, before mailing out these circulars, we knew how many of them would reach people who would take them into consideration!"

The sentence in itself meant little, but he was too pleased with it and he began to fling the sealed circulars into the air, thinking to mail only the ones that landed with the address facing up. The experiment recalled something similar I had done in the past, but still it seemed to me I had never carried it this far. Naturally I didn't collect or send out the circulars he eliminated, because I couldn't be sure his idea hadn't been a really genuine inspiration, guiding him in that selection, and I shouldn't waste stamps he had to pay for.

My good fortune kept me from being ruined by Guido, but the same good fortune also prevented me from playing too active a role in his affairs. I say this openly because others in Trieste think it was a different story: during the time I spent with him, I never acted on any sudden inspiration, of the sort connected with the dried fruit. Never did I force him into a transaction, nor did I ever talk him out of one. I was the admonisher! I urged him to be active, to be canny. But I would never have dared throw his money on the green table.

At his side I turned quite inert. I tried to set him on the straight and narrow path, and perhaps I failed out of excess inertia. For the rest, when two people are together, it is not up to them to decide which must be Don Quixote and which Sancho Panza. He conducted the transaction and I, like a good Sancho, followed him very slowly in my ledgers, after having examined and criticized it, as I saw my duty.

The commission business was a complete fiasco, but it did us no harm. The only person who sent us some merchandise was a paper manufacturer in Vienna, and a part of those items of stationery were sold by Luciano, who gradually came to learn how much commission was due us and then made Guido turn almost all of it over to him. Guido finally agreed because those sums were trifling, and because the first venture, thus concluded, should bring us luck. This first venture left us with a quantity of stationery in the little storeroom, which we had to pay for and keep. There would have been enough to fill, for many years, the office needs of a firm much more thriving than ours.

For a couple of months this sunny office in the center of the city was a pleasant refuge for us. Very little work was done there (I believe we concluded two deals in all, involving empty packing cases for which the supply and the demand coincided on the same day, bringing us a slight profit) and we chattered a lot, amiably, also with that innocent Luciano, who, when we spoke of business, grew agitated, as do other boys his age when the talk is of women.

At that time it was easy for me to amuse myself innocently with the innocents, because I hadn't yet lost Carla. And from that period I remember entire days with pleasure. In the evening, at home, I had many things to tell Augusta, and I could tell her all the events of the office, without exception, and without having to add anything to falsify them.

I wasn't the least worried when Augusta occasionally cried out with concern: "But when are the two of you going to start earning some money?"

Money? We hadn't even thought of that yet. We knew that first you had to take time, look around, study the merchandise, the market, and also our hinterland. A business firm wasn't something you could just improvise. And even Augusta was reassured by my explanations.

Then a very noisy guest was introduced into our office: a hunting dog, a few months old, frisky and curious. Guido loved him very much and organized a regular provision of milk and meat for him. When I had nothing to do or to think about, I also was pleased to see him bounding about the office in those four or five canine attitudes that we can interpret and which endear a dog to us. But I didn't feel he was in the right place, with us, noisy and dirty as he was! For me that dog's presence in our office was the first sign Guido gave of being unfit to run a business. It proved a complete lack of seriousness. I tried to explain to him that the dog couldn't benefit our business, but I didn't have the courage to insist, and with some sort of answer he silenced me.

Therefore it seemed to me that I had to devote myself to the training of this colleague, and I took great pleasure in giving him an occasional kick when Guido wasn't in. The dog whimpered and at first would come back to me, believing I had struck him by mistake. But a second kick always made things clearer than the first, and then he would hide in a corner, and until Guido arrived in the office there was peace. I later repented having raged against an innocent creature, but it was too late. I showered kindness on the dog, but he no longer trusted me, and in Guido's presence he clearly indicated his dislike.

"How strange!" Guido said. "A good thing I know you, because otherwise I wouldn't trust you. Dogs as a rule never get their dislikes wrong."

To dissipate Guido's suspicions, I was almost prepared to tell him how I had managed to win the dog's dislike.

I soon had a skirmish with Guido over a question that really shouldn't have mattered that much to me. Having grown so passionately concerned with accounting, he took it into his head to enter his household expenses under our general expenses. After consulting Olivi, I opposed this plan and defended the interests of old *Cada Vez*. It was, in fact, impossible to enter under that heading everything that Guido spent, and also Ada, and later the expenses of the twins, when they were born. These were expenses chargeable to Guido personally and not to the firm. To compensate for this, I then suggested writing to Buenos Aires, to fix a salary for Guido. His father refused to grant one, pointing out that Guido already enjoyed seventy-five percent of the profits, whereas his father received only what was left. This reply seemed fair to me, but Guido started writing long letters to his father to argue the question from a higher point of view, as he put it. Buenos Aires was very far away, and so the correspondence lasted as long as our firm lasted. But I won my point! The general expenses account remained pure and was not infected by Guido's personal expenditures, and so the entire capital was polluted by the failure of the firm, all of it, without deductions.

The fifth person admitted to our office (counting Argo as a person) was Carmen. I witnessed her hiring. I came to the office after having been at Carla's and I was feeling very serene, that 8:00 a.m. serenity of Prince Taillerand.* In the dim corridor I saw a young lady, and Luciano told me she wanted to speak with Guido in person. I had something to do and I asked her to wait outside there. Guido came into our room a little later, obviously not having seen the young lady, and Luciano entered and gave me the calling card she had supplied.

Guido read it, then said "No!" sharply, taking off his jacket because of the heat. But a moment later he had second thoughts. "I must speak with her, out of respect for the person who has recommended her."

He had her shown in, and I looked at her only when I saw that Guido, with one leap, had flung himself at his jacket, put it on, and was addressing the girl with the beautiful, dark, blushing face and the sparkling eyes.

Now, I am sure I have seen girls just as beautiful as Carmen, but not with a beauty so aggressive – so apparent at first glance, I mean. As a rule women create themselves first according to their own desire, whereas this girl had no need of a similar preliminary phase. Looking at her, I smiled and I also laughed. She was like an industrialist running about the world asserting the excellence of his products. She had come to apply for a job, but I would have liked to interrupt the interview, to ask, "What sort of job? In a boudoir?"

I saw that her face was not made up, but its colors were so precise, so cerulean was its purity and so like that of ripe fruit its ruddiness, that artifice was simulated to perfection. Her

* Zeno's spelling of Talleyrand.

great dark eyes refracted such a quantity of light that their every movement assumed great importance.

Guido had asked her to take a seat, and she was modestly looking at the tip of her umbrella or, more probably, at her little patent-leather boots. When he spoke to her, she quickly raised her eyes and turned them on his face; they were so radiant that my poor employer was absolutely bowled over. She was dressed modestly, but that was of no help to her because all modesty, on her body, was annihilated. Only the little boots were a luxury, and recalled a bit the very white paper that Velázquez set under the feet of his models. Velázquez, too, to set Carmen apart from her surroundings, would have placed her on black enamel.

In my serenity I began listening with curiosity. Guido asked her if she knew shorthand. She confessed she hadn't the slightest knowledge of it, adding, however, that she had considerable experience in taking dictation. Strange! That tall, slender, and so harmonious figure emitted a hoarse voice. I couldn't conceal my surprise.

"Do you have a cold?" I asked her.

"No!" she answered. "Why do you ask?" And she was so surprised that the glance with which she enveloped me was all the more intense. She was unaware that she had such a jarring voice, and I had to suppose that her little ear, too, was less perfect than it looked.

Guido asked her if she knew English, French, or German. He left the choice to her, as we didn't yet know which language we would need. Carmen replied that she knew a little German, very little, however.

Guido never came to a decision without reasoning. "We don't need German, because I speak it very well myself."

The young lady was awaiting the deciding word, which, it seemed to me, had already been spoken; but to hasten it, she said that in seeking a new job she also sought a chance to learn, and therefore she would be satisfied with very modest wages.

One of the first effects of female beauty on a man is to strip him of avarice. Guido shrugged, to signify that he didn't concern himself with such trifles; he named a salary, which she gratefully accepted, and he urged her very seriously to study shorthand. He made this recommendation only for my benefit, as he had previously compromised himself with me, declaring that the first employee he hired would be a perfect stenographer.

That same evening I told my wife about my new colleague. She was terribly upset. Though I said nothing, she immediately imagined Guido had hired this girl intending to make her his mistress. While admitting that Guido had behaved rather like a suitor, I argued with her and insisted he would recover from this infatuation, which would have no consequences. The girl, all in all, seemed respectable.

A few days later – whether by chance or not, I don't know – we received a visit at the office from Ada. Guido hadn't come in yet, so she tarried with me for a moment, to ask me when he would arrive. Then, hesitantly, she stepped into the next room, where, at that moment, Carmen and Luciano were alone. Carmen was practicing at the typewriter, completely absorbed in picking out the individual letters. She raised her lovely eyes to look at Ada, who was staring at her. How different the two women were! They resembled each other slightly, but Carmen seemed an intensified Ada. I thought that truly the latter, though dressed more richly, was made to be a wife or mother, while the other, though at that moment she wore a modest smock to avoid soiling her dress at the machine, was cast as mistress. I don't know if, in this world, there are learned men who could tell why Ada's beautiful eye collected less light than Carmen's and so was genuinely an organ for looking at things and people and not for dazzling them. Therefore Carmen easily tolerated its scornful but curious glance: did it contain also a touch of envy, or am I adding that myself?

This was the last time I saw Ada still beautiful, just as she had been when she rejected me. Her disastrous pregnancy followed, with the twins, who required a surgeon's intervention to come into the world. Immediately afterwards she was stricken by the disease that robbed her of all her beauty. This is why I remember that visit so well. I remember it also because at that moment all my compassion went out to her and to her meek and modest beauty, defeated by the very different beauty of the other woman. I certainly didn't love Carmen and I knew nothing of her beyond the magnificent eyes, the splendid coloring, the hoarse voice, and finally the circumstances – of which she was innocent – surrounding her employment here. I was truly fond of Ada at that moment, and it is a very strange thing to feel fondness for a woman one once ardently desired, did not possess, and who now matters not at all. All things considered, in this fashion you arrive at the same state you would be in if she had succumbed to your desires, and it is surprising to realize once again how certain things for which we live have really scant importance.

I wanted to curtail her pain, and I led her into the other room. Guido, entering a moment later, turned deep red at the sight of his wife. Ada gave him a highly plausible reason for her being there, but immediately afterwards, as she was leaving, she asked: "You've hired a new secretary for the office?"

"Yes!" Guido said, and to conceal his confusion he could find nothing better than to change the subject, asking if anybody had come looking for him. Then, after my negative answer, he made another grimace of displeasure, as if he had hoped for an important visit, whereas I knew that we were expecting no one at all, and only then did he say to Ada, with an indifferent expression, which he finally managed to assume: "We needed a stenographer!"

I was highly amused to hear that in his confusion, he used the masculine noun.

The arrival of Carmen brought much life into our office. I'm not speaking of the vivacity that came from her eyes, from her charming form, and from the color in her face; I am actually speaking of business. In the presence of that young woman, Guido felt impelled to work. First of all, he wanted to prove to me and to everyone else that the new employee was necessary, and every day he invented new tasks in which he also took part. Further, for a long time, his activity was a means of courting the girl more efficiently. He achieved an unheard-of efficiency. He had to teach her the form of the business letter, which he would dictate, and he would correct the spelling of very many words. He always did this delicately. No reward on the girl's part would have been excessive.

Few of the transactions he fondly thought up bore any fruit. Once he worked at length on a transaction involving an article that proved to be illegal. At a certain point we found ourselves facing a man, his face distorted with pain, on whose toes we had unwittingly trod. This man wanted to know what our interest was in that article, and he presumed we had been engaged by powerful foreign competitors. At our first encounter he was beside himself, and I feared the worst. When he realized our naïveté, he laughed in our faces and assured us we'd never achieve anything. It turned out he was right, but before we could accept this verdict, much time had to pass, and many a letter had to be written by Carmen. We found that the article in question was beyond our reach because it was surrounded by entrenched forces. I said nothing about this transaction to Augusta, but she spoke of it to me because Guido had spoken of it to Ada, to show her how busy our stenographer was. But the deal that didn't come off still remained important for Guido. He talked about it every day. He was convinced that in no other city of the world would such a thing have happened. Our commercial ambiance was deplorable, and any enterprising businessman was stifled here. And such was his fate also.

In the mad, disordered sequence of transactions that passed through our hands in that period, there was one that really scorched them. We didn't seek it out; it was the deal that took us by storm. We were pushed into it by a certain Tacich, a Dalmatian who had worked in Argentina with Guido's father. He first came to see us only to ask for some commercial information that we were able to provide for him.

Tacich was a very handsome young man, indeed too handsome. He was tall and strong, his face was olive-skinned, and the dark blue of his eyes harmonized charmingly with his long eyelashes and the short, thick, dark mustache with golden glints. In short, there was in him such a harmonious study of color that to me he seemed the man born to match Carmen. He was of the same opinion, and he dropped in on us daily. The conversation in our office then lasted for hours every day, but it was never boring. The two men fought to win the woman, and like all animals in love, they showed off their finest qualities. Guido was a bit cramped by the fact that the Dalmatian also called on him at home and hence knew Ada, but by now nothing could harm him in Carmen's eyes; I, who knew those eyes so well, realized this at once, whereas Tacich learned it only much later, and in order to have a pretext to see her frequently, he bought from us — or rather from the manufacturer — various carloads of soap for which he paid a slightly higher percentage. Then, again because of his love, he plunged us into that disastrous affair.

His father had noticed that, regularly, at certain seasons, copper sulfate went up and at other times its price went down. He decided therefore to speculate, buying some sixty tons in England at the most favorable moment. We discussed this venture at length, and indeed we prepared for it, getting in touch with an English firm. Then his father cabled Tacich that the right moment seemed to have arrived, and he cited also the price at which he would be willing to close the transaction. Tacich, enamored as he was, rushed to us and delivered the deal, receiving as reward a beautiful, long, caressing look from Carmen. The poor Dalmatian accepted the look gratefully, unaware that it was a sign of her love for Guido.

I remember Guido's calm and confidence as he set about the business, which, in fact, seemed very easy because from England we could arrange direct shipment to our purchaser, without handling the goods ourselves. Guido calculated exactly the sum he wanted to earn and, with my help, established the maximum price that our English friend should pay. With the dictionary's help, together we worked out the cable in English. Once it was sent, Guido rubbed his hands and started calculating how many crowns would pour into the cash box as a reward for that brief and easy effort. To maintain the favor of the gods, he found it proper to promise a little bonus for me and then, somewhat slyly, also for Carmen, who had contributed to the venture with her eyes. We both wanted to refuse, but he begged us at least to pretend to accept. Otherwise he was afraid we would all suffer bad luck, and I obeyed him at once to reassure him. I knew, with mathematical certainty, that he would be the recipient of only my warmest wishes, but I understood that he could be dubious about that. In this world, when we don't wish one another ill, we all love one another, but our most vital desires accompany only the affairs to which we are personally committed.

The affair was scrutinized in every respect and, in fact, I remember Guido calculated even the number of months during which, with his profits, he could maintain his wife and the office, his two families, in other words, or his two offices, as he sometimes called them when at home he was particularly vexed. It was overscrutinized, that affair, and this is perhaps why it didn't work out. From London came a brief dispatch: *Bought*, then the indication of that day's price for sulfate, much higher than what our buyer had stipulated. Good-bye, profit. Tacich was informed, and a short time later he left Trieste.

At that time, for about a month I stopped going to the office, and therefore a certain letter that arrived there didn't pass through my hands; apparently inoffensive, it was nevertheless to have serious consequences for Guido. In it, that English firm confirmed its dispatch to us and informed us finally that it considered our order valid, unless it was revoked. It didn't occur to Guido to revoke that order, and when I came back to the office, I had forgotten about the whole transaction. And so several months later, one evening Guido came to see me with a dispatch he couldn't understand and he thought had been sent to us by mistake, despite the fact that it clearly bore our cable address, which I had naturally made public as soon as we were settled in our office. The dispatch contained only three English words: *60 tons confirmed*. I understood it immediately, which was not hard inasmuch as the copper sulfate affair was the only big transaction we had initiated. I said to him: From that dispatch it was clear that the price, which we had stipulated for executing our order, had been reached and therefore we were the proud owners of sixty tons of copper sulfate.

Guido protested: "How can they think I'd accept such a belated filling of my order?"

I immediately thought that the letter confirming the first dispatch must be in our office, whereas Guido had no recollection of having received it. Uneasy, he suggested rushing to the office at once to see if it was there, and this suited me very well because I was annoyed at our having this argument in front of Augusta, who didn't know that for the past month I had never shown up at the office.

We hurried to the office. Guido was so displeased to see himself forced into that first big deal that, to be rid of it, he would have run all the way to London. We opened the office; then, groping in the darkness, we found our way to our room and reached the gas and lighted it. Then the letter was quickly found and it was as I had supposed, a confirmation that our order, valid until revoked, had been executed.

Guido looked at the letter, his brow furrowed, either with displeasure or with an effort to make his gaze annihilate what was announced as real, in such verbal simplicity.

"Just think!" he said. "It would have been enough to write two words, and this damage would have been avoided!"

It was certainly not a reproach aimed at me because I had been absent from the office and – though I had been able to find the letter immediately, knowing where it should have been – had never seen it before. But to absolve myself more completely of any reproach of his, I addressed him firmly.

"During my absence you should have read all the letters carefully!"

Guido's frown vanished. He shrugged and murmured: "This deal could prove a stroke of luck in the end."

A little later he left me, and I returned home.

But Tacich was right: at certain seasons copper sulfate went down, way down, farther every day, and in the filling of our order and in our immediate impossibility of selling the goods at that price to others, we had occasion to study the phenomenon thoroughly. Our loss increased. The first day Guido asked my advice. He could have sold at a loss small compared to what he had to bear later. I was unwilling to give advice, but I didn't fail to remind him of Tacich's conviction that the fall in value would continue for over five months.

Guido laughed. "Now all I need is that provincial telling me how to run my business!"

I remembered that I tried also to correct him, saying that this provincial had for many years spent his time in his little Dalmatian city following copper sulfate. I can have no remorse for the loss Guido suffered in that venture. If he had listened to me, it would have been spared him.

Later we discussed the copper sulfate affair with an agent, a short, tubby little man, brisk and bright, who scolded us for having made that purchase, though he seemed not to share Tacich's opinion. According to him, copper sulfate, though it was a market unto itself, still was affected by the fluctuation of the general price of metal. From that interview Guido gained a certain confidence. He asked the agent to keep him informed of every shift in price, he would wait, as he wanted to sell not only without loss, but with a small profit. The agent laughed discreetly, then, in the course of the conversation, said something I remarked because it seemed to me very true.

"Strange, how few people in this world can resign themselves to small losses; it's the great losses that immediately produce great resignation."

Guido paid no attention. But I admired him, too, because he didn't tell the agent how we had happened to make that purchase. I told Guido this, and he was proud. The agent, he said, would have tried to discredit us and also our goods, spreading the story of that purchase.

Afterwards, for a long time, we didn't mention sulfate again – that is, until a letter arrived from London asking us to make payment and wire instructions for the shipment. Sixty tons! To receive and then to store! Guido's head began to spin. We calculated how much it would cost us to warehouse that merchandise for several months. A huge amount! I didn't say anything, but the broker, who would have been glad to see the goods arrive in Trieste, because sooner or later he would then have been given the job of selling them, pointed out to Guido that this sum, which seemed huge to him, was not so great if expressed in percentage on the value of the goods.

Guido started laughing, because the observation seemed strange to him: "I don't have a mere hundred pounds of sulfate; I have sixty tons, unfortunately!"

In the end he would have allowed the agent's calculation, obviously correct, to convince him that with a slight upward shift in the price, the expenses would have been more than covered; but at that moment he was struck by one of what he called his inspirations. When he happened to conceive a commercial idea all on his own, it became an absolute obsession, and there was no room in his mind for other considerations. This was his idea: The merchandise would be sent him FOB Trieste, so the English shippers would pay for transport. If he were now to sell the goods back to his English purchasers, they would thus save the expenses of the shipment, and he would benefit by setting a more advantageous price than the one being offered him in Trieste. This was not entirely true, but, to please him, nobody debated it. Once the affair was concluded, he had a slightly bitter smile on his face, like that of a pessimist philosopher, and he said: "We'll say no more about it. It was a pretty costly lesson; now we have to learn how to profit by it."

But we did say more about it. He never recovered his fine confidence in rejecting offers, and at the end of the year, when I showed him how much we had lost, he murmured: "That damned copper sulfate was my downfall! I kept feeling I had to make up for that loss!"

My absence from the office had been provoked by Carla's leaving me. I could no longer witness the dalliance of Carmen and Guido. They looked at each other, smiled at each other, in my presence. I went off indignantly with a resolution I formed that evening at the moment of closing the office, and I said nothing about it to anyone. I would wait until Guido asked me the reason for this desertion, and then I would let him have it. I could be very severe with him, since he knew absolutely nothing of my excursions to the Public Garden.

It was a form of jealousy on my part, because Carmen appeared to me as Guido's Carla, but a milder, more submissive Carla. With his second woman, as with his first, he had been luckier than I. But perhaps – and this motivated another of my reproaches to him – he owed his luck also to those qualities of his that I envied, yet continued to consider inferior: parallel to his ease with the violin there ran also his nonchalance toward life. I now knew for certain that I had given up Carla for Augusta. When my thoughts returned to those two years of happiness Carla had granted me, it was hard for me to understand how she – being the sort of person I now knew she was – could have tolerated me so long. Hadn't I offended her daily, out of love for Augusta? Guido, I knew for a fact, would on the contrary enjoy Carmen without giving Ada a thought. In his carefree spirit, two women were no more than enough. Comparing myself to him, I seemed downright innocent. I had married Augusta without love, and yet I had been unable to betray her without suffering. Perhaps he had also married Ada without loving her, but – though by now Ada meant nothing to me – I remembered the love she had inspired in me, and it seemed to me that since I had loved her so much, in his situation I would have been even more delicate than I was now in my own.

It wasn't Guido who came looking for me. It was I who, on my own, returned to that office, to seek relief from a great boredom. He behaved according to the terms of our contract, whereby I had no obligation to take any part regularly in his affairs, and when he ran into me at home or elsewhere, he acted toward me with the usual great friendship and didn't seem to recall that I had left vacant my place at that desk he had bought for me. Between the two of us there was only one embarrassment: mine. When I returned to my desk, he received me as if I had been absent just a single day, warmly expressed his pleasure at having regained my company and, hearing my intention to resume my work, he cried: "Then I was right not to allow anyone to touch your books!"

In fact, I found the ledger and the daybook exactly where I had left them.

Luciano said to me: "Let's hope that now that you're here, we'll start moving again. I believe Signor Guido is discouraged because of a couple of deals he tackled, which then went sour. Don't say anything to him about me talking to you like this, but see if you can give him some encouragement."

I realized, in fact, that little work was being done in that office, and until the loss on the copper sulfate agitated us, we led a truly idyllic life there. I immediately concluded that Guido no longer felt such an urgent need to make Carmen work under his direction, and that the period of courtship between them was over and she had by now become his mistress.

Carmen's welcome brought me a surprise because she promptly felt the need to remind me of something I had completely forgotten. Apparently, before leaving that office, in those days when I had run after so many women because it was no longer possible for me to go and see my own, I had also pestered Carmen. She spoke to me with great seriousness and some embarrassment: She was glad to see me back because she believed I was fond of Guido and my advice could be useful to him, and she wanted to maintain with me – if I would permit it – a warm, fraternal friendship. She said something to this effect, extending her hand in a broad gesture. On her face, beautiful as it was, a very grave expression underlined the fraternal purity of the relationship now being offered me.

I remembered then, and I blushed. Perhaps if I had remembered earlier, I would never have gone back to that office again. It had been such a brief thing, crammed in among so many other actions of the same import, that if I had not now been reminded of it, I could have believed it had never happened. A few days after Carla's abandonment, I had set myself to examine the books, enlisting Carmen's help and, little by little, the better to see the same page, I had put my arm around her waist, which I then continued to squeeze harder and harder. With a leap, Carmen had escaped me and I had then left the office.

I could have defended myself with a smile, inducing her to smile with me, because women are so inclined to smile at such crimes! I could have said to her: "I attempted something that didn't succeed, and I'm sorry for it, but I bear you no grudge

and I want to be your friend until you prefer it to be otherwise."

Or I could have replied as a serious person, apologizing to
her and also to Guido: "Forgive me and don't judge me until
you know the condition in which I found myself at that time."

Instead, words failed me. My throat — I believe — was
blocked by a lump of bitterness and I was unable to speak.
All these women who firmly rejected me gave my life a
downright tragic cast. I had never endured such a miserable
period. Instead of uttering a reply, I would have been prepared
only to grind my teeth, hardly comfortable, as I had to maintain silence. Perhaps speech failed me also because of the pain
at seeing firmly denied a hope I still cherished. I can't help
confessing it: for me, no one better than Carmen could have
replaced the mistress I had lost, that girl who, so far from being
compromising, had asked for nothing save the permission to
live at my side until she asked never to see me again. A mistress
shared is the least compromising mistress. To be sure, I hadn't
yet entirely clarified my ideas, but I sensed them, and now
I know them. Becoming Carmen's lover, I would have contributed to Ada's well-being and I wouldn't have harmed
Augusta too much. Both would have been betrayed far less
than if Guido and I had had a whole woman each.

I gave Carmen my reply several days later, but even now it
embarrasses me. The turmoil into which Carla's abandonment
had thrown me must have still survived, impelling me to such
a juncture. I feel a remorse for it worse than for any other
action in my whole life. The bestial words we allow to escape
us prick the conscience more than the most unspeakable
actions our passion inspires. Naturally, by words I mean only
those that are not actions, because I know very well that the
words of Iago, for example, are out-and-out actions. But
actions, including Iago's words, are performed to produce
some pleasure or some benefit and then the whole organism,
including that part which should set itself up as judge,

participates and becomes consequently a very benevolent judge. But the stupid tongue acts on its own and for the satisfaction of some little part of the organism that, without words, feels defeated and proceeds to simulate a struggle after the struggle is over and lost. The tongue wants to wound or it wants to caress. It moves always amid mastodonic metaphors. And when words are red-hot, they scorch their speaker.

I had observed that she no longer had the coloring that had won her such prompt admittance to our office. I imagined she had lost it through some suffering that I refused to admit might have been physical, and I attributed it, instead, to her love for Guido. For that matter, we men are quite inclined to commiserate with those women who surrender to others. We never see what advantage they can expect. We may perhaps love the man in question – as was my case – but even then we can't forget how the vicissitudes of love on this earth usually end up. I felt a sincere compassion for Carmen, as I had never felt for Augusta or for Carla. I said to her: "And as you have been so kind as to invite me to be your friend, will you allow me to give you some advice?"

She wouldn't allow it, because, like all women in such situations, she also believed that advice is always an aggression. She blushed and stammered: "I don't understand. Why are you saying that?" And, immediately afterwards, to silence me: "If I really needed advice, I would certainly turn to you, Signor Cosini."

Therefore I was not allowed to preach morality to her, and it was too bad for me. In preaching morality to her I would surely have arrived at a higher level of sincerity, perhaps attempting again to take her into my arms. I would not torment myself any more for having wanted to play that false role of Mentor.

Several days each week, Guido never even put in an appearance at the office, for he was an impassioned hunter and fisherman. I, on the contrary, after my return, was assiduous for a while, occupied with bringing the books up to date. I was often with Carmen and Luciano, who considered me their manager. It didn't seem to me that Carmen suffered at Guido's absence, and I imagined she loved him so much that she was overjoyed to know that he was having a good time. She must also have been advised which days he would be absent, because she showed no sign of anxious expectation. I knew from Augusta that with Ada, on the contrary, it was a different story, for she complained bitterly of her husband's frequent absences. In any case, that wasn't her only complaint. Like all unloved women, she complained of great wrongs and small ones with the same fervor. Not only was Guido unfaithful to her, but when he was at home he constantly played the violin. That violin, which had caused me such suffering, was a kind of Achilles' spear in the variety of its functions. I learned that it had also passed through our office, where it had enriched the wooing of Carmen with some beautiful variations on the *Barber*. Then it had moved on, as in the office it was no longer needed, and had returned home, where it spared Guido the boredom of having to converse with his wife.

There was never anything between me and Carmen. Quite soon I felt an absolute indifference toward her, as if she had changed sex, something similar to what I felt for Ada. A keen sympathy for both, and nothing more. That was it!

Guido showered me with kindnesses. I believe that in that month when I had left him alone, he had learned to value my company. A girl like Carmen can be pleasant from time to time, but you can't really bear her for whole days. He invited me hunting and fishing. I detest hunting, and firmly refused to accompany him. But one evening, driven by boredom, I did end up going fishing with him. A fish lacks any means of communicating with us, and cannot arouse our compassion. He gasps even when he's safe and sound in the water! Death itself doesn't alter his appearance. His suffering, if it exists, is perfectly concealed beneath his scales.

One day, when Guido had invited me to go fishing in the evening, I put off my decision until I could see if Augusta would allow me to stay out so late that night. I told him I wouldn't forget that his boat would be casting off from the Sartorio dock at 9:00 p.m. and, if it was possible, I'd be there. So I assumed he, too, would immediately know he wouldn't see me that evening and, as I had done so many other times, I would fail to turn up at the appointed hour.

Instead, that evening I was driven out of the house by my little Antonia's screams. The more her mother caressed her, the more the little one screamed. Then I tried a system of mine that consisted of shouting insults into the tiny ear of that yelling monkey. The only result was to alter the rhythm of her screams, because she began to cry out also in fright. Then I thought to try another system a bit more vigorous, but Augusta recalled Guido's invitation just in time and accompanied me to the door, promising to go to bed by herself if I was late coming home. Indeed, if it would send me away, she would even contrive to take her coffee without me the next morning, if I were still out then. There is a little divergence of opinion between me and Augusta – our only one – about how to treat troublesome babies: it seems to me that the baby's suffering is less important than ours and that it's worth letting the infant endure it in order to spare the adult greater distress; she, on the contrary, feels that as we made the children, we must also put up with them.

I was in plenty of time to reach the dock, and I crossed the city slowly, looking at the women and at the same time devising a mechanism that would prevent any disagreement between me and Augusta. But for my device mankind was not yet sufficiently mature! It was destined for the distant future and could be of no help to me except in showing me the trivial cause that made my disputes with Augusta possible: the lack of a little device! It would have been simple, a domestic tramway, a high chair equipped with wheels and tracks on which my child would spend her day: an electric switch, at one touch, would send chair and screaming baby off, at top speed, toward the most remote point in the house, whence its voice, muted by the distance, would actually seem pleasant. And Augusta and I would remain together where we were, serene and loving.

It was a night rich in stars and without a moon, one of those nights when you can see a great distance, a night that therefore softens and soothes. I looked at the stars that might still bear the mark of my dying father's farewell glance. The horrible period in which my children soiled and screamed would pass. Then they would be like me; I would love them dutifully and effortlessly. In the beautiful, vast night I was completely reassured and had no need to make resolutions.

At the end of the Sartorio dock, the lights from the city were cut off by the old building from which the point itself extends like a brief pier. The darkness was perfect, and the water, deep and dark and still, seemed to me lazily swollen.

I no longer looked at either heaven or sea. A few paces from me there was a woman who aroused my curiosity, thanks to a patent-leather boot that for an instant gleamed in the darkness. In this brief space and in the darkness, to me it seemed this woman, tall and perhaps elegant, and I were enclosed in a room together. The most enjoyable adventures can occur when least expected, and, seeing that woman suddenly and deliberately approach me, for an instant I had a most pleasant sensation, which vanished immediately when I heard the hoarse voice of Carmen. She tried to act pleased at discovering that I, too, was one of the party. But in the darkness and with that voice, she couldn't pretend.

I said to her roughly: "Guido invited me. But if you want, I'll find something else to do and leave you to yourselves!"

She protested, declaring that, on the contrary, she was happy to see me for the third time that day. She told me that the entire office would be united in this little boat, because

Luciano was there, too. What a disaster for our business if we were to sink! Surely she had told me about Luciano's being there only to prove to me that the meeting was innocent. Then she continued chatting volubly, at once informing me that this was the first time she was going fishing with Guido, then confessing it was the second. She had involuntarily let me know that she didn't mind sitting on the bottom of the boat, the bilges, and it seemed strange to me that she should know the term. Thus she had to confess that she had learned it when she had gone out fishing with Guido the first time.

"That day," she added, to reveal the complete innocence of her first excursion, "we went fishing for mackerel, not bream. In the morning."

Too bad I didn't have time to encourage her to chatter more, because I could have learned everything that mattered to me, but Guido's boat was emerging from the darkness of the Sacchetta and rapidly coming toward us. I still hesitated. Since Carmen was there, shouldn't I go away? Perhaps Guido hadn't even meant to invite us both, because, as I recalled, I had practically refused his invitation. Meanwhile the boat tied up and, jauntily, confident even in the darkness, Carmen stepped down, not bothering to take the hand Luciano held out to her. As I hesitated, Guido cried: "Don't waste our time!"

With one bound, I was also in the boat. My leap was almost involuntary: a result of Guido's cry. I looked at the land with great desire, but a moment's indecision sufficed to make it impossible for me to go ashore. Finally I sat at the prow of the not-large boat. When I grew accustomed to the darkness, I saw that at the stern, facing me, sat Guido and at his feet, on the bottom, Carmen. Luciano, who was rowing, separated us. I felt neither very confident nor very comfortable in the little boat, but I soon grew accustomed to it and I looked at the stars, which again soothed me. It was true that in the presence of Luciano – a devoted servant of the family of our wives – Guido would not risk betraying Ada, and so there was nothing wrong in my being with them. I keenly desired to be able to enjoy that sky, that sea, and the vast calm. If I were going to feel remorse and therefore suffer, I would have done better to stay at home and submit to the torture of my little Antonia. The cool night air swelled my lungs and I realized that I could enjoy myself in the company of Guido and Carmen, of whom I was, after all, fond.

We rounded the lighthouse and were out at sea. A few miles farther on, the lights of countless sailing boats were shining: there, quite different traps were being set for the fish. From the Military Baths — a massive, blackish establishment on stilts — we began to move up and down along the Sant'Andrea seafront. It was a favorite spot with fishermen. Beside us, silently, many other boats were following our same course. Guido prepared the three lines and baited the hooks, spearing some shrimp by the tail. He gave each of us a pole, saying that mine, at the prow — the only one provided with a sinker — would attract the most fish. In the darkness I could discern the pierced tail of my shrimp, and it seemed to be moving slowly the upper part of its impaled body, that part that hadn't become a sheath. This movement made it seem to be meditating rather than writhing in pain. Perhaps whatever produces pain in large organisms can be reduced, in the very small, until it becomes a different experience, a stimulus to thought. I dropped the shrimp into the water, lowering it, as I had been instructed by Guido, about thirty feet. After me, Carmen and Guido dropped their lines. Guido, at the stern, now also had an oar, which he used to propel the boat with the skill required to keep the lines from tangling. Apparently, Luciano wasn't yet sufficiently skilled to guide the boat like that. In any case, Luciano was now assigned the little net with which he would lift from the water the fish our hooks brought to the surface. For a long time he had nothing to do. Guido chattered a lot. Who knows? Perhaps he was drawn to Carmen more by his passion for instruction than by love. I would have preferred not to sit there listening, but rather to think of the little animal I kept exposed to the voracity of the fish, suspended in the water, and that, nodding its tiny head – if it continued to do so in the water – would lure fish all the better. But Guido called to me repeatedly, and I had to hear his theory of fishing. The fish would nibble the bait several times and we would feel them, but we should take care not to pull on the line until it became taut. Then we should be ready to give it the jerk that would drive the hook squarely into the fish's mouth. Guido, as usual, was lengthy in his explanations. He wanted to explain clearly to us what we would feel in our hands when the fish nibbled the bait. And he continued his explanations when Carmen and I already knew from experience the almost aural sensation produced on the hand by every contact the hook underwent. Several times we had to draw in the line to replace the bait. The little pensive animal remained unavenged in the maw of some clever fish able to elude the hook.

On board was some beer and sandwiches. Guido spiced everything with his ceaseless garrulity. Now he talked about the enormous riches that lay in the sea. He didn't mean fish, as Luciano believed, or the riches sunk there by man. In the water of the sea, gold was dissolved. Suddenly he recalled that I had studied chemistry, and he said to me: "You should also know something about this gold."

I didn't remember much, but I nodded, venturing a remark of whose truth I was unsure. I asserted: "The gold of the sea is the most expensive of all. To acquire one of those napoleons lying dissolved down here, you would have to spend five."

Luciano, who had eagerly turned to me to hear me confirm the riches on which we were floating, now looked away, disappointed. He no longer cared about that gold. But Guido agreed with me, believing he could recall that the price of such gold was exactly five times its market value, just as I had said. He even glorified me, confirming my assertion, which I knew was a total invention of my brain. Obviously he felt I represented no great threat, and he harbored not a shadow of jealousy regarding that woman curled up at his feet. I thought for an instant of embarrassing him by declaring that now I remembered more clearly, and to extract one of those napoleons from the sea, ten would be necessary, or perhaps a mere three would be enough.

But at that moment I was summoned by my line, which suddenly tautened at a mighty tug. I gave a tug in reply, and I shouted. With a leap, Guido was beside me; he snatched the line from my hand. I gladly let him have it. He started pulling it up, first in short lengths, then, as the resistance lessened, in great ones. And in the murky water the silvery body of a big animal could be seen shining. It now swam rapidly and without resistance, following its pain. So I understood also the pain of the silent animal, because it was shouted by that haste in rushing toward death. Soon I had it, gasping, at my feet. Luciano had drawn it from the water in the net and, yanking the hook with no consideration, he removed it from the fish's mouth.

He squeezed the heavy fish.

"A seven-pound bream!"

In admiration, he quoted the price it would have fetched at the fish market. Then Guido observed that at this hour the water was still, and it would be hard to catch any more fish. He told how fishermen believed that when the water neither waxed nor waned, the fish didn't eat and therefore couldn't be caught. He philosophized on the danger an animal risked because of its appetite. Then, starting to laugh, unaware that he was compromising himself, he said: "You're the only one able to fish this evening."

My catch was still wriggling in the boat when Carmen let out a cry. Without stirring, and with a great desire to laugh audible in his voice, Guido asked: "Another bream?"

Confused, Carmen answered: "I thought so! But it's already let go of the hook!"

I'm sure that, overwhelmed by his desire, Guido had given her a pinch.

At this point I felt uncomfortable in that boat. I no longer followed the activity of my hook with my desire, indeed, I jerked the line so much that the poor fish couldn't bite. I declared I was sleepy, and I asked Guido to put me ashore at Sant'Andrea. Then I wanted to allay his suspicion that I was leaving because I was annoyed by what Carmen's cry must have revealed to me, so I told him of the scene my little girl had made that evening, and of my desire now to make sure she wasn't sick.

Obliging as always, Guido drew the boat up to the shore. He offered me the bream I had caught, but I refused it. I suggested giving it back its freedom by throwing it into the sea, which provoked a cry of protest from Luciano, as Guido good-naturedly said: "If I knew I could give it back health and life, I would. But by now the poor animal can go nowhere but into a pan!"

I followed them with my eyes, and I could verify that they didn't exploit the space I had left free. They were huddled close together, and the boat went off a bit high at the prow and too heavy at the stern.

It seemed to me a divine punishment when I learned that my baby had come down with a fever. Hadn't I caused her illness, feigning for Guido a concern for her health that I didn't feel? Augusta had not yet gone to bed, but Dr. Paoli had been there a short time before and had reassured her, saying he was sure the fever, as sudden as it was violent, could not indicate any serious illness. We stood a long time watching Antonia, who lay limp on her little cot, the skin of her face dry and flushed intensely below her disheveled dark curls. She didn't cry out, but moaned now and then, a brief lament arrested by an imperious torpor. My God! How close her sickness brought her to me! I would have given a part of my life to free her respiration. How could I dispel my remorse for thinking

I couldn't love her, and having spent all that time, when she was suffering, far from her and in that company?

"She looks like Ada!" Augusta said with a sob. It was true! We noticed it then for the first time, and that resemblance became more and more obvious as Antonia grew, so that sometimes I feel my heart quake at the thought that she could suffer the fate of the poor woman she resembles.

We lay down, after setting the baby's cot beside Augusta's bed. But I couldn't sleep: I had a weight on my heart as I did on those evenings when my misdeeds of the day were reflected in nocturnal images of suffering and remorse. The baby's illness weighed on me as if it were my own doing. I rebelled! I was pure and I could speak, I could tell everything. And I did tell everything. I told Augusta about the meeting with Carmen, the position she occupied in the boat, and then her cry, which I suspected had been provoked by a brutish gesture of Guido's, though I couldn't be sure. But Augusta was sure. Because otherwise, immediately afterwards, why would Guido's voice have a tone of hilarity? I tried to temper her conviction, but then I had still more to tell. I confessed also my own part, describing the boredom that had driven me from the house, and my remorse at not loving Antonia more. I immediately felt better and I fell sound asleep.

The next morning Antonia had improved; the fever was almost gone. She lay there, calm and breathing freely, but she was pale and drawn as if she had been consumed by a struggle disproportionate to her little organism; obviously she had emerged from the brief battle victorious. In the consequent peace, which also affected me, I recalled with regret how horribly I had compromised Guido, and I wanted Augusta to promise me she would communicate her suspicions to no one. She objected that they weren't suspicions, but obviously certainties, which I denied, without managing to convince her. Then she promised everything I wished, and I went off to the office with an easy mind.

Guido hadn't yet come in, and Carmen told me they had had quite a run of luck after I left. They had caught another two bream, smaller than mine, but nice and plump. I was reluctant to believe it, and I thought she was trying to convince me they had abandoned the occupation in which they had been involved while I was there. Hadn't the water become still? How late had they stayed out on the water?

To convince me, Carmen also made Luciano confirm the catching of the two bream, and from that time on I imagined that, to ingratiate himself with Guido, Luciano was capable of anything.

Still during the idyllic calm that preceded the copper-sulfate affair, something fairly strange occurred in that office, which I have been unable to forget, both because it confirms Guido's boundless presumption and because it places me in a light where I can hardly recognize myself.

One day all four of us were in the office, and the only one who was talking about business was, as always, Luciano. Something in his words sounded, to Guido's ear, like a reproach, which in Carmen's presence was hard for him to tolerate. But it was equally hard for him to defend himself, because Luciano had the proofs that a transaction he had advised months before, which Guido had rejected, had later earned a large sum of money for the person who accepted the offer. Guido ended by declaring that he scorned commerce, and he asserted that if fortune failed to assist him in business, he would find a way of making money through other, far more intelligent activities. Playing the violin, for example. All were in agreement with him, including me, though I expressed one reservation: "Provided you study a lot."

My reservation displeased him, and he said at once that if it were just a matter of studying, then he could have gone into many other fields – literature, for example. Here, too, the others agreed, and so did I, but with some hesitation. I didn't recall clearly the physiognomies of our great men of letters, and I tried to evoke them, to find one that resembled Guido.

He then cried: "Would you like some nice fables? I'll improvise some, like Aesop!"

All laughed, except Guido himself. He asked for the typewriter and, fluently, as if he were writing under dictation, with broader gestures than practical typewriting demands, he wrote down his first tale. He was about to hand the little page to Luciano, but then he thought better of it, took it back, replaced it in the machine, and wrote a second; but this one cost him greater effort than the first, and so he forgot to keep simulating inspiration with his gestures, and he had to revise his words several times. So I believe the first of the two fables wasn't his and only the second truly issued from his brain, of which it seems to me worthy. The first tale was about a little bird who happened to notice that the door of his cage had been left open. At first he thought to take advantage of this oversight and fly away, but then he changed his mind, fearing that if, during his absence, the door was closed, he would have lost his freedom. The second concerned an elephant, and it was truly elephantine. Suffering from weak legs, the heavy animal went to consult a man, a famous physician, who, seeing those ponderous limbs, cried, "I never saw stronger legs!"

Luciano didn't let those tales affect him, because he didn't understand them. He laughed abundantly, but it was clear that what seemed comic to him was the notion that something of this sort had been presented to him as salable goods. He laughed also out of courtesy when it was explained to him that the bird was afraid of being deprived of its freedom to return to the cage, and the man admired the elephant's legs, no matter how weak. But then Luciano asked: "What can you get for a pair of stories like that?"

Guido assumed a superior tone. "The pleasure of having created them, and then, after creating some more, also a great deal of money."

Carmen, on the contrary, was overcome with emotion. She asked permission to copy out those two little stories and she gratefully thanked Guido when he made her a present of the page on which he had written them, after he had also signed it with his pen.

What did I have to do with this? I didn't have to fight to win Carmen's admiration, which, as I have said, meant nothing to me; but remembering my behavior then, I have to believe that even a woman who is not an object of our desire can drive us to fight. In fact, didn't the medieval heroes fight over women they had never seen? To me that day it so happened that the shooting pains in my poor organism suddenly became acute, and I thought I could alleviate them only by dueling with Guido, immediately writing some fables of my own.

I had them give me the typewriter, and I really did improvise. True, the first tale I wrote had been in my thoughts for many days. I improvised the title: "Hymn to Life." Then, after reflecting an instant, I wrote below that: "Dialogue." It seemed to me easier to make animals speak than to describe them. Thus my fable took the form of a brief dialogue:

The pensive shrimp: Life is beautiful, but you have to take care where you sit.

The bream (rushing to the dentist): Life is beautiful, but we should eliminate those traitorous little animals that, inside their tasty flesh, conceal sharp metal.

Now I had to make up the second fable, but I had run out of animals. I looked at the dog lying in his corner, and he looked back at me. Those timid eyes evoked a memory: a few days earlier Guido had returned from hunting covered with fleas, and had gone to clean himself up in our little closet. I immediately had my fable, and I wrote it in one breath: "Once upon a time there was a prince, bitten by many fleas. He called on the gods, beseeching them to inflict a single flea on him, big and ravening, but just one, and the others were to be assigned to the rest of mankind. But none of the fleas would agree to remain alone with that beast of a man, and so he had to keep them all."

At that moment my fables seemed splendid to me. The things that issue from our brains have a supremely lovable appearance, especially when you look at them the moment they're born. To tell the truth, I like my dialogue even now, when I have had plenty of practice in creating. The hymn to life made by the doomed creature is something very pleasurable for those who are watching his sentence being executed, and it is also true that many who are moribund expend their dying breath to tell what, to them, seems the cause of their death, thus intoning a hymn to the life of the others, who will be able to avoid that misfortune. As for the second fable, I don't wish to speak of it, and it was wittily commented on by Guido himself, who shouted, laughing: "That's not a fable: it's a way of calling me an animal."

I laughed with him, and the pains that had impelled me to write immediately abated. Luciano laughed when I explained to him what I meant, and he believed nobody would pay anything for my fables or for Guido's. But Carmen didn't like my stories. She gave me an inquisitorial glance, truly new for those eyes, and I understood it as if it had been spoken aloud: You don't love Guido!

I was absolutely distraught because at that moment she surely was not mistaken. I thought I was wrong to behave as if I didn't love Guido – I, who, after all, worked altruistically for him. I had to be more careful of my behavior.

I said meekly to Guido: "I'm willing to admit that your fables are better than mine. But you must remember these are the first fables I've ever written."

He didn't back down. "Do you think I've written others?"

Carmen's gaze had already softened and, to make it even less harsh, I said to Guido: "You surely have a special talent for fables."

But the compliment made them both laugh and me, too, immediately afterwards, but all good-naturedly, because it was obvious I had spoken without any malicious intent.

The copper-sulfate deal brought a greater seriousness to our office. There was no more time for fables. Almost all the offers proposed to us now were accepted. Some brought in a profit, but slight; others entailed losses, large ones. A strange avarice was the chief defect in Guido, who, outside of business, was so generous. When a deal worked out, he liquidated it hastily, eager to collect the small profit he gained by it. When, on the contrary, he found himself involved in a losing venture, he could never seem to extricate himself, not if he could postpone the moment when he had to dig into his own pocket. This, I believe, is why his losses were always considerable and his profits slight. A businessman's qualities are only what is generated by his whole organism, from the ends of his hair to his toenails. A saying the Greeks have could be applied to Guido: "clever fool." Truly clever, but also truly foolish. He was full of cunning, which served only to grease the slope down which he slid farther and farther.

Along with the copper sulfate, the twins unexpectedly arrived. His first impression was of surprise, and far from pleasant, but then, immediately after announcing the event to me, he managed to make a witticism that made me laugh heartily, and so, pleased with its success, he couldn't go on looking angry. Connecting the two babies with the sixty tons of sulfate, he said: "I'm doomed to operate wholesale!"

To console him, I reminded him that Augusta was again in her seventh month and that soon, in the baby department, my tonnage would equal his.

He answered, still wittily: "To me, good bookkeeper that I am, it doesn't seem the same."

A few days afterwards, he was overcome with great affection for the two little mites. Augusta, who spent a part of every day at her sister's, told me he devoted several hours to them daily. He petted them and sang them to sleep, and Ada was so grateful to him that between the two a new fondness seemed to blossom. During those days he deposited a fairly conspicuous sum with an insurance firm so that when the children turned twenty, they would receive a little nest egg. I remember it, because I debited that sum to his account.

I, too, was invited to see the twins; actually, Augusta had told me that I could also say hello to Ada, who, as it afterwards turned out, was unable to receive me, having to remain in bed even though ten days had gone by since the delivery.

The two babies lay in two cradles in a little room adjoining their parents' bedchamber. From the bed, Ada cried to me: "Aren't they beautiful, Zeno?"

I remained surprised by the sound of that voice. It seemed softer to me: it was a genuine cry, because you could hear the effort it cost, and yet it remained so sweet. No doubt the sweetness in that voice came from motherhood, but it moved me because I had discovered it only when it was addressed to me. That sweetness made me feel as if Ada hadn't called me simply by my first name, but had also prefixed to it an affectionate qualifier, such as "dear" or "dear brother"! I felt a keen gratitude, and I became kind and affectionate.

I replied gaily: "Beautiful and dear, pictures of you, two wonders." To me they looked like two blanched little corpses. Both were whimpering, and not in harmony.

Soon Guido returned to his former life. After the sulfate affair, he came more regularly to the office, but every week, on Saturday, he went off hunting and didn't return until late Monday morning, barely in time to look in at the office before lunch. He went fishing at night, and often spent the night on the water. Augusta told me of Ada's sorrows, for she suffered not only from frantic jealousy but also from being alone so much of the day. Augusta tried to calm her, reminding her that hunting and fishing don't involve women. But – from someone, there was no finding out whom – Ada had been informed that Carmen sometimes accompanied Guido fishing. Guido, then, had confessed as much, adding that there was nothing wrong in his being kind to an employee who was so useful to him. And besides, wasn't Luciano always present, too? In the end he promised not to invite her again, as it made Ada unhappy. He declared he was unwilling to give up either his hunting, which cost him so much money, or his fishing. He said he worked hard (and, in fact, at that time there was a great deal to do in our office) and it seemed to him that he was entitled to a little distraction. Ada was not of this opinion, and it seemed to her that he would have enjoyed a finer distraction with his family, and on this score she had the unconditional agreement of Augusta, whereas for me this latter distraction was a bit too noisy.

Augusta then exclaimed: "Aren't you at home every day, at the proper hours?"

It was true, and I should have confessed that between me and Guido there was a great difference, but I couldn't bring myself to boast about it. I said to Augusta, caressing her: "The merit is all yours, because you used some very drastic methods of training."

Moreover, for poor Guido, things were worsening every day: first there were two babies all right, but only one wet nurse, because everyone hoped that Ada would be able to feed one of the children. But she couldn't, and they had to engage a second wet nurse. When Guido wanted to make me laugh, he would walk up and down the office beating time to the words: "One wife . . . two babies . . . two wet nurses!"

There was one thing Ada particularly hated: Guido's violin. She put up with the babies' crying, but she suffered horribly at the sound of the violin. She once said to Augusta: "I want to bark like a dog when I hear those sounds!"

Strange! Augusta, on the contrary, was blissful when she passed my little study and heard my faltering sounds coming from it!

"But Ada's marriage also was a love-marriage," I said, amazed. "Isn't the violin Guido's greatest asset?"

This sort of talk was completely forgotten when I saw Ada again for the first time. It was I, indeed, who first became aware of her illness. One day early in November – a cold, damp, sunless day – against my usual practice I left the office at three in the afternoon and hurried home, thinking to rest and to dream for a few hours in my warm little study. To reach it, I had to walk down the long passage, and outside Augusta's workroom I stopped, because I heard Ada's voice. It was sweet or tentative (which is the same thing, I believe), as it had been that day when it was addressed to me. I entered the room, impelled by the strange curiosity to see how the serene, the calm Ada could assume that voice, slightly reminiscent of one of our actresses when she wants to make others weep without weeping herself. In fact, it was a false voice, at least that's how I heard it, simply because even without even seeing its owner, I perceived it, for the second time after so many days, still equally moved and moving. I assumed they were talking about Guido, for what other subject could have made Ada so emotional?

On the contrary, the two women were taking a cup of coffee together, discussing domestic matters: linen, servants, and so on. But it sufficed for me to see Ada to understand that the voice was not false. Her face, too, was touching, and for the first time I found it so changed; if that voice was not inspired by a feeling, still it mirrored precisely an entire organism, and for this reason it was real and sincere. This I sensed at once. I am not a doctor, and therefore I didn't think of an illness, but I tried to explain to myself the change in Ada's appearance as an effect of her convalescence after giving birth. But how to explain the fact that Guido hadn't noticed this change that had taken place in his wife? Meanwhile, I, who knew those eyes by heart, those eyes I had so feared because I had promptly realized how coldly they examined things and people before accepting them or rejecting them, I could now verify at once that they were changed, enlarged, as if, in order to see better, they had forced their sockets. Those great eyes were a false note in that dejected, faded little face.

She held out her hand to me with great affection. "Yes, I know," she said to me. "You seize every possible moment to come and see your wife and your little girl."

Her hand was moist with sweat, and I know that signifies weakness. So I was all the more convinced that, upon recovering her health, she would regain her former color and the firm line of her cheeks and brow.

I interpreted the words she had addressed to me as a reproach directed at Guido, and good-naturedly I replied that Guido, as head of the business, had greater responsibilities than I, thus he was tied to the office.

She gave me a questioning look to make sure I was speaking seriously. "But still," she said, "it seems to me he could find a little more time for his wife and children." And her voice was full of tears. She recovered herself with a smile that craved indulgence, and added: "Besides business, there is also hunting and fishing! They are what take up so much of his time."

With a volubility that amazed me, she talked about the choice dishes they ate at their table as a result of Guido's hunting and fishing.

"All the same, I'd gladly do without!" she went on, with a sigh and a tear. She wouldn't say, however, that she was unhappy – no, quite the contrary! She said that now she couldn't even imagine being without her two babies, whom she adored! A bit coyly she added, smiling, that she loved them even more now that each had his wet nurse. She didn't sleep much, but at least, when she did manage to doze off, nobody disturbed her. And when I asked her if she really slept so little, she turned serious again and, with emotion, told me that sleep was her greatest problem.

Then, gaily, she added: "But it's already better!"

A little later she left us, for two reasons: Before evening she had to go and see her mother, and moreover she couldn't stand the temperature of our rooms, equipped with great stoves. I, who considered this temperature barely comfortable, thought it was a sign of strength to feel it was excessively hot.

"It doesn't seem you're all that weak," I said, smiling. "Wait and see how different you feel at my age."

She was very flattered to hear herself defined as too young.

Augusta and I accompanied her to the landing. Apparently she felt a great need for our friendship, because, in taking those few steps, she walked between us, grasping first Augusta's arm and then mine, which I immediately stiffened in fear of succumbing to my old habit of squeezing every female arm offered to my touch. On the landing she still talked a good deal, and as she recalled her father, her eyes were again moist, for the third time in a quarter of an hour. When she had gone, I said to Augusta that Ada was not a woman but a fountain. Although I had noticed her sickness, I attached no importance to it. Her eyes were enlarged, her little face was thin, her voice had changed, and even her character, with that displayed affection, so unlike her, but I attributed everything to the double motherhood and to weakness. In short, I proved myself an excellent observer because I saw everything, but also a big ignoramus because I didn't pronounce the true word: illness!

The following day, the obstetrician who was treating Ada asked for a consultation with Dr. Paoli, who immediately uttered the words that I had been unable to say: *morbus basedowii*. Guido told me about it, describing the disease with great erudition and sympathizing with Ada, who suffered greatly. No malice intended, I think his erudition and his sympathy were not great. He struck a heartbroken attitude when he spoke of his wife, but when he dictated letters to Carmen, he displayed all his joy in living and teaching; he believed, too, that the man who had given his name to the disease was the same Basedow who was the friend of Goethe's, whereas when

I looked up that sickness in an encyclopedia, I realized at once that it was a different person.

Basedow's is a great, significant disease! For me, becoming acquainted with it was highly important. I studied it in various monographs and thought I was finally discovering the essential secret of our organism. I believe that many people, like me, go through periods of time when certain ideas occupy, even cram, the whole brain, shutting out all others. Why, the same thing happens to society! It lives on Darwin, after having lived on Robespierre and Napoleon, and then Liebig or perhaps Leopardi, when Bismarck doesn't reign over the whole cosmos!

But only I lived on Basedow! It seemed to me that he had shed light on the roots of life, which is made thus: All organisms extend along a line. At one end is Basedow's disease, which implies the generous, mad consumption of vital force at a precipitous pace, the pounding of an uncurbed heart. At the other end are the organisms depressed through organic avarice, destined to die of a disease that would appear to be exhaustion but which is, on the contrary, sloth. The golden mean between the two diseases is found in the center and is improperly defined as health, which is only a way station. And between the center and one extreme – the Basedow one – are all those who exacerbate and consume life in great desires, ambitions, pleasures, and also work; along the other half of the line, those who, on the scales of life, throw only crumbs and save, becoming those long-lived wretches who seem a burden on society. It seems this burden, too, is necessary. Society proceeds because the Basedowians push it, and it doesn't crash because the others hold it back. I am convinced that anyone wishing to construct a society could do so more simply, but this is the way it's been made, with goiter at one end and edema at the other, and there's no help for it. In the middle are those who have either incipient goiter or incipient edema, and along the entire line, in all mankind, absolute health is missing.

In Ada, too, goiter was absent, according to what Augusta told me, but she had all the other symptoms of the disease. Poor Ada! She used to seem to me the picture of health and equilibrium, so that for a long time I thought she had chosen her husband in the same cold spirit with which her father chose his merchandise, and now she had been seized by a sickness that drew her into quite another regime: psychological perversion! But, along with her, I also fell ill, a slight but prolonged sickness. For too long I thought of Basedow. I already believe that at any point of the universe where you are settled, you end up being infected. You have to keep moving. Life has poisons, but also some other poisons that serve as antidotes. Only by running can you elude the former and take advantage of the latter.

My sickness was a ruling passion, a dream, and also a fear. It must have originated from a process of reasoning; by the term *perversion* we mean a deviation from health, that kind of health that accompanied us for a stretch of our life. Now I knew what Ada's health had been. Mightn't her perversion lead her to love me, whom – when she was healthy – she had rejected?

I don't know how this terror (or this hope) was born in my brain!

Was it perhaps because Ada's sweet, broken voice seemed a voice of love when she addressed me? Poor Ada had become really ugly, and I was unable to desire her any longer. But I kept reviewing our shared past, and it seemed to me that if she were overcome suddenly by love for me, I would find myself in a nasty situation somewhat reminiscent of Guido's position with the English friend and the sixty tons of copper sulfate. The same situation exactly! A few years ago I had declared my love to her, and I hadn't issued any notice of revocation beyond the act of marrying her sister. In that transaction she was not protected by the law, but by chivalry. It seemed to me I had committed myself to her so firmly that if now, many many years later, she were to come to me, complete with a fine goiter, thanks to Basedow, I would have had to honor my signature.

I remember, however, that this prospect made my thoughts of Ada more affectionate. Previously, when I had learned of Ada's sufferings caused by Guido, I surely had not felt pleasure, but I still had turned my thoughts with some satisfaction to my own home, which Ada had refused to enter and where there was no suffering whatsoever. Now things had changed: the Ada who had scornfully repulsed me no longer existed, unless my medical books were mistaken.

Ada's illness was serious. Dr. Paoli, a few days later, advised removing her from the family and sending her to a sanatorium in Bologna. I learned this from Guido, but Augusta then told me that even at a time like this, poor Ada was not being spared serious distress. Guido had had the nerve to suggest bringing in Carmen to run the household during his wife's absence. Ada lacked the courage to say openly what she thought of such a proposal, but she declared that she would not move from the house unless she was allowed to entrust its management to Aunt Maria, and Guido immediately fell in with this idea. However, he continued to cherish the notion of having Carmen at his disposal in the place vacated by Ada. One day he said to Carmen that if she hadn't been so busy in the office, he would gladly have entrusted the management of his household to her. Luciano and I exchanged a glance, and surely each of us discovered a sly expression on the face of the other. Carmen blushed, and murmured that she wouldn't have been able to accept.

"Of course," Guido said, enraged, "because of that stupid concern about what people think, it's impossible to do something really helpful!"

But he, too, soon fell silent and, surprisingly, he truncated his sermon on that interesting topic.

The whole family went to the station to see Ada off. Augusta had asked me to bring some flowers for her sister.

I arrived a bit late with a fine bunch of orchids, which I handed to Augusta. Ada was observing us, and when Augusta passed the flowers to her, she said: "I thank you both with all my heart!"

She meant she was receiving the flowers also from me, but I felt this as a show of sisterly affection, sweet and also a bit cold. Basedow certainly had nothing to do with it.

Poor Ada looked like a young bride, those enormous eyes enlarged with happiness. Her disease seemed to simulate every emotion.

Guido was leaving with her, to accompany her to Bologna and then return after a few days. We waited on the platform for the train to leave. Ada remained at the window of her compartment and went on waving her handkerchief as long as she could see us.

Then we took the weeping Signora Malfenti home. At the moment of our separation, my mother-in-law, after kissing Augusta, kissed me, too.

"Forgive me!" she said, laughing through her tears, "I did it without thinking. But if you'll allow me, I'll give you yet another kiss."

Little Anna, now twelve, also wanted to kiss me. Alberta, who was about to abandon the nation's theater to become engaged, and who as a rule was a bit reserved with me, that day warmly gave me her hand. They all loved me because my wife was bursting with health, and in this way they demonstrated their dislike of Guido, whose wife was ill.

But just then I risked becoming a less good husband. I caused my wife a great sorrow, through no fault of mine, because of a dream I innocently told her.

Here is the dream: There were the three of us, Augusta, Ada, and I, leaning out of a window, specifically the smallest window there was among our three houses – mine, my mother-in-law's and Ada's. We were, in short, at the window of my mother-in-law's kitchen, which overlooks a small yard, though in the dream it was right on the Corso. There was so little space on the sill that Ada, who was in the middle, holding our arms, was sticking close to me. I looked at her and I saw that her eye had again become cold and sharp and the lines of her face very pure all the way to the nape, which I saw was covered by her delicate curls, those curls that I had seen so often when Ada turned her back on me. Despite this coldness (as her health seemed to me), she remained pressed against me as I had believed she was that evening of my engagement around the speaking table. Jokingly, I said to Augusta (surely making an effort to pay attention also to her): "You see how she is cured? Where's Basedow now?" "Can't you see?" asked Augusta, the only one of us who managed to look into the street. With an effort we leaned out also and we could see a great crowd advancing, with threats and shouts. "But where is Basedow?" I asked once more. Then I saw him. It was he who was advancing, followed by that crowd: an old beggar wrapped in a huge cloak, tattered but of stiff brocade, his great head covered by disheveled white locks flying in the air, his eyes protruding from their sockets, anxiously looking forward with a gaze I had observed in fleeing animals, of fear and of menace. And the crowd was shouting: "Kill the disease-spreader!"

Then there was an interval of empty night. And then, immediately, Ada and I were alone on the steepest stair of our three houses, the one that leads to the attic of my villa. Ada was perched on some higher steps, but turned toward me, as I was about to climb up, though she seemed to want to come down. I was embracing her legs and she was bending toward me, whether out of weakness or the desire to be closer to me I don't know. For an instant she seemed to me disfigured by her sickness, but then, looking at her breathlessly, I could see her as she had appeared to me at the window, beautiful and healthy. She was saying to me in her solid voice: "Go ahead, I'll follow you at once!" I promptly turned to precede her, running, but not fast enough not to notice that the door of my attic was very slowly opening and Basedow's head, with its white mane and that face, half-afraid, half-menacing, emerged. I saw also his unsteady legs and the poor, wretched body that the cloak was unable to hide. I managed to run off, but I don't know whether it was to precede Ada or to escape her.

Now it seems that, gasping, I awoke in the night, and in my dozing state I told all or part of the dream to Augusta, before resuming my sleep, calmer and deeper. I believe that, in my semiconsciousness, I blindly followed my old desire to confess my misdeeds.

In the morning, on Augusta's face, there was the waxen pallor of major occasions. I remembered the dream perfectly, but not exactly how much of it I had reported to her. With an expression of pained resignation, she said: "You are unhappy because she's ill and has gone away, and so you dream about her."

I defended myself, laughing and teasing. It wasn't Ada who was important to me, but Basedow, and I told her of my studies and also of the applications I had envisaged. But I don't know if I succeeded in convincing her. When you are caught dreaming, it's hard to defend yourself. It's quite a different thing from returning to your wife, wide awake, immediately after having betrayed her. For that matter, in these jealousies of Augusta's, I had nothing to lose because she loved Ada so much, and for that reason her jealousy cast no shadow; as far as I was concerned, she treated me with even more affectionate respect and was all the more grateful to me for my slightest show of affection.

A few days later Guido returned from Bologna with the best of news. The director of the sanatorium guaranteed a definitive cure provided that, on her return, Ada found great serenity at home. Guido reported simply and fairly shamelessly the doctor's prognosis, not realizing that in the Malfenti family that verdict merely confirmed many suspicions regarding him.

And I said to Augusta: "Now I'm threatened with more kisses from your mother."

It seemed that Guido didn't feel quite comfortable in the house under Aunt Maria's management. Sometimes he paced up and down the office, murmuring: "Two babies...three wet nurses...no wife."

He also remained absent from the office more often because he released his ill humor in a rage against the poor animal victims of his hunting and fishing. But when, toward the end of the year, we received from Bologna the news that Ada was considered cured and was preparing to come home, he didn't seem all that happy to me. Had he become used to Aunt Maria, or did he see so little of her that it was easy and pleasant for him to tolerate her? With me, naturally, he showed no sign of his ill humor except perhaps in expressing the suspicion that Ada was in too much of a hurry to leave the sanatorium before she was assured there would be no relapse. In fact, a short time later, even before the end of that winter, when she had to return to Bologna, he said to me triumphantly: "What did I tell you?"

I don't, however, believe that there was any other joy in that triumph beyond his always keen pleasure in having successfully predicted something. He wasn't wishing Ada any ill, but he would have been glad to keep her in Bologna for a long time.

When Ada returned, Augusta was confined to bed for the birth of my little Alfio, and on that occasion she was truly moving. She insisted I go to the station with flowers and I was to tell Ada that she wanted to see her that same day. And if Ada couldn't come to her directly from the station, she begged me to return home at once so I could describe Ada to her and report whether Ada's beauty, of which the family was so proud, had been completely restored to her.

At the station there was Guido, me, and only Alberta, because Signora Malfenti spent most of every day with Augusta. On the platform, Guido tried to convince us of his immense joy over Ada's arrival, but Alberta, listening to him, made a great show of inattention in order – as she later told me – not to have to reply to him. As for me, simulation with Guido by now cost me little effort. I was accustomed to pretending not to notice his indulgence toward Carmen and I had never dared refer to his wrongs toward his wife. It was therefore not hard for me to assume an attitude of attention as if I were admiring his joy at the return of his beloved wife.

On the stroke of noon, when the train entered the station, he ran ahead of us to reach his wife as she stepped down. He took her in his arms and kissed her affectionately. Seeing him from behind, as he bent in order to be able to kiss his wife, who was shorter than he, I thought: What a good actor!

Then he took Ada's hand and led her toward us. "Here she is, restored to our devotion!"

Then he revealed himself for what he was, namely false, a simulator, because if he had taken a closer look at the poor woman's face, he would have realized that, instead of our devotion, she was being delivered to our indifference. Ada's face was badly put together, because it had recovered the cheeks, but they were misplaced, as if the flesh, returning, had forgotten where it belonged and had settled too low. They looked therefore like swellings rather than cheeks. And her eyes were back in their sockets, but no one had been able to undo the damage done by their absence. Some precise and important lines had been shifted or destroyed. When we bade our good-byes outside the station, in the dazzling winter sun, I saw that all the color of that face was no longer what I had so loved. It had faded, and on the fleshy parts it was flushed, splotchy. Apparently health no longer belonged to that face, and they had succeeded only in putting a pretense of it there.

I immediately told Augusta that Ada was beautiful just as she had been as a girl, and Augusta was overjoyed. Then, after seeing Ada, to my surprise she confirmed several times my pitiful lies as if they had been obvious truths.

She said: "She's as beautiful as she was as a girl, and as my daughter will be!"

Obviously a sister's eye is not very sharp.

For a long time I didn't see Ada again. She had too many children, and so did we. Still, Ada and Augusta managed to meet several times each week, but always at hours when I was away from the house.

Inventory time was approaching, and I had a great deal to do. Indeed, it was the period of my life when I worked most. On some days I stayed at my desk for as much as ten hours. Guido offered to call in an accountant to help me, but I wouldn't hear of it. I had assumed an obligation, and I had to maintain it. I meant to compensate Guido for that month of grim absence, and I was happy also to show Carmen my diligence, which could only have been inspired by my fondness for Guido.

But as I went ahead ordering the accounts, I began to discover the heavy losses we had incurred in that first year of activity. Concerned, I said something about it privately to Guido, but he was preparing to go hunting and wouldn't stay to hear me out.

"You'll see: it won't be as bad as it looks. And anyway the year isn't over yet."

Then I confided in Augusta. At first all she could see in this matter was the damage I might suffer. That's how women are made, but Augusta was extraordinary, even for a woman, when she lamented her own harm. Wouldn't I — she asked me — also be held somewhat responsible finally for the losses suffered by Guido? She wanted to consult a lawyer at once. Meanwhile it was necessary to make a break with Guido and stop going to that office.

It wasn't easy for me to convince her that I couldn't be held responsible for anything, since I was no more than an employee of Guido's. She insisted that one who doesn't have a fixed salary cannot be considered an employee, but some-

thing similar to a co-owner. When she was thoroughly convinced, she naturally remained of her opinion because then she
discovered I would lose nothing if I were to cease going to that
office, where I would surely in the end win myself a bad
reputation in the business world. Good heavens! My business
reputation! I, too, agreed that it was important to save it,
and though she may have been wrong in her arguments, in
conclusion I should do as she wished. She allowed me to
complete the ordering of the accounts, since I had begun
it, but afterwards I would have to find a way of returning to
my little study, where no money was earned, but none was
lost, either.

I then learned something curious about myself. I was unable
to abandon that activity of mine, even though I had decided
to. I was amazed! To understand things properly, you have to
work through images. I remembered then that once in England a sentence to forced labor was administered by suspending
the condemned convict over a wheel turned by water, thus
forcing the victim to move his legs at a certain rhythm to avoid
their being crushed. When you are working, you always have
the sensation of a similar constriction. It's true that when you
don't work the position is the same, and I believe it correct to
assert that I and Olivi were always equally dangling; only I was
hung in such a way that I didn't have to move my legs. Our
position therefore produced a different result, but now I know
for certain that it deserved neither blame nor praise. In short,
chance determines whether you're attached to a moving
wheel or to one that is motionless. Freeing yourself is inevi-
tably difficult.

For various days, after the accounts were closed, I continued going to the office, though I had resolved not to go
there again. I left my house, uncertain. Uncertain, I headed in
a direction that was almost always that of the office, and as
I proceeded, that direction became clearer until I found myself
seated in my usual chair opposite Guido. Luckily at a given

moment I was asked not to leave my place, and I immediately agreed, since in the meantime I had realized I was nailed there.

For the fifteenth of January my books were closed. An out-and-out disaster! We closed with a loss of half our capital. Guido was reluctant to show it to young Olivi, fearing some indiscretion on his part, but I insisted, hoping that he, with his great experience, would find some error capable of changing the whole position. There could be some amount shifted from credit, when it belonged to debit, and with a rectification we would arrive at an important difference. Smiling, Olivi promised Guido the maximum discretion, and he then worked with me for a whole day. Unfortunately he found no mistake. I must say that, from this review carried out by the two of us together, I learned much, and now I would be able to face and handle balance sheets far more intimidating than that one.

"And what will you do now?" the bespectacled young man asked before leaving. I already knew what he would suggest. My father, who often had talked about business with me in my infancy, had already taught me. According to the laws of finance, given the loss of half of the capital, we should liquidate the firm and perhaps revive it immediately on a new basis. I allowed him to repeat this advice.

He added: "It's a formality." Then, smiling, he said: "But failure to do this can be very costly!"

That evening Guido also started looking over the accounts, which he still wasn't able to grasp. He did it without any method, checking this or that sum at random. I wanted to stop that useless work, and I transmitted Olivi's advice to go immediately into liquidation, but only as a formality.

Until then Guido's face had been contracted by the effort to find in those accounts the redeeming error. A frown complicated by the grimace of one who has a disgusting taste in his mouth. At my communication, he raised his face, which relaxed as he tried to pay attention. He didn't understand at once, but when he did understand, he burst immediately into

hearty laughter. I interpreted the expression on his face in this
fashion: harsh, acid, as long as he was confronting those figures
that couldn't be altered; happy and resolute when the painful
problem was thrust aside by a proposal that allowed him to
recover the feeling of being master and judge.

He didn't understand. It seemed to him the advice of an
enemy. I explained to him that Olivi's advice had its value,
especially considering the danger obviously looming over the
firm, of losing more money and going under. A possible bank-
ruptcy would be criminal if, after this situation, by now recorded
in our books, we didn't take the measures Olivi suggested.

And I added: "By our laws the mandatory punishment for
fraudulent bankruptcy is prison!"

Guido's face turned so red that I feared he was on the verge
of a stroke. He yelled: "In this case Olivi doesn't need to give
me advice! If that should ever happen, I would take things into
my own hands!"

His decision impressed me, and I had the feeling I had
before me a person perfectly aware of his own responsibility.
I lowered the tone of my voice. I threw myself entirely behind
him and, forgetting that I had already defined Olivi's advice as
worthy of being taken into consideration, I said: "That's what
I said to Olivi, too. The responsibility lies with you, and we
can have no part of any decision you may make concerning the
fate of the firm that belongs to you and to your father."

Actually I had said this to my wife and not to Olivi, but it
was true that I had said it to someone. Now, after having heard
Guido's manly assertion, I would also have been capable of
saying it to Olivi, because decision and courage have always
conquered me. I already loved enormously even the mere
nonchalance that can derive from those qualities, but also
from other, far inferior ones.

Since I wanted to report all of his words to Augusta to
reassure her, I insisted: "You know what they say about me –
probably rightly – that I have no talent for business, I can carry

out what you order me to do, but I can't assume responsibility for what you do."

He heartily agreed. He felt so comfortable in the role I attributed to him that he forgot his sorrow over the bad accounts. He declared: "I am solely responsible. Everything is in my name, and I would never allow anyone else to assume responsibilities, even if he wished."

That went beautifully as far as reporting to Augusta was concerned, but it was much more than I had asked. And you had to see the attitude he assumed as he made that declaration: instead of a semi-failure, he seemed an apostle! He had comfortably adapted to his debit balance, and from that position he was becoming my lord and master. This time, like so many others in the course of our life in common, my impulse of affection for him was stifled by his expressions revealing his disproportionate self-esteem. He struck a false note. Yes, it had to be said: That great musician was out of tune!

I asked him brusquely: "Do you want me to make a copy of the accounts tomorrow for your father?"

For a moment I had been on the verge of making a far more cruel declaration, telling him that immediately after the books were closed, I would stop coming to his office. I didn't do this, not knowing how I would spend all the free hours I would then have. But my question replaced almost perfectly the declaration I had repressed. For I had reminded him that, in that office, he wasn't the only master.

He looked surprised by my words because they didn't seem to be in line with what had been said thus far, and with my obvious assent. And in his previous tone he said: "I'll tell you how that copy must be made."

I protested, shouting. In all my life I have never shouted as much as I did with Guido, because sometimes he seemed to me deaf. I declared to him that in law there is a responsibility also for the bookkeeper, and I was not prepared to pass off invented clumps of figures as exact copies.

He blanched and admitted I was right, but, he added, he was entitled to order that no extracts from his books should be given out. On this point I was willing to admit he was right, and then, relieved, he declared that he himself would write to his father. It even seemed he wanted to start writing immediately, but then he changed his mind and suggested we go out for a breath of air. I chose to content him. I supposed he hadn't yet thoroughly digested the balance sheet, and wanted to move about, the better to swallow it.

Our walk reminded me of the one we took on the night of my engagement. The moon was absent, as there was a great deal of fog up above, but below it, the sky was the same, as we walked, confidently, through clear air. Guido also recalled that memorable evening.

"This is the first time we've taken a walk together since that night. Remember? That time, you explained to me how on the moon they kissed the same way we do on earth. Now, on the moon they continue that kiss eternally, I'm sure, even though we can't see them this evening. But down here . . . "

Did he mean to start speaking once more against Ada? Against the poor sick woman? I interrupted him, though mildly, as if agreeing with him (hadn't I come with him to help him forget?).

"True! Down here we can't always kiss! But up above, there is only the fixed image of the kiss. A kiss is, above all, movement."

I was trying to remove myself from all his concerns, namely the accounts and Ada; in fact, just in time I managed to suppress a phrase I was on the point of saying, namely that up above, a kiss did not generate twins. But, to rid himself of the debit, he could find nothing better to do than complain of his other misfortunes. As I had anticipated, he complained about Ada. He began by regretting how disastrous that first year of marriage had been for him. He didn't speak of the twins, who were so dear and handsome, but of Ada's disease.

He thought that being ill made her irascible, jealous, and at the same time unaffectionate. He concluded with a disheartened exclamation: "Life is unfair and hard!"

I felt it was absolutely forbidden for me to utter a single word that suggested any judgment concerning him and Ada. But I also felt a duty to say something. He had ended by mentioning life and by applying two predicate adjectives to it, neither of them supremely original. I found something better precisely because I had set myself up as critic of what he said. Often we say things following the sound of the words as they are casually connected. Then, as soon as you look to see if what was said was worth the breath it consumed, you sometimes discover that the casual association generated an idea.

I said: "Life is neither ugly nor beautiful, but it's original!"

When I thought about it, it seemed to me I had said something important. Thus defined, life seemed to me so new that I stood there looking at it as if seeing it for the first time, with its gaseous, liquid, and solid bodies. If I were to narrate it to someone unfamiliar with it and therefore lacking our common knowledge, that listener would remain mute in the face of the enormous, aimless construction. He would ask me: "But how have you borne it?" And, having inquired into every single detail, from those celestial bodies suspended up above so that they can be seen and not touched, to the mystery that surrounds death, he would surely exclaim: "Very original!"

"Original? Life?" Guido said, laughing. "Where did you read that?"

I didn't bother to assure him I hadn't read it anywhere, because otherwise my words would have held less importance for him. But the more I thought about it, the more original I found life to be. And it wasn't at all necessary to come from outside in order to see how it was put together. Simply recalling everything we humans expected from life sufficed for us to see how strange it was, and to arrive at the conclusion that perhaps mankind is located in its midst by mistake and doesn't belong there.

Having made no agreement about the direction of our stroll, we ended up, as we had the last time, on the Via Belvedere. Finding the little wall where he had stretched out that night, Guido climbed onto it and lay down just like the other time. He was humming, perhaps still oppressed by his thoughts, and he was surely pondering the inevitable figures of his books. I, on the contrary, remembered how in this place I had wanted to kill him, and, comparing my feelings then with my present ones, I admired once again the incomparable originality of life. But suddenly I remembered that, a short while before, and because of an ambitious person's whim, I had inveighed against poor Guido, and on one of the worst days of his life. I devoted myself to an inquiry: I was witnessing with great pain the torture inflicted on Guido by the accounts I had kept with such care, and I felt a curious doubt and immediately an even more curious memory. The doubt: Was I good or bad? The memory, provoked suddenly by the doubt, which was not new to me: I saw myself as a child and dressed (of this I'm sure) still in short skirts, as I raised my face to ask my smiling mother: "Am I good or bad?" Then the doubt must have been generated in the child by the many people who had said he was good and by the many others who had called him bad. It was not surprising that the child was bewildered by that dilemma. Oh, incomparable originality of life! It was wonderful that the doubt it had already inflicted on the child in such a puerile form had not been resolved by the adult who had already passed the midpoint of his life.

On that dark night, in the very place where once before I had desired to kill, that doubt tormented me profoundly. To be sure, the child, sensing that doubt stirring in his head, only recently freed from its baby bonnet, had not suffered much from it, because children are told that badness can be cured.

To be rid of this anguish I tried to believe that again, and I succeeded. If I hadn't succeeded, I would have had to weep for myself, for Guido, and for our terribly sad life. My resolve renewed the illusion! I resolved to remain at Guido's side and collaborate with him in the development of his business, on which his and his family's lives depended, and with no idea of profit for myself. I glimpsed the possibility of running, transacting, and investigating for him; and, to help him, I admitted the possibility of becoming a great, enterprising, brilliant trader. This is exactly what I was thinking on that dark night of this highly original life!

Guido meanwhile stopped thinking of the balance sheet. He left his place and he seemed resigned. As if he had come to a conclusion after some reasoning of which I was ignorant, he told me he would say nothing to his father because otherwise the poor old man would undertake that enormous voyage from his summer sun to our winter fog. He then said that at first sight the loss seemed huge, but it wasn't so much after all, if he didn't have to bear it alone. He would ask Ada to be responsible for half of it, and in return he would assign her a share in next year's profits. The other half of the loss he would assume himself.

I said nothing. I thought that I was also bound not to give advice, because otherwise I would end by doing what I absolutely did not want to do, setting myself up as judge between husband and wife. For that matter, at the moment, I was so filled with fine intentions that it seemed to me Ada would be making a good bargain, taking part in a venture under our direction.

I accompanied Guido to the door of his house, and I clasped his hand at length to renew silently my resolve to love him. Then I cast about for something nice to say to him, and I came up with this sentence: "May your twins have a good night and allow you also to sleep, because you certainly need rest."

Going off, I bit my lips regretting I hadn't hit on something better. But I knew that the twins, now that each had his own wet nurse and they slept a mile apart, couldn't trouble his sleep! In any event he understood the intention of my wish because he accepted it gratefully.

On reaching home, I found that Augusta had retired to the bedroom with our children. Alfio was clinging to her bosom while Antonia slept in the cot, turning her curly nape to us. I had to explain the reason for my tardiness, and so I told her also the method Guido had conceived to be free of his debit. To Augusta, Guido's proposal seemed outrageous.

"In Ada's place I'd refuse!" she exclaimed violently, though in a low voice, so as not to frighten the little one.

Led by my good intentions, I argued: "So if I happened to have the same difficulties as Guido, you wouldn't help me?"

She laughed. "It's quite a different thing! Between the two of us we'd see what was most advantageous for *them*!" – and she nodded toward the baby in her arms and toward Antonia – "And if we now advised Ada to contribute her money to continuing that business in which you will soon have no part, wouldn't we then be obliged to compensate her if she lost it?"

It was an ignorant idea, but in my new altruism I exclaimed: "And why not?"

"But can't you see we have two children to think about?"

Oh, I could see them! The question was a rhetorical figure, truly without meaning.

"And don't they also have two children?" I asked, victoriously.

She began laughing loudly, frightening Alfio, who stopped nursing immediately in order to cry. She tended him, but still laughing, and I accepted her laughter as if I had won it with my wit, whereas, in truth, at the moment I asked that question, I had felt stirring in my breast a great love for all parents of children and for the children of all parents. Having now been laughed at, the affection had completely vanished.

But my distress at knowing I was not essentially good diminished also. I seemed to have resolved the troubling problem. We were neither good nor bad, just as we were also not many other things. Goodness was the light that, in flashes and for moments, illuminated the dark human spirit. The flaming torch was necessary to give light (it had been in my spirit, and sooner or later it would also return), and in that brightness any thinking person could choose the direction in which to move through the ensuing darkness. We could therefore show ourselves to be good, very good, always good, and this was what mattered. When the light returned, it would not take us by surprise, it would not dazzle. I would blow on it to put it out first, since I had no need of it. Because I would know how to maintain the resolution, in other words, the direction.

The resolution to be good is calm and practical, and now I was calm and cold. Strange! The excess of goodness had made me excessive in estimating myself and my power. What could I do for Guido? True, in his office I stood head and shoulders above the others as, in my office, the senior Olivi stood above me. But this didn't prove much. And, to be quite practical: what advice would I give Guido the next day? Perhaps some hunch of mine? But you don't follow hunches, even at the gambling table, when you're gambling with the money of others! To keep a business firm going, you have to create everyday work for it, and this can be achieved by working every hour on organization. I wasn't the man who could do such a thing, nor did it seem right to me to sentence myself, because of my goodness, to a lifetime of boredom.

I still felt the impression made on me by my access of goodness as a commitment I had made to Guido, and I couldn't get to sleep. I sighed several times profoundly, and once I even moaned, surely at the moment when I seemed to be bound to Guido's office as Olivi was to mine.

Half-waking, Augusta murmured: "What's wrong? Have you had another argument with Olivi?"

Here was the idea I'd been seeking! I would advise Guido to take on young Olivi as manager! So serious and hardworking, that youth, whom I was so unwilling to allow into in my own affairs – because he seemed to be preparing to succeed his father in their management and thus exclude me definitively – obviously belonged, to everyone's advantage, in Guido's office. Creating a position in the firm for him, Guido would save himself, and young Olivi would be more useful in that office than in mine.

The idea thrilled me, and I roused Augusta to inform her of it. She was also so enthusiastic that she woke up completely. It seemed to her that I could thus free myself more easily from the compromising affairs of Guido. I fell asleep with a clear conscience: I had found the way to save Guido, and I wouldn't doom myself. Far from it.

There is nothing more disgusting than to see your advice rejected, after it has been sincerely studied, with an effort that cost whole hours of sleep. In my case there had also been another effort: that of trying to rid myself of the illusion that I could be of help in Guido's affairs. An immense effort. I had first achieved true goodness, then absolute objectivity, and then I was told to go to hell!

Guido rejected my advice with downright disdain. He didn't believe young Olivi capable, and anyway he didn't like the young man's old-man appearance, and even more he disliked those eyeglasses that glistened so on the boy's insipid face. His arguments tended to make me believe that only one of them had any foundation: a desire to spite me. He ended up by telling me he would accept as his manager not the young Olivi, but the older one. But I didn't believe I could procure him the latter's collaboration, and besides, I didn't think I was ready to assume, on a moment's notice, the junior Olivi as manager of my affairs. I made the mistake of arguing, and I said to Guido that old Olivi wasn't worth much. I told him how much money Olivi's stubbornness had cost me, through his refusal to buy that dried fruit at the right moment.

"Well!" Guido cried. "If the old man's worth no more than that, how much can the young one be worth, since he's merely his father's disciple?"

Here, at last, was a sound argument, and all the more irksome to me, as I had supplied it myself through my foolish chatter.

A few days later, Augusta told me that Guido had proposed to Ada that she cover half of the losses on the books with her money. Ada refused, as she said to Augusta: "He's unfaithful to me and he wants my money as well!"

Augusta hadn't had the courage to advise her to give it to him, but she assured me she had done her best to make Ada reconsider her view of her husband's fidelity. Ada had replied in a way that suggested she knew far more on this score than we thought. And, with me, Augusta reasoned in these terms: "For a husband, a wife should be able to make any sacrifice." But did that axiom apply also to Guido?

In the days that followed, Guido's demeanor became truly extraordinary. He appeared in the office from time to time, but never stayed for more than half an hour. He would rush off like someone who's forgotten his handkerchief at home. I later learned that he went to confront Ada with new arguments, which seemed to him decisive, sure to make her do as he wished. He really looked like a man who has wept too much or shouted too much or who has actually fought, and even in our presence he was unable to control the emotion that choked him and brought tears to his eyes. I asked him what was wrong. He answered with a sad but friendly smile, to show he didn't hold anything against me. Then he collected himself so he could talk to me without becoming too agitated. Finally he said a few words. Ada was making him suffer with her jealousy.

He then told me that they quarreled over their personal matters, whereas I knew that there was also that question of debit and credit between them.

But apparently this had no importance. He told me so himself, and Ada said the same to Augusta, speaking of nothing but her jealousy. Also the violence of those arguments, which left such profound traces on Guido's face, suggested that they were all telling the truth.

On the contrary, it turned out that husband and wife talked of nothing but the money question. Though she let herself be driven by her passionate sufferings, Ada, out of pride, had never mentioned them, and Guido, perhaps through awareness of his guilt and although he sensed that womanly rage persisted in Ada, continued to discuss business affairs as if the rest didn't exist. He more and more desperately pursued that money, while she, who wasn't the least bit interested in financial matters, protested against Guido's proposal with a single argument: the money had to be kept for the children. And when he found other arguments – his peace, the benefits the children themselves would derive from his work, the security of being in compliance with the law – she dismissed them with a sharp "No!" This exasperated Guido and – as happens with children – also his desire. But both, when they spoke about it to others, believed they were truthful in asserting they were suffering for love and jealousy.

It was a kind of misunderstanding that prevented me from acting at the right time to end the unfortunate debate about money. I could prove to Guido that it effectively lacked importance. As an accountant I am a bit slow, and I don't understand things until I have entered them in the books, in black and white, but it seems to me I quickly understood that the investment Guido demanded of Ada would not have changed things much. What, in fact, was the use of making her deposit a sum in cash? The loss, in that case, did not appear any smaller, unless Ada agreed actually to add her money to the balance sheet, and Guido was not asking this of her. The law would surely not be mollified by finding that after having lost so much, we wanted to risk even more, attracting new capital into the firm.

One morning Guido didn't show up in the office, which surprised us because we knew he hadn't left to go hunting the previous evening. At lunch I learned from a distressed and agitated Augusta that, the night before, Guido had attempted to take his own life. Now he was out of danger. I must confess that the news, which to Augusta seemed tragic, made me angry.

He had resorted to that drastic measure to overcome his wife's resistance! I learned, also immediately, that he had done so with every precaution, and before taking the morphine, he had made sure he was seen holding the unstoppered bottle in his hand. Thus, at the first signs of drowsiness, Ada called the doctor, and Guido was quickly out of danger. Ada had spent a horrible night because the doctor felt it was proper to express some uncertainty about the effect of the poisoning, and then her distress was prolonged by Guido, who, when he came to, perhaps not yet fully conscious, covered her with reproaches, calling her his enemy, his persecutor, an obstacle to the healthy work he was trying to undertake.

Ada immediately granted him the loan he was asking, but then, finally, with the intention of defending herself, she spoke openly and uttered all the reproaches she had repressed for so long. Thus they came to an understanding because he – so Augusta thought – had managed to dispel all Ada's doubts about his fidelity. He was vehement, and when she spoke to him of Carmen, he cried: "Are you jealous of her? All right, if you want, I'll discharge her this very day."

Ada hadn't replied, and she believed she had thus accepted his offer and he had committed himself.

I was amazed that Guido had been able to act like this while half asleep, and I came to believe he hadn't swallowed even the small dose of morphine that he claimed. I thought one of the effects of clouding the brain through drowsiness was to weaken the most hardened spirit, prompting the most ingenuous confessions. Hadn't I only recently experienced something of the sort? This increased my outrage and my scorn for Guido.

Augusta wept, telling me the condition in which she had found Ada. No! Ada was no longer beautiful, with those eyes that seemed widened in terror.

My wife and I then had a long argument about whether or not I should immediately visit Guido and Ada, or whether it wasn't better to feign ignorance and wait to see him next in the office. To me, that visit seemed an intolerable nuisance. Seeing him, how could I refrain from expressing my feelings? I would say: "It's an action unworthy of a man! I've no desire to kill myself, but there's no doubt that if I did decide to, I would succeed immediately!"

This is truly how I felt, and I wanted to say as much to Augusta. But I thought I was doing Guido too much honor in comparing him with myself.

"You don't have to be a chemist to know how to destroy this organism of ours, which is all too sensitive. Almost every week in our city, isn't there some seamstress who swallows a solution of phosphorus prepared secretly in her humble room, and then that rudimentary poison, despite every care, carries her off, her face still distorted by the physical pain and by the moral suffering of her innocent little soul?"

Augusta wouldn't agree that the soul of the suicidal little seamstress was all that innocent, but after some faint protest, she renewed her efforts to make me pay that visit. She said I shouldn't be afraid of any embarrassment. She had spoken to Guido, who had conversed with her with absolute tranquillity, as if he had performed the most common of acts.

I left the house without giving Augusta the satisfaction of appearing convinced by her arguments. After a slight hesitation I set off firmly to satisfy my wife. Though the distance was short, my pace allowed an attenuation of my judgment of Guido. I remembered the direction indicated for me by the light that a few days earlier had illuminated my spirit. Guido was a boy, a boy to whom I had promised my indulgence. If he didn't manage to kill himself first, sooner or later he, too, would reach maturity.

The maid showed me into a little room that must have been Ada's study. It was a gloomy day and the cramped space was dark, its one window covered by a heavy curtain. On the wall were portraits of the parents of Ada and of Guido. I remained there only a short time, because the maid returned for me and led me to Guido and Ada in their bedroom. This was vast and bright even on that day, thanks to the two broad windows and the pale wallpaper and furniture. Guido was lying in his bed, his head bandaged, and Ada was seated beside him.

Guido received me without any embarrassment, indeed with the keenest gratitude. He appeared drowsy, but to greet me and then to give me instructions, he managed to recover himself and seem completely awake. Then he sank back on the pillow and closed his eyes. Did he remember he was to simulate the great effect of the morphine? In any case he inspired pity rather than anger, and I felt I was being very good.

I didn't look immediately at Ada: I was afraid of the Basedow countenance. When I did look at her, I was pleasantly surprised because I was expecting worse. Her eyes were really exceptionally enlarged, but the facial swellings that had replaced her cheeks were gone, and she seemed more beautiful to me. She was wearing a loose red gown, buttoned up to her chin, in which her poor little body was lost. There was about her something very chaste and, because of those eyes, something very stern. I couldn't entirely clarify my feeling, but I truly thought that before me was a woman who resembled that Ada I had loved.

At a certain moment Guido widened his eyes, took from beneath the pillow a check, on which I immediately saw Ada's signature, and gave it to me, asking me to cash it and deposit the sum in an account I was to open in Ada's name.

"In the name of Ada Malfenti or Ada Speier?" he jokingly asked Ada.

She shrugged and said: "You and Zeno will know which is better."

"I'll tell you later how you must make the other entries," Guido added, with a curtness that I found offensive.

I was on the point of interrupting the languor to which he then promptly succumbed, and tell him that if he wanted any more entries he could make them himself.

Meanwhile a great cup of black coffee had been brought, which Ada held out to him. He lifted his arms from under the covers and raised the cup to his mouth with both hands. Now, his nose in the cup, he really seemed a child.

When I took my leave, he assured me that the next day he would be in the office.

I had already said good-bye to Ada, and so I was considerably surprised when she joined me at the front door. She was out of breath.

"Please, Zeno! Come in here for a moment. There's something I have to tell you."

I followed her into the sitting room where I had been a little earlier, from which I now heard one of the twins crying.

We remained standing, face to face. She was still gasping, and for this reason, and no other, for a moment I thought she had shown me into this dark room to ask of me the love I had offered her.

In the darkness her great eyes were terrifying. Filled with anguish, I was wondering what I should do. Wouldn't it have been my duty to take her into my arms and thus spare her the necessity of asking anything of me? What a cyclone of resolutions in the space of an instant! One of the most difficult things in life is guessing what a woman wants. Listening to her words is no use, because a whole speech can be erased by one look, nor can that look guide us when we are with her, at her invitation, in a convenient, dark little room.

Unable to read her, I tried to read myself. What was my desire? Did I want to kiss those eyes and that skeletal body? I couldn't give a firm answer because just a moment earlier I had seen her in the stern chastity of that soft robe, desirable as the girl I had loved.

Her anxiety was now accompanied by tears, thus prolonging the time in which I was unsure what she wanted or what I desired. Finally, in a broken voice, she told me once again of her love for Guido, hence I had neither duties nor rights toward her.

She stammered: "Augusta told me you would like to leave Guido and not occupy yourself with his affairs. I must beg you to keep on helping him. I don't think he's capable of doing it on his own."

She was asking me to continue doing what I already did. It was little, very little, and I tried to offer more: "Since you ask me, I'll go on helping Guido. Indeed, I'll do my best to help him more effectively than I've done so far."

Another exaggeration! I realized as much at the very moment I blundered into it, but I couldn't give it up. I wanted to assure Ada (or perhaps lie to her), saying that she was important to me. She didn't want my love but rather my support, and I spoke to her in a way that could lead her to believe I was ready to give her both.

Ada immediately seized my hand. I shuddered. When a woman gives you her hand, she is offering a great deal! I have always felt that. When I was granted a hand, I felt I was grasping an entire woman. I sensed her stature, and in the obvious comparison between mine and hers, I felt as if I were performing an act that resembled an embrace. Without doubt, it was an intimate contact.

342

She added: "I have to go back to Bologna immediately, to the sanatorium, and it would be a great reassurance to know you were with him."

"I'll stay with him!" I answered with a resigned look. Ada was to believe that my look of resignation signified the sacrifice I was agreeing to make for her. Instead, I was resigning myself to returning to a common, a very common, life, for she had no thought of following me into that exceptional life I had dreamed of.

I made an effort to come down to earth completely, and I immediately discovered in my mind a far-from-simple problem of accounting. I had to deposit the amount of that check in my pocket in Ada's account. This was clear, and yet it was not at all clear how such an entry could affect the balance sheet. I said nothing, suspecting that perhaps Ada had no idea what in this world a daybook was, which contained accounts of various nature.

But I was reluctant to leave that room without having said more. So it was that instead of mentioning accounts, I uttered a sentence, dropped nonchalantly at that moment, simply to be saying something to Ada, but then I felt it was of great importance for me, for Ada, for Guido, but most of all for myself, whom I was compromising yet again. That sentence was so important that for long years I remembered how, with a careless gesture, I moved my lips to say it in that dark little room in the presence of the four portraits of the parents of Ada and Guido, married to each other also on the wall.

I said: "In the end, you married a man even more peculiar than I am, Ada!"

How a word can traverse time! It becomes an event in itself, connecting with other events! My words became an event, a tragic event, because they were addressed to Ada! In my thoughts I would never afterwards be able to evoke so vividly the house where Ada had chosen between me and Guido, on that sunny street where, after days of waiting, I had contrived to meet her and walk beside her and wear myself out trying to win her laughter, which I foolishly hailed as a promise! And I remembered, too, that then I was already made inferior by the clumsiness of my leg muscles, while Guido moved even more freely than Ada herself and wasn't marked by any inferiority, unless we were to consider that strange stick he was in the habit of carrying.

She said in a low voice, "It's true!"

Then she smiled affectionately. "But I'm happy for Augusta that you're so much better than I believed you." Then, with a sigh: "So happy, that it makes me a little less sad that Guido isn't what I expected."

I remained silent, still dubious. It seemed to me what she had said was that I had become the man she had expected Guido to become. Was this love, then?

And she went on: "You're the best man in our family, our mainstay, our hope." She took my hand again and I squeezed hers, perhaps too hard. But she withdrew it again so quickly that any doubt was dispelled. Perhaps to soften her gesture, she sent me another caress. "And because I know the man you are, I'm so sorry for having made you suffer. Did you really suffer that much?"

At once I thrust my eye into the darkness of my past to find that suffering again, and I murmured: "Yes!"

Little by little I recalled Guido's violin, and then how they would have cast me out of that living room if I hadn't clung to Augusta, and again that Malfenti living room, where, around the Louis XIV table, we wooed while at the other little table they were watching. Suddenly I recalled also Carla, who told me I belonged to my wife, namely Ada.

I repeated, as the tears came into my eyes: "Yes, very, very much!"

She summoned her strength and said: "But now you love Augusta!"

A sob interrupted her for an instant, and I started, not knowing whether she had paused to hear if I would affirm or deny that love. Luckily for me, she didn't give me time to answer, but went on: "Now, between the two of us there exists, and there must exist, a fraternal love. I need you. For that boy in there, I must now be also a mother, I must protect him. Will you help me with this difficult task?"

In her great emotion, she was almost leaning on me, as in my dream. But I strictly followed her words. She asked a fraternal affection of me; the loving pledge that I had thought bound me to her was thus transformed into another right she could claim, therefore I immediately promised to help Guido, to help her, to do whatever she wanted. If I had been calmer, I should have spoken to her of my inadequacy for the task she was assigning me, but I would have destroyed all the unforgettable emotion of that moment. In any case, I was so moved that I had no sense of my inadequacy. At that moment I thought that no inadequacies existed for anyone. Even Guido's could be dispelled with a few words that would instil in him the necessary enthusiasm.

Ada accompanied me to the landing and remained there, leaning on the banister, watching me go down. Just as Carla had always done, but it was strange that Ada did it, she who loved Guido, and I was so grateful to her for it that, before moving to the second flight of steps, I also raised my head once to see her and wave to her. This was how people in love behaved, but obviously it was appropriate also in a question of fraternal love.

Thus I went off happy. She had accompanied me out onto that landing, but no farther. There were no longer any doubts. We would remain like this: I had loved her and now I loved Augusta, but my former love gave her the right to my devotion. She continued, then, to love that boy of hers, but for me she retained a great fraternal affection, and not only because I had married her sister, but also to compensate me for the

345

sufferings she had caused me, which constituted a secret bond between us. All this was quite sweet, a sweetness rare in life. Couldn't such sweetness give me true health? In fact, I walked that day without clumsiness and without pains, I felt magnanimous and strong and, in my heart, a feeling of confidence that was new to me. I forgot I had betrayed my wife and also in the foulest way, or rather I determined never to do it again, which amounted to the same thing, and I felt I was truly as Ada saw me, the best man in the family.

When this heroism eventually faded, I would have liked to rekindle it, but meanwhile Ada had left for Bologna, and my every effort to draw a new stimulus from what she had said to me proved vain. Yes! I would do what little I could for Guido, but such a resolution didn't increase either the air in my lungs or the blood in my veins. For Ada in my heart there remained a great new sweetness, renewed every time she, in her letters to Augusta, recalled me with some affectionate word. I returned her affection with all my heart, and followed her treatment with the most sincere best wishes. If only she could succeed in recovering all her health and all her beauty!

The next day Guido came to the office and immediately started pondering the entries he wanted to make. He suggested: "Let's shift half the debit-and-credit account into Ada's."

This was precisely what he had wanted, and it did no good at all. If I had been the indifferent executor of his wishes as I had been until a few days before, without blinking I would have made those entries, and without another thought. But instead I felt it my duty to tell him everything; I thought it would stimulate him to work if I informed him it was not so easy to erase the loss we had incurred.

I explained to him that, as far as I knew, Ada had given him that money to be deposited to her credit in her account, and that would not happen if we cashed the check and slipped into her account, from another direction, half of our losses.

Further, that part of the loss that he wanted to assume himself had indeed to be entered in his personal account, where it belonged, and where, in fact, the entire debit really belonged. And none of this meant annulling the losses, but rather confirming them. I had given it so much thought that it was easy for me to explain everything to him, and I concluded: "Supposing that we happened to be – God forbid! – in the situation foreseen by Olivi, the loss would still be obvious from our books, the moment they were examined by a knowledgeable expert."

He looked at me, stunned. He knew enough of accounting to understand me, and yet he couldn't grasp it because his desire prevented him from coming to terms with the evidence. Then I added, to make him see everything clearly: "You see there was no point in Ada's making that payment?"

When he finally understood, he turned quite pale and began nervously gnawing his fingernails. He remained in a daze, but wanted to master himself, and with his comical commanding-officer manner, he still ordered that all those entries be made, adding: "To exempt you from all responsibility, I am prepared to write them in the book myself and even to sign my name!"

I understood! He wanted to go on dreaming at a stage where there is no more room for dreams. Not with double entry!

I remembered what I had promised myself, up on the hill of Via Belvedere, and later to Ada in the dark little sitting room of her house, and I spoke generously: "I will make the entries you want at once: I don't need your signature to protect me. I am here to help you, not to stand in your way!"

He clasped my hand affectionately. "Life is hard," he said. "And it's a great comfort to have a friend like you at my side."

Moved, we looked into each other's eyes. His were glistening. To evade the emotion that was threatening me as well, I laughed and said, "Life isn't hard, but it's very original."

And he also laughed with all his heart.

Then he remained with me to see how I would deal with that debit-and-credit account. All was done in a few minutes. That account vanished into nothingness, dragging the account of Ada after it. However, we recorded a credit to her in a little notebook, so that in case all other documentation were to vanish in some cataclysm, her loan would be documented, along with the fact that we were to pay her interest. The other half of the debit-and-credit account went to increase the debits, already considerable, in Guido's account.

By nature, accounts are a breed of animal much inclined to irony. Making those entries I thought: "One account – the one listed as profit-and-loss – had been assassinated, the other – Ada's – had died a natural death because there was no way of keeping it alive, whereas we didn't know how to kill off Guido's: a dubious debtor's, it remained an open grave, ready for our firm."

We continued to talk of bookkeeping for a long time, in that office. Guido racked his brain to find another way that might better protect him against possible snares (as he called them) of the law. I believe he also consulted some accountant, because one day he came into the office and proposed that he and I destroy the old books after making some new ones in which we would enter an invented sale to someone or other, some bogus figure; and the sale would then appear to have repaid the amount lent by Ada. It was painful to have to disillusion him, because he had rushed into the office, animated by such hope! He proposed a fraud that truly revolted me. Until now we had done nothing more than juggle some realities, threatening harm only to those who had implicitly agreed. Now, on the contrary, he wanted to invent actual transactions. I could also see that in this way, and only in this way, it was possible to eliminate every trace of the loss incurred, but at what cost! It was necessary also to invent the name of the buyer, or to gain the consent of the person we wanted to portray as such. I had nothing against seeing the books destroyed, though I had written them with such care, but it was annoying to make new ones. I raised some objections, and they finally convinced Guido. Such documents cannot be easily counterfeited. One would have to be able to falsify the documents proving the existence and the ownership of the merchandise.

He gave up his plan, but the next day he turned up in the office with another one, which also involved the destruction of the old books. Tired of seeing all other work stalled by these arguments, I protested, "You're thinking so much about it, anyone would believe you really want to prepare for bank-ruptcy! Otherwise why would such a small reduction of your capital matter? So far, no one has the right to look into your books. The important thing now is to work, to work and stop thinking about such foolishness."

He confessed to me that this thought had become an obsession with him. How could it have been otherwise? With a bit of bad luck he could incur that penal sanction and end up in jail!

From my study of law, I knew that Olivi had explained very precisely the duties of a businessman who kept such books, but to free Guido and also myself from this obsession, I advised him to consult some lawyer friend.

He replied that he already had done so, or, rather, he hadn't gone to a lawyer for that specific purpose, because he didn't want to confide his secret even to a lawyer, but he had encouraged a lawyer friend of his to chat while they were out hunting together. Therefore he knew that Olivi had not been mistaken, nor had he exaggerated – unfortunately!

Seeing the inanity of it, he stopped discovering ways to falsify his accounts, but that didn't restore his peace of mind. Every time he came into the office he turned grim, looking at his great ledgers. He confessed to me, one day, that on entering our room he felt he was in the anteroom of the prison and wanted to run off.

One day he asked me: "Does Augusta know everything about our books?"

I blushed because I seemed to sense a reproach in the question. But obviously if Ada knew about the books, Augusta could also know. I didn't think of this immediately, but, on the contrary, I felt I deserved his reproach. So I murmured: "She must have learned from Ada, or perhaps from Alberta, who heard it from Ada!"

I could see all the little streams that could flow to Augusta. With those words I didn't feel I was denying the fact that she had learned everything from the prime source, namely me, but I was asserting that it would have been pointless for me to remain silent. Too bad! If, on the contrary, I had confessed at once that I had no secrets from Augusta, I would have felt so loyal and honest! A simple act like that, or rather the dissimulation of an act it would have been better to confess and pronounce innocent, is enough to strain the most sincere friendship.

I will record here, though it has no importance for Guido or for my story, how a few days afterwards that talkative agent with whom we had dealt in the copper-sulfate affair stopped me on the street, looked up at me, compelled by his short stature, which he exaggerated by bending his knees slightly, and said ironically: "They say you two have done some good business, like the sulfate deal!"

Then, seeing me blanch, he shook my hand and added: "Personally, I wish you lots of good deals. I hope you have no doubt about that!"

And he left me. I suppose that our affairs had been reported to him by his daughter, who was a classmate of little Anna at the Liceo. I didn't mention this slight indiscretion to Guido. My main job was to defend him against useless troubles.

I was amazed that Guido made no decision about Carmen, because I knew he had formally promised his wife to discharge her. I thought Ada would come home in a few months, as she had the first time. But, without passing through Trieste, she went to stay in a villa on Lago Maggiore, where Guido took the children a short time later.

When he returned from that journey – and I don't know if he remembered his promise on his own, or whether Ada had reminded him of it – he asked me if it wouldn't be possible to employ Carmen in my office, that is to say Olivi's. I knew that all positions in that office were already filled, but because Guido asked me with such insistence, I agreed to go and talk about it with my manager. By a lucky chance, one of Olivi's employees was leaving just then, but his wages were lower than what Carmen had been paid during these last months, with great prodigality, by Guido, who, in my opinion, thus had his women paid from the general expenses account. Old Olivi asked me about Carmen's abilities, and though I gave her the most glowing recommendation, he offered to hire her on the same terms as the clerk who had quit. I reported this to Guido, who scratched his head, upset and embarrassed.

"How can she be given a lower salary than what she's now earning? Couldn't Olivi be persuaded to give her at least what she already makes?"

I knew that was impossible, and besides, it wasn't Olivi's way to consider himself married to his staff, as we did. If he were to realize Carmen was worth one crown less than the salary he'd given her, he would subtract it mercilessly. And in the end things remained like this: Olivi didn't receive and never asked for a firm reply, and Carmen continued to roll her lovely eyes in our office.

Between me and Ada there was a secret, and it remained important precisely because it continued to be a secret. She wrote constantly to Augusta, but never told her about having had an explanation with me, or even that she had recommended Guido to my care. Nor did I speak of it. One day Augusta showed me a letter of Ada's that concerned me. First she asked for news of me, and finally she appealed to my kindness, asking me to tell her something about the progress of Guido's affairs. I was uneasy when I heard that she was addressing me, and I was reassured when I saw that as usual she addressed herself to me only to learn more about Guido. Once again there was no call for me to presume anything.

With Augusta's assent and without saying anything to Guido, I wrote to Ada. I sat at my desk with the intention of writing her a genuine business letter, and I informed her that I was quite pleased by the way Guido now ran the business, with attention and cleverness.

This was true, or at least I was pleased with him that day, as he had managed to earn a bit of money selling some goods he had stored in the city for several months. It was also true that he seemed more assiduous, but he still went hunting and fishing every week. I gladly exaggerated my praises because it seemed to me this would speed Ada's recovery.

I reread the letter, and it didn't satisfy me. Something was missing. Ada had turned to me, and surely she wanted also my own news. Therefore I was being discourteous in not giving her any. And little by little – I remember it as if it were happening to me now – I felt embarrassed at that desk, as if I were again facing Ada, in that dark little sitting room. Was I to squeeeze the little hand being offered me?

I wrote, but then I had to rewrite the letter because I had allowed certain words, downright compromising, to escape me: I was yearning to see her again, and I hoped she was regaining all her health and all her beauty. This was like clasping the waist of the woman who had offered me only her hand. My duty was merely to shake that hand, to press it gently and at length, to signify that I understood everything, all that should never, ever, be said.

I won't repeat all the vocabulary I had to review in order to find something to replace that long and sweet and meaningful handshake, but only those sentences that I then wrote. I spoke at length of my incipient old age. I couldn't sit still a moment without growing older. At every course of my blood, something was added to my bones and my veins that meant old age. Every morning, when I woke, the world appeared grayer and I didn't notice because everything remained in the same palette; and in that day there wasn't a brushstroke of the color of the day before, otherwise I would have noticed it and regret would have driven me to despair.

I remember very well mailing the letter with complete satisfaction. I had in no way compromised myself by those words, but it also seemed certain to me that if Ada's thoughts were identical to mine, she would understand that loving handshake. It took little insight to grasp the fact that the long discourse on old age signified only my fear that, finding myself speeding through time, I would no longer be overtaken by love. I seemed to be shouting to love: "Come, come!" Instead, I'm not sure I wanted that love, and if any doubt exists, it stems only from the fact that I know what I wrote was more or less in those terms.

I made a copy of that letter for Augusta, omitting the disquisition on old age. She wouldn't have understood it, but precaution never does any harm. I might have blushed, feeling her observation of me as I was shaking her sister's hand. Yes! I could still blush. And I blushed also when I received a note of thanks from Ada, in which she made absolutely no mention of my prattle about my old age. It seemed to me she was compromising herself far more with me than I had compromised myself with her. She was not withdrawing her hand from my pressure. She allowed it to lie, inert, in mine, and for a woman, inertia is a form of consent.

A few days after I had written that letter, I discovered that Guido had started playing the stock exchange. I learned this through an indiscretion of Nilini, the broker.

I had known him for many years because we had been together at the Liceo, but he had been obliged to leave abruptly, to take a position in an uncle's office. Later we ran into each other now and then, and I recall that the difference between our fates had given me a superior position in our relations. He used to greet me first and occasionally he tried to become closer to me. To me this seemed only natural, but what appeared less explicable was that, in a period I can't pin down, he became very haughty toward me. He no longer greeted me first, and barely returned my own greeting. I was a little concerned by this because I am very thin-skinned and easily bruised. But what could be done? Perhaps he had discovered I was in Guido's office, where it seemed to him I occupied a subaltern position, and therefore he despised me, or, with equal probability, I could suppose that, since his uncle had now died and left him an independent broker on the exchange, his pride had grown. In narrow environments, such attitudes are frequent. Without any hostile action having taken place, one fine day two men regard each other with aversion and contempt.

I was surprised, therefore, to see him enter the office, where I was alone, and inquire about Guido. He had removed his hat and offered me his hand. Then, with great liberty, he slumped into one of our big chairs. I looked at him with interest. I hadn't seen him this closely for years, and now, with the aversion he was displaying toward me, he won my keenest attention.

He was then about forty, and was quite ugly thanks to an almost total baldness interrupted only by an oasis of thick, black hair on his nape and another at his temples, his face yellow and too heavy despite the big nose. He was short and thin and he held himself as erect as he could, so that when I spoke with him I felt a slight, sympathetic ache in my neck, the only sympathy I felt for him. That day he seemed to be restraining his laughter, and his face was contracted by an irony or by a contempt that couldn't wound me after he had greeted me so cordially. On the contrary, I later discovered that this irony had been printed on his face by a whim of

Mother Nature. His little jaws did not close precisely, and between them, on one side of his mouth, a gap remained, where his stereotyped irony dwelt. Perhaps to conform to the mask from which he was unable to liberate himself except when he yawned, he enjoyed mocking his fellow man. He was far from being a fool, and he fired off some poisonous arrows, but preferably at those who were absent.

He chattered a great deal and was full of imagination, especially in dealing with matters of the Bourse. He talked about the Bourse as if it were a person, a female, whom he described as fearing a threat or sleeping soundly, and with a face that could laugh and also weep. He saw her climbing the steps of a rising stock, dancing ahead, or then rushing down, with a risk of falling headlong; and yet he admired her as she caressed one stock, strangled another, or also how she taught people to control themselves or to take a plunge. For only people with sense could handle her. There was a lot of money strewn over the ground in the Bourse, but to bend down and gather it wasn't easy.

I invited him to wait, having offered him a cigarette, and I busied myself with some correspondence. After a little while he grew tired and said he couldn't stay any longer. For that matter he had come only to tell Guido that certain shares with the strange name of Rio Tinto, which he had advised Guido to buy the day before – yes, exactly twenty-four hours ago – had soared that day by about ten percent. He burst into hearty laughter.

"So while we're talking here, or while I'm waiting for him, the Bourse rumor-mill will have done the rest. If Signor Speier now wanted to buy those shares, heaven only knows what he would have to pay. I anticipated the direction the Bourse was taking."

He boasted of his eye for the Bourse due to his long intimacy. He interrupted himself to ask: "Who do you think is the better teacher, the University or the Bourse?"

His jaw dropped a little bit further, and the gap of irony was enlarged.

"Obviously, Bourse!" I said with conviction. This won me an affectionate handshake when he left.

So Guido was playing the stock market! If I had been more alert I could already have guessed as much, because when I presented him an exact account of the not insignificant sums we had earned with our latest transactions, he looked at it with a smile, but also with some scorn. He considered we had had to work too hard to earn that money. And, mind you, with a few dozen of those transactions, we could have made up the loss we had incurred the previous year! What was I to do now, I who only a few days before had written his praises?

A little later Guido came into the office, and I faithfully reported Nilini's words to him. He listened with such anxiety that he didn't even realize I had thus learned of his gambling; then he ran out.

That evening I spoke of it with Augusta, who felt we should leave Ada in peace, but should instead warn Signora Malfenti of the risks Guido was taking. She also asked me to do my best to restrain him from committing such follies.

I spent a long time preparing the words I would say to him. Finally I carried out my resolution of active goodness, and I kept the promise I had made to Ada. I knew how to grasp Guido and induce him to obey me. Anyone who plays the market – I would explain to him – is being foolish, especially a businessman with a balance sheet like his behind him.

The next day I began very well: "So you're now playing the market?" I asked him sternly. I was prepared for a scene, and I was keeping in reserve a declaration that, because he was behaving in such a way as to jeopardize the firm, I would promptly abandon the office.

Guido was able to disarm me at once. He had kept the secret till now, but now, boyish and open, he told me every detail of those affairs of his. He was trading in mining stocks in some country or other, which had already produced a profit that was almost enough to cover the loss on our books. Now all risk was past, and he could tell me everything. If he were to run into bad luck and lose what he had gained, he would simply stop playing. If, on the other hand, luck continued to favor him, he would quickly put the accounts in order, as he still felt threatened by them.

I saw there was no use in being angry, and that, on the contrary, he should be congratulated. As for questions of bookkeeping, I told him he could now rest easy, because where cash was available it was very easy to adjust the most troublesome accounts. As soon as we had recorded Ada's account properly and had at least begun to fill what I called the abyss of our firm, namely Guido's own account, our books would be as clean as a whistle.

Then I suggested to him that we put the accounts in order at once and enter the Bourse operations into the firm's books. He didn't agree, luckily for me, otherwise I would have become the accountant of the gambler, and I would have incurred even greater responsibility. On the contrary, things still proceeded as if I didn't exist. He rejected my suggestion with reasons that seemed valid to me. It was a bad idea to pay debts so quickly, and there is a widespread superstition at all gaming tables that other people's money brings luck. I don't believe it, but when I gamble, I, too, never neglect any precaution.

For a while I reproached myself for having accepted Guido's communications without any protest. But then I saw Signora Malfenti behave in the same way, telling me how her husband had been capable of making good money on the market, and I even heard from Ada, who considered gambling just another form of business, so I understood that on this score no one could make any complaint against me. No protest of mine could arrest Guido on that precipitous slope unless I was supported by all the members of the family.

So it was that Guido continued gambling, and the whole family with him. I, too, was a party to it, and indeed I entered into a curious kind of friendship with Nilini. To be sure, I couldn't bear him because I found him ignorant and presumptuous, but out of regard for Guido, who expected good tips from him, I was apparently so good at concealing my feelings that in the end he believed he had a devoted friend in me. I won't deny that perhaps my politeness toward him was due also to the desire to avoid that illness his hostility had caused, largely because of that laughing irony on his ugly face. But I never showed him any courtesies other than that of giving him my hand and greeting him when he arrived and when he left. He, on the contrary, was extremely cordial, and I couldn't fail to receive his courtesy with gratitude, which is truly the greatest kindness that one can display in this world. He procured contraband cigarettes and charged me only what they had cost him, namely very little. If I had found him more likable, he could have persuaded me to let him gamble for me; I never did, but only because, that way, I would have had to see him more often.

I saw him too much as it was! He spent hours in our office despite the fact – as it was easy to realize – that he was not in love with Carmen. He came specifically to keep me company. It seems he proposed to educate me in the field of politics, in which he was deeply versed thanks to the stock exchange. He introduced me to the Great Powers and explained how one day they shook hands and the next were knocking one another about. I don't know if he divined the future, because, in my dislike, I never listened to him. I maintained a foolish, printed smile. Our misunderstanding no doubt derived from an erroneous interpretation of my smile, which to him must have seemed admiring. It's not my fault.

I know only the things he repeated every day. I could divine that he was an Italian of suspect coloration because it seemed to him Trieste would be better off remaining Austrian.

He adored Germany and especially German railway cars, which arrived with such precision. He was a socialist in his own way, and would have liked any individual person to be forbidden to possess more than one hundred thousand crowns. I didn't laugh when, one day, conversing with Guido, he admitted that he possessed exactly one hundred thousand crowns and not a penny more. I didn't laugh, nor did I ask him whether, if he were to earn another penny, he would revise his theory. Ours was a truly strange association. I couldn't laugh with him or at him.

When he had rattled off some assertion of his, he would pull himself up in his chair so that his eyes would be directed at the ceiling, whereas I was left facing what I called the mandibular gap. And he could see through that gap! Sometimes I wished to take advantage of that position of his and think of something else, but he would recall my attention, abruptly asking: "Are you listening to me?"

After that friendly outburst of his, for a long time Guido didn't talk to me about his affairs. At first Nilini told me a little of them, but then he also became a bit more reserved. From Ada herself I learned that Guido was continuing to make money.

When she returned, I found her quite ugly again. She was not just fatter: she was bloated. Her cheeks, restored, were once again misplaced and gave her an almost square countenance. Her eyes had continued to distend their sockets. My surprise was great, because from Guido and others who had gone to visit her, I had heard that with every passing day she gained new strength and health. But a woman's health is, first of all, her beauty.

Ada also brought me other surprises. She greeted me affectionately, but no differently from the way she had greeted Augusta. There was no longer between us any secret, and certainly she no longer remembered having wept on recalling how she had made me suffer. So much the better! She was forgetting even her rights over me! I was her good brother-in-law, and she loved me only because she found unchanged my affectionate relations with my wife, which always remained the admiration of the Malfenti family.

One day I made a discovery that greatly surprised me. Ada believed she was still beautiful! Far away from home, at the lake, she had been courted, and obviously she had enjoyed her successes. Probably she exaggerated them, because it seemed to me excessive to claim she had had to leave that resort to escape a suitor's persecution. I admit there may have been an element of truth there, because she would no doubt seem less ugly to those who hadn't known her before. But still, not that much less, with those eyes and that complexion and that deformed face! To us she seemed uglier because, remembering what she had been, we saw more clearly the devastation wrought by the illness.

One evening we invited her and Guido to our house. It was a pleasant gathering, just family. It seemed the continuation of that four-way betrothal of ours. But Ada's hair was not illuminated by the glow of any light.

When we were separating, as I was helping her on with her cloak, I remained alone with her for a moment. I immediately had a slightly different feeling about our relations. We were left alone, and perhaps we could say to each other what we were unwilling to say in the presence of the others. As I was helping her, I reflected and finally I found what I had to say to her.

"You know he's gambling now," I said to her in a serious voice. I sometimes suspect that with those words I wanted to recall our last meeting, which I could not believe was so forgotten.

"Yes," she said, smiling, "and very successfully. He's become quite clever, from what they tell me."

I laughed with her, a loud laugh. I felt relieved of all responsibility. As she went off, she murmured: "Is that Carmen still in your office?"

Before I could answer, she had run off. Between us there was no longer our past. There was, however, her jealousy. That was alive, as at our last meeting.

Now, thinking back, I find that I should have realized, long before I was precisely informed, that Guido had begun losing on the market. His face was no longer illuminated by that air of triumph and it showed again his great anxiety over that balance sheet, left in that state.

"Why are you worrying about it?" I asked him, in my innocence, "when you already have in your pocket enough to make those false entries completely real? When you have all that money, you don't go to jail." At that time, I later learned, he no longer had a cent in his pocket.

I was so firmly convinced he had fortune bound to his chariot that I paid no heed to the many clues that might have persuaded me otherwise.

One evening in August, he dragged me off fishing again. In the dazzling light of an almost full moon there was scant likelihood of catching anything on our hooks. But he insisted, saying that out on the water we would find some relief from the heat. In fact, that was all we found. After a single attempt, we didn't even bait the hooks, and we allowed the lines to trail from the little boat as Luciano rowed out to sea. The moon's rays must surely have reached the seabed, sharpening the sight of the big animals, making them aware of the trap, and even of the little animals capable of nibbling the bait, but not of taking the hook in their tiny mouths. Our bait was simply a gift to the minnows.

Guido lay down at the stern, and I at the prow. A little later he murmured: "How sad, all this light!"

Probably he said that because the light prevented him from sleeping, and I agreed, to please him, and also so as not to disturb with foolish argument the solemn peace in which we were proceeding. But Luciano protested, saying he liked that light very much. As Guido didn't answer, I tried to silence the youth, saying the light was certainly sad because we could see all the things of this world. And besides, it spoiled the fishing. Luciano laughed and kept quiet.

We were silent for a long while. I yawned several times in the moon's face. I regretted having let myself be induced to climb into that boat.

Guido suddenly asked me: "You're a chemist, could you answer me this: which is more effective, pure veronal or sodium veronal?"

To tell the truth, I didn't even know that a sodium veronal existed. You can't expect a chemist to know the whole world by heart. I know enough chemistry to enable me to find any information promptly in my books, and further to be able to discuss – as is obvious in this case – the things I don't know.

Sodium? Why, it's a well-known fact that sodium compounds are those most easily assimilated. Also, in connection with sodium, I recalled – and I repeated more or less exactly – an encomium of that element expressed by a professor of mine in the only lecture of his I attended. Sodium is a vehicle on which the elements climb in order to move more rapidly. And the professor had recalled how sodium chloride passed from organism to organism, and how it collected simply as a result of gravity in the deepest pit of the earth, the sea. I'm not sure I reproduced my professor's thought precisely, but at that moment, faced by that vast expanse of sodium chloride, I spoke of sodium with infinite respect.

After some hesitation, Guido asked further: "So someone who wants to die should take sodium veronal?"

"Yes," I answered.

Then, remembering that there are cases in which a person may want to simulate a suicide and, not thinking just then that I might be reminding Guido of a painful episode in his life, I added: "And if the person doesn't want to die, he should take the pure veronal."

Guido's study of veronal might have made me stop and think. Instead, I didn't realize anything, concentrating on sodium as I was. Over the next few days I was able to bring Guido new evidence of the qualities I had attributed to sodium: to accelerate amalgams, which are simply intense embraces between two bodies, embraces that substitute combination or assimilation, some sodium was also added to mercury. Sodium was the mediator between gold and mercury. But Guido was no longer interested in veronal, and now I think that his visits to the Bourse had then taken a turn for the better.

In the course of a week, Ada came to the office all of three times. Only after the second visit did it occur to me that she wanted to talk with me.

The first time, she ran into Nilini, who had once again set himself to educating me. She waited a full hour for him to leave, but she made the mistake of chatting with him and he therefore believed he should stay. After having made the introductions, I heaved a sigh of relief, as Nilini's mandibular gap was no longer directed at me. I didn't participate in their conversation.

Nilini was actually witty and surprised Ada, telling her how there was as much wicked gossip in the Tergesteo as in a lady's sitting room. Only, according to him; at the Bourse, as always, they were better informed than elsewhere. To Ada it seemed he was slandering women. She said she didn't even know the meaning of the word gossip. At this point I spoke up, confirming that in all the long years I had known her, I had never heard from her lips a word that even remotely resembled gossip. I smiled while saying that, because I seemed to be reproaching her. She wasn't a gossip because other people's affairs didn't interest her. Before, in perfect health, she had minded her own business, and when her sickness overcame her, she could maintain only one little space free, which was reserved for her jealousy. She was a true egoist, but she welcomed my testimony with gratitude.

Nilini pretended not to believe her or me. He said he had known me for many years and he believed I possessed a great ingenuousness. This amused me, and it amused Ada, too. I was very annoyed, on the other hand, when he — for the first time in the presence of a third party — proclaimed that I was one of his best friends and that therefore he knew me profoundly. I didn't dare protest, but that shameless declaration offended my modesty, I was like a young woman publicly accused of fornication.

I was so ingenuous, Nilini said, that Ada, with her familiar female cleverness, could easily have uttered some slander in my presence without my being aware of it. It seemed to me that Ada continued to be amused by these dubious compliments, but I later learned that she was letting him talk in the hope that he would wear himself out and leave. She had quite a wait.

When Ada came back the second time, she found me with Guido. Then I read on her face an expression of impatience, and I guessed that it was actually me she was seeking. Until she returned, I toyed with my usual dreams. She wasn't asking me for love, actually, but too frequently she wanted to be alone with me. For men it was difficult to understand what women wanted because at times women themselves didn't know.

But her words then inspired no new feeling. As soon as she could talk to me, her voice was choked with emotion, but not because it was me she was addressing. She wanted to know the reason why Carmen had not been discharged. I told her all I knew about it, including our attempt to procure her a position with Olivi.

She was immediately calmer because what I told her corresponded exactly to what she had been told by Guido. Then I learned that her fits of jealousy struck her at intervals. They arrived without apparent cause, and they were dispelled by any convincing word.

She asked me two more questions: if it was really all that difficult to find a position for an employee, and if Carmen's family was in such straits that they depended on the girl's earnings.

I explained to her that, in fact, in Trieste it was hard to find an office job for a woman. And as for the second question, I couldn't answer, because I didn't know any member of Carmen's family.

"But Guido knows everyone in that house," Ada murmured wrathfully, and tears bathed her cheeks again.

Then she pressed my hand to say good-bye, and thanked me. Smiling through her tears, she said she knew she could rely on me. I liked her smile because it was certainly not meant for a brother-in-law, but rather for one bound to her by secret ties. I tried to give her proof that I deserved that smile, and I murmured: "What makes me fear for Guido isn't Carmen, but his gambling on the stock market!"

She shrugged. "That's not important. I've talked about it with Mamma, too. Papà also played the stock market, and he made lots and lots of money!"

I was disconcerted by this answer, and I insisted: "I don't like that Nilini. It's not true that I'm his friend!"

She looked at me, surprised. "He seems a gentleman to me. Guido is also very fond of him. I believe, furthermore, that Guido is now paying great attention to business."

I was determined not to speak ill of Guido, so I remained silent. When I found myself alone, I didn't think about Guido, but about myself. It was perhaps just as well that Ada finally appeared to me as a sister and nothing more. She didn't promise and didn't threaten love. For several days I ran about the city, restless and unbalanced. I couldn't manage to understand myself. Why was I feeling as if Carla had left me at that very moment? Nothing new had happened to me. I sincerely believe that I have always needed adventure, or some complication resembling it. My relations with Ada no longer involved the least complication.

From his easy chair one day Nilini preached more than usual: on the horizon a storm cloud was advancing, neither more nor less than an increase in the cost of money. The market all of a sudden was saturated and could absorb nothing more!

"Let's give it a dose of sodium!" I suggested.

My interjection didn't please him at all, but rather than become angry, he ignored it. Suddenly money in this world had become scarce and therefore costly. He was surprised that this was happening now, for he had foreseen its coming a month hence.

"Perhaps they sent all the money off to the moon!" I said.

"These are serious matters, not to be laughed at," Nilini declared, still looking at the ceiling. "Now we'll see who has the stuff of the true fighter and who is knocked down by the first blow."

As I didn't understand how money in this world could become scarcer, so I didn't realize Nilini was placing Guido among those fighters who had to prove their worth. I was so accustomed to defending myself against his sermons by paying no attention that this one, though I heard it, also passed by me without leaving the slightest mark.

But a few days later Nilini quite changed his tune. Something new had happened. He had discovered that Guido had conducted some transactions through another broker. Nilini began protesting in an agitated tone that he had never failed Guido in anything, not even in maintaining proper discretion. On this question he called me to bear witness. Hadn't he kept Guido's affairs a secret even from me, whom he continued to consider his best friend? But at this point he was released from any reticence, and he could shout in my face that Guido was in debt up to his ears. For those affairs that had been conducted through him, Nilini could guarantee that at the very slightest improvement it would be possible to hold out and await better times. It was, however, outrageous that at the first sign of trouble Guido had wronged him.

Talk about Ada! Nilini's jealousy was intractable. I wanted to dig more news out of him, but he, on the contrary, became increasingly exasperated and went on talking of the wrong that had been done him. Therefore, despite his best intentions, he still remained discreet.

That afternoon I found Guido in the office. He was lying on our sofa in a curious intermediate state between despair and sleep. I asked him, "Are you in debt up to your ears?"

He didn't reply at once. He raised his arm and covered his haggard face. Then he said: "Have you ever seen a man with worse luck than me?"

He lowered his arm and changed his position, lying supine. He closed his eyes again and seemed already to have forgotten my presence.

I was unable to offer him any comfort. It really offended me that he should believe himself the unluckiest man in the world. This wasn't an exaggeration: it was an outright lie. I would have helped him, had I been able to, but it was impossible for me to comfort him. In my opinion, even some-one more innocent and more unlucky than Guido doesn't deserve compassion, because otherwise in our lives there would be room only for that feeling, which would be very tiresome. Natural law does not entitle us to happiness, but rather it prescribes wretchedness and sorrow. When something edible is left exposed, from all directions parasites come running, and if there are no parasites, they are quickly gener-ated. Soon the prey is barely sufficient, and immediately afterwards it no longer suffices at all, for nature doesn't do sums, she experiments. When food no longer suffices, then consumers must diminish through death preceded by pain; thus equilibrium, for a moment, is reestablished. Why complain? And yet everyone does complain. Those who have had none of the prey die, crying out against injustice, and those who had a share feel that they deserved more. Why don't they die, and live, in silence? On the other hand, the joy of those who could seize a good part of the food is pleasant, and it should be displayed in broad daylight, to applause. The only admissible cry is that of the triumphant. The victor.

As for Guido! He lacked any ability to gain or even simply to hold on to riches. He came from the gambling table and wept at having lost. He didn't behave, therefore, like a gentleman, and he nauseated me. For this reason, and only for this one, at the moment when Guido would have had great need of my affection, he didn't find it. Not even my repeated resolutions could carry me that far.

Meanwhile, Guido's respiration was becoming gradually more regular and noisy. He was falling asleep! How unmanly he was in his misfortune! They had taken away his food, and he closed his eyes perhaps to dream that he still possessed it, instead of opening them wide to see if he could somehow snatch a little morsel.

I became curious to know if Ada had been informed of the misfortune that had befallen him. I asked him in a loud voice. He started, and needed a moment to adjust to his disaster, which suddenly he saw again, complete.

"No!" he murmured. Then he closed his eyes once more.

To be sure, all those who are severely stricken have a tendency toward sleep. Sleep restores strength. I went on watching him, hesitant. But how could he be helped if he was sleeping? This wasn't the moment to doze off. I grabbed him roughly by one shoulder and shook him.

"Guido!"

He had actually slept. He looked at me, uncertain, his eyes still clouded by sleep, and then he asked me: "What do you want?" A moment later, infuriated, he repeated his question: "Well, what do you want?"

I wanted to help him, otherwise I wouldn't have had any right to wake him. I became angry, too, and I shouted that this wasn't the moment for sleeping because he had quickly to see if some remedy could be found. He had to figure things out and discuss them with all the members of our family and with his family in Buenos Aires.

Guido sat up. He was still rather distraught, having been wakened in that manner. He said to me bitterly: "You would have done better to let me sleep. Who's going to help me now? Don't you remember how far I had to go last time, to be given the little I needed to be saved? Now there are substantial amounts involved! Where do you think I could turn?"

With no affection, but rather with anger at having to contribute and thus deprive myself and my family, I cried: "I'm here, aren't I?" Then avarice prompted me to temper my sacrifice right at the start: "And what about Ada? And our mother-in-law? Can't we all join hands to save you?"

He stood up and came toward me with the obvious intention of embracing me. But this was exactly what I didn't want. Having offered him my help, I now had the right to upbraid him, and I made full use of it. I reproached him for his present weakness and then also for his presumption, which had continued until this moment, and had lured him to his ruin. He had acted on his own, not consulting anyone. Time and again I had tried to communicate with him, to restrain him and save him; but he had rejected me, continuing to trust only Nilini.

Here Guido smiled. He actually smiled, the wretch! He told me for two weeks he had no longer worked with Nilini, having got it into his head that the man's ugly mug brought him bad luck.

His character was evident in all, in that sleep and in that smile: he was ruining everyone around him, and still he smiled. I played the stern judge because, to be saved, Guido had first to be educated. I insisted he tell me how much he had lost, and I was angry when he said he didn't know exactly. I became still angrier when he mentioned a fairly small sum, which then proved to be the amount he had to pay at the settlement on the fifteenth of the month, which was only two days off. But Guido insisted that things could be put off until the month's end, and the situation might still change. The scarcity of money on the market wouldn't last forever.

I shouted: "If money is scarce in this world, do you expect to get it from the moon?" I added that he was not to gamble again, not even for one day. He wasn't to risk increasing the already enormous loss. I also said that the loss would be divided into four parts, which would be covered by me, him (or rather his father), Signora Malfenti, and Ada, that we had to return to our normal commerce, which involved no risks, and I never wanted to see Nilini in our office again, or any other broker.

Very meekly, he begged me not to shout so, because the neighbors might hear us.

I made a great effort to calm myself, and I succeeded, also because, keeping my voice down, I could go on insulting him. His loss was in effect a crime. You had to be an idiot to get yourself into such a situation. I really felt it was necessary to subject him to the entire lesson.

Here, Guido mildly protested. Who didn't play the market? Our father-in-law, who had been such a sound businessman, hadn't spent a day of his life without some trading. And besides – as Guido knew – I myself had gambled.

I protested that there were different kinds of gambling. He had risked his entire patrimony on the market; I had risked a month's income.

It made me sad to see Guido childishly trying to slough off his responsibility. He insisted Nilini had induced him to risk more than he wanted, convincing him that he was on his way to a great fortune.

I laughed and mocked him. Nilini wasn't to blame, he was attending to his own business. And – for that matter – after leaving Nilini, hadn't Guido rushed to another broker and raised his stakes? He could have boasted of this new association if he had begun selling short without Nilini's knowledge. To remedy the situation, it surely wasn't enough to change brokers while continuing the same ill-starred course. Guido wanted only to persuade me finally to leave him alone, and with a sob in his throat, he admitted that he had been wrong.

I stopped upbraiding him. Now he really aroused my compassion, and I would even have embraced him if he had wanted me to. I told him I would immediately set about procuring the money I was to provide, and I would also take it upon myself to speak with our mother-in-law. He, on the other hand, would deal with Ada.

My compassion increased when he confided that he would gladly have spoken with our mother-in-law in my place, but he was tormented at the thought of speaking with Ada.

"You know how women are! They don't understand business, not unless it has a happy outcome!" He wouldn't talk with her at all, and would ask Signora Malfenti to inform her of the whole situation.

This decision relieved him greatly, and we left together. I saw him walking beside me with his head down and I felt remorse for treating him so roughly. But how could I do otherwise, when I loved him? He had to mend his ways if he didn't want to continue heading for ruin! What could his relations with his wife be like, if he was so afraid of speaking with her!

But meanwhile he discovered a way of vexing me again. Walking along, he had mentally perfected the plan that had so appealed to him. Not only would he not have to talk with his wife, but he would find a way not to see her that evening, because he would go off hunting. After that decision, he was free of every cloud. Apparently the prospect of going out into the open air, far from every concern, sufficed to make him look as if he were already there and enjoying himself fully. I was infuriated! With the same look, surely, he could go back to the Bourse and resume his gambling, with which he risked the family fortune and also mine.

He said to me: "I want to allow myself this last pleasure, and I invite you to come with me, on condition that you swear not to remind me of today's events, not even with a single word."

Thus far he had been smiling as he spoke. Confronted by my serious face, he also turned serious. He added: "You, too, must see that I need some relief after such a blow. Then it will be easier for me to resume my place in the struggle."

His voice had an edge of emotion whose sincerity I couldn't doubt. So I was able to curb my irritation, indicating it only by my refusal of his invitation, informing him that I had to stay in the city to raise the required money. My reply was in itself a reproach! I, the innocent one, would remain at my post, while he, the guilty, could go off and enjoy himself.

We had reached the front door of the Malfenti house. He hadn't managed to recover his expression of joy at the prospect of a few hours of pleasure, and while he stayed there with me, he retained, imprinted on his face, the suffering expression I had caused. But before leaving me, he found release in a display of independence and as it seemed to me resentment. He told me he was truly amazed to discover such a friend in me. He hesitated to accept the sacrifice I meant to make for him, and he wanted (really wanted) me to know that he didn't consider me committed in any way and I was therefore free to give or not to give.

I'm sure I blushed. To spare myself embarrassment, I said to him: "Why do you think I would want to back out, when just a few minutes ago, without your having asked anything of me, I volunteered to help you?"

He looked at me, somewhat uncertain, and then said: "Since it's your wish, I'll accept it, of course, and I thank you. But we will make a contract, a brand-new partnership, so that each will receive what is his due. In fact, if we have a business, and you want to continue handling it, you must have a salary. We'll set up the new firm on quite a different basis. That way, we'll no longer have to fear further harm from having concealed the loss in our first year of activity."

I replied: "That loss no longer has any importance, and you mustn't think any more about it. Try to win our mother-in-law over to your side. That, and only that, is what matters now."

So we parted. I believe I smiled at the naïveté with which Guido revealed his most intimate feelings. He had made me that long speech only so that he could accept my gift without showing me any gratitude. But I demanded nothing. It was enough for me to know that he really owed me such gratitude.

For that matter, on leaving him, I also felt a relief as if, only then, had I stepped into the open air. I truly felt again the freedom that had been taken from me by my resolution to educate him and put him back on the right path. Basically, the pedagogue is enchained worse than the pupil. I was fully determined to procure that money for him. Naturally I can't say whether I was doing this out of affection for him or for Ada, or perhaps to rid myself of that small share of responsibility I might bear for having worked in his office. In short, I had decided to sacrifice a part of my inheritance, and even today I look back on that day in my life with great satisfaction. That money saved Guido, and assured me a great serenity of conscience.

I walked until evening in the greatest serenity, and so I missed the right moment to go to the Bourse and find Olivi, to whom I had to turn to raise such a large sum. Then I decided the matter wasn't all that urgent. I had a considerable amount of money at my disposal, and that was enough for the present, to contribute to the payment we had to make on the fifteenth of the month. For the end of the month I would provide later.

That evening I thought no more of Guido. Later, when the children had been put to bed, I began several times to tell Augusta of Guido's financial disaster and the harmful consequences for me, but I didn't want to be bored with discussion, and I thought it would be better to hold off and convince Augusta at the moment when the settling of those affairs would be decided by the whole family. And besides, while Guido was off enjoying himself, it would be odd for me to be irritated.

I slept very well, and in the morning, with my pocket not heavily loaded with money (I had the envelope rejected by Carla, which till now I had religiously kept for her or for some successor of hers, plus a bit more money I'd been able to withdraw from a bank), I went to the office. I spent the morning reading newspapers, between Carmen, who was sewing, and Luciano, who was practicing addition and subtraction.

When I returned home at lunchtime, I found Augusta dejected and puzzled. Her face was covered by that great pallor produced only by sorrows caused by me. Mildly, she said: "I'm told you've decided to sacrifice a part of your inheritance to save Guido! I know I had no right to be informed – "

She was so doubtful of her right that she hesitated. Then she went on reproaching me for my silence: "But it's also true that I'm not like Ada, because I have never opposed your wishes."

It took me some time to learn what had happened. Augusta had dropped in on Ada, just as she was discussing Guido's situation with her mother. Seeing her sister, Ada burst into floods of tears and told Augusta of my generosity, which she absolutely didn't want to accept. She even begged Augusta to urge me to desist from my offer.

I realized at once that Augusta was suffering from her old sickness: jealousy of her sister; but I paid no attention. I was surprised by the attitude Ada had assumed: "Did she seem offended?" I asked, my eyes widening in surprise.

"No, no, not that!" the sincere Augusta cried. "She kissed me and hugged me . . . perhaps so I would hug you."

This seemed to me quite a comical way of expressing herself. She was looking at me, studying me, distrustful.

I protested: "Do you believe Ada is in love with me? What's got into your head?"

But I was unable to calm Augusta, whose jealousy was annoying me dreadfully. True, Guido by this time was no longer off enjoying himself, but was no doubt undergoing a nasty quarter-hour between his wife and his mother-in-law, but I was highly annoyed, too, and it seemed to me I was being made to suffer too much, as I was completely innocent.

I tried to calm Augusta, caressing her. She moved her face away from mine to see me better, and gently expressed a mild reproach that moved me deeply.

"I know that you love me, too," she said.

Obviously, Ada's state of mind held no importance for her, but mine did; and I had an inspiration, to prove my innocence to her. "So Ada is in love with me?" I said, laughing. Then, stepping back from Augusta to be seen better, I puffed out my cheeks a little and widened my eyes unnaturally so that I resembled the ailing Ada. Augusta looked at me, dumbfounded, but soon guessed my intention. She was seized by a fit of laughter, of which she was promptly ashamed.

"No!" she said to me. "Please don't make fun of her." Then she confessed, still laughing, that I had succeeded in imitating those very protuberances that gave Ada's face such a surprising appearance. And I knew it, because in imitating Ada, it was as if I were embracing her. And when I was alone, I repeated that effort several times, with desire and repulsion.

In the afternoon I went to the office, hoping to find Guido there. I waited awhile, then decided to go to his house. I had to know if it was necessary to ask Olivi for some money. I had to do my duty, even though it annoyed me to see Ada, once again distorted by gratitude. Who knows what surprises that woman might still have in store for me!

375

On the front steps of Guido's house I ran into Signora Malfenti, who was climbing them ponderously. She told me in full detail what had so far been decided about Guido's plight. When they had separated the previous evening, they were more or less agreed in the conviction that that man, who had undergone such a disastrous misfortune, should be rescued. Only in the morning had Ada learned that I would contribute to covering Guido's loss, and she had firmly refused to accept. Signora Malfenti excused her: "What can we do? She doesn't want to bear the burden of remorse at having impoverished her favorite sister."

On the landing, the Signora stopped to catch her breath and also to talk, and she said to me, laughing, that the matter would be concluded with no harm to anyone. Before lunch, she, Ada, and Guido had called on a lawyer for advice, an old family friend who was also little Anna's trustee. The lawyer had said that there was no need to pay because by law they were not obligated. Guido had objected sharply, speaking of honor and duty, but once all of them, including Ada, had decided not to pay, no doubt he, too, would have to resign himself.

"But will his firm be declared bankrupt in the Bourse?" I asked, puzzled.

"Probably!" Signora Malfenti said, with a sigh, before tackling the last flight of steps.

Guido was accustomed to rest after lunch, and so we were received by Ada alone, in that little sitting room I knew so well. Seeing me, she was confused for a moment, but just for one moment, which I, however, grasped and clung to, clear and evident, as if her confusion had been spoken aloud. Then she recovered herself and held out her hand with a firm, virile gesture, meant to erase the feminine hesitation that had preceded it.

She said to me: "Augusta must have told you how grateful I am to you. I couldn't now tell you what I feel, because I'm confused. I'm also ill. Yes, very ill! I should go back to the sanatorium in Bologna!"

A sob interrupted her: "Now I must ask you a favor. I beg you to tell Guido that you, too, are in no position to give him that money. Then it will be easier to persuade him to do what he must do."

First she had sobbed, recalling her illness; then she sobbed again before continuing to talk about her husband: "He's a boy, and he must be treated as such. If he knows that you will give him that money, he'll be all the more obstinate about his idea of sacrificing the rest as well, pointlessly. Pointlessly, because now we know with absolute certainty that bankruptcy in the Bourse is not illegal. The lawyer told us so."

She was communicating to me the opinion of a high authority without asking me for mine. Coming from an old habitué of the Bourse, my opinion, along with the lawyer's, could have carried some weight, but I didn't actually remember my opinion, if, indeed, I had one. I couldn't renege on the commitment I had made to Guido: it was that commitment that had authorized me to shout all those insults into his ear, thus pocketing something like interest on the capital that now I could no longer refuse him.

"Ada," I said, hesitantly. "I don't believe I can contradict myself like this, on a moment's notice. Wouldn't it be better for you to convince Guido to do things the way you wish?"

Signora Malfenti, with the great fondness she always showed me, said she understood my special position perfectly, and, for that matter, when Guido saw at his disposal only a quarter of the amount he needed, he would be obliged in any case to bow to their wishes.

But Ada hadn't wept all her tears. Crying, her face hidden in her handkerchief, she said: "You were wrong, very wrong, to make that truly extraordinary offer! Now it's clear, the wrong you've done!"

She seemed to me to hesitate between a great gratitude and a great bitterness. Then she added that she didn't want that offer of mine to be discussed any further, and she begged me not to provide that money, because she would prevent me from giving it, or would prevent Guido from accepting it.

I was so embarrassed that in the end I told a lie. I told her, in fact, that I had already procured that money, and I pointed to my breast pocket, where that very slim envelope was nestled. Ada looked at me this time with an expression of real admiration, which would have pleased me if I hadn't been aware of not deserving it. In any case, it was that very lie of mine, for which I can offer no explanation except a strange tendency I have to portray myself to Ada as greater than I am, that kept me from waiting for Guido, and drove me from that house. It could also have happened that, at a certain point, contrary to appearances, I might have been asked to hand over the money I had said I had with me, and then what kind of figure would I cut? I pleaded urgent business in the office and I ran off.

Ada saw me to the door and assured me she would induce Guido to come to me himself, thank me for my kind offer, and refuse it. Her resolve in pronouncing this declaration surprised me; it seemed her determination affected also me in part. No! At that moment she didn't love me. My act of kindness had been too great. It crushed the people on whom it fell, and it was no wonder that the beneficiaries protested. Going to the office, I tried to rid myself of the uneasiness that Ada's attitude had caused me, remembering that I was offering this sacrifice to Guido and to no one else. What did Ada have to do with it? I promised myself I would say this to Ada herself at the first opportunity.

I went to the office precisely to escape any remorse for having lied once again. Nothing awaited me there. Since morning a fine rain had been falling, which had considerably cooled the air of that tentative spring. A few steps and I would have been at home, whereas to go to the office I had to cover a much longer route, and this was fairly tiresome. But I felt I had a commitment to maintain.

A little later I was joined there by Guido. He sent Luciano out of the office in order to remain alone with me. He had that overwhelmed expression that assisted him in his struggles with his wife; I knew it very well. He must have wept and shouted.

He asked me what I thought of the plans of his wife and our mother-in-law, which he knew had been communicated to me. I acted hesitant. I didn't want to express my opinion, which could not agree with that of the two women, but I knew that if I were to adopt theirs, I would provoke further scenes on Guido's part. Yet it would have pained me too much if my help were to seem hesitant, and besides, Ada and I had agreed that the decision should come from Guido and not from me. I told him it was necessary to calculate, observe, listen also to other people. I wasn't such a businessman that I could give advice on an important subject like this. And, to gain time, I asked him if he wanted me to consult Olivi.

This was enough to make him shout. "That imbecile!" he cried. "Please leave him out of this!"

I surely wasn't going to become overheated defending Olivi, but my calm wasn't enough to soothe Guido. We were in the identical situation of the day before, but now it was he who was shouting and I who had to be silent. It's a matter of disposition. I was filled with an embarrassment that paralyzed my limbs.

But he absolutely insisted on hearing my opinion. Thanks to an inspiration I believe divine, I spoke very well, so well that if my words had had any effect whatsoever, the catastrophe that followed would have been avoided. I told him that, to begin with, I would have separated the two questions, that of the payment on the fifteenth from that at the end of the month. After all, on the fifteenth the sum to be paid wasn't so large, and therefore the women should be persuaded to accept

that relatively light loss. Then we would gain the time necessary to arrange wisely for the other payment.

Guido interrupted me to ask: "Ada told me that you have
the money all ready in your pocket. Do you have it here?"

I blushed. But I promptly found another lie at hand, which
saved me: "Since they wouldn't accept that money at your
house, I deposited it in the bank just now. But we can
withdraw it whenever we like, even first thing tomorrow
morning."

Then he reproached me for having changed my mind. Just
the day before I had declared I didn't want to wait for the
second payment before clearing up everything! And here he
had an outburst of violent wrath that finally flung him,
drained, on the sofa! He was going to throw Nilini out of
the window, and all those other brokers who had lured him
into gambling. Oh! While he was gambling he had clearly
glimpsed the possibility of ruin, but never that of being sub-
jugated to women who didn't understand a thing.

I went to shake his hand, and if he had allowed me, I would
have embraced him. I wanted nothing more than to see him
arrive at that decision. No more gambling, but day-to-day
work!

This would be our future and his independence. Now it
was a matter of getting through this brief, hard period, and
then everything would be easy and simple.

Downcast but calmer, he left me a little later. He, too, in his
weakness was pervaded with strong determination.

"I'm going back to Ada," he murmured, with a bitter but
confident smile.

I saw him to the door and I would have accompanied him
home if he hadn't had a carriage outside, waiting for him.

Nemesis was persecuting Guido. Half an hour after he left
me, I thought it would have been prudent on my part to go to
his house and lend him a hand. Not that I suspected there
might be any danger threatening him, but by now I was totally

on his side and I could help persuade Ada and Signora Malfenti to assist him. Failure in the Bourse was not something I liked, and while the loss divided among the four of us was not insignificant, it didn't represent ruin for any of us.

Then I remembered that my greatest duty at this moment was not to help Guido, but to make sure that the next day he would find the sum I had promised him. I went at once to look for Olivi, and I prepared myself for another struggle. I had worked out a system to repay to my firm the gross amount over various years, depositing, however, over a few months' time, all that remained of my mother's estate. I was hoping that Olivi would not create difficulties, because until now I had never asked him for more than was my due from profits and interest, and I could also promise never to trouble him again with such demands. Obviously, I could also hope to recover at least a part of that sum from Guido.

That evening I wasn't able to find Olivi. He had just left his office when I reached it. They assumed he had gone to the Bourse. I didn't find him there, either, and then I went to his house, where I learned he was at a meeting of an economic association in which he occupied some honorary position. I could have gone to him there, but by now it was night, and a heavy rain was falling steadily, transforming the streets into so many little streams.

The downpour lasted all night, and its memory persisted for long years thereafter. The rain fell very calmly, actually perpendicular, always with the same abundance. From the heights surrounding the city, the mud descended and, mingling with the refuse of our city life, soon clogged up our few canals. After having waited in vain in a shed for the rain to stop, I decided to go home, since I could clearly see that the weather had settled on rain and it was useless to hope for any change. I had to wade through water even when I chose the highest part of the cobbles. I hurried home, cursing and soaked to the skin. I was also cursing because I had wasted so much useful time hunting for Olivi. My time may not be all that valuable, but I surely suffer horribly when I can see I have labored in vain. And as I hurried home, I was thinking: "We'll leave everything till tomorrow when it will be clear and fair and dry. Tomorrow I'll see Olivi and tomorrow I'll go to Guido. Maybe I'll get up early, but it will be clear and dry." I was so convinced of the rightness of my decision that I told Augusta everyone had agreed to postpone all decisions to the next day. I changed, dried myself, and first, with my warm, comfortable slippers on my tortured feet, I had supper, then I went to bed and slept soundly until morning while, at the panes of my window, the rain pounded, in streams as thick as cables.

Thus I was late in learning of the night's events. First we found out that the rain had provoked flooding in various parts of the city, and then that Guido was dead.

Much later I found out how such a thing could happen. At about eleven in the evening, when Signora Malfenti had gone off, Guido told his wife that he had swallowed an enormous quantity of veronal. He wanted to convince his wife that he was doomed. He embraced her, kissed her, asked her forgiveness for having caused her suffering. Then, even before his speech turned into a stammer, he assured her that she had been the only love of his life. At that moment she believed neither that assurance nor that he had swallowed all that poison in order to die. She didn't even believe he had lost consciousness, but imagined he was shamming in order to get more money out of her.

Then, when almost an hour had gone by, seeing that he was sleeping more and more profoundly, she felt some terror and wrote a note to a doctor who lived not far from her house. In the note she said that her husband needed help at once because he had swallowed a great quantity of veronal.

Until then, there had been no emotion in that house that might have suggested to the maid, an old woman who had been with them only a short while, the gravity of her mission.

The rain did the rest. The maid found herself up to her calves in water, and she lost the note. She realized this only when she was in the doctor's presence. She did tell him, however, that it was urgent and she persuaded him to come with her.

Dr. Mali was a man of about fifty, far from brilliant, but an experienced physician who had always performed his duty as best he could. He didn't have a great clientele of his own, but he was kept very busy by a partnership with many other doctors, which paid him less than generously. He had just come home, and had finally managed to warm and dry himself at his fire. It's easy to imagine his state of mind, as he now abandoned his warm little nook. When I began investigating more closely the causes of my poor friend's death, I took care also to make the acquaintance of Dr. Mali. From him I learned only this: when he came outdoors and felt the rain soaking him despite his umbrella, he regretted he had studied medicine instead of agriculture, recalling that a peasant, when it rains, stays home.

Reaching Guido's bedside, he found Ada completely calmed. Now that she had the doctor with her, she recalled more clearly how Guido had fooled her months before, simulating suicide. It was no longer she who had to assume responsibility, but rather the doctor, who should be informed of everything, including the motives that might suggest a simulation of suicide. And these motives the doctor learned, all of them, at the same time that he pricked up his ear to hear the waves that were sweeping through the street. Not having been warned that he was called to deal with a case of poisoning, he lacked all the necessary implements for the treatment. He deplored this, muttering some words that Ada didn't understand. The worst of it was that, to initiate a gastric cleansing, he couldn't send for the necessary pump, but would have to go and fetch it himself, retracing his steps twice. He touched Guido's pulse and found it magnificent. He asked Ada if

Guido by chance had always been a sound sleeper. Ada answered yes, but not to this degree. The doctor examined Guido's eyes: they reacted promptly to the light! He went off, recommending that from time to time she give him a few teaspoons of very strong black coffee.

I learned also that, once in the street again, he muttered angrily: "It ought to be against the law, to fake suicide in weather like this!"

I, when I met him, didn't dare reproach him for his negligence, but he sensed my feeling and defended himself: He told me he was amazed to learn, the next morning, that Guido was dead, and had even thought the patient might have regained consciousness and taken more veronal. Then he added that those ignorant of the medical art couldn't imagine how a doctor, in the course of his practice, became accustomed to defending his life against patients who jeopardized it, thinking only of their own.

After little more than an hour, Ada tired of thrusting a teaspoon between Guido's teeth and seeing him sip less and less of it, letting the rest spill and dampen the pillow; she took fright again and asked the maid to go to Dr. Paoli. This time the maid was careful with the note. But it took her over an hour to reach the physician's house. It's natural, when it's raining that hard, to feel the need now and then to stop under some portico. That sort of rain doesn't just wet you: it lashes you.

Dr. Paoli wasn't at home. He had been summoned a short time before by a patient, and had gone off saying he hoped to be back quickly. But then, apparently, he had preferred to wait at the patient's house for the rain to stop. His housekeeper, a very kind elderly person, invited Ada's maid to sit by the fire and gave her some refreshment. The doctor hadn't left his patient's address, and so the two women spent several hours together by the fire. The doctor returned only when the rain had stopped. Then, when he reached Ada's with all the instruments he had used once before on Guido, dawn was breaking. At that bedside he had only one duty: to conceal from Ada the fact that Guido was already dead and, before Ada could realize it, send for Signora Malfenti, to assist the widow in her immediate grief.

This was why the news that reached us was delayed, and vague.

Getting out of bed, I felt for the first time an access of rage against poor Guido. He complicated every misfortune with his histrionics! I went off without Augusta, who couldn't leave the baby on such short notice. Outside, I was stopped by a doubt! Couldn't I wait until the banks opened and Olivi was in his office, so as to appear at Guido's supplied with the money I had promised? This is how little I believed in the gravity of Guido's condition, even though it had been announced to me!

I had the truth from Dr. Paoli, whom I encountered on the stairs. I was so overwhelmed that I almost fell down. Guido, since I had been living beside him, had become for me an individual of great importance. As long as he was alive, I saw him in a certain light, which was the light of a part of my days. With his dying, that light was transformed as if it had suddenly passed through a prism. And it was this that dazzled me. He had erred, but I immediately saw that, as he was dead, nothing of his error remained. According to me he was an imbecile, that clown who, in a cemetery paved with laudatory epitaphs, asked where they bury the sinners around there. The dead are never sinners. Guido now was pure! Death had purified him.

The doctor was moved, having witnessed Ada's grief. He told me something of the dreadful night she had gone through. Now they had succeeded in making her believe Guido had swallowed such a great quantity of poison that no succor would have been of help. It would be disastrous if she were to learn otherwise!

"The fact is," the doctor added, disheartened, "if I had arrived a few hours earlier, I would have saved him. I found the empty bottles of poison."

I examined them. A strong dose, but only slightly stronger than the last time. He showed me some bottles on which I read the printed word: Veronal. Not sodium veronal, then. No one else could now be certain, as I was, that Guido had not wanted to die. But I never told anyone.

Paoli left me, saying that for the moment I should not try to see Ada. He had given her a strong sedative, and he had no doubt that it would soon take effect.

In the passage, from that little room where Ada had twice received me, I heard her soft weeping. Isolated words I couldn't understand, but steeped in sorrow. The word *he* was repeated several times, and I could imagine what she was saying. She was reconstructing her relations with the poor dead man. They must in no way have resembled those she had had with the living man. For me it was obvious that with her living husband she had made a mistake. He died for a crime committed by all of them together, because he had played the market with the assent of them all. When it came time to settle accounts, then they had abandoned him. And, alone, he had hastened to pay up. Only one of his relatives – I, who had nothing to do with any of it – had felt called upon to help him.

In the bedroom on the nuptial double bed, poor Guido lay alone, covered by a sheet. Rigor, already advanced, expressed here not a force, but rather a great stupefaction at being dead without having wanted to be. On his dark and handsome face was imprinted a reproach. Certainly not addressed to me.

I went home to Augusta, to urge her to go to her sister's aid. I was deeply moved, and Augusta wept, embracing me.

"You were a brother to him," she murmured. "Now, finally, I agree with you: we must sacrifice a part of our money to redeem his memory."

I took care to render all honor to my poor friend. First, I affixed to the door of the office a bulletin that announced our closing because of the owner's death. I myself composed the death notice. But it was only on the following day, with Ada's consent, that the funeral arrangements were made. I learned then that Ada had decided to follow the bier to the cemetery. She wanted to give him all the evidence of affection that she could. Poor thing! I knew the pain of remorse at a grave. I myself had suffered it so after my father's death.

I spent the afternoon shut up in the office with Nilini for company. Thus we arrived at a little balance sheet of Guido's situation. Frightful! Not only was the firm's capital wiped out, but Guido was also in debt for an equal amount, if the whole debt were to be paid.

I should have started working, really working, for the sake of my poor deceased friend, but I was unable to do anything save dream. My first idea would have been to sacrifice my whole life in that office and to work for Ada and her children. But was I, then, sure of being able to do good?

Nilini, as usual, chattered away as I stared into the far, far distance. He also felt called upon to revise radically his relations with Guido. Now he understood everything! Poor Guido, when he had wronged Nilini, had already been affected by the sickness that was to lead him to suicide. So all was now forgotten. And he preached on, declaring this was his nature. He was incapable of bearing anyone a grudge. He had always loved Guido, and he loved him still.

In the end, Nilini's fantasies merged with mine and over-lapped. It was not in time-consuming commerce that we would find the remedy for such a catastrophe, but on the Bourse itself. And Nilini told me about a person, a friend of his, who at the last moment had been able to save himself by doubling his stakes.

We talked together for many hours, but Nilini's proposal to continue the gambling begun by Guido came at the end, shortly before noon, and I accepted it at once. I accepted it with joy, as if I were bringing my friend back to life. In the end I bought, in the name of poor Guido, a number of other stocks with exotic names: *Rio Tinto*, *South French*, and so on.

Thus for me began fifty hours of the hardest work I have done in my whole life. First, and until evening, I remained striding up and down the office, waiting to hear if my instructions had indeed been followed. I was afraid that in the Bourse they had heard of Guido's suicide and his name would no longer be considered valid for further commitments. Instead, for several days that death was not attributed to suicide.

Then, when Nilini finally could inform me that all my orders had been executed, for me a real agitation began, aggravated by the fact that at the moment I received the documents, I was informed that on all of them I was already losing some fairly large fraction. I remember that agitation as true toil. In my memory I have the curious sensation that uninterruptedly, for fifty hours, I remained seated at the gambling table, nursing the cards. I don't know anyone who has ever been able to tolerate similar exertion for fifty hours. Every shift in price I recorded, brooded over, and then (why not say it?) mentally urged shares forward, or held them back, as best suited me, or rather my poor friend. Even my nights were sleepless.

Fearing that some member of the family might intervene and prevent the salvage operation I had undertaken, I mentioned to no one the midmonth payment. When it came due, I paid everything myself, because none of the others remembered their commitment, as all were gathered around the corpse, awaiting the interment. For that matter, in that settlement there was less to be paid than had been originally established, because luck had favored me quickly. Such was my sorrow at Guido's death, that I seemed to alleviate it by compromising myself in every possible way, both with my signature and with the risk of my money. I had been accompanied to this point by the dream of goodness I had had a long time ago, at his side. I suffered so from this agitation that I never again played the stock market on my own account.

But because of all my absorption with the market (this was my chief occupation) in the end I missed Guido's funeral. Here is what happened. That very day, the shares in which we were involved made an upward leap. Nilini and I spent our time calculating how much of the loss we had recovered. Old Speier's original investment now turned out to be only halved! A magnificent result, which filled me with pride. What happened was just what Nilini had predicted, in a very tentative tone, though now, of course, when he repeated his former words, that tone vanished and he portrayed himself as a confident prophet. According to me, he had predicted this and also its opposite. There was no way he could have erred, but I didn't say so because it suited me for him to remain in the transaction, with his ambition. His urging could also influence prices.

We left the office at three and began to run because we remembered that the funeral was to take place at two-forty-five.

Reaching the Chiozza arcades, I saw the procession in the distance and I even seemed to recognize a friend's carriage, sent to the funeral for Ada. With Nilini, I jumped into a hack, ordering the driver to follow the funeral. And in that vehicle Nilini and I continued our mental exertions to influence the market. So far were we from thinking of the late lamented that we complained of the coach's slow pace. Who could say what was happening meanwhile on the Bourse, without us to keep watch over it? Nilini, at a certain moment, looked me straight in the eye and asked me why I didn't do something with the Bourse on my own.

"For the moment," I said, and I blushed, I don't know why, "I am working only for my poor friend."

Then, after a slight hesitation, I added: "Afterwards I'll think of myself." I wanted to leave him the hope of being able to induce me to gamble, part of my effort to keep him wholly friendly to me. But, silently, I formulated the very words I didn't dare say to him: "I will never place myself in your hands."

He started preaching. "Who knows if there will be another opportunity like this!" He was forgetting: he had taught me that on the Bourse there are opportunities every hour.

When we arrived at the place where, as a rule, the vehicles stop, Nilini stuck his head out of the window and emitted a cry of surprise. The carriage was proceeding, following a funeral cortege toward the Greek Orthodox cemetery.

"Was Signor Guido Greek?" he asked, surprised.

In fact, the funeral was passing beyond the Catholic cemetery and advancing toward some other cemetery, Jewish, Greek, Protestant, or Serbian.

"He might have been Protestant!" I said at first, but immediately recalled having attended his wedding in the Catholic church.

"It must be a mistake!" I exclaimed, thinking first that they wanted to bury him in some remote spot.

Nilini suddenly burst out laughing, uncontrollable laughter that flung him, his strength exhausted, against the back of the carriage, his ugly mouth wide open in his little face.

"We've made a mistake!" he cried. When he managed to restrain the explosion of his hilarity, he showered reproaches on me. I should have seen where we were going, because I should have known the time and the people and the rest. It was somebody else's funeral!

Irritated, I hadn't laughed with him, and now it was difficult for me to put up with his reproaches. Why didn't he also pay more attention? I controlled my ill temper only because the Bourse mattered more to me than the funeral. We got out of the carriage to get our bearings, and headed for the gate of the Catholic cemetery. The carriage followed us. I realized that the survivors of the other deceased looked at us with surprise, unable to figure out why, having honored the poor man to this extreme place, we were now abandoning him just at the supreme moment.

Nilini, impatient, walked ahead of me. He asked the gatekeeper, after a brief hesitation: "Has Dr. Guido Speier's funeral already arrived?"

The gatekeeper didn't seem surprised by the question, which to me seemed comical. He answered that he didn't know. He knew only that in the last half hour two funerals had passed the gates.

Puzzled, we held council. Obviously there was no knowing whether the funeral was already inside or not. Then I decided for myself. It was not admissible for me to arrive when the service had already begun, disturbing it. So I wouldn't enter the cemetery. But, on the other hand, I couldn't risk encountering the funeral on its way out. Therefore I gave up the idea of attending the interment, and I would return to the city taking a long way around, by Servola. I left the carriage to Nilini, who wanted at least to put in an appearance, out of deference to Ada, whom he knew.

With a rapid step, to avoid any encounter, I climbed the country road leading to the village. At this point I wasn't the least displeased to have mistaken funerals, not paying my last respects to poor Guido. I couldn't linger over those religious practices. Another duty weighed on me: I had to save my friend's honor and defend his patrimony, for the sake of his widow and children. When I could tell Ada that I had managed to recover three-quarters of the loss (and in my mind I returned to the whole calculation redone so many times: Guido had lost double the amount of his father's capital, and after my intervention the loss was reduced to half of that. So it was exact. I had actually recovered three-quarters of the loss), she would surely forgive me for not having attended his funeral.

That day the weather had turned fine again. A splendid spring sun was shining, and, in the still-soaked countryside, the air was clear and healthy. My lungs, taking the exercise I hadn't allowed myself for several days, swelled. I was all health and strength. Health is evident only through comparison. I compared myself to poor Guido and I climbed, higher and higher, with my victory in the very struggle where he had fallen. All was health and strength around me. The country, too, with its young grass. The long and abundant watering, the other day's catastrophe, now produced only beneficent effects, and the luminous sun was the warmth desired by the still-frozen earth. Surely, the more we moved away from the catastrophe, the more disagreeable that blue sky would be, unless it could darken in time. But this was the forecast of experience and I didn't remember it; it grips me only now as I write. At that moment there was in my spirit only a hymn to my health and all of nature's: undying health.

My steps quickened. I was overjoyed to feel them so light. Coming down the Servola hill, my pace picked up until I was almost running. Having reached the flat Sant'Andrea promenade, it slowed again, but I retained the sensation of great ease. The air was carrying me along.

I had perfectly forgotten that I was coming from the funeral of my closest friend. I had the stride, the respiration of a victor. But my joy in victory was a tribute to my poor friend in whose interest I had entered the fray.

I went to the office to see the closing prices. They were a bit weak, but not enough to undermine my confidence. I would go back to my mental focus, and I had no doubt that I would arrive at my goal.

I finally had to go to Ada's house. Augusta came to the door. She asked me immediately: "How could you miss the funeral? You? The only man in our family."

I put down my umbrella and hat and, a bit puzzled, I told her I would like to speak at once with Ada as well, so I wouldn't have to repeat myself. Meanwhile I could assure her that, as for missing the funeral, I had had my own good reasons. I was no longer all that sure of them, and suddenly my side started hurting, perhaps from fatigue. It must have been that remark of Augusta's that made me doubt the possibility of justifying my absence, which must have caused a scandal; I could see before me all the participants at the sad function, distracted from their grief by wondering where I was.

Ada didn't come. I learned later that she hadn't even been informed that I was waiting for her. I was received by Signora Malfenti, who began speaking to me with a frown more stern than any I had ever seen; I began apologizing, but I was quite far from the self-confidence with which I had flown from the cemetery into the city. I stammered. I told her also something less than true, in support of the truth, which was my courageous initiative on the Bourse for Guido's benefit. What I said was that shortly before the time of the funeral I had had to send a dispatch to Paris to place an order, and I had felt compelled to remain in the office until I had received the reply. It was true that Nilini and I had had to cable Paris, but that was two days ago, and two days ago we had also received the reply. In other words, I understood that the truth wouldn't suffice to excuse me, perhaps because I couldn't tell all of it, relating the important operation that I had been carrying on for days, namely regulating, with my mental willpower, the international stock exchanges. But Signora Malfenti forgave me when she heard the sum to which Guido's loss had now been reduced. She thanked me with tears in her eyes. I was again not simply the sole man in the family, but the best.

She asked me to come that evening with Augusta to see Ada, to whom in the meanwhile she would tell everything. For the moment, Ada was in no condition to receive anyone. And I gladly went off with my wife. Even she, before leaving that house, didn't feel it necessary to say good-bye to Ada, who alternated between weeping and a dejection that didn't allow her even to notice the presence of anyone who spoke to her.

I had a hope: "Then it wasn't Ada who realized I was absent?"

Augusta confessed that she would have liked to remain silent, since Ada's display of indignation at my absence had seemed excessive to her. Ada demanded explanations from her, and when Augusta had to say she knew nothing, not having yet seen me, Ada again gave way to despair, crying that Guido had been driven to that end, for the whole family hated him.

It seemed to me Augusta should have defended me, reminding Ada how I alone had been prepared really to help Guido. If they had listened to me, Guido would have had no motive for committing or simulating suicide.

But Augusta, on the contrary, had remained silent. She was so moved by Ada's desperation that she feared enraging her, if she tried to argue. For that matter, she was confident that Signora Malfenti's explanations would now convince Ada of her own injustice toward me. I must say that I felt that same confidence myself, and indeed I must confess that from that moment on, I anticipated the certain satisfaction of witnessing Ada's surprise and her manifestations of gratitude. For with her, thanks to Basedow, everything was excessive.

I returned to the office, where I learned that on the market there was another slight indication of a rise, very slight, but already sufficient to allow me to hope I would find, at tomorrow's opening, the high level of that morning.

After supper I had to go to Ada's alone, because an indisposition of our little girl prevented Augusta from accompanying me. I was received by Signora Malfenti, who told me she had to attend to something in the kitchen, and therefore she would have to leave me alone with Ada. Then she confessed to me that Ada had asked to be left alone with me because she wanted to say something to me that shouldn't be heard by others. Before leaving me in that sitting room where I had already been with Ada twice, Signora Malfenti said to me, smiling: "You know, she isn't yet ready to forgive your absence from Guido's funeral, but . . . almost!"

In that little room, my heart was again beating. Not, this time, out of fear of finding myself loved by one I didn't love. Only a few moments before, and only through Signora Malfenti's words, had I recognized that I had committed a grave breach of respect to poor Guido's memory. Ada herself, now aware that pardoning this error would bring her a fortune, still couldn't forgive me immediately. I sat down and looked at the portraits of Guido's parents. Old Cada Vez had a pleased expression that seemed to me due to my endeavor, whereas Guido's mother, a thin woman wearing a full-sleeved dress and a little hat perched on a mountain of hair, looked very severe. Of course! In front of the camera, everyone assumes another appearance, and I looked away, outraged with myself for studying those faces. The mother surely couldn't have foreseen that I wouldn't attend her son's burial!

But the way Ada spoke to me was a painful surprise. She must have rehearsed at length what she wanted to say to me, and she actually took no notice of my explanations, my protests, and my rectifications, which she couldn't have foreseen and for which therefore she was not prepared. She raced along her track, like a frightened horse, to the very end.

She entered, dressed simply in a black house robe, her hair in great disorder, disheveled, and perhaps torn by hands, which insist on doing something when they cannot otherwise soothe. She reached the little table at which I was seated, and leaned forward, pressing both hands on the surface, to get a better look at me. Her little face was thin again, and freed from that strange health that swelled there discordantly. She was not beautiful, as when Guido had won her, but no one looking at her would have remembered the sickness. It was gone! In its place there was a sorrow so great that it completely mastered her. I understood it so well, that enormous sorrow, that I was unable to speak. As I looked at her, I thought: "What words could I say to her that would be the equivalent of taking her fraternally into my arms to comfort her and induce her to cry and unburden herself?" Then, when I heard myself being assailed, I tried to react, but too weakly, and she didn't hear me.

She spoke and spoke and spoke, and I can't repeat all her words. If I'm not mistaken, she began by thanking me soberly, but without warmth, for having done so much for her and for her children. Then immediately she reproached me: "Thanks to what you've done, he actually died for something that wasn't worth it!"

Then she lowered her voice as if she wanted to keep secret what she was saying to me, and in that voice there was greater warmth, a warmth caused by her affection for Guido and (or was this only an appearance?) also for me: "And I pardon you for not coming to the funeral. You couldn't, and I pardon you. He, too, would pardon you if he were still alive. What would you have done at his funeral, anyway! You, who didn't love him! Good as you are, you could have wept for me, but not for him, whom you ... hated! Poor Zeno! My brother!"

It was outrageous that such things could be said to me, altering the truth so. I protested, but she didn't hear me. I believe I shouted, or at least I felt that urge in my gullet: "But this is wrong, a lie, a slander. How can you believe such a thing?"

She continued, still in a low voice: "But neither was I able to love him. I never betrayed him, not even in my thoughts, but my feelings didn't allow me to protect him. I looked at your relationship with your wife and I envied it. It seemed better than what he offered me. I'm grateful to you for not having come to the funeral, because if you had, even now, I would have understood nothing. As it is, on the contrary,

I see and understand everything. Also that I didn't love him: otherwise how could I have hated even his violin, the most complete expression of his great spirit?"

It was then that I lay my head on her arm and hid my face. The accusations she was making were so unjust that they couldn't even be debated, and their irrationality was so tempered by her affectionate tone that my reaction couldn't be as harsh as it should have been, in order to be victorious. Moreover, Augusta had already given me an example of considerate silence, not to offend and exacerbate such sorrow. When my eyes closed, however, in the darkness I saw that her words had created a new world, like all words that are not true. I seemed to realize, myself, that I had always hated Guido and had constantly been at his side, waiting for the opportunity to strike him. Like me, she, too, had coupled Guido with his violin. If I hadn't known that she was groping blindly in her sorrow and in her remorse, I could have believed that the violin had been brought in as part of Guido to convince my spirit of the accusation of hatred.

Then in the darkness I saw again Guido's corpse and, still imprinted on his face, the stupor of being there, robbed of life. Frightened, I raised my head. It was preferable to confront Ada's accusation, which I knew was unjust, than to stare into the darkness.

But she was still speaking of me and of Guido. "And you, poor Zeno, without knowing it, went on living at his side, hating him. You did good things for him out of love for me. It was impossible! It had to end like this! I also thought once of being able to take advantage of the love I knew you still bore me, to increase the protection around him that could serve him. He could only be protected by someone who loved him, and among us, nobody loved him."

"What more could I have done for him?" I asked, weeping hot tears to make her – and myself – feel my innocence. Tears sometimes can substitute for a scream. I didn't want to scream, and I was even in doubt about whether I should speak. But I had to drown out her assertions and I wept.

"Save him, dear brother! I, or you – we should have saved him. Instead, I stayed with him and couldn't save him, because I lacked true affection, and you remained distant, absent, always absent, until he was buried. Then you appeared sure of yourself, armed with all your affection. But before, you cared nothing for him. And yet he was with you until evening. And you could have imagined, if you had been concerned for him, that something serious was about to happen."

My tears prevented me from speaking, but I blurted something intended to establish the fact that the previous night he had spent enjoying himself in the marsh, hunting, so no one in this world could have predicted the use to which he would put the night that followed.

"He needed his hunting! He needed it!" she cried, in loud reproach. And then, as if the effort of that cry had been excessive, all of a sudden she collapsed and fell senseless to the floor.

I remember that I hesitated for a moment before calling Signora Malfenti. It seemed to me that this swoon revealed something about what she had said.

Signora Malfenti and Alberta rushed in. Signora Malfenti, supporting Ada, asked me: "Did she talk with you about that wretched trading on the market?" Then: "This is her second fainting fit today!"

She begged me to step out for a moment, and I went into the passage, where I waited to be told if I should go back into the room or leave the house. I was preparing myself for further explanations with Ada. She was forgetting that if things had been carried forward as I had suggested, the tragedy would surely have been averted. It would suffice to tell her this, and she would be convinced of her injustice toward me.

A little later, Signora Malfenti joined me and said Ada had come round and wanted to bid me good-bye. She was resting on the sofa where, until a short time before, I had been seated.

Seeing me, she started crying, and these were the first tears I saw her shed. She extended her little hand, moist with sweat: "Good-bye, dear Zeno! I beg you: remember! Remember always! Don't forget him!"

Signora Malfenti spoke up, asking what it was I should remember, and I told her Ada wanted Guido's position on the Bourse to be settled at once. I blushed at my lie and I also feared a denial on Ada's part. Instead of contradicting me, she started screaming: "Yes, yes! Everything must be cleared up! That horrible Bourse! I never want to hear it mentioned again!"

She grew pale once more, and Signora Malfenti, to calm her, assured her that what she desired would be done immediately.

Then Signora Malfenti accompanied me to the door and begged me not to rush things: I was to do whatever I thought was in Guido's best interests. But I replied that I had lost confidence. The risk was enormous and I no longer dared deal with another's interests in that way. I no longer believed in the Bourse and in playing it, or at least I had lost faith that my mental energies could control the market's movement. I therefore had to liquidate at once, quite happy that things had gone as they had.

I didn't repeat to Augusta what Ada had said. Why should I distress her? But those words, also because I repeated them to no one, continued to pound in my ear, and remained with me for long years. They still reecho in my soul. Again and again, even today, I analyze them. I can't say I loved Guido, but this is only because he was a strange man. But I stood by him like a brother and helped him as best I could. I don't deserve Ada's reproach.

I never again found myself alone with her. She didn't feel the need to say anything else to me, nor did I dare demand an explanation, perhaps to avoid renewing her sorrow.

At the Bourse the matter ended as I had foreseen, and Guido's father, after having been informed by the first dispatch that he had lost his entire fortune, was surely pleased to find half of it intact. All my doing, but I wasn't able to enjoy it as I had anticipated.

Ada treated me affectionately always, until her departure for Buenos Aires, where she and the children went to live with her husband's family. She enjoyed seeing me and Augusta. I sometimes chose to imagine that her whole speech had been due to a genuinely mad outburst of pain, and that not even she remembered it. But then once when Guido was mentioned again in our presence, she repeated and confirmed in a few words everything she had said to me that day: "He wasn't loved by anybody, poor thing!"

At the moment of boarding ship, carrying one of her babies, slightly indisposed, in her arms, she kissed me. Then, in a moment when there was nobody near, she said to me: "Goodbye, Zeno, dear brother. I will always remember that I wasn't able to love him enough. You must know that! I am glad to be leaving my country. I feel as if I'm leaving my remorse behind!"

I scolded her for tormenting herself like that. I avowed she had been a good wife and I knew it and could bear witness to it. I don't know if I succeeded in convincing her. She no longer spoke, overcome with sobs. Then, a long time afterwards, I sensed that, in bidding me farewell, she had meant those words also to renew her reproaches of me. But I know she misjudged me. Surely, I don't have to reproach myself with not having loved Guido.

It was a dark, murky day. It was as if a sole cloud, outspread but not at all threatening, darkened the sky. From the port, a great fishing vessel, its sails hanging limp from the masts, was trying to move out, rowed by the sailors. Only two men were at the oars, and despite repeated efforts, they managed barely to shift the heavy vessel. Out at sea they would find a favoring breeze, perhaps.

Ada, from the deck of the liner, waved her handkerchief. Then she turned her back. Of course, she was looking toward

Sant'Anna, where Guido lay at rest. Her trim little form became more perfect, the farther it moved off. My eyes were blurred with tears. Now she was abandoning us, and never more would I be able to prove my innocence to her.

PSYCHOANALYSIS

I'M THROUGH WITH psychoanalysis. After having practiced it faithfully for six whole months, I'm worse off than before. I still haven't discharged the doctor, but my decision is irrevocable. Yesterday, in any case, I sent him word that I was tied up, and for a few days I'll keep him waiting. If I were quite sure of being able to laugh at him and not lose my temper, I might even see him again. But I'm afraid I'd end up coming to blows.

In this city, after the outbreak of the war, we are more bored than ever, and, as a substitute for psychoanalysis, I have returned to my beloved papers. For a year I hadn't written a word; in this, as in everything else, obeying the doctor, who commanded that during my therapy I was to reflect only when I was with him, because unsupervised reflection would reinforce the brakes that inhibited my sincerity, my relaxation. But now I find myself unbalanced and sicker than ever, and, through writing, I believe I will purge myself of the sickness more easily than through my therapy. At least I am sure that this is the true system for restoring importance to a past no longer painful, and the dispelling the dreary present more quickly.

I had put myself in the doctor's hands with such trust that when he told me I was cured, I believed him completely and, on the contrary, I didn't believe in my pains, which still afflicted me. I said to them: "You're not real, after all!" But now there can be no doubt! It's them, all right! The bones in my legs have been converted into vibrant scales that hurt the flesh and the muscles.

402

But this wouldn't matter all that much to me, and it isn't for this reason that I am giving up my therapy. If those hours of reflection at the doctor's had continued to be interesting bearers of surprises and emotions, I wouldn't have abandoned them, or before abandoning them, I would have waited until the end of the war, which makes all other activity impossible for me. But now that I know everything, namely that it was nothing but a foolish illusion, a trick designed to affect some hysterical old woman, how could I bear the company of that ridiculous man, with that eye of his, meant to be penetrating, and that presumption that allows him to collect all the phenomena of this world within his great new theory? I will spend my remaining free time writing. To begin with, I will write sincerely the story of my therapy. All sincerity between me and the doctor has vanished; now I can breathe. No stress is imposed on me any longer. I don't have to force myself to have faith, or to pretend I have it. The better to conceal my true thoughts, I believed I had to show him a supine obsequiousness, and he exploited that to invent something new every day. My therapy was supposedly finished because my sickness had been discovered. It was nothing but the one diagnosed, in his day, by the late Sophocles for poor Oedipus: I had loved my mother and I would have liked to kill my father.

And I didn't become angry! Spellbound, I lay there and listened. It was a sickness that elevated me to the highest noble company. An illustrious sickness, whose ancestors dated back to the mythological era! And I'm not angry now, either, alone here with my pen in hand. I laugh at it wholeheartedly. The best proof that I never had that sickness is supplied by the fact that I am not cured of it. This proof would convince even the doctor. He should set his mind at rest: his words couldn't spoil the memory of my youth. I close my eyes and I see immediately, pure and childish and ingenuous, my love for my mother, my respect and my great fondness for my father.

The doctor puts too much faith also in those damned confessions of mine, which he won't return to me so I can revise them. Good heavens! He studied only medicine and therefore doesn't know what it means to write in Italian for those of us who speak the dialect and can't write it. A confession in writing is always a lie. With our every Tuscan word, we lie! If he knew how, by predilection, we recount all the things for which we have the words at hand, and how we avoid those things that would oblige us to turn to the dictionary! This is exactly how we choose, from our life, the episodes to underline. Obviously our life would have an entirely different aspect if it were told in our dialect.

The doctor confessed to me that in all his long practice, he had never witnessed emotion as strong as mine on discovering myself in the images that he thought he had been able to evoke from me. For this reason, too, he was so prompt to declare me cured.

And I didn't simulate that emotion. It was, indeed, one of the most profound I have felt in my whole life. Bathed in sweat when I created the image, in tears when I held it. I had already cherished the hope of being able to relive one day of innocence and naïveté. For months and months that hope supported me and animated me. Didn't it mean producing, through vital memory, in full winter the roses of May? The doctor himself guaranteed that the memory would be vivid and complete, such that it would amount to an extra day in my life. The roses would have all their scent and perhaps also their thorns.

Thus, after pursuing those images, I overtook them. Now I know that I invented them. But inventing is a creation, not a lie. Mine were inventions like those of a fever, which walk around the room so that you can see them from every side, and then they touch you. They had the solidity, the color, the insolence of living things. Thanks to my desire, I projected the images, which were only in my brain, into the space where

I was looking, a space whose air I could sense, and its light, and even the blunt corners that were never lacking in any space through which I passed.

When I achieved the drowsiness that should have facilitated illusion, though it seemed to me nothing but the association of a great effort with a great inertia, I believed those images were real reproductions of distant days. I might have suspected at once that they were not, because the moment they vanished, I remembered them again, but without any excitement or emotion. I remembered them the way you remember an event narrated by someone who was not present. If they had been true reproductions, I would have continued laughing and crying over them as when I had experienced them. And the doctor made notes. He said: "We have had this, we have had that." To tell the truth, we had had nothing more than graphic marks, skeletons of images.

I was led to believe this was an evocation of my childhood because the first of the images placed me in a relatively recent period of which I had retained, even previously, a pale memory that this image seemed to confirm. There was a year in my life when I went to school before my brother had begun there. I saw myself leave my house one sunny morning in spring, and cross our garden to descend into the city, down, down, with an old maidservant of ours, Catina, holding me by the hand. My brother, in this dream scene, didn't appear, but he was its hero. I sensed him in the house, free and happy, while I was going to school. I went off, choked with sobs, dragging my feet, an intense bitterness in my spirit. I visualized only one of those walks to school, but my rancor told me that I went to school every day, and every day my brother stayed home. To infinity, though in reality I believe that, after a fairly short time, my brother, only a year younger than I, also went to school. But then the dream's truth seemed to me beyond debate. I was condemned to go always to school while my brother was permitted to stay home. Walking at Catina's side, I calculated the duration of the torture. Until noon! While he's at home! Further, I recalled that, during the preceding days, I must have been upset at school by threats and scolding, and then, too, I had thought: They can't touch him. It had been a vision of enormous immediacy. Catina, whom I had known as a small woman, seemed to me huge, surely because I was so little. Even then she had seemed very old, but, as is well known, the very young always see older people as ancient. And along the streets I had to follow to reach school, I glimpsed also the strange little columns that in those days bordered the sidewalks of our city. True, I was born long enough ago to see still, as an adult, those little columns in our downtown streets. But the ones along the street I took that day with Catina were gone by the time I emerged from childhood.

My faith in the authenticity of those images persisted in my spirit even when, quite soon, stimulated by that dream, my cold memory discovered further details of that period. The chief one: my brother also envied me because I went to school. I was sure I had noticed it, but that did not immediately suffice to invalidate the truth of the dream. Later it despoiled the evocation of any semblance of truth: the jealousy had in reality existed, but in the dream it had been transferred.

The second vision also took me back to a recent time, though long before the first: a room in my house, but I don't know which, because it is vaster than any room actually there. It is strange that I saw myself closed in that room, and that I immediately knew a detail that the mere sight of it could not have provided: the room was far from the place where my mother and Catina then stayed. And another detail: I hadn't yet started attending school.

The room was all white and, indeed, I never saw a room so white or so completely illuminated by the sun. Did the sun then pass through the walls? It was certainly already high, but still I was in my bed, holding in my hand a cup from which I had drunk all the milky coffee and in which I continued to scrape the spoon, extracting the sugar. At a certain point the spoon could collect no more, and then I tried to reach the bottom of the cup with my tongue. But I failed. So, finally, I was holding the cup with one hand and the spoon with the other and I was watching my brother, lying in the bed beside mine, as, belatedly, he was still sipping his coffee, with his nose in the cup. When he finally raised his face, I saw it all somehow contracted in the rays of the sun, which struck it fully, whereas mine (God knows why) was in shadow. His face was pale and a bit disfigured by a slight prognathism.

He said: "Will you lend me your spoon?"

Only then did I realize that Catina had forgotten to bring him a spoon. Immediately, and without hesitation, I answered him: "Yes! If you'll give me a bit of your sugar in return."

I held up the spoon to underscore its value. But Catina's voice immediately resounded in the room: "Shame on you! Little shark!"

Fright and shame plunged me again into the present. I would have liked to argue with Catina, but she, my brother, and I – as I was then, small, innocent, and a usurer – disappeared, sinking into the abyss.

I regretted having felt that shame so strongly that it destroyed the image which I had achieved with such effort. It would have been so much better if, instead, I had offered the spoon, meekly, and gratis, and had not argued over that bad deed of mine, probably the first I committed. Perhaps Catina would have enlisted my mother's help to mete out a punishment to me, and finally I would have seen her again.

I saw her, however, a few days later, or thought I saw her. I might have realized at once it was an illusion, because the image of my mother, as I had evoked it, resembled too closely her portrait, which hangs over my bed. But I must confess that in the apparition my mother moved like a living person.

Great, immense sunlight, enough to blind you! From what I believed was my youth, there came so much of that sun that it was hard to believe this was not that time. Our dining nook in the afternoon hours. My father has come home and is sitting on a sofa beside Mamma, who is marking with a certain kind of indelible ink some initials on much linen spread over the table at which she sits. I find myself under the table, where I am playing with some marbles. I move closer and closer to Mamma. Probably I want her to join in my game. At a certain point, to stand on my feet between them, I clutch the linen cloth hanging from the table; a disaster occurs. The bottle of ink falls on my head and stains my face, my clothes, Mamma's skirt, and also produces a little spot on Papà's trousers. My father raises his leg to give me a kick.

But I had returned from my long journey in time, and I was safe here, an adult, an old man. For an instant I suffered at the threatened punishment, and immediately afterwards I was sad that I couldn't witness the protective gesture that no doubt came from Mamma. But who can arrest those images when they start fleeing through that time, which had never before so resembled space? This was my notion as long as I believed in the authenticity of those images! Now, unfortunately (oh! how it saddens me!), I believe no longer and I know that it wasn't the images that sped away, but my clear eyes that looked again into real space, where there is no room for ghosts.

I will say more about the images of another day, to which the doctor attributed such great importance that he pronounced me cured.

In the doze to which I abandoned myself, I had a dream, immobile as a nightmare. I dreamed of myself, a baby again, but seeing only that baby and how he also dreamed. He lay mute, overcome by a joy that pervaded his tiny organism. He seemed finally to have achieved his old desire. And yet he lay there alone and abandoned! But he could see and hear with the clarity that enables us to see and hear even distant things in dreams. The child, lying in a room of my house, saw (God knows how) that on its roof there was a cage, fixed in very

solid foundations, without doors and windows, but illuminated with the most pleasing light and filled with pure and
sweet-smelling air. And the child knew that only he could
reach that cage, and without even going there, because the
cage would come to him. In that cage there was just one piece
of furniture, an easy chair, and in it sat a shapely woman,
delightfully formed, dressed in black, a blonde with great
blue eyes, snow-white hands, and little feet in patent-leather
pumps from which, below her skirts, only a faint glow
escaped. I must say that the woman seemed to me all one
with her black dress and her patent-leather pumps. She was a
whole! And the child dreamed of possessing that woman, but
in the strangest way. He was sure, that is, that he could eat
some little pieces at the top and at the base.

Now, thinking back, I am amazed that the doctor, who,
according to what he says, has read my manuscript so carefully,
didn't recall the dream I had before going to see Carla. To me,
some time afterwards, as I thought it over, it seemed that this
dream was simply the other one, slightly altered, made more
childish.

But the doctor recorded everything carefully, then asked
me with a somewhat syrupy attitude: "Was your mother blond
and shapely?"

I was amazed by the question, and answered that my grand-
mother also had been the same. But for him I was cured, quite
cured. I opened my mouth to rejoice with him and I adjusted
myself to what was to come next: namely, no more investigations, no research or meditations, but rather a genuine and
diligent reeducation.

From then on, those sessions were downright torture, and
I continued them only because it has always been so difficult
for me to stop when I am moving or to move when I am still.
On occasion, when he exaggerated, I would venture some
objection. It wasn't really true – as he believed – that my every
word, my every thought was criminal. He would then widen

his eyes. I was cured, and I refused to realize it! This was true blindness: I learned that I had desired to steal my father's wife – my mother! – and yet I didn't feel cured? My stubbornness was unheard of. However, the doctor admitted that I would be even more cured when my reeducation was finished, after which I would be accustomed to considering those things (desire to kill father and to kiss mother) quite innocent matters for which there was no need to suffer remorse, because they occurred often in the best families. Basically, what did I have to lose? One day he told me that now I was like a convalescent who still wasn't accustomed to living without a fever. Well, I would wait until I was accustomed.

He felt that I was not yet entirely his, and, besides the reeducation, from time to time he returned also to the therapy. He tried dreams again, but we didn't have a single one that was authentic. Annoyed with all this waiting, in the end I made up one. I wouldn't have done so if I could have foreseen the difficulty of such simulation. It isn't all that easy to stammer as if we were immersed in a half-dream, or to cover ourselves with sweat or turn pale, not giving the game away, or perhaps turning scarlet from strain, and yet not blushing. I spoke as if I had gone back to the woman in the cage and had persuaded her to extend, through a hole suddenly produced in the wall of the little room, her foot for me to suck and eat. "The left one! The left one!" I murmured, putting into the vision a curious detail that might make it resemble the previous dreams more closely. Thus I demonstrated that I had understood perfectly the sickness that the doctor demanded of me. The child Oedipus had in fact done just this: he had sucked his mother's left foot, leaving the right one for his father. In my effort to concoct a reality (far from a contradiction, this), I deceived also myself and could taste the flavor of that foot. I wanted to vomit.

Not only the doctor but I, too, would have liked to be revisited by those dear images of my youth, authentic or not, which I hadn't had to invent. Since, in the doctor's presence, they no longer came, I tried to summon them when I was away from him. By myself, I ran the risk of forgetting them, but I wasn't looking for therapy, after all! I wanted again May roses in December. I had had them once, why couldn't I have them again?

In solitude, too, I was fairly bored, but then, instead of the images, something else came and for a while replaced them. Simply, I believed I had made an important scientific discovery. I thought I had been called upon to complete the whole theory of physiological colors. My predecessors, Goethe and Schopenhauer, had never imagined what could be achieved by deftly handling complementary colors.

I should say that I spent my time sprawled on the sofa opposite my study window, from which I had a view of a stretch of sea and horizon. Now, one evening, as the sunset colored a sky jagged with clouds, I lingered at length to admire, along a limpid edge, a magnificent color, a pure and soft green. In the sky there was also a good deal of red, along the outlines of the clouds to the west, but it was a still-pale red, diluted by the white rays of the direct sun. Dazzled, after a certain time, I shut my eyes and it was obviously the green to which my attention had been directed, along with my affection, because on my retina now its complementary color was produced, a brilliant red that had nothing to do with the luminous but pale red of the sky. I looked, I caressed that color I had created. My great surprise came when, after I opened my eyes, I saw that dazzling red invade the whole sky and cover also the emerald green that for a long time I couldn't then find again. So I had discovered the way to color nature! Naturally, I repeated the experiment several times. The wonderful thing was that there was also movement within that coloration. When I reopened my eyes, the sky would not accept immediately the color of my retina. There was an instant of hesitation, during which I was still able to see the emerald green that had generated that red by which it would be destroyed. The latter rose from the background, unexpected, and spread like a frightful fire.

When I was convinced of the exactness of my observation, I took it to the doctor in the hope of enlivening our boring sessions. The doctor settled the question for me, saying that my retina was more sensitive because of nicotine. I was almost ready to say that, if so, then the images we had considered reproductions of events of my childhood could also have been generated through the effect of the same poison. But then I would have revealed to him that I wasn't cured, and he would have tried to persuade me to start the therapy all over again.

And yet that brute didn't always believe I was poisoned like that. This was clear also in the reeducation he undertook, to heal me of what he called my smoking sickness. These are his words: smoking wasn't bad for me, and if I were convinced it was harmless, it would really be so. And he went further: now that the relationship with my father had been revealed and subjected to my adult judgment, I could realize I had contracted that vice to compete with my father, and had attributed a poisonous effect to tobacco thanks to my unconscious moral feeling that wanted to punish me for my rivalry with him.

That day I left the doctor's house smoking like a chimney. A test was necessary, and I gladly subjected myself to it. That whole day I smoked uninterruptedly. Then a totally sleepless night followed. My chronic bronchitis returned, and there could be no doubt about that, because it was easy to discover the consequences in the spittoon.

The next day I told the doctor I had smoked a great deal and now it no longer mattered to me. The doctor looked at me, smiling, and I could sense his bosom swelling with pride. Calmly he resumed my reeducation! He proceeded with the confidence of one who sees flowers blossom from every clod on which he sets his foot.

I remember very little of that reeducation. I submitted to it, and when I emerged from that room I shook myself like a dog coming out of the water, and also like the dog remained damp but not soaked.

I remember, however, with indignation that my educator asserted that Dr. Coprosich had rightly addressed to me the words that had so provoked my ill-feeling. But would I then have deserved as well the slap my father tried to give me, as he was dying? I don't know if the doctor also said this. But I do know for certain that he declared I had hated also old Malfenti, whom I had installed in my father's place. Many in this world believe they cannot live without a given affection; I, on the contrary, according to him, became unbalanced if I lacked a given hatred. I married one or another of the daughters, and it didn't matter which, because it was a question of putting their father in a place where my hatred could reach him. Then I defaced, as best I could, the house I had made mine. I betrayed my wife and, obviously, if I could have succeeded, I would have seduced Ada and also Alberta. Naturally I have no thought of denying this, and indeed the doctor made me laugh when, in telling it to me, he assumed the attitude of Christopher Columbus arriving in America. I believe, however, that he is the only one in this world who, hearing I wanted to go to bed with two beautiful women, would ask himself: Now let's see why this man wants to go to bed with them.

It was even more difficult for me to tolerate what he thought himself entitled to say about my relations with Guido. From my own account he had learned of the dislike that had marked the beginning of my acquaintance with Guido. This dislike never ceased, according to the doctor, and Ada was right to see my absence from the funeral as its final manifestation. The doctor forgot how, at that moment, I was intent on my labor of love, saving Ada's fortune, nor did I deign to remind him.

It seems that, on the subject of Guido, the doctor had even made some inquiries. He asserts that, having been chosen by Ada, Guido couldn't be the way I've described him. He has discovered that an important lumberyard, very close to the house where he practices psychoanalysis, belonged to the firm of Guido Speier & Co. Why hadn't I mentioned it?

If I had mentioned it, it would have been an added difficulty in my already quite difficult exposition. This omission is simply the proof that a confession made by me in Italian could be neither complete nor sincere. In a lumberyard there are enormous varieties of lumber, which we in Trieste call by barbarous names derived from the dialect, from Croat, from German, and sometimes even from French (*zapin*, for example, which is by no means the equivalent of *sapin*). Who could have given me the appropriate vocabulary? Old as I am, should I have found myself a job with a lumber dealer from Tuscany? For that matter, the lumberyard belonging to the firm of Guido Speier & Co. produced only losses. So I had no call to mention it, as it remained always inactive, except when thieves broke in and made that barbarously named wood move, as if it were destined to make little tables for spiritualist séances.

I suggested to the doctor that he seek information on Guido from my wife, from Carmen, or from Luciano, who is now a well-known, successful merchant. To my knowledge, the doctor consulted none of them, and I must believe he refrained for fear of seeing, thanks to their information, the collapse of all his construction of accusations and suspicions. Who knows why he has been overcome by such hatred of me? He must be another hysteric who, having desired his mother in vain, takes it out on someone totally extraneous.

In the end I grew very tired of the struggle I had to sustain with the doctor, whom I was paying. I believe also that those dreams didn't do me any good, and then the freedom to smoke whenever I liked finally depressed me totally. I had a good idea: I went to Dr. Paoli.

I hadn't seen him for many years. He had gone rather white, but his grenadier figure had not yet been fattened by age, or bent. He still looked at things with a gaze that seemed a caress. This time I discovered why he seemed like that to me. Obviously he enjoys looking, and he looks at the beautiful and the ugly with the satisfaction that others derive from a caress.

I had gone up to see him with the intention of asking him if he believed I should continue my psychoanalysis. But when I found myself facing that coldly investigative eye, my courage failed me. Perhaps I would make myself ridiculous, telling him that at my age I had let myself be taken in by such charlatanism. I was sorry to have to remain silent, because if Paoli had forbidden me psychoanalysis, my position would have been greatly simplified, but I definitely would not have liked to see myself caressed at length by that great eye of his.

I told him about my insomnia, my chronic bronchitis, a rash on my cheeks that was tormenting me, about certain shooting pains in my legs, and finally about my strange memory gaps.

Paoli analyzed my urine in my presence. The mixture turned black, and Paoli became thoughtful. Here, finally, was a real analysis and not a psychoanalysis. I remembered with affection and emotion my remote past as a chemist and some real analyses: me, a test tube, and a reagent! The other, the analyzed, sleeps until the reagent imperiously wakens him. Resistance in the test tube doesn't exist or else it succumbs to the slightest increase of temperature, and simulation is also completely absent. In that test tube, nothing happens that could recall my behavior when, to please Dr. S., I invented new details of my childhood, which then confirmed the diagnosis of Sophocles. Here, on the contrary, all was truth. The thing to be analyzed was imprisoned in the tube and, remaining always itself, it awaited the reagent. When it arrived, the thing always said the same word. In psychoanalysis there is never repetition, neither of the same images nor of the same words.

It should be called something else. Let's call it psychic adventure. That's right: when you begin such an analysis, it's as if you were going into a wood, not knowing whether you will encounter an outlaw or a friend. And even when the adventure is over, you still don't know. In this, psychoanalysis recalls spiritualism.

But Paoli didn't believe it was a question of sugar. He wanted to see me again the next day, after he had analyzed that liquid by polarization.

Meanwhile, I went off, basking in the glory of diabetes. I was about to go to Dr. S. to ask him how he would now analyze, in my bosom, the causes of such a disease in order to nullify them. But I had had enough of that individual, and I wouldn't see him again, not even to make fun of him.

I must confess that diabetes for me was infinitely sweet. I talked of it with Augusta, who immediately had tears in her eyes. "You've talked so much about diseases all your life, that you had to end up having one!" she said, then tried to console me.

I loved my illness. I fondly remembered poor Copler, who preferred real sickness to the imaginary. Now I agreed with him. Real sickness was so simple: you just let it have its way. In fact, when I read in a medical volume the description of my sweet sickness, I discovered a kind of program of life (not death!) in its various stages. Farewell, resolutions: at last I was free. Everything would take its course without any intervention on my part.

I also discovered that my sickness was always, or almost always, very sweet. The sick person eats and drinks a great deal, and there are no great sufferings if you are careful to avoid ulcers. Then you die in a very sweet coma.

A little later, Paoli called me on the telephone. He informed me that there was no trace of sugar. I went to him the next day and he prescribed a diet, which I followed only a few days, and a potion that he described in an illegible prescription, which did me good for a whole month.

"Did diabetes give you a great fright?" he asked me, smiling.

I protested, but I didn't tell him that since diabetes had abandoned me, I felt very much alone. He wouldn't have believed me.

In that period I happened upon Dr. Beard's famous work on neurasthenia. I followed his advice and changed medicines every week according to his prescriptions, which I copied out in a clear hand. For some months the treatment seemed to do me good. Not even Copler had had such an abundant consolation of medicines in his life as I did at that time. Then that faith also faded, but meanwhile I had postponed from day to day my return to psychoanalysis.

I then ran into Dr. S. He asked me if I had decided to give up therapy. He was, however, very polite, far more so than when he had had me in his hands. Obviously he wanted to get me back. I told him I had some urgent business, family matters that occupied and preoccupied me, and that once I found peace again, I would return to him. I would have liked to ask him to give me back my manuscript, but I didn't dare; it would have been tantamount to confessing that I wanted nothing more to do with the treatment. I postponed such an attempt to another time, when he would have realized that I no longer gave therapy any thought, and he would have to resign himself.

Before leaving me, he said a few words, meant to win me back: "If you examine your consciousness, you will find it changed. As you will see, you will return to me only if you realize that I was able, in a relatively short time, to bring you close to health."

But, to tell the truth, I believe that, with his help, in studying my consciousness, I have introduced some new sicknesses into it.

I am bent on recovering from his therapy. I avoid dreams and memories. Thanks to them, my poor head has been so transformed that it doesn't feel secure on my neck. I have frightful distractions. I speak with people, and while I am saying one thing, I try involuntarily to recall something else that, just a moment before, I said or did and now no longer remember, or I even pursue a thought of mine that seems to me enormously important, with the importance my father attributed to those thoughts he had just before dying, which he, too, was unable to recall.

If I don't want to end up in the lunatic asylum, I must throw away these playthings.

15 May 1915

We have spent a two-day holiday at Lucinico, in our villa there. My son, Alfio, has to recuperate from influenza and will remain in the villa with his sister for a few weeks. We'll come back here for Pentecost.

I have finally succeeded in returning to my sweet habits, and stopped smoking. I am already much better since I have been able to abolish the freedom that foolish doctor chose to grant me. Today, as we are in midmonth, I have been struck by the difficulty our calendar creates for regular and orderly resolutions. No one month is the same as another. To underline better one's inner resolve, one likes to end smoking together with the end of something else: for example, the month. But except for July and August, and then December and January, there are no two successive months that form a pair thanks to their equal number of days. Time involves true disorder!

To collect my thoughts more readily, I spent the afternoon of my second solitary day on the shores of the Isonzo. Nothing is more conducive to meditation than watching the flow of water. You stand motionless, and the running water supplies the distraction needed, because it is never identical to itself, in its color and its pattern, not even for a moment.

It was a strange day. Certainly up above, a strong wind was blowing, because the clouds constantly changed shape; but below, the atmosphere was unmoving. It happened that from time to time, among the shifting clouds, the already-hot sun found an aperture through which to lavish its rays on this or that patch of hill or mountaintop, emphasizing the sweet green of May amid the shadow covering the landscape. The temperature was mild and there was also something springlike in that flight of clouds in the sky. There could be no doubt: our weather was regaining health!

Mine was genuine meditation, one of those rare instants that our miserly life bestows of true, great objectivity, when you finally stop believing and feeling yourself a victim. In the midst of all that green, emphasized so delightfully by those patches of sun, I could smile at my life and also at my sickness. Woman had an enormous importance in it. Perhaps in fragments: her little feet, her waist, or her mouth filled my days. And seeing my life again and also my sickness, I loved them, I understood them! How much more beautiful my life had been than that of the so-called healthy, those who beat or would have liked to beat their women every day, except at certain moments. I, on the contrary, had been accompanied always by love. When I hadn't thought of my woman for a while, I then called her to mind again, to win forgiveness for thinking of other women. Other men abandoned their women, disappointed and despairing of life. I had never stripped life of desire, and illusion was immediately, totally reborn after every shipwreck, in the dream of limbs, of voices, of more-perfect attitudes.

At that moment I remembered that among the many lies I had dished out to that profound observer Dr. S., there was also the story that I had never again betrayed my wife after the departure of Ada. This lie, too, had helped him construct his theories. But there, on the bank of that river, suddenly and with fear, I remembered that it was true that, for a few days now, perhaps since I had given up the therapy, I hadn't sought the company of other women. Am I perhaps cured, as Dr. S. claims? Old as I am, for some time women have no longer looked at me. If I stop looking at them, then all ties between us are severed.

If a suspicion like this had come to me in Trieste, I could have resolved it at once. Out here, that is much more difficult.

A few days before, I had picked up the memoirs of Da Ponte, the adventurer, contemporary of Casanova. He, too, had surely passed through Lucinico, and I dreamed of encountering those ladies of his, faces powdered, limbs concealed by crinolines. My God! How did those women manage to surrender so quickly and so frequently, defended as they were by all those rags?

It seemed to me that the thought of the crinoline, despite my therapy, was rather arousing. But my desire was fairly artificial, and it wasn't enough to reassure me.

The experience I sought came to me a little later, and it sufficed to reassure me, but only at great cost. To have that experience, I altered and spoiled the purest relationship I had had in my life.

I ran into Teresina, the older daughter of the tenant of a farm situated next to my villa. Her father had been left a widower two years ago, and his numerous brood had found a new mother in Teresina, a sturdy girl who got up every morning to work, and stopped only to go to bed and rest in order to be able to resume her work. That day she was leading the donkey habitually entrusted to the care of her little brother, and she was walking beside the cart loaded with fresh grass, because the far-from-large animal would have been unable to carry up the slight slope the added weight of the girl.

A year ago, Teresina had seemed to me still a child, and I had felt for her nothing but a smiling, paternal fondness. But even the day before, when I saw her again for the first time, despite the fact that I found her grown, her dark little face more serious, her slight shoulders broadened and the bosom rounder in the scant ripening of the overworked little body, I continued to regard her as an immature child in whom only her extraordinary activity could be loved, and the maternal instinct from which her little charges benefited. If it hadn't been for that accursed therapy and the necessity to verify immediately the state of my sickness, I could have left Lucinico once again without have disturbed such innocence.

She had no crinoline. And the round, smiling little face was ignorant of powder. Her feet were bare, and half of her legs were also visibly naked. The little face and the feet and the legs were unable to excite me. The face and the limbs that Teresina allowed to be seen were of the same color; they all belonged to the air, and there was nothing wrong in their being exposed to the air. Perhaps for this reason they were unable to stir me. But on feeling myself so cold, I was frightened. After the treatment, did I now require crinolines?

I began by stroking the donkey, for whom I had won a bit of respite. Then I tried to return to Teresina, and I put into her hand a ten-crown note. It was a first assault! The year before, with her and the other children, to express my paternal affection, I had pressed only a few pennies into their hands. But paternal affection, of course, is a different thing. Teresina was dumbfounded by the rich gift. Carefully she raised her little skirt to put the precious piece of paper into some concealed pocket or other. Thus I saw a further bit of leg, but it, too, was still tanned and chaste.

I returned to the donkey and gave him a kiss on the head. My affection provoked his. He stretched his muzzle and emitted his great cry of love, which I heard always with respect. How it crosses distances, and how significant it is, that initial cry that invokes and then is repeated, diminished, ending in a desperate lament. But, heard at such close range, it hurt my eardrum.

Teresina laughed, and her laughter encouraged me. I returned to her and promptly grasped her by the forearm, where my hand moved up, slowly, toward the shoulder, as I studied my sensations. Thank heaven I was not yet cured! I had given up the therapy in time.

But Teresina, hitting the donkey with a stick, made the animal move on, following him and leaving me behind.

Laughing heartily, because I remained happy even if the little peasant girl would have none of me, I said to her: "Do you have a boyfriend? You should. Too bad you don't have one already!"

Still moving away from me, she said: "If I do take one, he'll surely be younger than you!"

My happiness was not marred by this. I would have liked to give Teresina a little lesson, and I tried to remember from Boccaccio how "Maestro Alberto of Bologna virtuously shamed a woman who wanted to shame him, as he was in love with her." But Maestro Alberto's reasoning didn't have the desired effect, because Madonna Malgherida de' Ghisolieri said to him: "Your love is dear to me as that of a wise and worthy man should be; and therefore, save for my virtue, ask surely of me any pleasure, as if it were yours to demand."

I tried to do better: "When will you give old men some time, Teresina?" I shouted, to be heard by her who was already far away from me.

"When I'm old myself!" she cried, laughing wholeheartedly and without pausing.

"But then the old men will want nothing to do with you. Mind what I say! I know them!"

I was shouting, pleased with my wit, which came directly from my sex.

At that moment, in some part of the sky, the clouds opened to release the sun's rays; they struck Teresina, who now was at least forty meters from me, and about ten or more higher than I. She was tanned, small, but luminous!

The sun didn't illuminate me! When you are old, you remain in shadow, even when you have wit.

26 June 1915

The war has overtaken me! I, who was listening to the stories of war as if it were a war of olden days, amusing to narrate, but foolish to worry about! I stumbled into its midst, bewildered and at the same time amazed at not having already realized that sooner or later I would have to be involved. I had lived, completely calm, in a building whose ground floor was on fire, and I hadn't foreseen that sooner or later the whole building, with me in it, would collapse in flames.

The war grabbed me, shook me like a rag, deprived me at one stroke of my whole family and also of my business manager. Overnight I was an entirely new man, or rather, to be more precise, all twenty-four of my hours were entirely new. Since yesterday I have been a bit calmer because finally, after waiting a month, I received the first news of my family. They are safe and sound in Turin, whereas I had given up all hope of ever seeing them again.

I have to spend the whole day in my office. I have nothing to do there, but the Olivis, as Italian citizens, have had to leave, and my few able employees have all gone off to fight on this side or that, and so I have to remain on guard at my post. In the evening I go home, burdened with the heavy keys of the warehouse. Today, feeling so much calmer, I brought with me to the office this manuscript, which might help me endure the long hours better. In fact, it has provided me with a wonderful quarter-hour in which I learned that there was in this world a period of peace and silence that allowed one to concern himself with such trivial matters.

It would also be beautiful if someone now seriously invited me to sink into a state of semiconsciousness so as to be able to relive even one hour of my previous life. I would laugh in his face. How can anyone abandon a present like this, to go hunting for things of no importance? It seems to me that I have only now definitively separated myself from my health and from my sickness. I walk through the streets of our wretched city, feeling privileged, not going to the war, finding each day what food I require. Compared with everyone else, I feel so happy – especially since I've had news of my family – that I would feel I was provoking the wrath of the gods themselves if I were also perfectly well.

The war and I met in a violent fashion, though now it seems a bit comical to me.

Augusta and I had gone back to Lucinico to spend Pentecost with the children. On 23 May, I got up early. I had to take my Karlsbad salts and also go for a walk before my coffee. It was during this cure at Lucinico that I became aware that the heart, when you are fasting, attends more actively to other repairs, spreading a great well-being through the whole organism. My theory was then to be perfected that very day, when it forced me to suffer the hunger that did me so much good.

Bidding me good morning, Augusta raised her head, now totally white, from her pillow and reminded me that I had promised my daughter to find her some roses. Our only rosebush had withered, and something therefore had to be done. My daughter has become a beautiful girl and resembles Ada. From one moment to the next, I had forgotten to play the gruff educator with her, and I had turned into the cavalier who respects womanhood even in his own daughter. She immediately became aware of her power, and to my great amusement and Augusta's, she abused it. She wanted roses, and roses had to be found.

I planned to walk for a couple of hours. There was a bright sun, and since my intention was to keep walking and not to stop until I had returned home, I didn't take even a jacket and hat. Luckily, I recalled that I would have to pay for the roses, and therefore I didn't leave my wallet behind with the jacket.

First of all I went to the nearby farm, to Teresina's father, to ask him to cut the roses, which I would collect on my way home. I entered the great yard girded by a dilapidated wall, and I found no one. I shouted the name of Teresina. From the house came the smallest of the children; he must then have been about six. I put a few coins in his hand and he told me that the whole family had crossed the Isonzo early that morning for a day's work in a potato field, where the clods had to be broken up.

This news didn't displease me. I was acquainted with that field and I knew that it would take me about an hour to reach it. Since I had determined to walk for two hours, I liked the idea of being able to give my walk a specific purpose. Thus there was no danger of its being interrupted by a sudden fit of laziness. I set off across the plain, which is higher than the road, of which I could therefore see only the edge, and the crowns of a few flowering trees. I was really in great spirits: in my shirtsleeves as I was, and hatless, I felt very light. I breathed in that pure air and, as I often did at that time, while I walked I performed the Niemeyer pulmonary exercises, which a German friend had taught me, very useful for a man who leads a rather sedentary life.

Having reached that field, I saw Teresina working near the road. I went toward her and then noticed that, up ahead, her father and her two little brothers were working, boys of an age I couldn't have said precisely, between ten and fourteen. Working perhaps makes the old feel exhausted, but, thanks to the excitement that accompanies it, still younger than when they are not doing the work.

Laughing, I said to Teresina: "You're still in time, Teresina. Don't wait too long."

She didn't understand me, and I explained nothing to her. Since she didn't remember, it was possible to resume our former relations. I had already repeated the experiment, and with a favorable result. Addressing those few words to her, I had caressed her not just with my eyes alone.

I quickly made an arrangement with Teresina's father for the roses. He would allow me to cut as many as I wanted, and afterwards we would agree on the price. He wanted to go back to work at once, while I turned toward home, but then he changed his mind and ran after me. Overtaking me, in a very low voice he asked: "Didn't you hear something? They say the war's broken out."

"Yes! We all know that! About a year ago," I answered.

"I don't mean that one," he said, out of patience. "I'm talking about the one with — " And he nodded toward the other side of the nearby Italian border. "Do you know anything about it?" He looked at me, anxious to hear my reply.

"As you must realize . . . " I said with great confidence, "if I don't know anything, that means there isn't anything to know. I've come from Trieste, and the latest news I heard there was that the war has been averted for good. In Rome they've overthrown the Cabinet that wanted war, and now they have Giolitti."

He was immediately relieved. "That's why we're covering these potatoes, which are very promising and will be ours! The world is so full of big talkers!" With the sleeve of his shirt he wiped away the sweat trickling down his brow.

Seeing how happy he was, I tried to make him even happier. I love happy people, I honestly do. So I said some things I really don't like to recall. I declared that even if the war were to break out, it wouldn't be fought up here. First of all there was the sea, where it was high time they did some fighting; and besides, in Europe there was no lack of battle-fields for anyone who wanted them. There was Flanders, there were various departments of France. I had also heard — I no longer remembered from whom — that in this world there was now such a need for potatoes that they carefully dug them up even on the battlefields. I spoke quite a while, looking steadily at Teresina; tiny, minute, she had crouched on the ground, to test its hardness before taking her hoe to it.

The peasant, perfectly reassured, returned to his work. I, on the contrary, had transferred a part of my own serenity to him and was left with much less for myself. It was certainly true that at Lucinico we were too close to the border. I would discuss it with Augusta. It might be a good idea for us to return to Trieste and perhaps go on even farther in that direction or another. To be sure, Giolitti had returned to power, but there was no knowing if, arriving there, he would continue to see things the way he had seen them when that high position had been occupied by someone else.

I was made even more nervous by a casual encounter with a platoon of soldiers, marching along the road in the direction of Lucinico. They were not young soldiers, and were very badly outfitted. At their hip hung what we in Trieste call the *durlindana*, that long bayonet that, in the summer of 1915, the Austrians had had to take from the old storehouses.

For some time I walked behind them, anxious to be home quickly. Then I was irritated by a certain gamey odor that they emanated, and I slowed my pace. My uneasiness and my haste were foolish. It was also foolish to be uneasy just because I had observed the uneasiness of a peasant. Now I could see my villa in the distance, and the platoon was no longer on the road. I quickened my steps to arrive finally at my coffee and milk.

It was here that my adventure began. At a turn in the road I found myself halted by a sentinel, who shouted: "*Zurück*," putting himself actually in the position to fire. I wanted to speak to him in German, since he had shouted in German, but that was the only German word he knew, so he repeated it, more and more menacingly.

I had to go *zurück*, and, looking always over my shoulder in fear that the other man, to make his meaning clearer, might fire on me, I withdrew with a haste that remained with me even when I could no longer see the soldier.

But I hadn't yet given up the idea of reaching my villa promptly. I thought that by crossing the hill to my right, I could pass well behind the threatening sentinel.

The climb was not hard, especially as the tall grass had been trodden down by many people who must have passed by there before me. They must surely have been driven by the prohibition against the use of the road. Walking, I regained my confidence, and I thought that on arriving at Lucinico, I would immediately go and complain to the mayor about the treatment to which I had been subjected. If he allowed vacationers to be treated like that, soon nobody would come to Lucinico anymore!

But, reaching the top of the hill, I had a nasty surprise, finding it occupied by that same platoon of soldiers with the gamey smell. Many soldiers were resting in the shade of a little peasant house I had known for a long time, at this hour completely empty; three of the men seemed to be on guard duty, but not facing the slope by which I had come; and some others were in a semicircle before an officer, who was giving them instructions, which he illustrated with a map he held in his hand.

I didn't have even a hat, which could serve me for greeting. Bowing several times and with my best smile, I approached the officer, who, seeing me, stopped speaking to his soldiers and started looking at me. Also the five Mamelukes surrounding him bestowed all their attention on me. Under these stares and on the uneven terrain it was difficult to move.

The officer shouted: *"Was will der dumme Kerl hier?"* [What does this fool want?]

Amazed that, without the slightest provocation, he would offend me like this, I wanted to demonstrate, in a manly fashion, that I was offended, but still with appropriate discretion, I altered my path and tried to arrive at the slope that would lead me to Lucinico. The officer started shouting that if I took even one more step, he would have his men shoot me. I immediately became very polite, and from that day to this, as I write, I have remained always very polite. It was barbaric to be forced to deal with such an idiot, but at least there was the advantage that he spoke proper German. It was such an advantage that, remembering it, I found it easier to speak to him politely. Animal that he was, it would have been a disaster if he hadn't spoken German. I would have been lost.

Too bad I didn't speak that language more fluently, for in that case it would have been easy for me to make that surly gentleman laugh. I told him that at Lucinico my morning coffee was awaiting me, and I was separated from it only by his platoon.

He laughed, I swear he laughed. He laughed, still cursing, and without the patience to let me finish. He declared that the Lucinico coffee would be drunk by someone else, and when he heard that in addition to the coffee, my wife was also awaiting me, he yelled, *"Auch Ihre Frau wird von anderen gegessen werden."* [Your wife, too, will be eaten by someone else.]

By now he was in a better humor than I. Then, apparently sorry he had said words to me that, underlined by the laughter of the five clods, could seem offensive, he turned serious and explained that I must give up hope of seeing Lucinico for some days, and in fact his friendly advice was not to ask to go there, because my mere asking could get me into trouble!

"Haben Sie verstanden?" [Have you understood?]

I had understood, but it wasn't all that easy to adjust to giving up my coffee when it was less than half a kilometer away. Only for this I hesitated to leave, because it was obvious that if I were to descend that hill, toward my villa, on that day I would not arrive. And, to gain time, I meekly asked the officer: "But to whom should I speak in order to be able to go back to Lucinico and collect at least my hat and my jacket?"

I should have realized that the officer was anxious to be left alone with his map and his men, but I hardly expected to provoke such fury.

He yelled, making my ears ring, that he had already told me I wasn't to ask. Then he ordered me to go wherever the devil might wish to take me *(wo der Teufel Sie tragen will)*. The idea of being taken somewhere didn't displease me, because I was very tired, but still I hesitated. Meanwhile, however, with all his shouting, the officer became increasingly angry and, in a highly threatening tone, he called on one of the five men around him and, addressing him as *Herr Kaporal*, gave him orders to conduct me back to the bottom of the hill and to watch me until I had disappeared down the road to Gorizia, and to shoot me if I hesitated to obey.

Therefore I went down that hill fairly willingly: "*Danke schön*," I said, also with no intention of irony.

The corporal was a Slav who spoke rather decent Italian. He felt he had to be brutal in the officer's presence, and to encourage me to descend the hill, he shouted *"Marsch!"* at me, but when we were a bit distant he became gentle and friendly. He asked me if I had news of the war, and if it was true that Italian intervention was imminent. He looked at me anxiously, awaiting my reply.

So not even they, who were waging the war, knew if it existed or not! I wanted to make him as happy as possible, and I repeated to him the words with which I had calmed Teresina's father. Afterwards they weighed on my conscience. In the horrible storm that broke, all the people I had reassured were probably killed. Who knows what surprise there must have been on their faces, crystallized by death? My optimism was incoercible. Hadn't I heard the war in the officer's words and, even more, in their sound?

The corporal rejoiced, and to reward me, he also advised me not to attempt to reach Lucinico. Given my news, he believed the order preventing me from going home would be revoked the next day. But meanwhile he advised me to go to Trieste, to the *Platzkommando*, from which I could perhaps obtain a special pass.

"All the way to Trieste?" I asked, frightened. "To Trieste, without my jacket, without my hat, without my coffee?"

As far as the corporal knew, while we were talking, a heavy cordon of infantry was closing off all transit into Italy, creating a new and impassable frontier. With the smile of a superior person, he declared that, in his opinion, the shortest way to Lucinico was the one that passed through Trieste.

Hearing this counsel repeated, I resigned myself and set off toward Gorizia, thinking to catch the noon train and go on to Trieste. I was agitated, but I must say I felt fine. I had smoked very little, and hadn't eaten at all. I felt a lightness that I had missed for a long time. I wasn't at all displeased to have to walk more. My legs ached slightly, but it seemed to me I could hold out till Gorizia, for my respiration was free and deep. Warming my legs with a brisk pace, the walking, in fact, did not tax me. And in my well-being, beating time as I walked, jolly because the tempo was unusually fast, I regained my optimism. Threats from this side, threats from that, but it wouldn't come to war. And thus, when I arrived at Gorizia, I hesitated, wondering if I shouldn't take a room in the hotel, spend the night, and return the next day to Lucinico to make my complaints to the mayor.

I rushed first to the post office to telephone Augusta. But at the villa there was no answer.

The clerk, a little man with a wispy beard, who, in his small, rigid person, seemed ridiculous and obstinate – the only thing I remember about him – hearing me curse angrily at the dumb telephone, approached me and said, "That's the fourth time today that Lucinico has failed to answer."

When I turned to him, in his eye a great, joyous malice gleamed (I misspoke! there's another thing I still remember!) and that gleaming eye of his sought mine, to see if I was really so surprised and angered. It took a good ten minutes for me to understand. Then there were no more doubts for me. Lucinico was, or a few minutes from now would be, in the line of fire. When I finally understood that eloquent look, I was on my way to the café, to have, anticipating lunch, the cup of coffee that had been due me since morning. I immediately changed direction and headed for the station. I wanted to be closer to my family, and – following the suggestions of my corporal friend – I went to Trieste.

431

It was during that brief journey of mine that the war broke out.

Thinking to arrive so early in Trieste, though there would have been time at the Gorizia station, I didn't even have the cup of coffee I had so long been yearning for. I climbed into my carriage and, alone, addressed my thoughts to my loved ones, from whom I had been separated in such a strange way. The train proceeded normally until beyond Monfalcone.

It seemed the war had not reached there yet. I regained my serenity thinking that at Lucinico probably things would have taken more or less the same course as on this side of the border. At this hour, Augusta and my children would be traveling toward the interior of Italy. This serenity, together with my enormous, surprising hunger, procured me a long sleep.

It was probably that same hunger that woke me. My train had stopped in the midst of what is called the Saxony of Trieste. The sea wasn't visible, though it must have been very close, because a slight haze blocked any view into the distance. The Carso has a great sweetness in May, but it can be understood only by those not spoiled by the exuberantly colorful and lively springtimes in other regions. Here the stone crops out everywhere from a mild green that isn't humble because soon it becomes the predominant note of the landscape.

In other conditions I would have been hugely enraged not to be able to eat, suffering such hunger. But that day the grandeur of the historic event I had witnessed cowed me and led me to resignation. The conductor, to whom I gave some cigarettes, couldn't procure me even a crust of bread. I told no one about my experiences of the morning. I would talk about them in Trieste, with a few intimate friends. From the border, toward which I pricked up my ear, no sound of fighting came. We had been stopped at that place to allow eight or nine trains to pass, storming down toward Italy. The gangrenous wound (as the Italian front was immediately called in Austria) had opened and needed matériel to nourish its purulence. And the poor men went there, snickering and singing. From all those trains came the same sounds of joy or drunkenness.

When I reached Trieste, night had already descended on the city.

The night was illuminated by the glow of many fires, and a friend who saw me heading home in my shirtsleeves shouted to me: "Did you take part in the looting?"

Finally I managed to eat something, and immediately went to bed.

A true, great weariness drove me to bed. I believe it was produced by the hopes and the doubts that were combating in my mind. I was still quite well, and in the brief period preceding the dream whose images my psychoanalysis had enabled me to retain, I remembered that I concluded my day with a last, childish, optimistic idea: On the frontier no one had yet died, and therefore peace could be regained.

Now that I know my family is safe and sound, the life I lead doesn't displease me. I haven't much to do, but it can't be said I'm idle. No buying or selling is allowed. Trade will be reborn when we have peace. From Switzerland, Olivi had some advice transmitted to me. If he only knew how hollow his counsels sound in this atmosphere, which is totally changed! I, for the moment, do nothing.

24 March 1916

Since May of last year, I haven't again touched this little book. Now, from Switzerland, Dr. S. writes me, asking me to send him everything I have so far recorded. It's a curious request, but I have no objection to sending him also this notebook, from which he will clearly see what I think of him and of his therapy. Since he possesses all my confessions, let him keep also these few pages and a few more that I will gladly add for his edification. I haven't much time, because my business occupies my day. But with Doctor S., I still want to have my say. I have given it so much thought that now my ideas are clear.

Meanwhile he believes he will receive further confessions of sickness and weakness, and on the contrary he will receive the description of sound health, as perfect as my fairly advanced age will allow. I am cured! Not only do I not want to undergo psychoanalysis, but also I don't need it! And my healthiness doesn't come only from the fact that I feel privileged in the midst of so much martyrdom. I do not feel healthy comparatively. I am healthy, absolutely. For a long time I knew that my health could reside only in my own conviction, and it was foolish nonsense, worthy of a hypnagogue dreamer, to try to reach it through treatment rather than persuasion. I suffer some pains, true, but they lack significance in the midst of my great health. I can put a sticking-plaster here or there, but the rest has to move and fight and never dawdle in immobility as the gangrenous do. Sorrow and love – life, in other words – cannot be considered a sickness because they hurt.

I admit that before I could be convinced of my health, my destiny had to change and warm my organism with struggle and above all with victory. It was business that healed me and I want Dr. S. to know it.

Stunned and inert, I contemplated the upheaval of the world until the beginning of August of last year. Then I began to *buy*. I underline this verb because it has a higher meaning now than it had before the war. On a businessman's lips, then, it meant he was prepared to acquire a given article. But when I said it, I meant that I was the buyer of any goods that might be offered me. Like all strong people, I had in my head a sole idea, and by that I lived and it made my fortune. Olivi wasn't in Trieste, but it is certain that he would never have allowed such risk and would have left it all for others. But for me it was no risk. I knew its happy outcome with complete certainty. First, following the age-old custom of wartime, I had

434

set about converting all my wealth to gold, but there was a certain difficulty in buying and selling gold. Gold that might be called liquid, as it was more mobile, was merchandise, and I stocked up on it. From time to time I also do some selling, but always to a lesser extent than my buying. Because I began at the right moment, my buying and my selling have been so fortunate that the latter provided me with the great means I needed for the former.

With great pride, I remember that my first purchase was actually an apparent foolishness and was intended solely to put my new idea immediately into effect. A not-large stock of incense. To me the seller broached the possibility of using incense as a substitute for resin, which was already growing scarce, but, as a chemist, I knew with absolute certainty that incense could never replace resin, which was different *toto genere*. The way I looked at it, the world was going to reach such a state of poverty that they would have to accept incense as a surrogate for resin. And so I bought! A few days ago I sold a small part of it, and I received the amount I had had to pay out for the whole stock. At the moment I pocketed that money, my chest swelled, as I felt my strength and my health.

The doctor, when he has received this last part of my manuscript, should then give it all back to me. I would rewrite it with real clarity, for how could I understand my life before knowing this last period of it? Perhaps I lived all those years only to prepare myself for this!

Naturally I am not ingenuous, and I forgive the doctor for seeing life itself as a manifestation of sickness. Life does resemble sickness a bit, as it proceeds by crises and lyses, and has daily improvements and setbacks. Unlike other sicknesses, life is always fatal. It doesn't tolerate therapies. It would be like stopping the holes that we have in our bodies, believing them wounds. We would die of strangulation the moment we were treated.

Present-day life is polluted at the roots. Man has put himself in the place of trees and animals and has polluted the air, has blocked free space. Worse can happen. The sad and active animal could discover other forces and press them into his service. There is a threat of this kind in the air. It will be followed by a great gain . . . in the number of humans. Every square meter will be occupied by a man. Who will cure us of the lack of air and of space? Merely thinking of it, I am suffocated!

But it isn't this, not only this.

Any effort to give us health is vain. It can belong only to the animal who knows a sole progress, that of his own organism. When the swallow realized that for her no other life was possible except migration, she strengthened the muscle that moves her wings, and it then became the most substantial part of her organism. The mole buried herself, and her whole body adapted to her need. The horse grew and transformed his hoof. We don't know the process of some animals, but it must have occurred and it will never have undermined their health.

But bespectacled man, on the contrary, invents devices outside of his body, and if health and nobility existed in the inventor, they are almost always lacking in the user. Devices are bought, sold, and stolen, and man becomes increasingly shrewd and weaker. His first devices seemed extensions of his arm and couldn't be effective without its strength; but, by now, the device no longer has any relation to the limb. And it is the device that creates sickness, abandoning the law that was, on all earth, the creator. The law of the strongest vanished, and we lost healthful selection. We would need much more than psychoanalysis. Under the law established by the possessor of the greatest number of devices, sickness and the sick will flourish.

Perhaps, through an unheard-of catastrophe produced by devices, we will return to health. When poison gases no longer suffice, an ordinary man, in the secrecy of a room in this world, will invent an incomparable explosive, compared to which the explosives currently in existence will be considered harmless toys. And another man, also ordinary, but a bit sicker than others, will steal this explosive and will climb up at the center of the earth, to set it on the spot where it can have the maximum effect. There will be an enormous explosion that no one will hear, and the earth, once again a nebula, will wander through the heavens, freed of parasites and sickness.